SPHERE

First published in Great Britain in 2023 by Sphere

1 3 5 7 9 10 8 6 4 2

A CIP catalogue record for this book
is available from the British Library.

HB ISBN 978-1-4087-2907-6
Trade Paperback ISBN 978-1-4087-2908-3

Typeset in Meridien by M Rules
Printed and bound in Great Britain by
Clays Ltd, Elcograf S.p.A.

Lines from 'The Smuggler' by Norman MacCaig from *The Poems of Norman MacCaig*
reproduced with permission of the licensor, Birlinn Limited, through PLSclear.

'let it go – the' © 1944, © 1972, 1991 by the Trustees for the E. E. Cummings
Trust, from *Complete Poems: 1904-1962* by E. E. Cummings, edited by
George J. Firmage. Used by permission of Liveright Publishing Corporation.

Papers used by Sphere are from well-managed forests
and other responsible sources.

Sphere
An imprint of
Little, Brown Book Group
Carmelite House
50 Victoria Embankment
London EC4Y 0DZ

An Hachette UK Company
www.hachette.co.uk

www.littlebrown.co.uk

Val
McDermid

PAST
LYING

SPHERE

Val McDermid is an international number one bestselling author whose books have been translated into more than forty languages. Her multi-award-winning series and standalone novels have been adapted for TV and radio, most notably the *Wire in the Blood* series featuring clinical psychologist Dr Tony Hill and DCI Carol Jordan. The Karen Pirie novels have now been adapted for a major ITV series.

Val has been chair of the Wellcome Book Prize and has served as a judge for both the Women's Prize for Fiction and the Man Booker Prize. She is the recipient of seven honorary doctorates and is an Honorary Fellow of St Hilda's College, Oxford. She is a visiting professor in the Centre of Irish and Scottish Studies at the University of Otago in New Zealand. Among her many awards are the CWA Diamond Dagger recognising lifetime achievement and the Theakston's Old Peculier award for Outstanding Contribution to Crime Writing. Val is also an experienced broadcaster and much-sought-after columnist and commentator across print media.

For McDermid Ladies FC:
every one a hero.

Gambit (n): an act or remark that is calculated to gain an advantage, especially at the outset of a situation.

Oxford English Dictionary

While the Scotch Game can be one of the slower games and can lead to very unexciting matches, the Scotch Gambit takes it to the other extreme as both sides have the opportunity to give up material early on in exchange for a non-material, yet crucial, advantage.

If you play this opening it's always important to know how to respond to your opponent's moves because one misstep and you will find yourself very behind.

The Chess Website

The perfect detective story cannot be written.

'Twelve Notes on the Mystery Story'
RAYMOND CHANDLER

Prologue

He really believed it was a madcap game. A joke. A dare, played out between old friends. Why would anyone imagine otherwise? Writing twisted scenarios didn't mean he believed they happened in the real world. *Strangers on a Train* had the brilliant premise of two unconnected people swapping murders, but he didn't believe anybody would be daft enough to try it for real. Not even a card-carrying psychopath like the character in Highsmith's novel.

It had genuinely never crossed his mind that his best friend would actually commit a murder solely to demonstrate that the perfect crime was possible, and that he was capable of committing it. Not until he had to deal with the revelation that there was now a dead body in his garage.

1

April 2020

Detective Chief Inspector Karen Pirie tucked her hands into the pockets of her down jacket. Even silk-lined leather gloves weren't enough to keep out a night wind that was whipping straight across from the Urals to this Edinburgh rooftop. It had been three weeks since lockdown began, but the novelty of street stillness hadn't worn off. Looking down across the New Town and beyond from this height, nothing was stirring. It was like the zombie apocalypse without the zombies.

Light and movement caught the corner of her eye, and she turned her head in time to spot a liveried police car slowing for a set of lights. Down by Canonmills, she reckoned. She checked her phone. Three minutes after midnight. It was officially tomorrow. Technically, she could go for her daily walk now.

She let herself back into the sunroom. She didn't want to think about how a previous owner had managed to obtain planning permission for the roof garden in a conservation area of Georgian buildings. It wasn't her problem; this wasn't her flat. Its owner, her – what was he? Karen baulked at

3

thinking of Hamish Mackenzie as her boyfriend. You didn't have boyfriends in your thirties. 'Lover' always sounded wrong to her. It suggested the only thing that mattered was the sex, and while there was no denying she enjoyed that, their relationship encompassed much more. To a cop, 'partner' had a whole different set of resonances. And even if she stripped that out of the equation, 'partner' implied a much more serious commitment than Karen believed she'd made to Hamish. And 'significant other' was downright embarrassing. There simply wasn't a word for what Hamish was to her.

Except that right now, she supposed he was technically her landlord, even though she wasn't paying him rent. When the COVID-19 lockdown had been announced, he'd persuaded Karen to move into his flat. 'I need you to take care of the place,' he'd said, after announcing he was heading back to his working croft in the Highlands. One of his two shepherds had decided to move to Lairg to spend lockdown with his girlfriend, leaving the croft perilously shorthanded. And no sooner had Hamish returned than he'd bought Duggie Brewster's struggling gin still and started making hand sanitiser, committing himself even further to Wester Ross.

He'd turned on the charm. 'You'd be doing me a favour – forwarding the post and making the place look occupied. I can't help being anxious about being burgled. It's not like your flat, where the whole block's festooned with CCTV.' There was no denying his place was more spacious than her waterside apartment in Leith, and closer to her Historic Cases Unit office in Gayfield Square. What had clinched the deal was Detective Sergeant Daisy Mortimer's swift acceptance of Karen's impetuous suggestion they could lock down together. That would never have worked in the confines of her own flat. But Hamish's place was a different story. They wouldn't be living on top of each other, thanks to two bedrooms, a study, a living room big enough to house a dining table as well as a sofa and armchairs, a spacious kitchen, two bathrooms and a roof terrace, complete with a garden room.

She'd made the uncharacteristic offer of sharing her space at the end of their first case together. Daisy had been seconded to the HCU from the Major Incident Team in Fife; they'd worked well together and Karen had persuaded her boss to expand the HCU to include her. Daisy had been living alone in a cramped flat in Glenrothes, isolated on the other side of the Forth; in the moment, Karen had thought being in lockdown together was a good idea. It would, she thought, make working together much easier and it'd prevent the two of them from slipping into bad ways. When it came to junk food and eating chocolate ice cream straight from the tub, they could keep each other honest. Or keep each other company.

Three weeks in, she wasn't so sure it had been one of her better ideas.

She made her way down the spiral staircase into the flat. Daisy was curled up in a comfortable tweed armchair, headphones on, absorbed in yet another bloody Netflix box set. She glanced away from the screen and hit pause on the remote. 'You OK?' she asked, peeling off one headphone. 'Get you anything?'

Karen shook her head. 'I'm away out. I'm going to walk down to my flat. Just to check everything's OK.'

Daisy frowned. 'Will that not take you more than an hour? To walk there and back?'

'Yeah. Technically, I should stay there till after midnight before I come back.'

Daisy's frown deepened. 'I bet nobody would notice if you walked back during daylight hours today.'

'Maybe not, but I am a polis. I'd know I was breaking the rules. More to the point, you'd know and you're a polis.' Karen grinned. 'One hour's outdoor exercise a day, that's the limit. I'm not about to give you blackmail material. I'll see you in about twenty-five hours.'

It was the absence of noise that she found most unsettling. Even in this side street sandwiched between Leith Walk and Broughton Street, the perpetual sound of traffic had been the background hum to her night walks. Now, the silence was only broken every ten minutes or so by the engine of a car or bus. Then the quiet descended again like a suffocating blanket. It unnerved her, so she'd taken to self-improvement. Headphones in, she was learning Gaelic. Not out of a sentimental nationalism but because some of the locals living near Hamish's croft spoke it among themselves and she hated to miss out on anything. Besides, she wanted to know what they really thought of her.

Karen cut through a narrow vennel and emerged on Leith Walk. Not another human in sight. A grey cat materialised from a basement, sinuously weaving through the railings. She made a soft clicking noise and the cat approached, rubbing against her leg. She'd never had much time for cats, but these days, contact with anything with a pulse felt obligatory.

Karen bent down and scratched the cat's head between its ears. It tired before she did and strolled nonchalantly into what would have been the path of a car or a van or a bus in what already felt like the olden days. She sighed and made off at a good pace down Leith Walk. Past the library, past the shuttered shops and deserted bars, not a creature stirring.

She passed the side street where her wingman, DC Jason 'The Mint' Murray, was locked down with his hairdresser fiancée. She wondered how they were doing. Jason would be playing FIFA on his games console; she was less certain how Eilidh would pass the long days.

Another fifteen minutes and Karen was on Western Harbour Breakwater, repeating, *'Is toil leam buntàta agus sgadan,'* under her breath, wondering whether she'd ever have to insist she liked potatoes and herring. She let herself into her flat, pulled out her earphones and felt her shoulders settle. This was her domain. It wasn't that Daisy or Hamish were difficult to be around. It was simply that, like the cat on Leith Walk, she liked company on her terms. She crossed the living room and opened the patio doors leading to the balcony. The night wind made her cheeks tingle in seconds.

In the years she'd been living on the edge of the Firth of Forth, she'd grown accustomed to the night-time light show. Ribbons of red from tail lights and pools of white from headlamps mapping the road network on both sides of the wide estuary. Dots of yellow appearing and disappearing as people moved around their houses on the way to bed, or off to a night shift. Now, three weeks into lockdown, the only constants were the warning beacons on the three bridges that spanned the narrows between North and South Queensferry.

There were still the lighthouses, of course, sending their messages to the boats that weren't there. A childhood rhyme ran round her head:

Inchgarvie, Mickery, Colm, Inchkeith,
Cramond, Fidra, Lamb, Craigleith;

7

Then round the Bass to Isle of May,
And past the Carr to St Andrew's Bay.

Back when she'd learned that, there hadn't been the brilliant orange flare of the Mossmorran gas cracking plant, an occasional warning of a different kind, its glow sometimes so bright that people miles away called the emergency services to report Fife on fire. But tonight, Mossmorran was nothing more than a tall smudge obliterating a column of stars.

Karen stood in the teeth of the wind for as long as she could bear it, then went back inside. Ten minutes later she was tucked up in bed, reading an old Marian Keyes novel. It was a struggle to grow tired enough to sleep. She missed her work. Running the Historic Cases Unit had always been demanding. That and her night walks, when the rhythm of her feet helped her thoughts to surface, were usually enough to wear her down. But right now, both of these occupations were beyond her reach. There was no active cold case to occupy them; they'd cleared two complicated investigations just before lockdown had started and they'd not had time to develop a new one. All they had were boxes of files of potential cases waiting for them to dig deep and find a loose thread to pull. And it hadn't yet occurred to anyone in senior management to draft them in to one of the thankless lockdown roles. Or maybe it had, and they'd decided the HCU team weren't the best option when it came to breaking up illicit gatherings. Either way, right now she was languishing for the lack of something meaningful to investigate, and it didn't suit her. Was she really one of those people who had no life outside the job?

It was a thought that shamed her.

2

The stadium erupted in cheers as Barcelona's star striker slotted home another cracking goal. Jason Murray, La Liga's leading scorer, ran back to the centre spot, bouncing up and down on the sofa every step of the way. 'Yaaas,' he shouted, punching the air with the hand that held the game controller.

His fiancée barely glanced up from her phone screen. Jason scoring yet another virtual goal was infinitely less interesting than her Instagram feed. It was good to have the time to keep abreast of what the stylists she rated were posting in lockdown, but frustrating not to be able to try out their recommendations in the salon. There was a limit to what she could do with her own hair, never mind Jason's. His ginger hair had a lovely texture, it was true, but there just wasn't enough of it for the exercise of true creativity.

Jason paused the game and leaned into Eilidh. 'Fancy a brew?'

'You drink too much coffee.'

'That's what comes from working with KP.' He stood up, tossing the controller to one side. 'Anyway, I've only had one this morning so far. You sure I can't tempt you?'

9

Eilidh looked up and gave him an adoring smile. 'Not with a cup of coffee.'

He chuckled and made for the tiny kitchenette. A penetrating chirping stopped him in his tracks. He frowned. 'Who's that?' He stretched across the back of the sofa for his vibrating phone.

'You're the detective, Jase. Only one way to find out,' Eilidh said.

Jason frowned. 'Unknown number' usually meant somebody trying to scam him or sell him something he didn't want. But Karen had drummed into him that, as a polis, he should always answer his phone. 'You never know when that unknown caller could be the one that breaks a case.' So far, that had never happened. But this might be the day. 'Hello?'

Never give anything away to the unknown caller. Another lesson from the boss.

'Is that Jason Murray? DC Murray?' It was a woman's voice. Vaguely familiar but he couldn't put a name to it.

'Aye, that's right. Who is this?'

'It's Meera Reddy. From the National Library?'

At once, Jason was alert. Thanks to the boss, he'd learned the library's extensive resources could be invaluable in cold case investigations. Along the way, he'd found an unexpected ally in Meera, whose fondness for true crime podcasts had made her happy to forge a bond with a real live polis. She never seemed to mind how much she had to explain to Jason, who was grateful for her indulgence. He knew he was slow off the mark, but not so slow that he didn't pick up on the exasperation he often provoked. 'Hey, Meera. Great to hear from you. How are you doing?'

'Ach, you know? Stuck at home by myself and talking to the telly. How about you?'

'Not so bad. I'm in the flat with my fiancée, Eilidh, so at least I've got company.' He hesitated. 'Is there something I can do for you?'

'I don't know. Are you still on the Historic Cases Unit?'

'I am. Not that we're getting much done right now. With lockdown, and all that. The boss says we better not go into the office in case they get us putting on uniforms and chasing down folk breaking the lockdown rules,' he scoffed.

'I-I'm maybe wasting your time, I don't know.'

'That's one thing nobody's short of right now. What's the matter?'

'Well ...' Meera's voice tailed off. 'It's something from work. I'm probably getting it all out of proportion.'

'Are you going in to work, then?'

'No, no. This was something I stumbled on before we were sent home for lockdown. It's been playing on my mind. I tried to convince myself I was imagining things, but the more I've thought about it since, the more it's got me worried.'

And she did sound worried. 'OK,' Jason said slowly. 'Why don't you run it past me? I'm in no hurry. Take your time, and start from the beginning.'

'Are you sure? I don't want to waste your time.'

'You've helped me out often enough. And what else would I be doing?' He caught Eilidh's eye-roll in his peripheral vision and pulled a face at her. He reached up to the top shelf for his notebook and pen and sat down at the dining table in the window. 'Fire away.'

'I've moved jobs since the last time we spoke,' Meera began. 'I'm working in the archives now. It's a bit different.'

'How? What do you do there?'

'I'm in the section that deals with new acquisitions.

11

Basically, when important people either die or decide it's time to sort out their paperwork, they box it up and send it to us. So if you're a writer, or a politician or a scientist or anybody that might have done something interesting to researchers in the future, we get sent it.'

'That's a thing?' Already Jason felt out of his depth. 'What? They leave you their letters and that? Their private stuff?'

'It varies. Like, some writers just donate their early drafts. But some folk? It's like a massive info dump. Electricity bills, VAT receipts, bank statements, invoices from their plumbers, love letters to other people's wives . . . You name it, we get it.'

'Why?'

'Because somebody in the future might want to write about them. A biography or a PhD or something.'

'Jeez.' Sometimes Jason felt overwhelmed by the burden of what he didn't know. 'So what do you do with all this stuff?'

'My job is to catalogue it. I go through the boxes and list what's in them. Then one of the trained archivists sorts them out. Arranges them, matches up items that go together. Tries to make sense of them, I suppose.'

Jason scratched his head with the end of his pen. 'You must have to work your way through some right crap.'

'Actually, what I've had so far has been pretty interesting. I've mostly avoided the shopping-list level of stuff.' She hesitated, then, in a rush, 'Have you ever heard of a writer called Jake Stein?'

The name sounded familiar but Jason had never been much of a reader. He had a vague notion that he'd seen his mum reading one of Jake Stein's books. Which gave him a clue. 'Is he a crime writer?'

That perked Meera up. 'Yeah, that's right. One of the pioneers of the so-called Tartan Noir school. He was a best-seller for years and then there was some sort of scandal. I don't know the details – for obvious reasons he didn't keep any of the newspaper clippings about that. Anyway, his career took a real dip, then last year he died very suddenly from a cerebral haemorrhage. And we got the papers.' She stopped abruptly.

'And what? You think there was something suspicious about the way he died?'

'No, no, I don't know anything about that. No, this is something completely different. It's an unpublished man-uscript. Well, the start of one anyway. It's only eleven chapters and a synopsis. It's called *The Vanishing of Laurel Oliver.*' She paused.

He wondered if that was supposed to mean something to him. Only, it didn't. 'OK. And something about this bothered you?'

A nervous laugh. 'Honestly, Jason, the more I tell you, the more stupid I feel.'

'Meera, you're one of the least stupid people I've ever met.' He cast a quick glance at Eilidh, who was looking more interested now. 'If you're feeling bothered, I'm guessing there's something to be bothered about.'

She cleared her throat. 'Does the name Lara Hardie mean anything to you?'

Now they were firmly on Jason's territory. There were very few cases of unsolved homicides in Scotland. Sometimes as few as one a year. The Historic Cases Unit reviewed them all regularly, alongside serious sexual assaults and disappearances in suspicious circumstances where there was no concrete evidence of foul play. So Lara

Hardie's name was firmly on Jason's radar. An Edinburgh University student, she had vanished into thin air a year before. There were no grounds for suspecting she'd committed suicide, nothing to suggest she'd chosen to disappear. She'd simply been there one day and gone the next. There had been a week-long manhunt around the street where she lived. Every rubbish skip, every bit of shrubbery, every garden shed, every obscure wee vennel had been combed by police and volunteers. Her parents and her sister had done a TV appeal where everybody cried. All the other students on her university course had faced questioning by police and interrogation by social media. Ill-informed speculation had ranged from Lara drowning in Duddingston Loch, the best part of three miles away, to having been abducted by aliens. 'I know who you're talking about,' he said. He had a strange feeling in his stomach.

'This book – it's full of echoes of Lara Hardie's story. Plus the victim's got the same medical condition. It's really creepy. But this is a crime novel. And even though it's unfinished, it's got a kind of solution.'

3

For once, Karen had slept well. She'd made porridge with some dried fruit and a carton of coconut water, in the absence of milk. The ingredients came courtesy of Hamish, who disdained traditional methods of making porridge in favour of store cupboard extravaganzas. It was usually grounds for mockery on Karen's part but that morning she was grateful.

The wind had dropped and the sun was shining, turning the Firth of Forth from gunmetal grey to picture postcard blue. She understood that lockdown was perilous for many people's mental health, but for her, it felt almost like a blessing. The usual pressure from on high for results was absent; the only detective work being conducted was on live cases, and even then, the constraints of social distancing were mostly being observed. These days, her perpetual nemesis ACC Ann Markie had more important things on her mind than making Karen's life more difficult.

Not that she was skiving. She might have grown up in a household with little regard for the Church of Scotland, but nevertheless the Protestant work ethic was ingrained in her. Not having Markie chittering in her ear like a monkey on her back had given Karen the opportunity to

15

take a more leisurely, granular approach to some of the intractable cold cases in her files. It felt like a luxury to be able to re-examine old cases with the closest possible attention.

She'd barely started on a comparison between two stabbings, one in Dundee and the other in Kilmarnock, when the familiar tomtom alert of a FaceTime call interrupted her search for common factors. 'Hamish,' she muttered, arranging her face into a welcoming look before she accepted the call. He loomed into sight, grinning, golden hair tumbled round his face in an unfamiliar style.

'Morning, Karen. I finished taking the feed round the sheep and I thought I'd give you a quick call before I head down to the still. What are you up to?'

'Digging into a couple of knife attacks from three years ago,' she said.

'You can't leave it alone, can you?' Affectionate, not critical.

'Keeps me out of trouble when you're not here to do that. What have you done to your hair?'

He gave a little shrug, pushing the curls back from his forehead. 'You like it? I've been doing a lot more work with the livestock since Donny buggered off at the start of lockdown and I was fed up with it getting in the way, so Teegan got the scissors out. And I thought, while you're at it, why not lighten it a bit?'

Karen felt a tug of something she didn't want to examine. 'A woman of many talents, Teegan,' she said. For fuck's sake, surely she wasn't feeling insecure over a twenty-something teuchter who'd never been further south than Inverness? 'She's done a good job, you look about six months younger.'

'I don't think she'll be giving Eilidh anything to worry

about any time soon,' he chuckled. 'But it does what I needed.'

'The colour suits you. Though it does make your beard look more gingery. So how's life on the farm? Any cases of the COVID up your way yet?'

He shook his head. 'Not that I've heard. People are being careful, though. Shona Macleod is turning out Harris Tweed face masks with the offcuts from the tailoring business, so we're all sweating like beasts whenever we go into the village shop.' He peered into the screen. 'Hey, you're in your place.'

'Yeah, I walked down during the night.'

'Is that even legal?'

'We're allowed to check on unoccupied properties as long as we don't come into contact with anyone outside our bubble. And there's nobody here to come into contact with, so I reckon I'm technically within the rules.'

'So you left Daisy in the flat alone?' He seemed faintly cross though she couldn't imagine why that might be.

'She's not a teenager, Hamish. She's not going to trash the place.'

'Come on, Karen, I never suggested she would. I guess it's that I don't know her too well.'

Sometimes, when he was annoyed, his American teenage self slipped the leash of his cultivated Scottish present, she thought. 'So, what? You're worried she's going to read your secret diaries? Examine your bank statements?'

'No, but—'

'Why would you imagine she'd be interested in you anyway? If anybody's got anything to fear from her prying eyes, it's me. And I trust the lassie.' Karen grinned at him.

He held his hands up, palms facing her, in a gesture of concession. 'I'm sorry, I was out of order.' He tutted. 'I hate

17

FaceTime. There's no nuance. I'm never sure when you're taking the piss.'

'Just assume I usually am,' she said, trying for a tease. She hated it when things became scratchy between them; this separation had seemed to make that happen more often. He began to speak, but she was distracted by her phone. 'Sorry, it's work, I have to take this,' she said, guiltily glad of the intrusion. 'Talk soon, handsome.' She blew him a kiss and cut the connection.

'Jason, what's up?' Karen said, switching straight into professional mode.

'Hi, boss. Sorry to bother you, but I've just had a funny phone call.'

'What kind of funny?'

'This is going to sound really weird.'

Karen smothered a sigh. One day the Mint might learn how to get to the point. 'Let me be the judge of that. What's happened?'

'Meera Reddy phoned—'

'Your National Library contact?'

'Aye.'

'Have they not been sent home?'

'Yeah, but this goes back to something before lock-down. She's been transferred to archives. You remember Lara Hardie?'

'Of course. You'd have to have been living under a stone when she disappeared not to know about her. I reviewed the papers when they passed it over to us before Christmas. What's Lara Hardie got to do with the National Library archives?'

'Meera found something. She thinks it's like a blueprint or a kind of explanation for what happened to Lara Hardie.'

Karen straightened up. 'What? Jason, go right back to the beginning and tell me exactly what Meera said.' She listened patiently while he stumbled through an outline of what Meera had told him. It begged more questions than it answered, inevitably. Jason was getting better at interviewing witnesses, there was no doubting that. But the one thing Karen couldn't teach him was an instinct for the key questions.

'You say this manuscript of Meera's mentions the victim suffering from epilepsy?' she asked.

'Not just any old epilepsy, boss. Drop attacks. It's a thing. I googled it. It's like all your muscles kind of drop out for a few seconds. You just collapse like somebody cut the strings. It's over almost before anybody knows it's happening, apparently. Mostly you totally recover in seconds and it's only dangerous if you hurt yourself falling, or bang into something on the way down. Its proper name is Atonic Seizure. It's what Lara Hardie suffered from. Remember how the internet true crime detectives fixed on it, convinced she'd collapsed outside her front door and been huckled into some passing maniac's car?'

As if she could forget the hysteria of the mob. 'I remember. And there were the fuckwits who wanted to drag the Union Canal. As if Lara Hardie could've walked more than a mile down to the canal basin without being spotted by a living soul or a CCTV camera, then just happened to have a seizure while nobody was looking.'

'Aye, right. Well, the lassie in this book, the lassie that disappears, she suffers from the drop attacks too. It's not like it's that common.' He drew breath, then said, 'So what do you think, boss? Is Meera imagining things or what?'

'Meera's a smart lassie, right?'

19

Jason gave a strangled laugh. 'She's a helluva lot smarter than me. I know that's not saying much—'

'Stop fishing. Do we know who her boss is?'

'Bethan Carmichael,' he said, sounding pleased with himself. 'I got her phone number. I'll ping it to you.'

'OK, Jason. Nice work. What I need you to do now is to write up your conversation with Meera. Every cough and spit.'

'Are we going to dig into it now?' He couldn't hide the excitement in his voice. After the bungled investigation that had led to him breaking his leg, ACC Markie had wanted to move him to a desk job. That would surely have doused the enthusiasm that was one of the reasons Karen had fought so hard to keep him on her team.

'Leave it with me,' she said. 'I need to figure out how we deal with this without breaking lockdown rules.'

He laughed. 'That would be something, eh? Senior polis breaking the lockdown law.'

On that wry note, Karen ended the conversation. She experienced a low buzz of adrenaline that she hadn't felt since they'd been sent home three weeks before, when she'd instructed Jason and Daisy to pack up all the physical files for unsolved murders and suspicious disappearances and move them to Hamish's flat. For the first time, it seemed possible that they had a genuine new lead to follow.

Karen pulled her laptop towards her and started typing up a skeleton of what Jason had told her. Now wasn't the time for detail; now was the time to form a plan of action.

It didn't take her long to outline the next steps on this particular journey. She'd been working cold cases for long enough to know the basic shape of an inquiry that delved into histories that some people wanted to stay buried. Exhumation was a skill she'd developed long ago.

She needed to get her hands on a copy of the manuscript in question, which would mean sweet-talking Meera's boss. Then she'd have to read the manuscript and refresh herself with the case papers to see whether the plot of the novel mapped on to the reality to any significant degree. Then maybe – and it was a big maybe – they might start to unravel what had happened to Lara Hardie.

Ideally, she'd like Daisy to go through the rest of Jake Stein's archive to see whether anything else might connect with Lara Hardie. Further down the line, Jason, who pro-voked the maternal instinct in so many women, could talk again to Lara's mother, her sister and her friends in the light of what they might uncover now. But access would be the big stumbling block, she feared.

Time to pick someone else's brains. DCI Jimmy Hutton had been on her 'favourites' list since her late partner Phil Parhatka had been his bagman. After Phil had died, Jimmy and Karen had become a support group of two, meeting reg-ularly to work through their loss and to sample the myriad gins that had appeared out of nowhere to flood the market. The impossibility of meeting over a glass or two was already something she missed keenly. Not because of the alcohol but because of the conversation.

Now, he answered his phone on the second ring. 'Listen, Karen,' he began without preamble. 'Do you think it would work if we met up on the Zoom for a drink and a blether?'

'It'd be a bit weird. Let's see how long this goes on for. See how desperate we get,' she chuckled.

'Right enough. So I'm guessing this isn't a social call? What can I do for you?'

'I've read all the memos and the briefings from on high about how we go about things in this weird new state of affairs. But I'll be honest, with me not being a front-line officer, it kind of went in one ear and out the other. So I don't really have a sense of how the policing is working on the ground. What happens when you need to talk to witnesses? Or get access to evidence?'

'Are you tidying up loose ends? Or have you managed to find a new case to work?' He sounded incredulous.

'Might have.' She tried to sound nonchalant. 'We were looking at old cases, but there's an outside chance we've got a fresh lead on a misper that's barely cold. Might be something and nothing but I need to check it out. And nobody seems to know how long this lockdown's going to last.'

'I should have known. Doing a jigsaw and watching box sets isn't your kind of thing. Well, we've been told that the beat goes on. There's no free pass for the villains or the toe-rags. We still go out and arrest folk, in their homes if we have to. But we've got to wear masks and use hand sanitisers and keep our distance. We're taking patrol cars with us to bring them in because they've got the Perspex screens between the front seats and the back. If we can get them into an interview room, we have to keep two metres distance.'

Karen snorted. 'That sounds totally impractical.'

'It's a nightmare, is what it is. You know what the neds are like – "I've got the COVID, I'm going to cough my germs on you, ya cunt." So we're doing our best. With witness statements, if they've got a computer or a smartphone, we're trying to do them on screen. Otherwise, it's kind of take your life in your hands.' He sighed. 'We're all going to get it.'

'It's scary,' she acknowledged. 'Nobody knows what's coming at us down the line. Is this going to be the one that sees us off? Like the asteroid and the dinosaurs? Or is it just going to be a jacked-up version of the flu?'

'Your guess is as good as mine. All we can do is drink gin and try to do our jobs. Have you got plenty masks and hand sanitisers?'

She groaned. 'Even the gin might be under threat, Jimmy. You're not going to believe Hamish's latest. He's taken over a wee still in the village and he's making heather hand sanitiser instead of gin.' Jimmy said nothing. 'And since he's had to close the coffee shops here in Edinburgh, he's talking about using his baristas to do home deliveries of the stuff.'

'He never misses a chance.' Jimmy's voice was flat. She knew he was comparing Hamish to Phil. The dead man would come out on top; the dead always did. 'So what's this new lead you're chasing?'

'I'll tell you if it comes to anything. It might be the deranged fantasy of a lockdown mind,' she said wryly.

'Plenty of that about. I don't even know why we're bothering, to be honest. The backlog in the courts was already horrendous. This is just going to make things way worse. They're already talking about more than two years between the offence and the court appearance.'

'That's a helluva long time for victims and their families to wait for justice. And I can just see the defence advocates rubbing their hands in glee.' She assumed a posh accent. '"So, Mrs McPhee, do you really expect the court to believe you can recall the events of a drunken night three years ago with such accuracy?" There's going to be a lot of free passes down the line.'

Jimmy sighed. 'No kidding. But we just have to press on. Let me know if there's anything I can help with.'

'Will do.' She ended the call, already running through

her options. For the first time since COVID had curtailed their lives, Karen felt invigorated. Maybe it wasn't such a bad thing to be so committed to her job. That was a damn sight better than having nothing more than the next Scandi crime drama to fire her up in lockdown.

4

The one advantage of lockdown was that, apart from their daily hour of exercise, everyone was exactly where they were supposed to be. Not only that – already they welcomed anything that broke the monotony. So she wasn't surprised when Bethan Carmichael answered her mobile on the second ring. Karen introduced herself and hastily added that there was nothing to be worried about.

The head of Archive Services didn't seem reassured. 'You'll appreciate, I'm responsible for a great deal of valuable material,' she said sternly. 'So you'll forgive me if I find a call from a senior police officer unsettling.'

Karen smiled. She knew that, though it wasn't visible, it injected warmth into her voice. 'As far as I'm aware, your archive is intact. It's not under threat.'

'So why are you calling?' No thaw so far.

'One of my team has had dealings with one of your colleagues. They've become pals, I suppose you'd say. Anyway—'

'Which one of my colleagues?' Sharpness in the tone now.

'Meera Reddy. She's been very helpful in our inquiries in the past, before she joined the archive team.' Karen paused but nothing came back. 'She called DC Murray from my unit this morning because something's been preying on her mind. Something she came across before lockdown.'

'Something in the archive?' Now she had Bethan Carmichael's attention. 'And she came to you with this? Without consulting me?'

'If she's right, it's a police matter.' Without waiting for a response, Karen ploughed on and outlined what the Mint had told her.

'Extraordinary,' Carmichael said. 'I understand now why you called me. It seems unlikely that there's any connection between the manuscript and the disappearance of this young woman, but I suppose you have to take it seriously. Just in case.'

'As you say, just in case. The first thing I need to do is to see this manuscript for myself.' Karen let the request hang in the air.

'I understand. And in normal circumstances, I'd be happy to let you do just that.' Carmichael spoke slowly. 'But as I'm sure you're aware, the library is closed just now. The staff have been sent home. The only presence on our estate right now are security staff.'

Karen rolled her shoulders as if preparing for battle. 'A photocopy would do at this point. Can Meera not go in and do that?'

'If anyone is going in, it will be me,' she said flatly. 'That way I know the guidelines are not being breached.'

'It's a police investigation, Bethan.' Dropping into the librarian's first name to make it clear who was top banana in this conversation. 'We are allowed to breach the terms of the lockdown rules if there's no other way to pursue it. I'd be happy to do it myself, except that I don't have a clue where to find the papers in question. I could come with you if you're concerned about being reported in breach?'

'I don't understand what the urgency is here. Surely this can wait till the lockdown is lifted? The archive isn't going anywhere. It's not as if anything you can do at this stage will affect this young woman's fate.' She sounded cross.

Karen stood up and walked to the window, taking a deep breath on the way. 'We've no idea when lockdown will be lifted, Bethan. Right now, all we're seeing is rising numbers of infections, rising numbers of deaths. People not allowed to visit their loved ones in care homes or hospitals. We don't know when we'll have a vaccine, or even *if* we'll get one. None of us likes living with that uncertainty. So imagine how it is for Lara Hardie's family. They've been living with uncertainty for a year now. Uncertainty and fear. They don't know what happened to their daughter, their sister. They don't even know whether she's alive or dead. And if she's alive, that's another argument against wasting time.' She paused and let her words sink in.

'It's my job to find answers to their questions,' she continued, her voice softening as she gazed out over the sea. 'Chances are, it won't be an answer that brings them anything other than more grief. But at least they'll know what happened to their lassie. That's why, in my job, every day counts, Bethan. That's why I don't want to hang about till somebody decides it's safe for us all to come out of our houses again.'

'Oh, fuck,' Daisy Mortimer sighed. The boss's number was on the phone screen and she couldn't refuse the call. She spread her arms in a frustrated shrug. 'I've got to take this, I'll message you later.' She ended FaceTime on her laptop and accepted Karen's call. 'Hi,' she said brightly. 'Did you forget something?'

'No. Something's come up. I'll explain when I get back. Those files we brought back from the office – can you pull the Lara Hardie case and call up the online details too?'

Daisy swung her legs off the sofa and sat up. 'Sure. Are you heading back now?' I thought you weren't coming back till past midnight?'

'Yeah, well, things have changed.' Karen chuckled. 'You sound panicked. Are you having a party?'

Was her boss psychic? 'No, just surprised.'

'I'll be with you inside the hour. It's police business, Daisy, not a whim.' The line went dead. Daisy cursed under her breath. She'd thought she had the flat to herself for the whole day. She'd had plans. Plans that involved someone else. Not in person, but certainly in the flesh. She opened WhatsApp on her phone and started typing.

> Sorry. I know I said I had all day, and I know we had plans but it turns out I have to work. Gutted! xxx

The reply came within seconds.

> Shit happens. Don't worry, I'm not going to go off you. Having to wait makes it all the sweeter.🖤

That was a relief, at least. Bloody KP Nuts, though. Why couldn't she stick to the arrangements? Sharing with Karen was generally pretty straightforward, and Daisy loved working on the cold cases team with her and the Mint. But when she'd agreed to moving in, what she hadn't bargained on had been starting a new relationship two days before

28

lockdown. That was hard enough without having to dodge around someone so unpredictable. At least their bedrooms were at opposite ends of the flat. But every now and again, Daisy would have liked to have an encounter outside the hours of darkness.

She went through to Hamish Mackenzie's spare room, its luxury a sharp contrast with her own flat. Daisy had stretched her finances to the limit to buy her place; when it came to furnishing it, she'd had to settle for an IKEA bed and sofa, with everything else coming from the monthly house clearance auction in Cowdenbeath. Staying here felt a bit like living in a hotel and the novelty had worn off.

Daisy gave herself a mental shake. Karen was mostly good company, and it was better than being stuck on her own with only the walls to talk to, like most of her friends. And there was no getting away from the fascination of poring over other officers' old files, looking for possible cracks in the surface. Now it sounded like they had something fresh to get their teeth into.

But still . . . There was no time for a shower, so she settled for a swipe of deodorant and a tumble of her hair. Ruefully, she pulled a T-shirt over her bra, and a pair of joggers over the sexy black pants she'd chosen for the expected day's fun.

She remembered the Lara Hardie disappearance. She'd still been working in Fife, recently promoted to sergeant and eager to prove herself. She'd watched the TV coverage, ashamed to admit to herself that she'd wished Lara had vanished from Fife so she could have worked the case. Daisy was only a few years older than the missing young woman; she remembered how it had felt to be on the brink of emerging from university into the real world of work; that exhilarating mixture of fear and desire. What could have derailed

Lara's life so thoroughly? It was hard not to believe that the student had been abducted. That she was dead. Daisy wondered what set of choices had taken Lara to the terrible convergence of her path and that of a killer? Was it simply a matter of being in the wrong place at the wrong time? Or did it run deeper than that? And what had Karen found that might answer those questions? It was, now she thought about it, a more exciting prospect than a digital date.

The HCU files they'd removed were in Hamish's office, a small room lined with filing cabinets, a utilitarian pine desk housing a Mac and a second monitor. The cardboard boxes of files were piled three high and two deep along the other wall, leaving only a narrow passage between door and desk. With a sigh, Daisy started. 'It'll be the last box in the last row,' she muttered. 'Bound to be.'

She was thrilled to be proved wrong. Second box in the second row was the jackpot. Daisy hauled it through to the living room, then rewarded herself with a couple of slices of sourdough toast dripping with butter. She was halfway through the second slice when Karen walked in.

Karen grinned. 'Don't drip butter on the files,' she said as she took off her jacket and slung it over a chair.

'What's happened?' Daisy wiped her fingers with a piece of kitchen towel and put her plate down. 'Are we properly back in business?'

'Maybe.'

'How come?'

Daisy perched on the edge of the sofa as Karen filled her in on what Jason had learned. 'That's weird,' she said. 'I mean, I know crime writers sometimes use real cases to kick-start their books, but they don't usually map on to the reality that accurately.'

'We don't know yet how close the manuscript is. And it's only part of the story. If I'm honest, I doubt it's as much of a match as Meera seems to think. But at least we can take another pass at it. Who knows? Reading the book might shake a few ideas loose.'

'So are we going to get our hands on the original?'

Karen gave a short bark of laughter. 'No chance.' She assumed a portentous accent. 'The National Library of Scotland are the custodians of the unpublished manuscripts of one of Scotland's most significant crime writers of his generation. It would be inappropriate to let *The Vanishing of Laurel Oliver* out of their custody.'

Daisy giggled. 'Right enough. We might drip butter on it.' *Or worse*, she thought with a smirk. 'What's the plan, then?'

'Bethan Carmichael is going to scan it and send a digital copy to me. I've asked her to send me a photocopy as well, just in case there are any annotations that don't come through clearly. She reckoned she can get it done by close of play tomorrow. So in the meantime, what I think we should do is work our way through the case papers and the online stuff.' She pulled a face. 'It'll be good to have something specific to focus on. I don't know about you, but some days it gets to bedtime and I've got no bloody idea what I've done to pass the hours.'

'I know, it's like my brain's turned to mush. Is that a secret COVID symptom?'

Karen groaned. 'I hope not. Here's how we do this. I'll read a statement or a report, then pass it to you, then you do the same. We both make notes as we go, then at the end, we compare what we've written. We'll probably duplicate a lot of the queries, but we'll also both come up with different takes on specific things. Does that make sense?'

31

Daisy had never worked an HCU case from the start and she was surprised at Karen's style. 'I guess. It's not an approach I've come across before.' Her expression was dubious.

'It's one of the luxuries of cold cases. When you're working a live case, time's your enemy. You don't have the opportunity to process things at such a granular level. And with the best will in the world, inevitably stuff gets overlooked or missed. It's nobody's fault. But we're the last chance saloon, so we owe it to the victims to give it all the attention we can muster.'

'That makes sense.'

'So you make us both a coffee while I get started.' Karen was already reaching for the first folder in the box.

'I'll open the shortbread as well.' At the start of lockdown, they'd unearthed a box containing dozens of packets of souvenir shortbread at the back of the pantry. Karen had joked that Hamish would have forgotten the existence of anything so unhealthy. Daisy had made it her mission to work her way through it as an act of kindness. Forensically unravelling a cold case was the perfect opportunity to make real inroads.

'Careful with the crumbs,' Karen said absently, Lara Hardie already her focus. 'We'll never hear the last of it if we have to hand over the case papers to the Fiscal Depute with shortbread between the pages.'

Daisy wished she could share her boss's optimism about the ultimate fate of the file. But still, she'd give it her best shot, even if it was interfering with her first chance at a love life in months. She jumped up with genuine enthusiasm. 'Right you are, boss. If anyone can nail this, we can.'

They were at the bottom of the file box when the call came through the following afternoon. Bethan Carmichael had found her mojo lurking somewhere by the photocopier. 'DCI Pirie? I made two copies of the manuscript and I've put the scanned text on a memory stick. I'll hand them over to you personally. I don't trust internet security.' She gave Karen directions to the back entrance of the library, off the Cowgate. 'How long will it take you to get here?'

Karen consulted her mental map of the city. 'I can be there in twenty minutes.'

'I'll wait for you outside. It's a nice afternoon, I'll enjoy the air.'

Karen left Daisy reading. The late afternoon sun dazzled her as she emerged from the tenement and she was glad to turn south up the steep hill of Broughton Street. It felt eerily still, pavements that usually bustled with shoppers almost empty. Those who were out and about gave each other a wide berth, even stepping into the gutter to avoid coming too close to anyone else. The bars and restaurants were shuttered; only the wholefood grocers, deemed an essential food shop, was open, a sign on the door limiting the number of customers to two at a time. The stream of traffic that usually stuttered up the hill was absent too. Karen counted only three cars, two going up and one down. She had no idea how all the wee shops and restaurants that dotted the streets around Hamish's flat would survive the shutdown. A lot of them wouldn't, she suspected.

Picardy Place, usually jammed in all directions because of the perennial roadworks, felt abandoned. Karen hurried across, up Leith Street to the point where the city became three-dimensional. Centuries of building wherever foundations could be set down – even when that place was a street already – had created a complex warren of streets that coexisted at different levels. The National Library's back door was approached via the Cowgate, a road that crossed beneath George IV Bridge three storeys below the front door of the building. It inevitably reminded Karen of an Escher drawing. She wasn't given to fancies, but she remembered that Hamish had once confessed that he'd wondered whether there were lost librarians wandering its aisles like the Flying Dutchman. She'd had to google that, and she had to admit to herself that it wasn't such a daft idea.

She turned into the vennel leading to the rear entrance of the library. It looked far too innocuous to house millions of books and maps, assorted bits of paper and the set of that electrifying play, *The Cheviot, The Stag and the Black, Black Oil*. Though she seemed to remember reading somewhere that particular two-metre-high pop-up book was on loan to the V&A in Dundee. Either way, nobody was going to be consulting it now.

A woman she took to be Bethan Carmichael was sitting on a polypropylene chair by the closed door. She was immersed in a paperback, a canvas tote bag leaning against one of the slender metal legs of the chair. A curtain of long dark hair obscured her face. Karen's trainers made no sound as she approached and she was almost upon the woman before some instinct made her look up. Startled, she jumped to her feet, the legs of the chair screeching as she pushed it back. 'God, you nearly gave me a heart attack!' She clamped the hand that held the book to her chest. 'Are you DCI Pirie?'

Karen registered the book title. *Around the World in 80 Trees*; appropriate enough for someone whose job depended upon the death of trees. She held out her ID. 'That's me. Bethan Carmichael, I presume?' She looked more like a model for a high-end clothes store. Sahara, or Oska, maybe. Unstructured linen, loose trousers, a jacket like a French labourer's. Her face was all planes and angles; not exactly attractive, but striking, Karen thought.

Carmichael bent to pick up the tote bag and hesitated. 'I've done what you asked,' she said. 'But if you think this is going anywhere, I should warn you that there are two whole archive boxes that date from roughly the same period. There are all sorts of scribbles on pieces of paper, some of them possibly related to this material. You may find that you need to go through them with a fine-tooth comb. If so, we'll have to make special arrangements.'

'What sort of special arrangements? Why can't we just take them away? Or have them copied?'

Carmichael rolled her eyes. 'Because they've not been catalogued and assessed by a fully qualified archivist. We've only had Jake Stein's papers for a few months. We've not had time to fully prepare the archive. If you did want to go down that road, I'd have to arrange for one of your people to be given access to a room and locked in while they were reading through the material. I'm really not sure even that would be lawful.' As with so many in these terrified times, her fear had translated itself to hostility.

Karen shrugged. 'In spite of the pandemic, we're still supposed to serve and protect. And that means carrying out investigations. This particular inquiry might be a cold case, but if Lara Hardie was murdered, there's somebody out there who's killed at least once and might well do so again. It becomes a public protection issue, Bethan. If there's a can to be carried, I'll cheerfully do that. But we'll burn that bridge if we come to it. In the meantime, let us look at what you've got for us and we'll take it from there.' She held out her hand and Carmichael reluctantly handed over the bag.

'Let me know how you get on,' she said.

Karen dipped her head in acknowledgement. 'When I can. Thanks for this.' She turned to walk away, then swung back as a thought occurred to her. 'Who delivered this material to you?'

'It was part of Jake Stein's estate,' she replied. 'It came from the lawyers who were handling the probate. I think they'd consulted Stein's ex-wife; there were probably considerations of privacy and Stein's own conditions to be met.'

'So someone could have weeded out material they didn't want anyone else to see?'

'It's always a possibility. An ex-wife might well pull letters or notes that showed her in an unfavourable light.'

Karen tutted. 'Great. Oh well, we'll have to make the best of what we've got.' She walked off, wishing she could head to the nearest café and dive into the text. But the nearest café, ironically one of Hamish's Perk chain, was closed, its baristas repurposed as delivery boys. She increased her pace as she pushed on up and over the ridge of the Canongate, hardly able to contain her impatience. In the meantime, she could set Jason to work.

He answered his phone with a cheerful, 'Hi, boss. So, was Meera right? Are we cooking with gas?'

'Too early to say, Jason. Daisy and I are going to wade through the manuscript and that will give us a better idea.'

'Oh. Right.' He sounded disappointed.

'In the meantime, I've got a job for you.'

'Oh. Right.' This time, he resembled a dog that's been shown the treat.

'I want you to get online and research Jake Stein. There'll be a lot of interviews and probably YouTube videos. Plus you'll need to dig down deep into the socials – Faceplant, Twatter, Slapchat—'

'That's not what they're called, boss.'

Karen rolled her eyes. 'I want a full timeline of the man's life and career. See how much you can get for a briefing, OK?'

'How are we going to do a briefing?'

'It'll have to be on the Zoom,' she sighed. 'So you'll need to get up in time to comb your hair.' She ended the call and forged on. Maybe this was something and nothing. But that was often the case with leads on cold cases. With a little digging in the right place, the unpromising could reveal a hidden path through the thicket of information. And when it came to finding the right place to dig, Karen Pirie was definitely more bloodhound than box-ticker.

That didn't mean she was optimistic that they'd been handed a revelation that would open the Lara Hardie case like a can-opener. Chances were, this would turn out to be nothing more than a couple of coincidences. But that would also be OK. Karen could run it as if it were the real thing, making it a training and team-building exercise for Jason and Daisy. That was just what they needed. The one case where Daisy had been seconded to the HCU hadn't told Karen enough about her skills and her practices. And Jason needed reassurance that the arrival of a new team member one rank up from him wasn't a threat to his standing with Karen. Walking through this odd situation might prove the perfect piece of serendipity.

Either way, it wouldn't hurt. And it would be more fun than a thousand-piece jigsaw.

6

The Lara Hardie case file contained few surprises, Daisy thought. There was a familiar pattern to this kind of disappearance. The initial report, from friends or family; the excluding of the trifecta of usual reasons – running away for love; ditto for escape; depression leading to suicide. Then the attempt to fill in the hours leading to the vanishing, the door-to-door, the questioning of anyone who knew the misper well. Then the absurd false leads thrown out by the internet and seized on by the conspiracy theorists. It wasn't easy to disappear without trace these days. Not with CCTV and digital footprints. But Lara had managed it. She'd left the flat she shared with two other students one Monday evening almost a year ago, saying she was going to the library. She never arrived.

She wasn't in a relationship. Her studies were going well. She wasn't the life and soul of the party, but she wasn't someone who provoked antagonism. There was no obvious reason for her to leave her life. One of the flatmates had said she thought Lara had an air of suppressed excitement that didn't fit with a trip to the library.

There was one distinctive element to this particular disappearance. Lara had suffered since childhood with atonic epileptic seizures. Every few months, she'd experience a moment where all her muscles stopped working. If she was standing or walking, she'd hit the deck. If she was sitting down, she'd slump forward. The last time it had happened, she'd been sitting at a desk in the library and her head had smacked into it with such force she'd ended up with a goose egg on her forehead. But suffering such damage had been rare. Usually, Lara recovered fully almost instantaneously, often not even realising she'd had an episode. She made no fuss about her ailment. She took regular medication; the only deprivation she'd ever commented on to her flatmates was she could neither drive nor cycle.

The media, both news and social, speculated that she'd experienced a seizure that had allowed a passing predator to exploit her illness. No matter how often medical experts expressed frustration at this misrepresentation of her illness, the inaccuracies persisted.

There had been a search, of course. Police dogs, volunteers, the usual. Nothing had turned up. There were some printouts from online news outlets, ranging from WHERE IS PRETTY BLONDE LARA? to EDINBURGH STUDENT GOES MISSING. Always the same, Daisy thought. Blonde white lassie = screaming headlines. Anybody else = a few paragraphs. Nevertheless, it hadn't made any difference. Lara had slid out of sight without a trace.

Finally, the TV appeal. Lara's mum and dad were joined by her elder sister, stoic at first, then tearful. *Have you seen Lara ... if you're keeping Lara ... Lara, we love you ... Lara come home.* Heartbreaking, but this time, as was usually the case, fruitless. Unless you counted the dozens of time-wasting 'sightings'.

Daisy was close to the end of the Lara Hardie case file

when Karen burst through the door, out of breath from hurrying up three flights of stairs. Daisy pushed her notes to one side and stood up expectantly. 'Did you get it?'

Karen waved the bag, triumphant as a successful bargain hunter at the sales. 'I did.' She moved the empty file box to the floor and spread out her spoils. Two disappointingly scant piles of paper and a memory stick. 'I managed to keep my hands off all the way home.' She sounded pleased with herself, and Daisy couldn't blame her. She'd have squatted in the nearest doorway and stolen a quick look if it had been her.

Daisy approached and they each picked up a set of pho-tocopies. 'Tell me we get to read it now,' she said.

'No reason to hold back,' Karen said, moving to one of the comfortable armchairs that flanked the fireplace. She tucked a pencil behind her ear and began to read.

THE VANISHING OF LAUREL OLIVER

PART ONE

Prologue

He really believed it was a madcap game. A joke. A dare, played out between old friends. Why would anyone imagine otherwise? Writing twisted scenarios didn't mean he believed they happened in the real world. *Strangers on a Train* had the brilliant premise of two unconnected people swapping murders, but he didn't believe anybody would be daft enough to try it for real. Not even a card-carrying psychopath like the character in Highsmith's novel.

It had genuinely never crossed his mind that his best friend would actually commit a murder solely to demonstrate that the perfect crime was possible, and that he was capable of committing it. Not until he had to deal with the revelation that there was now a dead body in his garage.

1

Jamie Cobain and Rob Thomas had met in a curry house in Perth. The one in Scotland, not Australia. They were both there for the crime writing festival the city had hosted for the previous decade. Jamie had never quite worked out why Perth ended up as the venue for the festival. As far as he knew, its only real claim to criminal fame was the maximum security prison celebrated in song by the late Dundee bard Michael Marra in his 'Letter from Perth'. Other than that, the only reason he could think of for choosing Perth was that it was well served by the motorway network, and by direct trains from Edinburgh and Glasgow. And there was the sleeper to and from London, which was always a consideration when it came to persuading the metropolitans to reach escape velocity from their orbital motorway.

Rob had appeared on the last panel of the Saturday afternoon on the thorny subject of *Mad or Bad: Dangerous to Know*. Alongside a criminal barrister, a former priest and an escaped wife and mother (her words, not Rob's), he'd explained his views on why people do the terrible things his imagination conjured up. There were a couple of hundred in the audience, several of whom had queued up afterwards to have their books signed. The other authors sloped off before Rob had finished, leaving him at a loose end. He was relatively new to the festival scene; the book he was promoting was only his second, and he hadn't managed to establish any friendships yet that went beyond an occasional drink in the hotel bar.

He ambled back from the theatre, aiming for nonchalance, and arrived at the hotel just as a group of guys were heading out. Half a dozen of them, early thirties to mid-fifties, full of good-natured swagger and nonsense, the way men get when they're let loose from their pedestrian lives and feel the need to prove themselves. He recognised most of them as fellow writers but the only one he could actually put a name to was Jamie Cobain. In his early forties, he already had a career to envy. More than a dozen books published, three or four major awards, bestseller status at home and abroad. Rumour had it that his series detective was in development for TV, starring one of the craggy-faced, piercing-eyed heart-throbs of the moment.

Jamie Cobain caught sight of Rob and stopped in mid-stride. 'It's Rob, right?' He turned to the others and said, 'Guys, this is Rob Thomas. You know? *Dereliction*. Shortlisted for the Golden Thistle.'

A general rumble of acknowledgement, recognition, greetings. 'Hi,' Rob said, gripped by the shyness he always felt when confronted by a bunch of strangers.

'We're going for a curry, Rob.'

'And a few sherbets,' one of the others chipped in.

'Are you spoken for, or do you want to join us?' Jamie Cobain again.

Rob swallowed. 'That'd be great, thanks.' He tacked on to

the edge of the crew and they hustled down the street, past the concrete monolith of Police Scotland, ending up in a time-warped Indian restaurant. Paper tablecloths, flock wallpaper, a list of different curries each with the option of chicken, lamb, beef or prawn. They could have been anywhere from Plymouth to Pitlochry, Rob thought. But definitely not the Punjab.

Not that it mattered. They were there for the beer and the chat. The curry was an incidental. Rob found himself sitting next to Jamie, surprised to be engaged in lively conversation with his new acquaintance. The table talk was mostly publishing gossip, lurid tales of bad behaviour among the crime writing community, gossip about who had fallen out with editor or agent, unlikely speculation about who might be shagging whom. A lot of laughter and anecdotage. But every now and then it would splinter into separate conversations. During one of those, Rob and Jamie discovered they lived not far from each other; Rob in his tiny flat in Leith, Jamie in the large detached house that his authorial success had brought him.

More to the point, they shared a common passion for chess. They'd both learned to play as schoolboys, Jamie at one of those Edinburgh private schools that trains its pupils to sound English, Rob at the local comprehensive in Dundee. But they'd both played at county level. Jamie was the elder by five years, otherwise they might have faced each other across the board as acned teenagers with bad haircuts. 'Come round sometime, we'll have a game,' Jamie offered warmly as the waiter cleared the dishes and the writers ordered another round.

Rob didn't think he meant it. He thought it was the kind of throwaway line that fills a space in the conversation. When they all staggered back to the hotel, genial and fuzzy with drink, Jamie was immediately swallowed up in a bigger crowd that included his agent and his editor. Forsaken now, Rob drifted to the fringes of the room, where a couple of intense readers collared him and insisted on a battery of detailed questions about his books and the earlier panel discussion. He didn't see Jamie again all weekend until he was driving off in one of those ugly SUVs that rumbled through the cobbled streets of Edinburgh like an invading army. In spite of his enjoyment of their dinner encounter, Rob felt Jamie drop a little in his estimation at the sight.

But Jamie rose again a few days later when he emailed Rob via his website. 'Mate, when are we going to get together over a board or two? I don't know about you, but it's a bitch to find a half-decent opponent.'

It was a friendly gesture, but at the same time, Rob recognised it was a gauntlet thrown down. Did he fancy his chances? Was he up to Jamie's standards? Would it be a humiliating one-off, or would it be enough of a mutual challenge to occupy a regular slot in their lives?

There was only one way to find out.

2

The house impressed Rob. He'd assumed Jamie was making a good enough living, but he hadn't expected it to provide a detached half-timbered monster that wouldn't have looked out of place in the leafy lanes of the Home Counties. Its double gables looked out on the woodland of Ravelston Dykes like a pair of sarcastically raised eyebrows disdaining Rob's approach.

The doorbell pealed the first four notes of the Westminster chimes. Through the stained-glass panels flanking the door he could see an indistinct figure approaching. The door swung open silently and Jamie Cobain broke into a grin. 'Hey, you came, mate. I was afraid you might bottle it.' He gestured expansively. 'Welcome to the humble abode.'

Humble it certainly wasn't, Rob thought. He followed Jamie down the tiled hallway and into a room towards the back of the house. He reckoned if a set designer had been told to produce a gentleman's study, it would have resembled Jamie's den. Bookshelves, a couple of dramatic Highland landscapes, a leather-topped desk and a pair of club chairs facing each other over a table with a marquetry chessboard, its dark squares black as ebony. The only object out of place was the silver MacBook Air folded shut on the desk.

'Let me take your coat.' Jamie fussed around, helping Rob out of his budget down jacket and disappearing with it. He returned with a tray – two decanters, two whisky tumblers, a jug of water. 'Speyside or Islay?' he said, putting the tray on the desk with a flourish.

'Islay, with a splash.'

Jamie chuckled as he poured a dark whisky whose phenolic fumes Rob could smell across the room. 'I expected as much. You don't strike me as a man who likes a breakfast whisky at this time of day.' It was a pitch-perfect performance; Rob recognised it as the very goal he was working towards. In Jamie's case, though, it was the real thing. Being a writer wasn't improbable for someone from his background. But Rob and Jamie both knew that people like him weren't supposed to become writers, never mind successful ones.

Jamie handed him a generous measure and they toasted each other. 'I've been looking forward to this,' he said. 'A worthy opponent who moves in the same world as me.'

Rob pulled a wry smile. 'Maybe not quite on the same plane.'

'Only a matter of time.' He waved Rob towards a chair and settled himself opposite. 'You're a class act, Rob.'

'Kind of you to say so, but there are no certainties in
our game.'

Neither of them had any way of knowing how prescient
Rob's words were. He sat watching Jamie set out the pieces,
both unaware that their lives were at a tipping point. They had
not the faintest notion that Rob's impending stratospheric rise
would be mirrored by Jamie's tragic fall.

All they were thinking about that first evening was what
lay immediately ahead. Jamie was confident in his ability;
he'd often been surprised by his knack of stringing together
a winning sequence of moves from apparently beleaguered
positions. But he'd already decided that if need be, he'd go easy
on Rob, at least for tonight. He enjoyed being looked up to by
the newbie on the scene – who wouldn't? – and he genuinely
appreciated the joy of finding a fresh opponent who might just
give him a battle worth winning.

Rob was apprehensive about the game, obviously anxious
about what this encounter could mean for him. But both
were hoping they'd be evenly matched. If Jamie outstripped
him easily, Rob reckoned he'd probably never be asked back.
He didn't think Jamie was the kind of man who'd favour the
delivery of humiliation over the pleasure of challenge. On the
other hand, if Rob commanded the board and made Jamie
feel small, he definitely wouldn't be asked back. And right
then, he wanted to be part of Jamie Cobain's charmed life.
Being his friend was an entrée into the easy camaraderie of
publishing's big dogs.

Because the big dogs still ran the game. Readers believed
that the books that garnered the golden reviews, the pole
positions in the bookshops, the eye-catching ads in the tube
and on train stations were there by virtue of their quality. Rob
knew the truth. They were there because an editor had sold

them at the marketing meeting, hooked them up with the best publicist, put them in front of the best cover designer. Sometimes that was because the book genuinely was the real deal. But just as often, it was because the author had a great smile, connected well on social media, and knew how to walk the fine line between attractively surprising and grotesquely shocking interviews. To get those plum slots, the big dogs had to know you. You had to be in it to win it.

Rob, at the start of his career, was determined to do whatever it took to be in it. Jamie understood that too, and if Rob turned out to be a worthy opponent, he'd do all he could to bring him into the club. It wasn't altruism; Rob would owe him and he'd use his rising position to big-up his benefactor. That was the way it worked.

They sipped their whisky and exchanged a few desultory comments about the Perth festival. But Rob could tell Jamie's heart wasn't in it. He sensed a suppressed excitement in the other man. They were each as eager as the other to get on with the game. Jamie kept glancing at a wooden box sitting on the side table next to him. It was a simple piece, its only decoration a half-moon indentation to facilitate the removal of the lid. But the wood had a beautiful grain. Rob couldn't name it then; he'd since learned it was bird's-eye maple.

'I've been looking forward to this,' he said.

Jamie's smile was impish. 'The game or the blether?'

Rob didn't have to pause for reflection. 'The game. Always the game.'

It was the entry point Jamie had been angling for. He grabbed the box, slid open the lid and tipped the contents out. Both men stared at the tumble of pieces for a moment before Jamie swiftly shifted them to their places on the board. Rob was pleased to see he'd avoided the cheesy temptation of a novelty set. Whether

it was Lord of the Rings, Star Wars or even a resin replica of the
Lewis chessmen, nothing screamed 'time-waster' more when it
came to a game of chess, in Rob's opinion. Jamie's pieces were as
plain as the box they came in, though the traditional shapes had
been carved from wood with as fine a grain.

'Nice set,' he said as Jamie laid them out with a care that
matched his speed.

He gave Rob a quick look, sizing him up. 'They were a
second-hand gift,' he said. 'My wife bought them for me. She
still thinks I'm worth spending a lot of my money on. They were
supposedly given to Garry Kasparov by an admirer to celebrate
his twenty years as world ranking number one.' He snorted. 'I
wish my game merited them.'

Jamie palmed two pawns, lowered his hands beneath the
level of the table, then offered his closed fists. Rob ended up
with black; to his surprise, Jamie kicked off with the English
Defence. The tempo of the game was slow; both were feeling
their way against an unfamiliar opponent. Rob answered with
the Hedgehog Defence, a cramped set-up but one with plenty
of possibilities for his pawns. He thought he had Jamie on the
run a couple of times, but his host was shrewd and smart, and
he outwitted Rob each time. In the end, Jamie caught him in a
pincer between a knight and a rook and forced him to resign.

Jamie leaned back in his chair, arms spread expansively in an
empty embrace. 'I haven't had to work that hard in a very long
time. You really pushed me, Rob.'

'Same for me.' Rob let out a long breath and caught sight of
his watch as he flexed his fingers. 'My God, we've been at it for
nearly three hours.'

Jamie reached for the decanter. 'Fastest three hours I've had
for quite a while. We definitely have to do this again. I love
feeling my brain working overtime.'

Rob put a hand over his glass. 'No more for me. I've got the car.'

Jamie grimaced. 'Fair enough. Next time, get a cab so we can celebrate a victory properly.'

Rob grinned. 'What if it's a draw?'

A single eyebrow rose. Rob wondered how long Jamie had practised that in the mirror. 'Half-measures, then,' his host said. 'But I warn you, I've never been a man for half-measures.'

Daisy looked up from the bundle of pages she was reading. 'If it wasn't for the prologue, you wouldn't know it was supposed to be a crime novel.'

'I don't read enough crime fiction to know what to expect.' Karen flicked back through what she'd already read. 'And I haven't read any Jake Stein, so I don't know whether this is his usual style.'

'I've read a few of his. I went through a mini-binge a few years ago. I read three on the bounce but then I took a scunner to them. You know how you eat a whole box of Tunnock's teacakes, then you feel kind of queasy and you swear you'll never eat another one?'

Karen shook her head. 'You scare me, Daisy. How come you're not the size of a house?'

'Lucky genes. Anyway, I felt like that about Jake Stein. He takes his time setting up the scene, then eases you into sudden violence. So far, this is spot on with the scene-setting.'

'Do you think there's any chance this has autobiographical elements?'

'Authors always deny that when readers ask them. But I had a quick look at some of the online interviews with

Stein while you were out, and there seemed to be a lot of similarities between Stein and Cobain. And I did read one piece that talked about Stein being a bit of a chess child prodigy.'

'So is Jamie Cobain a straightforward stand-in for Jake Stein? And who is "Rob Thomas" supposed to be, do you think? Do they really sail that close to the wind, these authors?'

Daisy shrugged. 'I'm not an expert on the lives and careers of Scottish crime writers. But it sounds a bit like what I know of Ross McEwen. His books are all one-word titles that start with "Re-". And Rob Thomas's book in the first chapter has a one-word title that starts with "De-". But that might just be a quirk that Stein seized on for a bit of verisimilitude.'

Karen frowned. Time for a little push? 'Or it might be more. Let's make the giant assumption that it's him, for now at least. What do you think the point of this is? I mean, I get that Meera made the connection to Lara Hardie because of the epilepsy thing, which I presume is going to show up in the novel at some point. And I get that crime writers sometimes piggy-back off real cases. But why bring this so close to home? Why would you write something that points a finger right at you?'

'Maybe Jake Stein has a theory about Lara Hardie's disappearance? Maybe the idea is that Jamie will become the intrepid investigator who solves the case that baffled the police?'

Karen tapped the small pile of papers. 'Let's hope he gets to the point before we run out of pages. Because as things stand we don't even know if the fictional body in the garage is a Lara Hardie lookalike or a chess-playing crime writer.'

3

The chess games became a fixture in the two men's diaries. Not exactly regular, because they both had to participate in book promotion events, to attend meetings with agents and editors, to endure foreign tours, to extend festivals for as long as possible to escape the humdrum. But once or twice a month, Jamie would lay out the pieces on his magnificent board and pour two generous Islay malts. And battle would commence.

Getting on for a year after that first encounter, honours were more or less even. Jamie had taken a narrow lead first, then Rob had overtaken him. There had been a series of draws, then Jamie had crept back ahead. For both men, their chess matches had found a place at the heart of their lives. It was as if the mental stimulus of the game gave an added fillip to their imaginations. Each in his own way was energised by the encounters; the chess engaged a different part of the brain to the writing process and somehow provoked a more active creativity.

On a couple of occasions, Rob had met Jamie's wife, Rachel. The first time, she'd poked her head round the door of the study at the start of the evening and suggested a light supper after they'd finished playing. Jamie had looked up, frowning. 'I don't think so, love. Rob's here for serious business, not the Waitrose snacks.'

Rob had winced inwardly at Jamie's rudeness, but Rachel's mouth had quirked in an ironic smile. 'Please yourselves. Enjoy your evening, Rob.'

The second time, it had been Rachel who had answered the door. 'Sorry, Rob. Jamie's flight has been diverted to Glasgow. He's only just touched down. He said—'

At that moment, his own mobile rang, the screen displaying

Jamie's name. He raised a finger and took the call. 'Jamie, I hear there's been a problem.'

'Bloody fog at Edinburgh,' Jamie said, curt and cross. 'I'll be an hour and a half. If you don't mind waiting, we could play some speed chess, rather than a proper game? Rachel will feed you while you're waiting.'

Rachel, who had clearly heard her husband's clipped words, nodded. 'I'd like that,' she said.

It wasn't quite the response he'd expected, but something to eat followed by the exciting prospect of speed chess was better than a solitary evening in his little flat. 'Great idea, Jamie. Rachel seems fine with it.'

'She likes the company of other writers,' he said. 'It's the only way she can find out what I'm up to.'

The line cut out. There had been an edge to Jamie's voice that made Rob uneasy, but Rachel simply shook her head. 'Always all about Jamie,' she said with a tight smile. 'Come through to the kitchen.'

Rob loved to cook, but his options were limited in his tiny galley kitchen. He'd have killed for the substantial room at the rear of the Cobains' house. It wasn't the black and white terrazzo tiles or the granite worktops or the cleverly designed lighting that he envied; those, he barely noticed. What drew his eye were the Aga, the Neff oven and gas rings, the sous-vide and the vacuum packing machine, the Kitchen Aid mixer and blender, the Dualit toaster and kettle and the two knife blocks. What impressed him yet more was that all the equipment looked as if it saw regular use. He gave a low whistle. 'Someone's a very lucky cook,' he said, trying to avoid falling into the easy assumption that it was the woman of the house.

'That would be me,' she said. 'The kitchen is my refuge. I don't know whether Jamie mentioned it, but I'm a lawyer?'

Rob shook his head. 'He never said. That's handy for a crime writer.'

She laughed, a soft sardonic sound. 'Not really, I do the dull stuff. Wills and probate. Jamie often complains that all my practice ever brings in is money, and he can make plenty of that.'

Rob wondered whether that was supposed to be a joke or a put-down. 'So you lawyer by day and cook by night?'

'I only work part-time now,' she said. 'More time for stress-busting culinary adventures.'

She didn't look like a woman who ate many of the products of her adventures. He knew she must be in her early forties, but Rachel Cobain showed no signs of over-indulgence. She was slender and shapely, dressed in tight-fitting yoga pants and a loose shirt tied artfully at the waist to show her off to her best advantage. Her face bore the faintest early traces of lines around the eyes and bracketing a mouth that seemed perpetually on the edge of a smile. Another reason to envy Jamie Cobain, Rob thought. His own recent excursions on the road to romance had led nowhere near the likes of Rachel Cobain.

She opened a vast American-style fridge and peered into the interior. 'So, there's a wild mushroom and porcini soup if you want something light. Sourdough or focaccia to go with it. Or I have some delicious venison loin from the game stall at Castle Terrace market. I've got roast Roscoff onions and artichoke puree to go with that. It won't take me ten minutes to cook it. Or—'

'Stop,' he said. 'You had me at "venison loin".'

While she put dinner together with swift efficiency, she asked Rob about his life before writing. He gave her the version he'd honed for his events, and she gave him a knowing smile.

'Very good,' she said. 'Apparent candour without actually being candid. I bet those audiences love you, Rob Thomas.'

Taken aback, he said, 'I don't know what you mean. It's true.'

'But very far from the whole truth and nothing but the truth.' She chuckled as she prodded the venison spitting in the hot pan. 'I've lived with a champion confabulator for fifteen years, Rob. I may not be able to unpick the seams of your story, but I do know there will be seams.' She lifted the lid on the wide pan where she was heating through the onions and sniffed. 'All these years with Jamie, I know the whiff of deception.'

Over the past months, his association with Jamie had promoted Rob to one of the lads. Not quite one of the big dogs, but certainly one who ran with them. One who could be trusted. So he knew there were plenty of Jamie's deceptions for Rachel to sniff out. He had charm, he was not unattractive and he was a bright star in their firmament. Rob knew Jamie had plenty of offers – hell, he even had a few himself, and he was a next-to-nobody. The difference was that Rob didn't have anyone at home to let down.

He watched Rachel dishing up his dinner with unexpected unease. He liked this woman. Her cooking for him had created an intimacy that hadn't existed when she was just a head poking round a door. In future, knowledge of Jamie's infidelities would confer an awkward complicity.

But there was far worse to come than complicity.

4

The first hint of trouble came at what should have been a night of triumph for Rob. His third novel, *Desecration*, had been published to rave reviews and, even better for sales, an entirely unexpected congruence with an appalling murder in France whose circumstances eerily mirrored those of the novel. Rob, who had only ever been to France under the aegis of his French publishers, clearly had clean hands when it came to accusations of exploitation. Nevertheless his publishers could barely keep up with the demand, as readers devoured the fiction in the hope that it would make the reality explicable.

Hitting the top of the bestseller list would have been enough, he felt, but no sooner had he hit that pinnacle than *Desecration* was shortlisted for two major awards, one on either side of the Atlantic. And it was chosen as one of the *Jackie and Jimmy Summer Reads*, a promotion run by a network magazine show and supported by a leading supermarket chain.

The success of *Desecration* drove readers to his earlier titles, pushing both into the paperback and e-book bestsellers. To celebrate, his publishers did what publishers always did – they threw a party.

The guest list read like a roster of the UK's leading crime writers. The social media back channels buzzed with resentment from those who hadn't made the cut. Agents and editors swirled through the chattering groups. There were journalists too, a smattering of MPs, a handful of actors hoping to be cast in the inevitable TV adaptations, and those booksellers deemed useful by the publishers.

Jamie was there, of course, Rachel at his side, splendid in an aquamarine dress that Rob imagined had come from the sort of shop so discreet he'd never even noticed it. Rob worked his way across the room to where Jamie was holding court. He'd no sooner reached his friend's side than a woman he vaguely recognised barged past him. She stopped inches from Jamie's face, her expression unreadable. He seemed disconcerted, but reached for her elbow and tried to steer her out of the group.

She shook herself free and shouted, 'You fucking bastard,' so loudly a hush fell on that end of the room. Then she swung her right arm back and delivered an open-handed slap that rocked him back on his feet. The shock was tremendous. People stared with dropped jaws. Rachel seemed utterly confounded. Jamie had a hand to his cheek, his other balled into a fist. He took a half-step towards his attacker, then thought better of it.

Before anyone else could react, Jamie's publisher stepped forward and wrapped an arm round the woman, who was now weeping noisily, and virtually dragged her away. For a moment, Rob thought Jamie was going to brazen it out, but one look at Rachel's face told him that wasn't an option. She was already turning from him, moving through the crowd in the opposite direction to the assailant. Hastily, Jamie followed her. As he passed Rob, he muttered, 'Fucking *cunt.*'

Now there was a hubbub of voices. Rob felt like he'd been catapulted back to his high school years, when he was always the one on the outside of the secret. He had no idea who the woman was who had hijacked his moment in the sun. Nor what her particular problem was; though, knowing Jamie, he guessed it was something to do with sex.

He spotted his pal Lucy Brazil nearby and moved towards her. He'd never worked out how she managed it, living up in Manchester, but Lucy was always plugged in to the gossip hotline. Whenever an author had been dropped, or an agent betrayed by a client, whenever a newbie had been suckered into bed by the promises of a bigger name, Lucy always knew the inside story. She cheerfully purveyed her gleanings to her friends, but somehow there was never any malice in it. It puzzled Rob; if he'd been writing such a character, he wouldn't have known how to avoid making her toxic, yet everybody adored Lucy. They even wore the 'I love Lucy' badges she'd handed out for the publication of her last book, her own image an ironic version of the late Lucille Ball.

When he reached her side, he spoke softly. 'What the actual fuck was that?'

Lucy arched her eyebrows. They were normally hidden behind the thick black circle of her glasses, so raising them created a strange duplicating effect. 'You don't know?'

'No, Lucy, I don't know.'

'That was Gala Faraday.'

The name rang faint bells with Rob, but he couldn't remember why. 'Should I know her?'

'She used to be Jamie's editor's assistant. She left about six months ago for a plum editorial job at Samson House. One of the hot young editors, everybody agreed. Until the proofs of Jamie's latest started making the rounds.'

Rob had a horrible presentiment of what was coming next. *Needs Killing* had landed on his doormat the previous week. It featured a female character who craved sexual humiliation, a craving whose satisfaction was outlined in the kind of gleeful detail that had made Rob feel more than a little queasy. He couldn't in all conscience call himself a feminist, but he really couldn't find a word to describe it other than 'misogynist'. It had ended inevitably in rape, torture and murder. For the first time, he'd found himself skimming a Jamie Cobain novel. 'You're not telling me ...'

Lucy nodded, her scarlet lips a tight line. 'Oh yes. Nobody who knows Gala could fail to recognise her. Physical description – well, I assume it's accurate because the relevant piercings are not on show – and even her verbal tics.

"Doomtastic" and "Born to chart", stuff like that. Darling, surely even Edinburgh's heard the horror story by now?'

Rob shook his head. 'Sorry, I've not been out and about. I'm on deadline, you know how it is.'

'But you play chess with Jamie. Did he not boast about it? Apparently, he'd been sniggering to the boys about teaching Gala who was in charge. But then she did the unforgivable and dumped him, you see?'

'We don't talk much when we're playing. It's all about the chess. He said nothing to me.' He looked around, rueful. 'So much for my celebration. The only thing anyone will remember about tonight is Gala Faraday lamping Jamie Cobain.'

Lucy put a hand on his arm. 'Don't worry. You're on the up and up. Not like Jamie.'

'What do you mean, "not like Jamie"?'

Her smile reminded Rob of a cat contemplating a bowl of tuna. 'Didn't you know? His sales are on the slide.'

'Surely not? His last book went straight in at number two. He only missed the top spot because it came out the same week as Jojo Moyes.'

Lucy shook her head, a pitying look in her eyes. 'Honestly, Rob, you've still got so much to learn. It's not the chart position that matters, it's the sales numbers. Jamie went in at number two but he dropped straight out again. His sales have been on a downward curve for the last three books. *You're* outselling him now.'

This was news to Rob. 'Really? Me?'

Lucy tittered. 'You sound like "The Ugly Duckling" song. "Me? A swan? Ah, go on ... "'

'I truly didn't know that, Lucy.'

She nodded portentously. 'He needs a big hit if he's going to avoid being yesterday's man.'

'Poor bastard.'

She groaned. 'You're far too nice, Rob. Think about the way he's just used Gala to create a storm. Obviously the mainstream media won't join up the dots, but they'll make headlines out of the sadism and general nastiness of it all. And the socials won't hold back. Gala's basically fucked in this industry now. That's what happens to women who refuse to play by the rules. So don't waste your kind heart on feeling sorry for Jamie. He'll come out the other end of this relatively unscathed. But Gala? This'll be the first thing everyone ever says about her. "Isn't that Gala Faraday? The one Jamie Cobain ...?"'

Rob understood the truth of Lucy's words. But he also understood the power of desperation. He knew how much Jamie valued his standing in their world. It would have hurt him deeply to see that threatened by falling sales. He'd hit on a quick and very dirty way to give them a boost – nothing sold better than scandal. Rob couldn't help wondering how far he'd go himself to preserve his own lesser but equally treasured status. Hopefully, he'd never have to find out.

Karen stood up and headed for the coffee machine. 'I need stimulation,' she said. 'If this is Jake Stein's attempt to resurrect his career, it's not working for me. I can see why he left it unfinished.'

'I think his natural readership will love the peek behind the curtain.' Daisy yawned and stretched her arms over her head. 'They'll be trying to map his characters on to real people and relishing the inside track on how their favourites really behave. And the slap? That really happened. There was a mention of it in the cuttings I read. No details, just a couple of lines about an incident where an unnamed woman assaulted Stein at a party.'

'That makes it look a helluva lot more autobiographical. You'd think Stein would want to sweep that under the carpet, not resurrect it in all its gory detail.'

'Maybe he thinks there's no point in trying to hide it when it's an open secret? We don't know yet how he's going to spin it. I've heard writers say nothing is ever wasted.'

'What I'm struggling with is how this relates to Lara Hardie. She was studying English, her family said she wanted to be a writer, but nothing anybody said about her suggested she was the kind of lassie who'd be daft enough to think she could sleep her way to a book deal. I still can't quite see why Meera's connecting this to Lara's disappearance.'

Daisy got to her feet and headed for the fridge. She peered inside and came out with a can of Sugar-Free Irn Bru. 'What day is it, by the way? I've totally lost track.'

'Thursday? I think it's Thursday.' Karen tapped her phone screen. 'Yeah. Thursday.'

Daisy grinned. 'We'd better keep an eye on the time. It's Clap for our Carers at eight o'clock. I had a thought about that. We don't need to go all the way down to the street, we can just hang out of the windows and bang a pot with a wooden spoon.'

Karen scoffed. 'Clap for our Carers. It'd be a damn sight more meaningful if the government paid them better.'

Daisy popped the top off her drink and took a swig. 'Don't be such a grinch. I think it's nice. It's about solidarity. And it's a way to show people they're appreciated.'

Karen shook her head. 'They're taking their lives into their hands every time they turn in for a shift. You must have seen the footage of them wearing bin bags because they've no proper protective gear? They're heroes, right enough, but some of them can't even afford to feed their kids. Sure, I'll bang a pot, though I don't think there's many nurses or cleaners or ambulance drivers or care home workers living in this part of town. The best thing we can do for the health service workers is to avoid catching COVID. Wear our masks and follow the rules.'

Not for the first time, Daisy could think of no effective riposte. She was slowly learning that her boss was a woman of strong opinions. And they were opinions it was hard to knock holes in. She picked up the next page and carried on reading about the secret life of crime writers.

5

Six months later

Rob set out the chess pieces and put the two bottles of whisky on the side table. He stepped back to take in the whole scene. He still wasn't accustomed to his new home, a generous detached villa south of the city centre. Over the years, the area had housed so many authors it had been dubbed 'Writers' Block' by journalists.

He'd been reluctant to move from his cramped one-bedroom flat, scared that his success was a flash in the pan, but his agent had told him he deserved better and his accountant had told him there was no better investment for the money that was flowing in. His father had told him not to get above himself, and that had been the deciding factor. Rob had spent his life hearing he would never make anything of himself; the house on Somerville Place was the perfect riposte.

It seemed as if his agent and accountant had been right. Rob had won the two major awards he'd been shortlisted for; pre-orders for *Depredation* were rolling in; principal photography for the TV adaptation of *Dereliction* was scheduled for the following month; if he'd accepted even half of the invitations in his inbox, he'd have had no time to write.

So now they played their chess games in Rob's book-lined study. His rise had been matched by Jamie Cobain's fall from grace. Rachel had filed for divorce the day after Rob's party. They'd been married since before Jamie published his first book; Scots law awarded half their assets to Rachel. Their lavish lifestyle had eaten most of Jamie's earnings; when the dust had settled, he'd ended up with little more than half the value of the house.

That wouldn't have been so bad if his earning power had remained undiminished. But the Gala Faraday incident had grown legs and stalked a wider world than publishing. Combined with Jamie's declining sales, it had made him toxic in a #MeToo world. After he delivered his next manuscript, the final book in his contract, his publisher told him they were done. The news spread schadenfreude throughout the crime fiction community. It turned out Jamie hadn't had as many friends as he'd thought. Or not ones who were comfortable with having a pint with a man who chained his lover to a radiator then told the world all about it.

Now he was living in a tiny two-bedroomed flat in the no man's land between Craigentinny and Portobello. He still talked a good game, saying how much he loved being within walking distance of the long prom that ran along Porty beach. There was talk that he'd found a new publisher willing to touch the untouchable, but the word was that it was a Scottish indie with a reputation for opportunism. When comedians were barred by the BBC, when historic racist tweets were excavated, when politicians were caught out, this was the publishing house where they ended up. There was no doubt in Rob's mind that Jamie still had plenty of potential readers but convincing them this was the book for them might be a trickier proposition than Stramash Press could manage.

But Rob had remained quietly loyal. He thought there were plenty of other men who had behaved as badly as Jamie had. The main difference was that they hadn't been caught out. And it was clear that Jamie was hurting. He'd tried to reach a rapprochement with Rachel, but she'd simply turned away. He'd grown so accustomed to his charmed life that it came as a bolt from the blue that Rachel had reached her limit and burned it to the ground.

So when the grand house in Ravelston Dykes had been sold, Rob had invited Jamie to continue their chess games at his new house. Over the months, he had watched his friend fray round the edges. Jamie started to go too long between haircuts. Sometimes he turned up unshaven, with the faint smell of badly dried clothes clinging to his hand-made shirts. He lost weight, which was fine to begin with, but then he began to look gaunt. He drank more of Rob's whisky than had been his habit when it was his own. All in all, it was a swift decline.

But his mind remained sharp as ever across the chessboard. He neither gave nor expected quarter. Sitting at a board, brow furrowed in concentration, was the last remaining place the old Jamie Cobain held sway, Rob thought. It was as if he shed his disgrace with the same disdain he'd show an old raincoat.

Jamie arrived promptly and they started to play with little preamble. Asking Jamie how he was doing felt brutal and awkward to Rob; he imagined the last thing Jamie wanted Rob to know was how he was. Jamie went straight on the attack with the King's Gambit, the most aggressive of white's openings. So that was how it was going to be, Rob thought. He took the offered pawn to buy time. Out came the King's Bishop, and it was game on.

When the struggle was over, leaving Jamie the victor, he said, 'You see I went straight on the attack tonight?'

Rob poured the whiskies. 'Hard to miss. I was on the back foot from the word go. I'm amazed I lasted so long with that block of pawns in the middle.' He handed Jamie his drink. He swallowed half of it in one gulp. Rob tried not to resent the waste of a good whisky.

'I've been thinking, Rob. There's only one way I'm going to redeem myself. I can't change the past. But I can make the world forget the damage that bitch Faraday has done to me.' He finished the drink and held his glass out.

Rob refilled it without comment.

'I'm writing an absolutely stonking book. An irresistible book. With a twist that will leave everybody else in the dust. Something that will make *The Girl with the Dragon Tattoo* and *Gone Girl* history.' He was almost feverish, his eyes bright and his cheeks pink.

'Easier said than done.' Rob sat down. 'That's what we're all looking for, every time we sit down at the keyboard.'

Jamie smiled, an echo of his former bonhomie. 'But I've cracked it. A perfect murder with a screamer of a twist in the tail.'

Rob shook his head. 'There's no such thing as the perfect murder in a crime novel. Because it has to be solved in the end.'

Jamie stood up and helped himself to more whisky. 'But what if it's the wrong solution? What if the perfect murderer also puts together the perfect frame?'

Rob frowned. 'So what's the twist? He gets away with it?'

'He gets away with it, yes. But the man he frames is a bigger criminal than him. So where does the justice lie?'

Rob sipped his drink, giving himself a moment to find words that wouldn't offend Jamie. 'So you end the book with a moral dilemma that doesn't get solved?'

'Exactly. And here's the twist. We go interactive. We invite the readers to vote on whether they think the killer should be caught or whether the victim of the frame should go to jail instead. We leave the poll up and running for, say, three months. And at the end of it, I write the final chapter based on the public vote.' The shit-eating grin signalled that in his head, Jamie Cobain was back. 'Nobody's ever done anything like that before.'

And with good reason, Rob thought. 'But how do the paying customers get the last chapter?'

Jamie shrugged, spreading his hands in a careless gesture. 'That's for the boffins to work out. Maybe each copy sold has a special one-off code you type into the website. Like in the olden days when you bought a download code for a computer game. I'm sure they can figure it out. I tell you, Rob, I'm writing like a runaway train. I haven't put words down this fast since the early days. I'm doing twelve-hour days and the ideas are spilling out on the page as fast as I can set them down.'

There was something almost manic in his speech, Rob thought. It wasn't surprising; few people would have been able to come out of the past year mentally unscathed. But the more he digested Jamie's words, the more Rob could see a glimmering of possibility in what he was suggesting. It was true, nobody had ever done anything like that before. And the technology could certainly support it. 'It's a novel idea, I'll grant you that. Do you think Stramash can handle something potentially that big?'

'If they can get the books out there, I'm sure we'll sell them. Think of the publicity, Rob. And we can milk it online like crazy. I'm telling you, this is the way back for me.'

Rob felt uneasy, but he managed a smile. After all, he needed Jamie to climb back to the top of the tree. That way, maybe he and Rachel wouldn't have to keep hiding. All it needed was the perfect crime to set the wheels in motion. And who better to come up with it than Jamie?

'Now we're starting to get somewhere,' Karen said. 'Time to let the dog see the rabbit.'

'I've never understood what that meant,' Daisy said absently.

'It means, we've been getting all excited about something we know is going on even though we couldn't see any evidence of it. And now it's time for the reveal. We're getting to the bit where we come face to face with the lassie who's vanished. Laurel Oliver.'

'That internet vote's a great idea,' Daisy said. 'I never heard about that.'

'I suspect it never happened. Whatever the endgame was for this book, it never got that far. I'm guessing Jake Stein's brain probably blew up before he got that far into the story. Don't you think?'

Daisy frowned. 'Either that or he gave up on it. He was trying to be really tricksy, and maybe he realised he couldn't pull it off?'

Karen leaned back in her chair and considered. 'Or maybe the enormity of what he'd done finally got to him? Killing someone isn't as straightforward as Stein or his crime writing pals make it seem. Even if you manage it in the moment, if you don't lose control when what you've done hits you . . .

it's got a way of creeping up on you. If he did kill her – and right now that's a very big if – it could be he woke up one morning and the horror of what he'd done freaked him out.'

'Would he not have destroyed the manuscript, if that was what happened?'

Karen shrugged. 'That might have been what he intended. Only his body let him down before he could do that.' She sighed. 'Just another one of the great unanswerable questions that plague the cold case investigator.'

'I don't suppose there was anything suspicious about his death?'

Karen shook her head. 'There were no red flags at the time. I don't think you can actually provoke a brain aneurysm.' She reached for her phone and googled. Daisy waited patiently, knowing better than to interrupt. Karen looked up, shaking her head. 'Apparently not. High blood pressure, a shit-ton of cocaine, but even then you'd have to have a natural weakness. And I don't think he could have afforded a serious coke habit towards the end of his life. Looks like it was just bad timing.'

'What I find interesting,' Daisy said slowly, 'is how self-critical he is. That is, if the character of Jamie is really how Stein saw himself. He's not going out of his way to make us feel sympathy for him.'

'Good point. But maybe we're not meant to like him at this point? He could have been planning to turn Jamie into the hero later on?'

'I suppose . . . ' Daisy didn't sound convinced. 'More likely, he just lacked insight into how he comes off.'

Karen grimaced. 'He wouldn't be the first man to suffer from that. But we might be wrong about this whole set-up. He could have been playing with an idea inspired by Lara's disappearance. Maybe he was trying it out for size. And it didn't fit. Let's not lose sight of that.'

6

'So, tell me about this perfect crime,' Rob said two weeks later, pouring a liberal Scotch for Jamie.

Jamie gave him a sly look. 'What? And give you a solid gold plot for free? Do you think I came up the Firth of Forth on a bike?'

Rob shrugged. 'We write very different kinds of book, Jamie. Even if I did steal your plot, the end result wouldn't be anything like yours.'

Jamie, in benevolent mood after beating Rob soundly with a twist on the Scotch Gambit, acknowledged the truth of the comment by raising his glass in a toast. 'True. So, the bad guy is a poet. The victim is a student who comes to one of his readings and lingers at the end of the signing queue. She confesses she's struggling with her own poetry. He's been looking for someone like her for a long time. So he arranges to meet her, he kills her, then he dumps the body in his patsy's garden. Then he stands back and waits for the right time to betray him.'

'That doesn't sound very perfect to me,' Rob said. 'There'd be evidence galore, surely?'

Jamie tapped the side of his nose. 'I've worked it all out, Rob. Every last detail.'

'But why? What's your killer's motivation?'

Jamie savoured a mouthful of Scotch. 'The dish best eaten cold.'

'Revenge? Revenge for what?'

Jamie shrugged. 'The usual. You know. Betrayal.'

Rob felt the inward shiver of someone walking over his grave. Surely Jamie couldn't know about him and Rachel? They'd both understood from the very start that there would be consequences for both of them if Jamie found out about their relationship. He had a very clear idea of what belonged to him; he had been genuinely hurt by the divorce and outraged at what he saw as a deeply unjust settlement. He'd raged for months about having to surrender the assets he'd worked so hard for. Rachel was a qualified lawyer; they could have been equal partners in building their life. But she'd chosen to go part-time, to contribute nothing to the household economy except cooking for their dinner guests. Deliveroo could manage that almost as well without demanding half his home.

Falling in love with his chess partner's wife had been so far off his agenda that Rob didn't notice it was happening. That first time Rachel had cooked for him had felt special, it was true, but only because it had been so long since anyone had shown him any culinary care. He'd asked for her recipe for the Roscoff onions, and that simple act had apparently sparked a fire in Rachel, accustomed for so long to being taken for granted.

The next time they'd met had been happenstance. He'd walked up to Valvona & Crolla at the top of Leith Walk for some of their exquisite nduja and he'd been diverted by a shelf of cannoli. A voice at his shoulder startled him. 'You know you want to,' in low tones. He swivelled to come face to face with Rachel.

He flushed and said, 'The trouble with cannoli is that one's never enough.'

'Like so many of the good things in life.' Rachel's tone was rueful but her smile was playful. 'Have you got time for a coffee? Or are you in one of those short breaks between frantic creativity?'

It was true that the walk up the hill to the Italian grocery had shaken loose a path through a thorny conversational thicket between two of his characters. But that could wait. Even if the idea evaporated before he got back to his keyboard, he knew he wouldn't care. Ideas were cheap; spending time with a woman like Rachel was not.

This time, they talked about books, about febrile Scottish politics, about what was coming up at the Film House. Jamie barely figured in the conversation. And the next time they'd played chess, Jamie had said nothing about their meeting. Now, thinking about it, Rob had a fleeting moment of unease. Had that been a test? Had Rachel told her husband and was Rob's silence indicative of guilt? It hadn't occurred to him at the time; rather, he'd assumed it had been so trivial an encounter that Rachel didn't consider it worth mentioning.

But now? Now he was being paranoid, he told himself. Because Rachel had felt that same spark that had lit up his day. She'd since told him so. That was why she'd said nothing to Jamie and also why she'd called him a few days later. 'Jamie has suddenly decided he's going to New York for that stupid awards ceremony. The one he's convinced he's got no chance of winning?' She sighed. 'Apparently, he needs to be in the room, to show his face. And I've got a lobster in the fridge that needs to be eaten tomorrow. I don't suppose you feel like sharing it?'

The uptick in his heart rate had nothing to do with the lobster and everything to do with the prospect of seeing Rachel. 'Hmm,' he mused. 'How were you thinking of cooking it?' They both knew the answer didn't matter. She could have placed a plate of beans on toast in front of him and they'd still

71

have ended up in bed afterwards. In the spare room, obviously. There was never anything tacky about Rachel.

Rob felt Rachel was who he had been waiting for all his life but had never quite believed he'd find. He'd had girlfriends, but none of them had ever made him feel that he'd want to spend the rest of the year, never mind the rest of his life with them. With Rachel, he felt completed in a way that he thought was only a fiction. The truly astonishing thing was that she claimed she felt the same way about him. That was harder to credit, but he was reluctantly coming round to believing her.

Of course, keeping their relationship under wraps did spice it with risk, giving it a frisson of excitement that might not have persisted so strongly had they been out in the open. But Rachel was adamant, even after the divorce, that they keep it from Jamie. 'You have no idea how dangerous he is,' she'd said.

'But it's over. You're divorced. He's got no claim on you.'

'He still says he loves me. That he'd get back together in a heartbeat.'

'He'll just have to get over it.'

Rachel had turned to face him, her expression grave, her dark eyes troubled. 'Rob, he will destroy you. Trust me, he'll make it his life's work to bring you down.'

'He can't do that.' Rob stroked her tousled hair back from her forehead. 'He's got no credit in the bank in the crime writing world. Nobody would take him seriously.'

She shook her head. 'You underestimate the power of social media. Ripped out of context, a throwaway joke can be turned toxic in the time it takes me to tell you this. Anybody who's ever begrudged your success can be weaponised. He'll pretend you're the reason our marriage went south, even though he had no idea it was happening. He'll turn his dirty little affairs into a response to my infidelity. Remember the shock of Gala

Faraday's slap? You think you're beyond provocation, Rob. But you're not.'

He pushed himself into a sitting position, the pillows scrunched into the small of his back. 'So, what? We skulk around in the dark forever? We let him win?'

'Not forever, my love.' She moved confidently to straddle him. 'I know the way his mind twists. As soon as he finds another woman he wants to make his property, he'll lose all interest in me. I'll be the one who failed, you'll be the mug who got stuck with her.' She leaned into him, lips caressing the line of his jaw. 'And it's not like we can only be together when he's out of town,' she added. 'We just have to be private.'

All of this flashed across Rob's mind in seconds. None of it showed on his face, he was certain. He'd perfected his blank face in poker schools at college; it had been one of the ways he'd managed to keep his head above the financial waves. He'd reawakened the old skills at US mystery conventions, where the American top dogs played late-night games for high stakes. He'd never come away from the table with less than he'd started with.

'Betrayal? Lots of possibilities there,' he said. 'Professional double-cross, marital infidelity, sibling rivalry, inheritance that doesn't go the way everyone expects, plagiarism. You're spoilt for choice.'

'Oh, I 've already decided. I told you, it's going like a train.' The old Jamie was back – smugly confident and untouchable. 'I'm all set. All I have to do is the final checks. Run a dress rehearsal.'

'What do you mean, a dress rehearsal?'

'The perfect crime. I just need a run-through to make sure it works.'

This time, Rob's poker face failed him. 'You're not going to *kill* someone, are you?'

Jamie roared with laughter. 'You are so easy, Rob. What do you take me for?' He finished his drink and stood up. 'Wait and see, mate. This will blow them away.'

7

Karen paused in her reading. 'So now the wife swims into focus. Bethan Carmichael mentioned Stein's ex-wife when she was explaining about the archive. It didn't seem important at the time. But now ... What do we know about Rosalind Stein?'

Daisy scrambled back through her notebook. 'Like the book says, she's a lawyer. Probate and wills. There's no personal stuff on Google, except that she divorced Stein after an "incident" at a publishing event. She's never given an interview as far as I could see.'

'So we've got no idea if she's having an affair or has ever had an affair, with Ross McEwen or anybody else?'

Daisy shook her head. 'If she has, she's kept it well out of the headlines.'

'Maybe she was as scared of her husband's reaction as the fictional wife.' Karen sighed. This was growing more complicated by the minute. 'Or maybe that's what we're being set up to think. It's still possible that we're being strung along here, that there never was an affair.'

'So what do we do?'

Karen ran a frustrated hand through her hair. It was flimsy, but she kept telling herself it was something for them to get their teeth into during these strange disconnected lockdown days. She was certainly learning how Daisy's mind worked; she thought she was beginning to draw her into the tight-knit unit of the HCU. 'Let's just move on very carefully. Take it at face value but interrogate it as we go along. First, how the hell did Jake Stein know about the beginnings of the affair between his wife and Rob McEwen? Surely neither of them would have told him, since they were determined to keep it secret?'

Daisy pondered. 'Well, if we're going to say for the sake of argument that this account maps on to reality then obviously Stein found out about the affair at some point. That's why he's got it in for Ross McEwen.'

'But how could he have known all the *details* of how they got together?'

'I just assumed he'd made it up.' Daisy looked perplexed. 'It's fiction, boss. Even if it's rooted in truth, he's got to put stuff on the page he can't know. Surely he would have known his wife well enough to understand what would excite her about a man? After all, they'd been in love once. He might even have used their own early connection and pasted it on to how he imagined Ross and Ros got together.'

'Wouldn't that have been a kind of torture?'

Daisy shrugged. 'Writers do it all the time. They give their own experiences to their characters, or they nick them off their friends. All it would have taken would have been somebody in his circle complaining about how rubbish their kitchen was compared to Stein's. That'd set him off down that road.'

It made sense, and it made Karen even more glad she'd never considered a career where you constantly had to pick the scabs of your past mistakes. She pondered what she'd read, and wondered once more what it was that had set alarm bells ringing for Meera Reddy. So far, what they had was pitifully thin. The chances of this going somewhere useful were diminishing by the hour.

'I'm not really seeing anything of interest to us yet.' She registered the flash of relief in Daisy's eyes. 'I tried a Jake Stein a couple of years ago, but I struggled to get past the first chapter – cardboard cut-out blonde with zero personality who's obviously going to get dead, you know the kind of thing. I only picked it up because it was the one book in English in the hotel where I was staying.' She scoffed. 'I have the same issue here if I've forgotten to bring a book with me.'

'He doesn't read much fiction, does he?' Daisy scanned the motivational paperbacks and the business manuals that filled Hamish's bookshelves.

'So what do you think's going on here? You're the one with the degree.'

Daisy shrugged. 'French and Legal Studies doesn't make me a literary critic. I read the same kind of thing as you do, I reckon. Like I said, I got sucked in once and read three on the bounce – he was a good storyteller but I started to feel uncomfortable about his female characters.'

Karen prodded the pages with her finger. 'This is quite clever, though. He writes in a way that makes it feel smarter than it really is. You get propelled along and don't stop to question how likely it all is. A cut above genre, kind of. Does that make sense?'

'It's something to do with the syntax, I think. The sentence structure.'

'Yeah, yeah, I know what "syntax" means, Daisy.' Karen caught herself sounding grumpy. It was always the same, waiting for a case to start moving. Even worse when there might not be a case at all.

Daisy cut her eyes at her boss. 'There's one wee thing that did strike me. And I don't know whether it means anything ...'

Karen perked up. 'Don't be shy, Daisy.'

'This is supposed to be a first draft, yeah?'

'I think so. I mean, there's not enough of it for it to be finished.'

Daisy thumbed through the pages she'd read. 'I'd have thought there would be scribbles all over it. Changing words, cutting bits out, adding bits. But this looks pretty polished.'

'Mibbes he does all the revisions on the screen and doesn't print it out till he's happy with it?'

'That's probably it.' Daisy seemed unconvinced.

'The trouble is, we don't know enough about this. Is it really the first draft of something Stein was planning to publish? Or is he just playing around with an idea? Was he going to rework it to make it more anonymous? So it wouldn't read like him confessing? Mibbes he had another version in mind where Ross McEwen was pointed to as the murderer? And if Stein was planning to publish it, why didn't he finish it? Was he still working on it or had he dumped it? The time frame in the novel probably doesn't correspond to real life either. Like the song says, more questions than answers ...' Karen let out a sigh that seemed to come from her boots. 'Either way, we shouldn't take anything it says for gospel.'

Daisy gave her boss an anxious look, clearly lost for a response. When in doubt, she knew there was one way to go. 'Do you want a coffee or will we just crack on?'

Karen picked up the next bundle of manuscript. 'Onwards. Save the coffee for a reward at the end. Let's see whether we can find whatever it is that's ringing the librarian's bell.'

THE VANISHING OF
LAUREL OLIVER

PART TWO

7

Cognitive dissonance. That was the posh term for it, and it was driving Jamie Cobain tonto. On the one hand, he'd become addicted to going head-to-head over the chessboard with Rob Thomas. Those nights were the only oasis of pure pleasure in this life he'd been shunted into. On the other hand, he hated Rob Thomas with every fibre of his being. Rob was fucking his wi— his *ex*-wife. Had been for more than a year now. Rob was the reason he'd not been able to salvage something from the wreckage. She'd only jumped ship when she finally thought she'd found a lifeboat. And he still loved her. The tension between love and hate was costing him sleep and any possibility of pleasure.

The thunderbolt realisation of the only resolution for this had come out of the blue a few weeks ago while he'd been watching the own-brand budget macaroni cheese slowly spinning in the microwave. He had to destroy Rob. In the process, he'd probably royally fuck up Rachel. But maybe out of the wreckage, they'd find a way to get back together. OK, somebody would have to die. But you can't make an omelette without breaking some chicken's heart.

What was that saying about the cobbler's kids being the worst shod? There should be a modern version about the tech-savvy crime writers being the easiest to spy on. Rob and Rachel thought they'd been so careful, sneaking around the city under cover of darkness. She'd even disabled the 'find my phone' feature on her iPhone. It never occurred to her to check her car for a tracker. Or inside the lining of her four favourite handbags. Mind you, she wouldn't have been any the wiser if she had. She wouldn't know a tracker from a tracksuit.

He'd had the car tracker installed when she'd bought the car, mostly to stop it being nicked by one of the neds who regularly infiltrated Ravelston Dykes on the hunt for plunder. But it was her own fault he'd resorted to the handbags. He'd been in New York, being passed over for an award that should have had his name written all over it. When he'd got home, she'd acted like that was no big deal. Instead, she was full of bounce and good cheer for no apparent reason. And the outside food waste bin was full of lobster shells. More lobster than one person could reasonably eat.

No bisque, either. Rachel always made bisque with the remains of lobsters and crabs. There was only one possible conclusion. She was hiding the fact that she'd had company. And company that, for some reason, she didn't want to tell Jamie about. It was a stab in the heart.

He'd run through the mental card index of men of their acquaintance. He couldn't picture any of them holding a candle to him. He flirted briefly with the idea of a woman, but dismissed it with regret. Rachel and another woman was his fantasy, not hers. But now Jamie was on the alert. He'd be checking those trackers every day now and if there was anything going on, it would only be a matter of time before he'd know all about it.

Three days later, he called her at work to say he was going to Glasgow for a curry with some of the lads and he'd be on the last train. Would she pick him up at Waverley?

Rachel agreed without a word of complaint, even telling him to enjoy himself, that there was some documentary on Netflix she wanted to watch.

Of course, he didn't go to Glasgow. He sat in a corner booth in a quiet bar in a side street in Stockbridge where they didn't mind him making each cocktail last an hour. He didn't have too long to wait. Just before seven, when he was near the end of his second Bloody Mary, one of the handbag trackers left the house and almost instantly overlapped with the car tracker.

Jamie leaned forward as if that would bring him closer to her. He followed the car's journey down Lothian Road, down Hanover Street and on to Canonmills. He couldn't think of anyone in their friendship group who lived in this part of town. She passed Rosebank Cemetery and Pilrig Park. There were a couple of good restaurants near Great Junction Street, the only reason he could think of for being in these parts after dark. Then she turned right.

His mouth dried and his cheeks flushed. Rachel's car had stopped in the middle of the dead-end street. But her handbag hadn't. It left the car and travelled a short distance ahead. Jamie could feel a pulse beating in his temple. He switched from the map to street view, unwilling to believe what the tracker was showing.

He knew that street. He knew the very building the tracker was hovering over. He knew it because he'd visited it once to drop someone off after they'd done an event together. OK, people said Edinburgh was a village. But unless this was the most preposterous coincidence, the person Rachel was visiting was Rob fucking Thomas. His friend. And he didn't think they'd be watching a Netflix documentary.

Jamie wanted to break something. To hurt someone, preferably Rob. It took all his willpower not to summon an Uber and confront the double-dealing bastards. He kept telling himself that he could hurt them much more if he took his time. Let them think they were safe and secure, then let the heavens rain fire on their treacherous fucking heads.

For now, he had to dissemble. He'd hold fast to the plan he'd already made for the evening. He finished his drink and walked up the hill towards Haymarket station. He stopped in a pub in the West End and ordered a burger and fries. He managed a couple of mouthfuls then barely made it to the toilet in time to throw up. When an eager fangirl came over to ask for an autograph, he gave her a blank look. 'I'm at my dinner,' he said, pushed the plate away and then, head down, bulled his way into the street.

He knew that some might say sauce for the goose was fair exchange after the gander had had his beak in the sauce boat. But he'd always maintained that men and women had different attitudes to sex. For men, for him anyway, it was about scratching an itch. If it was on offer, no strings attached, he wouldn't say no. It didn't steal anything from Rachel. But for women, he believed it was a different story. Certainly, for Rachel. Sex was inextricably bound up with love. For her to have an affair, she'd have to be emotionally engaged. And of all the people for her to be emotionally engaged with, Rob Thomas was the most profound insult of all. A man he'd trusted, a man whose company he had developed a need for. It was a double dagger to the heart.

At Haymarket, he sat in the waiting room for hours, holding on for the last train from Glasgow so he could make the short hop to Waverley, where Rachel would be waiting. He spent the time forcing himself into a state of composure. He had to get past his outrage to a place where he could plan.

But he kept coming back to the same refrain. How dare she? How could she? She was his wife. She was his. Bound to him. He knew she'd try to hide behind his own misbehaviour. But she knew that the women he'd fucked over the years had been just that, no more. A fuck. He'd never screwed any of her friends, never shat on his own doorstep. Because she was the one he loved. The rest were just about passing the time. So how could she say that shagging his chess partner, his literary rival, his *mate*, for fuck's sake, was the same as him having a random legover? No, this was different.

They were going to pay. There was no room in his head for any other thought. He simply had to stay calm enough for long enough to work out exactly how to destroy them.

8

The trouble with constructing a plot perfectly watertight in every detail was that it made you take your eye off the ball. Jamie had been so preoccupied with figuring out how to destroy Rob and Rachel that he simply hadn't paid enough attention to disguising that piece of shit Gala Faraday on the page. He should have been more subtle. Carefully calibrated nuances so that those in the know would put the pieces together and work out it was Gala. Instead, he'd used the truth like a blunt instrument and the bitch had turned it round and weaponised it against him.

Somebody should have been covering his back. His agent, his editor, his copy editor. Surely one of them must have heard the gossip, or at the very least, recognised Gala Faraday from the description? They'd all had their pathetic little excuses. His agent said she'd never run across Gala Faraday. His editor claimed he hadn't heard the gossip and thought that any resemblance to Gala was coincidental. His copy editor lived in the far north-west of Scotland and was so far out of the loop she might as well have been on Mars. Allegedly.

That slap had been like a full stop in Jamie's life. His career was in ruins, his reputation wrecked. If Rachel had stood by him, it would have been a different story. But in this post-#MeToo world, men who had fallen over themselves to buy him pints and curries now treated him as if he was toxic waste. The only ones who slapped him on the back these days were the ones whose bottom-of-the-heap books glamorised violence and rough sex in equal measure. And Rachel jumped on this excuse for a divorce before he'd even had the chance to gather evidence against her and that snake Rob Thomas.

The worst of it was that he couldn't give up the chess. At first Jamie told himself that was because he didn't want Rob to suspect he knew about him and Rachel. He still wanted his revenge to come like a thunderbolt from a blue sky. But deep down, he knew that their matches were like a drug. Over the chessboard, he felt like himself. For those few hours, he could put aside the horrors that life had visited on him. He could shut out everything except the hypnotic interplay of pieces on the board. And more often than not, he could beat the little shit who had helped to inflict these body blows on him.

For he was in no doubt that without Rob Thomas in the picture, Rachel would have stayed with him. Maybe not quite forgiven him, not right away. But without someone else to run to, she'd still be there on his arm, showing the world he wasn't a pariah. She'd have been his stepping stone back to his place in the sun. Her apparent acceptance and forgiveness would have paved the way for everyone else to move on to the next gobbet of salacious gossip. But no. Instead she'd left him to the wolves, happy to screw his reputation.

Jamie knew that if he was going to succeed in his elaborate plan he'd have to pack away his pain. Letting his hurt leak out would make him careless, and when it came to murder, he couldn't afford that. So for a few weeks, he spent his mornings drafting out the opening chapters of the book that would drive his plot towards fruition. He could move forward inch by inch in the story, examining each potential pitfall or problem and figuring out how to make it foolproof. Not that he thought the police were fools; far from it, in spite of the way some of his colleagues portrayed them.

In the afternoons, he punished his body. He needed to be on top physical form as well as mentally fit. He went on long loping runs along the beach at Portobello, through Joppa then into the grounds of Newhailes House, quartering the paths before returning via the prom. He'd persuaded the guy who ran the burger van near the toilets to let him store a pair of hand weights there, and he'd spend half an hour on the waste ground running through a set of exercises designed to build muscle and flexibility. All the while, his scheme was running through his head till he stumbled on something not quite right. Then he'd backtrack and figure out a way to fix it. Every step forward was like the application of balm to his wounds.

The first thing he had to do was find the perfect victim. He didn't think it would be hard. He was still doing events, albeit on a smaller scale. No Edinburgh International Book Festival for him this year, but there were booksellers and small festivals that could draw a half-decent crowd. Some were there to gawp at the man in the stocks, but there were plenty of others who recognised that the books were separate from the man. The signing queues were shorter, it was true. But nevertheless they were there.

In preparation, Jamie had bought a burner phone and created a new gmail account. Now it was about playing the waiting game. That didn't come naturally to him, but he was determined to control his impulses to serve his plot.

Three weeks later, in a village hall in an East Lothian town, a candidate appeared. She hung about at the back of the queue, the mark of someone who wanted to open up a conversation. Or at least, to ask a question. Medium height, shoulder-length dirty blonde hair, mildly pretty in a nondescript kind of way. Most people would have forgotten her five minutes after meeting her. Not Jamie. He prided himself on his observational skills. Every encounter was an entry in his mental database of potential characters.

He kept sneaking glances at her. A quick flick of the eyes to check she was still there and hadn't bottled it. At first, he dismissed her because he vaguely recognised her. It took him three or four automatic signatures, smiles and selfies before he nailed it down.

He'd done a workshop on plotting about a year before at a festival in Dundee. She hadn't made much impact because she was neither startlingly good or terrifyingly bad. He would have given her some feedback, but he had no notion what. There was something about her, some distinction, some difference but he couldn't quite remember what it was.

Then it dawned on him what it was. She might be the one.

Her turn. She put the book on the table, an uncertain smile not reaching her eyes. 'Hi, Jamie. You probably don't remember me, but I did your workshop in Dundee on Rob Thomas's recommendation? Laurel Oliver?'

He gave her the full hundred-watt smile. One of the few things he hadn't lost was the ability to be charming. It still worked on people who didn't know him. 'Of course I remember you. How are you doing?' Pen poised over the title page.

'OK, thanks. I'm in my final year at Edinburgh now.'

'And the writing? I remember your piece showed real promise.'

She pinked up. 'You're just saying that.'

'No, really. Have you stuck with it?'

'I chucked that story away – you were right, it didn't feel like it was going anywhere. I'm working on a novel now.'

'Good for you. The more you write, the better you get. Is this for you, Laurel?' She nodded and he scribbled, '*To Laurel. All the very best, Jamie Cobain.*' He pushed his chair back and stood up. 'Walk me out. Tell me about your book.'

He led the way to the door, turning to wave to the organisers. 'Thanks for a great night,' he said. When you can fake sincerity, you can get away with anything, an actor had once told him.

'To be honest, I'm struggling a bit with the structure. Are you doing any more workshops?' she asked as they emerged into the cold.

'I've nothing planned, I'm afraid.' Then he stopped, as if something had just struck him. 'Look, I've always believed in supporting new writing. I could take a look at what you've got and give you some personal feedback?'

She lit up. 'Really? You'd do that?'

'I've done it a few times before.' He shrugged, aiming for modesty. 'I've done it with three or four writers at the start of their career and I'm proud to say two of them have gone on to be very successfully published.' A smile. 'Obviously, you'll have to take my word for that. Nobody wants to share the credit for their success.'

'I would,' Laurel said, her voice wistful.

'Well, I wouldn't want you to. If you did, I'd have every aspiring author in Edinburgh chapping at my door.' A chuckle. 'Why don't you email it to me, and I'll take a look?'

She looked as if she might burst into tears. 'That's so amazing of you.' She pulled out her phone. 'What's your email address?'

He reached for the phone. 'I'll put it in.' He added the contact. *JC:* jcnumberone@gmail.com. 'I look forward to seeing it. But remember, don't tell anybody. Not even if they're not writers themselves. I'm still well known in Edinburgh, the word would get out and I'd be flooded.' Then he gave her the killer smile. 'Besides, you know what people are like. They'd say I was just taking pity on you because of your illness.'

She flushed. 'You remembered that?'

'You did have that episode in our session.' His voice was gentle. 'I remember thinking how hard it must be for you, never knowing when you'd lose all control.' And he remembered her insistence that there was nobody she wanted to be contacted in the wake of her momentary collapse. Flatmates would freak out, parents would go, 'We told you not to push yourself.'

'It doesn't happen too often,' she said, arms wrapped around her chest. 'It's usually stress that brings it on, and I was so worried you'd think I was crap . . .'

'So let's reduce the stress by not telling anyone you've got this opportunity. That way, if I can't manage to make a difference, you don't have the embarrassment of telling people.' He stopped by a silver hatchback. 'This is me.' He suddenly looked aghast. 'I've left my bag inside with my keys. I'll need to go back and get it. Be in touch, Laurel.' He turned on his heel and hurried away from the car that was not his but which looked like Rob's.

Inside the hall, Jamie went back to speak to the bookseller. 'Sorry, I should have said thank you,' he said. 'Appreciate it.' He went back into the foyer and checked for Laurel Oliver. He didn't have a bag with him; it had been an excuse to get away from the girl. He couldn't see any sign of her. Either she'd had her own car or she'd set off to walk to the station.

Jamie walked across to his own car, the black luxury SUV he'd managed to hang on to in the divorce on the grounds that he needed it for work. He climbed aboard and lowered the seat back. He took out his phone, googled 'Drop fall seizures' and started reading. He wanted to give her long enough to get away.

This time.

'There it is,' Karen said. 'That's the smoking gun. That's what Meera picked up on. It's in the files, it was in the media coverage. Lara Hardie suffered from Atonic Seizure epilepsy. And so does Laurel Oliver.'

'You might argue Stein just stole it from real life,' Daisy pointed out.

'Not if he was trying to frame his ex-wife's lover for murder.'

9

The file was already in his inbox by the time Jamie got home: THE VIEW FROM THE LAW by Laurel Oliver. There was no real need to read it but he was curious. Maybe she'd learned

89

something from him after all. His face creased in a predatory grin. Maybe there would even be something here worth stealing. He went to bed with his laptop propped up on his knees and began reading.

It was set in Dundee, hence the title – the Law being the conical hill that rose from the heart of the city. The central character was – surprise, surprise – a female cop struggling to be taken seriously by her male colleagues. Things took an awkward turn in chapter three when she came home from work to find her boyfriend lying dead on the kitchen floor, still warm. Her alibi was shoogly, but their relationship, by all accounts, wasn't. Nevertheless ... etc, etc. Jamie could see where it was going and although the prose was competent enough, there was little suspense and even less empathy.

The actual plot wasn't bad, with an interesting twist. But the story structure was far too linear. Jamie brought himself up short. Why the fuck was he bothering with practical criticism here? It wasn't as if she was going to have the chance to put any of it into practice. He'd reply to her tomorrow. It didn't do to seem too eager, like he had nothing better to do than sit about reading her immature draft. Jamie closed his laptop, turned out the light and slept like a man who had never contemplated murder.

Jamie did not vary his routine the following day, except that when he returned from his run, he sent an email from his burner phone.

Hi Laurel. I think this is fixable. Call me.

It took her seven minutes. She sounded breathless, whether from nerves or hurrying to find somewhere private, he couldn't tell. 'Jamie? Is that you?'

'Who else have you been asking to fix your book?' He managed to sound amused.

'Nobody, honestly.' Laurel was earnest. That gave him confidence that she'd keep her word about telling no one. 'You really think you can help me?'

'I think so. It's just a matter of rearrangement. You need to make the structure more complex, and I reckon I know how you can do it.'

'That's amazing. And you read it so quickly.'

'Once I started, I had to know how it finished. Shelley Maclean is a terrific character, she's the kind of protagonist we all root for. I loved the ending too. Listen, we should sit down together and work our way through this. What are you doing on Thursday evening?'

A moment's silence. 'Nothing,' Laurel said. 'Wow, you don't hang about.'

'Get it down while it's fresh, that's my motto.'

'That makes sense. Do you want to meet up somewhere?'

'I've got a wee place down the coast. It's where I go to write. I can pick you up and we can drive down together. It's only forty minutes down the road. If I pick you up at six, we'll have it all done by ten and I can drive you back again. How does that sound?'

'Amazing. I can't thank you enough.'

'Laurel, I get genuine pleasure from helping young writers along the road. Just ask Mari Gibson, she'll tell you.' He'd worked with Mari on her first novel. When *The Other Hangman* had been shortlisted for the best debut novel at the Daggers Awards, Mari had been full of praise for Jamie's helping hand. She wasn't the kind of woman who would kiss and tell. Not like bloody Gala Faraday. Besides, he happened to know Mari was off in Nepal for a month trekking in the

Himalayas. Laurel would have to have telepathic powers to reach her there.

'I can't believe you're doing this for me. I'm so grateful. Yes, Thursday evening will be great. I'll email you my address. Thank you, Jamie. Thank you so much.'

'And remember, not a word to anyone. I want to choose who I work with, not have people bothering me all the time for help.' *Like you did.*

'I get it. Honestly, I get it.'

'And bring your laptop. That way we can move blocks of text around easily.'

'That makes sense. God, Jamie, I'm overwhelmed that you'd do all this for me.'

'My reward will be to see you published.' He ended the call then, leaving her with the memory of his warmest tone of voice.

One more duck to put in the row and he was done with his preparations. He dialled Rob's number. 'Hi, mate,' he said.

'Jamie? How are you?'

'Fighting fit. We're still all set for the weekend, yeah?'

'I'm determined to exact revenge for that last game. And I have a new bottle to broach. A new iteration from Bruaichladdich.'

Jamie chuckled. 'I can't wait. Listen, I need a favour.'

'What's that?' Jamie could hear the wariness in Rob's voice.

'I've got to take my car in to the garage tomorrow. Something's fucked up with the gearbox and they need to keep it for a couple of days. But I've got to go down to Melrose tomorrow night for a meeting about the book festival. I'm trying to get my feet back under the table there, you know how it is. Can you lend me your car? Just for a couple of days.'

'Of course.' There was no mistaking the relief.

92

'Thank fuck,' Jamie breathed. 'You are the only friend I have left in the world.' *And I'm going to bring you to your knees.*

'Pop round tomorrow afternoon, I'll give you the keys.'

'Could I come now? I'm a bit tied up tomorrow.'

'Aye, that would be fine.'

'I owe you, mate.'

'No worries. You can repay me by giving me a pawn start on Saturday.'

Jamie tutted. 'Hard bargain. But yeah, that's cool.' He ended the call and did a little victory dance on the spot. It was all so easy. Rob's car. Mari's temporarily abandoned writing shed tucked away in a stand of trees near Tyninghame sawmill, the combination for the keybox on his phone. He'd head out there tomorrow and check she'd not added anything obviously pointing to her ownership since he'd last been there. He'd take some of his own awards to dress the set.

And he'd leave the fine cord he'd use to strangle Laurel.

In a couple of days, Laurel Oliver would be making her final journey. Jamie realised he should probably be apprehensive and nervous. But the thought of what lay ahead was strangely thrilling. Maybe he'd finally found his real calling.

8

Karen expelled an angry breath. 'Jesus,' she said. 'Whether or not this is the real thing, it's giving me the creeps.' She shuddered. 'There's a genuine cruelty here. It's almost gleeful.'

'You think it is the real thing?' Daisy sounded as anxious as Karen felt. 'Stein made up this sort of thing for a living, you'd expect him to be convincing, I suppose.'

Karen spoke slowly. 'I think it's because it's so clinical. I mean, most of us, we've got some level of empathy. I've sat in interviews where people have admitted some truly terrible things, but even so, I've always felt a bit of common humanity. A deep-down sense that maybe if I'd been backed into the same corner as them, with the same lack of choices as them and the same lack of any learned moral compass, I could possibly have seen that as the only way out. I can just about imagine being in their shoes. But this? It's beyond me.' She meant what she said; Jake Stein was making her feel queasy.

'I read quite a lot of crime novels, boss. And you're right. They don't want to turn us off. They want to shock us but not to disconnect us. And this is weirdly disconnected. See your woman Patricia Highsmith? Her that wrote the Ripley novels – *The Talented Mr Ripley* – and that *Strangers on a Train*? She created monsters who did monstrous things, but she never lets us forget they're human. She almost makes them reasonable. But this isn't like that. This character, Jamie, he's got no humanity. And it's like he doesn't care that he's showing that to us.' Daisy stood up and stretched, arching her back.

Karen nodded. 'Maybe he doesn't realise he is. There might be real people like that out there, but I've never come face to face with one. Or not that I know about. One thing ...' She flicked back a few pages. 'He says he spent his mornings drafting out the revenge plot. I think we need to search his archive for those pages. While you're on your feet, gonnae make a cup of coffee?'

'Sure.' Daisy departed, followed by the welcome and familiar sounds. Beans grinding, kettle filling, mugs clattering from cupboard to counter. At least lockdown hadn't suspended all the things that made life worth living. Karen crossed to the window and looked down on the empty city. What was going on behind all those windows? How was it for people cooped in a small space with young children? For women trapped indoors with abusive men? Were there couples glorying in each other's company or were they mostly feeling homicidal? And what about the ones running a bit of a temperature and coughing more than usual? How scared would she be in their shoes? How did the health service workers force themselves to turn in, shift after shift? And how did the First Minister stand at that podium every day and manage to tell them the truth at the same time as encouraging them to do the right thing for their community as well as themselves when she knew better than anyone the swathe this disease was carving through her country?

Abruptly she turned away as her phone pinged. A message from Miran, the Syrian refugee she'd helped set up a café in the heart of Leith. Like every other café, it was closed, a source of income and community shut down in the name of protecting lives. It was the right thing to do, but there was no escaping the hardship for people at the bottom of the pile.

Hi Karen, she read. I need to talk to you. I need your advice and maybe your help. Can we do a FaceTime? At your convenience, please? Sorry to ask. Miran.

She was intrigued. Miran was not a man who asked favours for himself. When he'd talked to her about opening the café, he'd talked about its importance to his community, about the need for the Syrians to have a corner they could call their own. And Aleppo had certainly become that – a café providing excellent Middle Eastern meze and pastries, it had developed a devoted clientele of both Syrians and Leithers. The profits from Aleppo all went straight back into supporting the tight-knit group who had lost everything when they'd left their wrecked homes and cities. Karen texted him back right away.

Hi Miran. Happy to help if I can. FaceTime me this evening? 7 p.m.? KP

Daisy returned with two steaming mugs, the aroma lifting Karen's spirits. 'There you go, boss.' She plucked a packet of biscuits from under her arm. 'Florentines.'

Karen grinned. 'Where did they come from?'

'I picked them up when I did the supermarket run last

96

night. They weren't on the list, but honestly, you're totally puritanical. I mean, fruit and vegetables and salad stuff and fish and chicken thighs are all very well, but where's the joy in that?' Daisy had the appetite of a teenage boy and the same enviable capacity to avoid putting on weight. There were moments when Karen hated her.

'Plus, I paid for them myself. I didn't take the money out of the kitty,' Daisy added, only slightly defensive.

'Don't do that again,' Karen said, pretending severity. Seeing Daisy's crestfallen expression, she laughed. 'Next time, pay for the goodies out of the kitty. Otherwise you'll guilt me into not eating them.'

Daisy laughed, relieved. 'Fair enough. There's ice cream in the freezer for tonight. The good stuff, with the wee chocolate fishes. God knows we deserve something to cheer us up after wading through all this.'

'Even with the epilepsy link, I'm still not sure I'm seeing enough lines of connection to Lara Hardie,' Karen said.

'One of her pals said in her witness statement she used to go to book events. That she talked about wanting to be a writer,' Daisy said.

'You could say the same about dozens, probably hundreds of folk in this city, though.' Karen had once had to interview one of the volunteers at the Edinburgh International Book Festival about an assault she'd witnessed on her way home one evening. She'd been taken aback at the hundreds of people spilling out of the huge marquee in Charlotte Square Gardens, not to mention the crowds milling around buying books and beer and baguettes. She enjoyed reading, but it had never occurred to her to go and listen to an author talking about their books. What was the point of that? You liked the book or you didn't. If you liked it, you looked out for another one by the same writer. If you didn't, you made a mental note to avoid them. Why would listening to the author make any difference to what you thought about the book?

But clearly there were a lot of smart people who held a different opinion. And she'd lay money on the fact that a sizeable number of them had ambitions to appear on those stages themselves one day.

'That witness statement from her pal, though. It's worth making a note. We can go back to her and see whether she remembers Lara mentioning Jake Stein in particular.' She paused for a moment, deep in thought. Where should she point Daisy next? 'I wonder if there's any way of checking whether Stein was doing any events in the Edinburgh area around the time Lara went missing?'

'His publisher? They'll have people who do publicity,' Daisy said. 'They keep lists of that sort of thing, don't they?'

'Didn't he get dumped by his publisher? After he trashed that poor woman in his book?'

Daisy frowned. 'Yeah, they couldn't distance themselves fast enough. But honestly, she must have been either really stupid or really gullible not to think she might end up in one of his books. We know that's what writers do all the time.'

Karen glared at Daisy. 'We don't do blaming the victim on this team, Daisy.'

Daisy flushed. 'But—'

'No buts. Writers must learn really quickly to disguise what they're doing if they don't want to end up in the libel courts. So either Stein was really careless or else he didn't give a flying fuck about destroying that woman's reputation.'

Daisy stared at the pile of paper in front of her. 'Sorry,' she mumbled. But she wasn't a woman who stayed squashed for long. 'But he got another publisher, didn't he?'

Karen googled. 'Jake Stein books . . . here we are. His last book came out with Stooshie Press. Never heard of them . . . OK, they're a small Scottish press with a weird-looking list. Put it this way, they're not going to make the Booker Prize shortlist any time soon.'

'Do you want me to follow it up?'

'First, we've got to finish wading through the sewer of Jake Stein's nasty mind. Let's get back to it. Then we can cleanse our palates with an episode of *Sex Education* and lust after lovely Ncuti Gatwa.'

Daisy gave a non-committal grunt.

'What? You don't think Ncuti Gatwa's the best thing to come out of Fife since . . . I don't know, Dougray Scott?'

'Who is Dougray Scott? How old do you think I am? Anyway Ncuti's not my type,' Daisy said. 'And I'd have thought you had your hands full with Hamish.'

Karen chuckled. 'Doesn't hurt to remind him he's not the only man in the world.'

'Just don't fall out with him till after lockdown. We don't want to be chucked out on the street.'

Karen gave Daisy an unreadable look and picked up the next sheet of paper. 'Onwards,' she said. 'Miles to go before we sleep.'

10

Laurel was sitting on the wall opposite the tenement where she shared a flat with three other students. Right where she'd said she would be. At that time of year in Edinburgh, as winter turned the corner into spring, twilight was creeping in by six o'clock, especially on a grey day with lowering skies. There was no pavement by the wall where she was perched, just a thin strip of scrappy grass, too narrow for anyone to walk along. From the other side of the street, he reckoned she'd be nothing more than a blur. And he certainly wouldn't be recognisable. She was, he reckoned, as good as invisible.

He pulled up alongside her in Rob's nondescript silver Toyota Prius. For the first time, he wasn't scornful of his chess partner's choice of car. The man could have afforded a top-of-the-line Tesla if he was that bothered about the environment, but no, he'd opted for a set of wheels that only a pensioner could be proud of. Jamie leaned across and opened the door, smiling at her through the dark. He'd turned off the interior light, obviously. 'Hi, Laurel. Good to see you. In you get.'

She climbed in without a second thought, placing her backpack between her feet and fastening her seat belt. 'This is amazing,' she said. 'I can't believe you think The View from the Law is worth your attention.'

He pulled away from the kerb. 'I told you, I think Shelley Maclean is exactly the kind of feisty female protagonist that publishers are looking for right now. I can already see her on the TV screen. We just need to do a bit of structural work to up the suspense and pace the revelations.'

'What do you think needs—'

'Not now, Laurel. I need to pay attention to the traffic. We'll have plenty of time to drill down into it once we get to the cabin. Well, I say cabin, it's more of a glorified shed. But it meets my needs. The atmosphere somehow lends itself to creativity. Close to the sea, but away from people. I'm lucky I hung on to it in the divorce.' He let a note of bitterness creep into his voice.

'That must have been difficult for you,' she said, hesitant. He thought she was probably trying not to think of the revelations that had precipitated the divorce.

'It was. I made a terrible mistake and I paid for it.' He forced a tight little laugh. 'But I insisted the cabin was one of the tools of my trade, so I was able to keep hold of it. And honestly? I'm happier now. I'm back to being my own boss, and I really believe my writing is the better for it. My next book is going to put me back on top of the chart again, I'm sure of it.'

She smiled, eyes and teeth glinting in the streetlights. 'I hope so. What's it about?'

He chuckled. 'A perfect crime,' he said.

'That sounds intriguing.'

'It will be. But I can't talk about it yet.' *And certainly not to you . . .* 'I'm superstitious about that. If I say too much about it, it'll somehow slip through my fingers. Vanish into the ether the way a vivid dream does as soon as you wake up.'

'Ah. OK. Sorry.'

'No, you weren't to know. So, tell me about your course. Who are you reading?' He really didn't give a toss, but it got her talking and that was the main thing. It turned out she was looking at the role of doppelgangers in Scottish literature, which was something he knew a bit about. They worked their way through Robert Louis Stevenson's Jekyll and Hyde to Iain Banks's *The Bridge* and had just begun to address Irvine Welsh's *Trainspotting* when they turned off the main A1 on to the side road that led to Tyninghame. The road was dark, the sky a low blanket of cloud. There would be nobody about to remember their passage, Jamie thought.

Just past the sawmill was a dense stand of trees. A track led off to the left and Jamie took it. A few hundred yards in, a gate barred the way. 'Can you jump out and get the gate?'

he asked. Another step on the road to lulling any unease. If he had a nefarious purpose, he surely wouldn't be offering her the chance to make a break for it, would he?

'Sure, yes,' Laurel said eagerly, getting out and trotting the few metres to the barrier. In the beam of the headlights he could see her fumbling with the stiff bolt. But she wrestled it free and swung the gate open. Jamie drove through slowly and waited on the far side for her to close it and return to the car.

'Not far now,' he said. Moments later, they rounded a curve and the cabin was before them at the far side of a clearing big enough for two cars. 'And here we are.' He smiled and stared at Mari's bolthole. It had started life as a shipping container, but she'd clad it in tongue-and-groove pine, added a pitched roof and inserted a couple of windows. It looked like a proper wooden cabin.

'Wow,' Laurel said. 'This is cool.'

'It's basic, but I like it,' he said. 'Come on, let's get down to business.'

She followed him obediently out of the car and on to the small porch. Jamie unlocked the door, flicked the light switch and stood back to let her enter. He tried to see it through her eyes, remembering the first time Mari had brought him here. The walls had been lined with plywood and painted in soft shades of sage green and duck egg blue. Nothing girly, thankfully. There was a desk, a bookcase, a table and a couple of chairs, a daybed with a Navajo rug. The only art on the walls was a print of an Alison Watt painting of cunningly folded fabric. At the far end, a couple of doors led to a tiny toilet and a kitchenette.

And now the bookshelf also displayed Jamie's Steel Dagger and both of his Golden Thistles. Mari's awards and photographs were tucked away in the drawer under the daybed.

'This is amazing,' Laurel breathed. He wouldn't be sorry to lose that constant amazement. She stepped closer to examine his awards. 'And this is where you write?'

'Mostly. I can do it in my flat or in hotel rooms, at a pinch. But this is where I feel at my most creative.'

'You've never mentioned it in interviews.'

He had to think on his feet. 'No, I don't want people knowing about it. I've got fans crazy enough to track it down and stalk me here. Not to mention I didn't like boasting that I was doing well enough to afford a bolthole like this. So, take a seat, get your laptop fired up. Would you like a drink? I've got red wine or coffee.' He dropped his own bag on the table, pointing her to the chair that faced away from the kitchenette door.

'Just a glass of water, please.' She sat down and opened her laptop. He headed for the back of the cabin, checking over his shoulder that she'd logged on. The miniature camera he'd installed on the bookcase should have captured her keystrokes so he could access the laptop later.

Jamie ran the tap while he opened the drawer and took out the gloves and the noose of strong cord he'd left there the day before. On with the gloves. Then he took a deep breath, turned off the tap and returned to the main room. She was focused on the screen, opening the file she still believed she'd be working on with her hero.

He moved quickly, holding the noose in his hands like someone assisting in the winding of wool. A few swift steps and he was behind her, dropping it over her head and yanking it tight, the slip knot obliging.

There were a few seconds when Laurel seemed not to understand what was happening. Then she convulsed, her hands clawing at her throat. But there was no gap between the biting cord and her swelling flesh. A terrible cawing sound came from her mouth. Jamie pulled harder, the muscles of his arms and shoulders straining. Her legs were thrashing as her feet sought purchase on the sisal floor covering, but she was already losing the battle. Then, in what felt like a long time but was less than a minute, she stopped. Limp, purple-faced and motionless, she slumped against the noose.

An amateur would have thought his job done. But Jamie was no amateur. When it came to murder, he'd been an expert for years. He hadn't had to leave a trail of online searches when it came to the mechanics of strangulation; he'd simply taken a couple of his many reference books off the shelf in his flat and read up on the subject. The victim would lose consciousness quickly; sometimes in as little as ten seconds. But to get the job done, you'd have to keep up the pressure for a good five minutes. Besides, she might have gone limp because of a seizure.

So he leaned back and used his weight as well as his strength to finish Laurel off. He counted the seconds out loud. When he reached the five-minute mark, he gave himself another sixty elephants to make sure. He let go of the cord, massaging his stiff hands through the leather gloves. The next bit was the dangerous part. He needed to check for a pulse, and that meant taking off one of his gloves. He'd leave a fingerprint on her skin, and he'd have to remember to wipe it clean.

Jamie stepped around Laurel, whose head fell forward on to the laptop keyboard with a chime of protest. He was grateful for that; he didn't want to have to look at her face any more than necessary. He wasn't the kind of sicko who got off on dead girls. He lifted her slack arm and laid it on the table, then took off one glove and felt for a pulse. He could find no trace, no matter how hard he pressed.

He'd done it. He'd killed someone. Agatha Christie had

been right. Murder is easy. Jamie was amazed at his lack of
emotional response.

He put his gloves back on and fetched a wet wipe from
Mari's toilet. He scrubbed Laurel's wrist to remove any trace
of his touch then opened the drawer from under the daybed.
He pulled out the snowboard bag he'd bought with cash from
a sports shop in a shopping mall near Glasgow and tucked
the wet wipe in it. Then he unzipped it next to the dead
woman's chair and tipped her into it, face down. There was just
enough room.

He dragged the bag the few feet to the door. Jamie checked
there was no sign of life outside, then with a grunt of effort, he
used the shoulder strap to hoist the bag, and staggered to the
car. With the back seat folded down, he managed to fit it in.
Nothing suspicious about a man with a snowboard bag in his
car, was there?

Jamie slammed the boot shut and went back to the cabin.
He closed Laurel's laptop and collected the mini camera from
the bookcase. He swapped his awards for Mari's, then put
everything in Laurel's backpack and slung it over his shoulder.
He looked around for a final check, then pushed the daybed
drawer shut and returned to the car.

He dropped Laurel's backpack in the passenger footwell and
started the car. Job done. Well, at least part of it was done.

11

Jamie parked Rob's car at the end of his street, nonchalantly
hefting the backpack over one shoulder. He walked back to his
flat and locked the door behind him. It was only when he took
off his rain jacket – chosen for its non-shedding fabric – that

he realised his shirt was damp with sweat. He must have been more stressed than he realised, he thought. He dropped the backpack and poured himself a tumbler of water from the cold tap. No more iced water from the big American-style fridge for him these days, he thought bitterly. It was the little things that cut deepest.

He settled down at his own laptop and played back the camera footage without actually downloading it. He prided himself on being too smart to leave that sort of digital trace. When Laurel appeared on the screen, he felt a jolt in his chest, the kind of shock he felt when a movie offered a moment of genuine surprise. He took a deep breath and kept watching as she opened the laptop. Her fingers moved fast over the keys and he had to replay it twice before he could be sure he'd got her password right. *StrangersOnATrain50*. He didn't have Laurel Oliver down as a Patricia Highsmith aficionado, but then he'd barely known her.

Back at the desk, he opened Laurel's laptop and tapped in the password. He recognised her wallpaper – a photograph of the cover of *All That Remains*, a memoir written by forensic anthropologist Sue Black, a book that sat on his own shelves. Laurel had certainly gone through the motions of studying her chosen genre. Before he went any further, Jamie unplugged the camera and dropped it in the sink. He took a hammer out of his toolbox and smashed the tiny spy beyond recovery, gathering the remains and dropping them in the kitchen bin with the banana skins and coffee grounds.

He opened the email account and checked her recent sent messages. Nothing there to worry about. She hadn't even told anyone she'd planned to go to his reading. WhatsApp, Twitter DMs and her Instagram account were all clean too. 'Good little girl,' he murmured. He skimmed through her Dropbox folder, opening anything that looked like it might have something to do with him. He did a global search for 'Jamie Cobain' and came up with nothing more incriminating than an advert for an event he'd done over a year before with some nobody from Aberdeen. Just after all the shit had come down, he recalled. It had been a grim, grim night. There would be no more of those, if everything went well.

He plugged in a new external hard drive he'd bought for cash in a backstreet electronics shop in Paisley. Jamie painstakingly downloaded the entire contents of Laurel's hard drive on to the little black box and put it in the kitchen drawer. He didn't just transfer a mirror of the hard drive; that would include fragments of the files he'd deleted, fragments a forensic computer analyst might be able to recover. Instead, he copied and pasted folder after folder on to the external drive. He had plans for that, plans to boost the evidence against his rival, but not until the weekend.

Then he reformatted Laurel's laptop and wiped it clean. A forensic specialist would be able to find fragments of the original files, but Jamie wasn't planning on it ending up in a digital detective's hands. Later, he'd walk down to the Shore at Leith and drop it over the Victoria Swing Bridge and watch it sink to the bottom. Bye bye, digital footprints.

Now all that remained was the physically demanding part. Just as well he'd devoted himself to his fitness regime.

It was after eleven when Jamie rolled silently into Rob's driveway. That was the one good thing about the Prius – he could cruise in on the electric motor, any sound swallowed by the ambience of the night city.

There were no lights visible in the house; he'd earlier tracked

Rachel's car to this house then away again, across the bridge to Fife. The car had driven to Cellardyke in the East Neuk and parked outside Rachel's favourite restaurant, where it had remained. It was safe to assume Rob was safely out of the way, enjoying a Michelin-starred dinner followed by an overnight stay. They wouldn't be heading back at this time of night, not with a skinful of wine.

Rob's garage was round the side, a single-skin brick building about ten metres away from the house itself. Jamie parked the car and opened the garage doors. Rob liked to take care of his possessions, so they were well-maintained, the hinges regularly oiled to prevent annoying squeaking.

Jamie had paid a visit to the garden earlier in the week, when he'd known Rob was in Glasgow recording some inane BBC radio panel show. He'd driven his car alongside the garage and unloaded the three packs of dry mix fast-setting concrete he'd bought at an agricultural supplies store in the Borders. He'd slipped them inside heavy-duty plastic sacks to protect them from the weather, and tucked them behind the large barbecue that was tightly covered for the winter. When he'd showed it off, Jamie had said sourly, 'If the arse ever falls out of the writing game, you can always wheel it down the street and set up a hot dog stand.' Now, he had to admit he was glad it was there.

One by one he carried the bags of concrete mix into the garage and leaned them against the wall. He stood for a moment, hands on hips, breathing heavily from the exertion. He stared down at the sheet of woodchip that covered the inspection pit in the garage floor, the very feature that had started his imagination on the journey that had led him here, now.

The previous owner of the house had been obsessed with veteran and vintage cars. He would scour the country for examples on their last legs, bring them here on a low loader and lovingly restore them. Rob had boasted that a Lagonda returned to its former glory here in his garage had featured in several episodes of *Downton Abbey*, as if that was something to be proud of. He'd waved at the oil-stained inspection pit and said airily, 'I'll have to get that covered, though. I don't want to misjudge my angle when I'm putting the car away.'

Even at the time, Jamie had thought that the pit offered interesting opportunities. But something had made him hold his tongue. And the more he'd thought about his project of revenge, the more the inspection pit began to loom large.

He wrestled the cover away from the pit and looked down into it. He'd remembered it correctly. It was just deep enough for a mechanic to stand in it and work on the chassis and brakes. Perfect.

Jamie walked to the back of the Prius and looked around once more. The garden was barely overlooked, and there was no sign of life in any of the few neighbouring windows. Rob's house stood dark and blank-eyed. Quickly, he opened the boot and grunted softly at the effort of lifting the snowboard bag clear of the boot lip. Congratulating himself on the foresight of buying a holdall with wheels, he ferried it into the garage. Once inside, he closed the doors.

It was a simple job to get the bag into the pit. Then he went back out to the car and grabbed a black bin bag containing the cans of polyurethane foam he'd been stockpiling over the previous weeks. It wouldn't provide a perfect seal but it would keep the putrefaction smells to a minimum. Not that that would be a problem; he had a belt and braces plan for that. He sprayed can after can of the foam around the snowboard bag to encase it. The used cans went back into the bin liner.

Once the foam had set, one by one, he emptied the sacks of

quick-drying cement mix into the pit. There was just enough to cover the bag and fill the gaps around it. The last act was to add water to the cement. There was a hose attached to a tap by the door, and Jamie let a slow trickle of water flow into the pit. He resisted the urge to hurry the job along, knowing he needed to let the cement thoroughly absorb the water. But he was twitchy all the same. This was the hardest part of the process. He wasn't patient at the best of times, and there was no other necessary activity to take his mind off what was happening.

He stirred the gloopy mix with a garden cane, one of a bundle stacked in a corner. At last, he was satisfied he had the right consistency, and that the water had penetrated throughout. Jamie turned off the tap and squatted by the pit. The surface of the cement was not quite smooth; there were some eddies and streaks visible. But nothing to indicate what lay beneath. He let out a sigh of satisfaction. The perfect murder, no doubt about it.

The last act of the night was to replace the woodchip cover in the right place. Jamie grabbed the bags that had contained the cement. He stuffed them along with the cement-contaminated cane in the black bin bag. He'd toss the bag in a builder's skip in the New Town. There were always plenty to choose from. Finally, he stepped back towards the door, checking everything was as it should be. Hose coiled on the hook as it had been before. No sign anyone had been here.

'I've got you,' he said softly. 'I have so got you.'

9

And that was the end of the manuscript. The strongest emotion it provoked in Karen was disgust. Disgust and a desire to scrub the words from her memory. Whatever was going on here, whether truth or dark fantasy, it was deeply unpleasant. By the looks of Daisy's face, she felt much the same. What had wormed its way past the defences her years in the job had built was the cold disdain for the humanity of the victim. Laurel Oliver was an object to be manipulated to satisfy the ends of a cruel and selfish killer. What was clear to her was that this was intentional. 'Jake Stein deliberately created a character devoid of empathy,' she said. 'He's deliberately made him repugnant. And I suppose that means he's succeeded in what he set out to do.'

Daisy's lip curled in scorn. 'But why would you do that? Jake Stein wrote big fat books. Four hundred pages or more. Nobody would want to spend four hundred pages inside Jamie Cobain's head.'

Karen picked up the pages of notes they still had to read. 'Maybe that wasn't the plan? Maybe the narrative shifts back to the perspective of Rob what's-his-name and we get his side of whatever the story ends up being?'

'Or Rachel. Can you imagine what being married to Stein

111

would have been like? Why did she not leave him sooner? Or put rat poison in his tea?'

'Women – and men too – stay in uncomfortable relationships for all sorts of reasons. Fear of the repercussions if they leave. Fear of being alone.' Karen scoffed. 'Fear of being skint, of losing the good life they've got used to. Have you never stayed with someone you really knew you should have given the jaggy bunnet?'

Daisy grinned. 'Chance would be a fine thing, boss. I do know what you mean, though.'

'I do wish we had more of it, disgusting though it is. I want to know how it all ends, this perfect murder plot. And I want to know why it ends where it does.'

'The answers – or at least some clues – might be in the notes? Shall we get stuck into them?'

Karen glanced at the clock. 'Let's leave it for tomorrow. The inside of my head feels like it needs disinfecting. We'll come at it with a clear head in the morning. And besides, I've got a FaceTime at seven.'

Daisy smirked. 'The handsome Highlander?'

'He's not really a Highlander,' Karen protested. 'He spent his teens in California. He's got more surfer in him than crofter, truth be told. But no, not Hamish. I got an odd wee message from Miran. You know, the guy who runs Aleppo?'

'The Syrian café? What's he after? Surely they're shut down just now?'

'They are, and I've no idea.' She stood up. 'I'll take the call through in my bedroom, just in case it's sensitive.'

Daisy nodded. 'OK. I've got plenty to watch on my laptop that you'll totally hate.'

She was probably right, Karen thought. The ten years between them sometimes felt like an entire generation.

In the bedroom she usually shared with Hamish, she set the laptop up on what she supposed she'd have to call the dressing table and pulled a chair across from the corner. On the dot of seven, the FaceTime stuttered its announcement and she accepted the call. Miran looked as if he was in a cupboard. She'd never been inside the tiny flat he shared with Amina and their baby daughter, so she had no idea of his exact location.

'Good evening, Karen,' he said, his diction careful and precise. 'How are you?'

'As good as can be expected in these strange days, Miran. I don't like being cooped up for so long, but I know compared to a lot of people, I'm very fortunate. And you?'

He shrugged. 'It's so much better than what we left in Syria, so I have no complaints. I like the chance to get to know my baby, and to spend time with Amina.'

'I miss getting to Aleppo. I can't wait for this to be over so I can get a good cup of coffee and a pastry.' Deep breath. 'So, what did you want to talk to me about, Miran?'

He frowned. 'It's complicated.'

'I do complicated just fine. Tell me.'

A deep sigh. 'We have a friend. Well, he is a distant cousin of Amina. His name is Rafiq. Rafiq Yasin. He is a doctor.' Another sigh. Miran looked pained, his dark eyebrows drawn together. 'You remember the torture photographs that escaped from Assad's prisons? The ones that shocked everyone over here?'

They were the kind of images that, once seen, you could never forget, she thought. 'I remember.'

'Rafiq was a doctor in one of the prisons. He hated what he was seeing there. He took some of the pictures. He passed them over to a journalist.' He cleared his throat.

'That was incredibly brave. I don't think I could have done that.'

Miran's mouth twisted. 'I pray you never have to make that choice. Rafiq paid a high price. The journalist, he was a man Rafiq did not know well. And when the photos appeared in the West, he was arrested and he gave them the name of Rafiq and the others who had passed photographs to him.'

Karen felt her stomach tighten. She had an idea of what was coming. 'They came for him?'

Miran nodded. 'But he was not there.' He pressed his eyes closed momentarily. 'They raped his wife in front of his five-year-old son. The boy tried to run away, but he fell on the stairs and . . .' His voice faltered. 'He broke his neck. One of the neighbours saw, he told Rafiq the boy died straight away. When Rafiq came home, he found his wife had hanged herself.'

There were no words, Karen knew that. But still, something had to be said. 'I'm so sorry, Miran.'

His eyes glistened with tears. 'I know.' A pause. 'Rafiq helped many people over the years, Karen. He is a good doctor, he is surgeon for . . .' He waved his hand in a circular motion, frowning because he didn't know the word. 'Bones,' he said at last. 'If you break your knee, Rafiq is the man who can fix it.'

'Orthopaedics?'

He nodded, doubtful. 'I think so. But he has helped many patients to walk again and one of them was able to help him to leave Syria. And now he is here in Edinburgh. He is in a hostel. And yesterday, one of the other men spoke to him and said, "They are still looking for you."' His eyes beseeched her. 'Someone knows where he is and they will kill him.'

114

'Surely, with lockdown, there's some sort of security? Some kind of control?' Karen wanted to believe that, but she knew she was probably whistling in the dark.

Miran shrugged. 'Rafiq says the staff don't pay much attention. He says we all look the same to them. He's scared for his life, Karen. We don't know what to do. He can't come here, there is no room, even if it wasn't against the law. Can you help?'

'I don't know.' He'd put her firmly on the spot. She needed time to work out whether there was anything she could do. 'I need to think about it. Talk to some people. Give me twenty-four hours, Miran. I'll try to come up with something.'

He broke into a smile. 'You have been our saviour before, Karen, Amina says you are the one who can help us.'

Karen shook her head. 'I don't know whether I can fix this, Miran. These are strange times. Even though I'm a polis, I can't just break the rules without good reason.'

'Is a man's life not good reason?' The smile was gone, a flash of frustration crossed his face.

Karen sighed. 'Believe me, I understand it seems absurd that I can't just sort this out. But it doesn't help anybody if I get this wrong. I have to figure out what might be possible. We're the ones who have to enforce the law. We can't be seen breaking the rules when it suits us.'

He bowed his head. 'I am sorry.'

'Leave it with me till tomorrow. I'll try, but I can't make any promises.'

Karen threw herself down on the bed and considered the options. She ran through all the people she'd usually turn to for advice. River Wilde, forensic anthropologist, her closest friend and professional ally, was locked down in the Lake District with her partner. But he was a senior police officer, and what Karen wanted to talk about was a breach of the COVID regulations for starters. Whatever she did next, she'd be doing something that could land her with a fixed penalty notice at the very least. So River was out.

There was no point in running it past Hamish. He'd either have some mad flamboyant 'solution' or else he'd tell her it wasn't her problem. Besides, he was too busy building another wee empire to replace the coffee shop one that COVID was holding to ransom. For a brief moment, she let herself be diverted. Really, was he the man for her? He'd been the right one at the right time when she was trying to get past her grief. But was he still the right one now she was further along the path towards healing? Sure, he was a lovely distraction – clever, funny, sexy and generous. Was that enough, though? Hamish always seemed to see her through the prism of what he wanted her to be; but Karen had known what it was to be seen for what she was, and sometimes that made anything less seem insubstantial.

She gave herself a mental shake and returned to the problem at hand. Obviously she couldn't discuss it with Daisy. It was never a good idea to let your subordinates see you bending the rules for your own ends, even if it was in a noble cause. Karen didn't want to give Daisy wriggle room for becoming one of those cops who always managed to find the right reason for doing the wrong thing. Daisy had already walked that line on their first case together. On that occasion, there was no argument that the outcome had justified her action. But it was the thin end of a wedge Karen didn't want to drive in any deeper.

Her thoughts skated across Craig Grassie, the SNP MP

whose help she'd enlisted when she had first crossed paths with Miran and the other Syrians. He'd refused to take no for an answer from the bureaucrats who had stood in the way of the community café and he'd stayed in touch with the refugees since. But he wasn't a natural comrade in arms for anything dodgy. And this was definitely going to have to be dodgy. Rafiq was a refugee; the Home Office wouldn't be about to devote any kind of police protection to him, in spite of his part in exposing the worst excesses of the Syrian regime. There would be no straight way of doing this, even in the best of times. Her mouth twisted in an ironic smile. Nobody in their right mind would call this the best of times.

Then there was DCI Jimmy Hutton. Their fortnightly Monday gin evenings had become a safety valve for both of them, a secure place to let off steam and bounce ideas off each other. Jimmy wouldn't betray her confidence, she knew that. But she didn't feel she had the right to put him in the position of knowing a colleague was breaking the rules. This was no trivial matter, like clearing off a parking ticket. The Prime Minister was in hospital with COVID; the Chief Medical Officer of Scotland had ended up having to resign after she'd made a couple of trips to her second home in Fife.

Karen knew she was likely skating on thin ice when it came to her own walks to her empty flat. It was too tempting when she felt overwhelmed with sharing her space with Daisy. Maybe the answer was to make it impossible?

She sighed again. Since she couldn't have a useful conversation, she might as well have an obligatory one. She dialled up a familiar number on FaceTime and let it ring more times than most people needed. At last, her father's face swam into view, his eyes screwed up in their usual

FaceTime mode. 'Och, it's you,' he said cheerily. He turned away and shouted, 'It's Karen, come and say hello.'

And they were off. The state of the allotment now he was only allowed an hour a day; the jams and pickles her mother was making to fill her days; who from the bowling club had got the COVID; what they'd been watching on TV. Their general bonhomie was reassuring; although their interests were not hers, there was a certain comfort in their apparent calm. As the conversation wound down, her mother said, 'You look after yourself, Karen. Don't do anything daft. And don't let yon Hamish do anything daft either.'

She'd given a wry chuckle. 'Hamish is in the Highlands. Whatever daftness he's up to, thankfully I don't have to give it a thought.' As she said the words, their truth struck home. She ended the call, wondering what this new revelation might mean for her.

10

Karen was up ahead of the sun. The faint glow of dawn was giving the streetlights a run for their money as she threaded her way through the silent streets to Gayfield Square police station. She fumbled a mask into place and walked in. The Historic Cases Unit was tucked away at the back of the shop, invisible from the reception area. But that wasn't her destination this morning.

She rang the bell and after a few moments, a uniformed PC emerged. A newly installed screen had replaced the former sliding glass window that separated them. 'DCI Pirie?' He sounded surprised, rather than dubious of her identity.

'That's right. I need the use of a patrol car,' she said. 'I need to talk to a witness and the Perspex screen means we can do it safely.'

He frowned. 'Is that right?'

'Trust me, that's right. I only need it for a couple of hours.'

He looked around, as if he'd expected a senior officer to have materialised. 'I'll need to go and check.'

Karen sighed. 'I outrank you by several degrees, son. I'm really not asking your permission. Away and get me a set of keys.' She tried to soften her words with a smile. By the look on his face, all it did was unnerve him further. He nodded several times and backed out.

A couple of minutes passed, then a sergeant Karen knew appeared. 'You're wanting a motor, then, Chief Inspector?'

'That's right. I need to interview a witness and I'm mindful of the COVID restrictions. And no, before you ask, it won't wait. You know my mantra – we might be historic, but every day counts to grieving families.'

He nodded with the weary air of a man who'd had to listen to Karen for longer than was reasonable. 'You'll get no argument from me,' he said, pulling a car key from his trouser pocket. 'You'll need to sign for it.'

Karen rolled her eyes. She really didn't want to leave a paper trail on today's excursion. If the Assistant Chief Constable (Crime) Ann Markie got wind that Karen was running operations off the books, she'd leap at the chance to cut her off at the knees. They were old adversaries and it wouldn't take much to set Markie's antennae quivering. 'Really?' she said.

'You know the rules, Karen.' His voice was patient and paternal.

It made her hackles rise. 'ACC Markie's got enough on her plate without me waving a red rag. And if you're the one who signed the key out to me ...'

Without another word, he gave a rueful smile and handed her the key. 'Second on the left in the car park. Don't hurt the paintwork and don't go blues and twos past the Dog Biscuit's office.'

Karen gave him the thumbs up and took the key before he could have second thoughts. It had cheered her up to be reminded of Ann Markie's nickname, inflicted because of a brand of dog treats that shared her surname, and because she was always trying to reward the top brass. 'Woof, woof,' she said under her breath as she got behind the wheel of the car. She didn't need blues and twos; the chequerboard markings along the side of the car were all the ID required in the deserted streets.

The hostel had been a residential children's home in a previous life, tucked away in a depressed side street near Saughton prison. Karen had no idea where the kids were now, but it could hardly be less uplifting than this scabby two-storey building with the dirty terracotta harling peeling off at the corners. There were bars on the windows on both floors and the door was a bare steel sheet. CCTV cameras festooned the building, giving full cover from the gate. The building and its tarmacked forecourt were surrounded by a wall, deterrent rather than preventative. Karen reckoned a reasonably fit and determined person could be over it and away within five minutes. But they'd have to get out of the building first and that was clearly a much bigger ask.

She parked on the street. Showtime. Karen felt the flush of adrenaline pulsing in her heart and consciously pushed down her nerves. If this went south, she'd be facing more than a rap on the knuckles for breaching COVID rules. 'Just be gallus,' she told herself. She walked up the pavement and pressed the intercom by the gate. Almost immediately it crackled into life. 'Yes?'

She held her ID up to the tiny camera lens. 'I'm Detective Chief Inspector Karen Pirie, Police Scotland. I'm here to collect a Rafiq Yasin.'

'I don't understand.'

'Can you let me in and I'll explain?'

Crackle and pause. She was about to press the button again when the gate buzzed loudly. Karen pushed it open and strode across the pitted tarmac. Fake it till you make it, she reminded herself. As she approached, putting on her mask again, the steel door swung open to reveal a whey-faced dumpy man in his thirties, stuffed into trackie bottoms and a Hibs replica shirt two sizes bigger than any actual footballer would ever need. His haircut had a careful fade at the sides to reveal a saltire flag tattoo. His mask covered his mouth but was tucked under his nose in what Karen was coming to consider a mark of stupidity. He peered at the ID card Karen held out in front of her, getting close enough for her to smell his onion breath. 'OK, you're a polis. I get that.'

'And you are?'

'Brian Ryan. I'm the duty manager.' Karen was surprised. She'd expected a uniform and an element of organisation. Things were really slipping in lockdown. He stood back to let her in.

Karen found herself in a sally port vestibule. At the far end, another steel door. To one side, an open door led to an office. It had a window on to the vestibule with a sliding glass partition. 'I'm here to collect this Rafiq Yasin,' she said.

He shook his head. 'I've got no notice of that.'

'That might be because you're not a member of Police Scotland.' She managed not to sound sarcastic. 'We don't always advertise our moves ahead of schedule.'

'Usually there's two of you.'

'We're keeping contacts to a minimum because of the COVID. And by the way, you need to wear that mask properly. Nose *and* mouth.' He flushed and yanked it over his nose. 'Now, if we can just get on? I need to take Yasin in for a witness interview. We believe he has information that could lead to a series of major arrests.'

He gave a self-satisfied grunt. 'Drugs, eh? I'm no' sur-prised. Half of this lot are dodgy as fuck, you ask me.'

'So, can you get Rafiq Yasin for me? And tell him to bring his stuff with him. He might not be coming back here. The people he knows about ... Well, let's just say he'll be safer someplace else.' Always keep the lies as close to the truth as possible.

'Sounds like a big deal.' He took a key card from his pocket and said, 'I'll be back.'

If he was going for Arnold Schwarzenegger, he'd scored an epic fail, she thought, watching him let himself into the main part of the building. Ten minutes passed slowly. The little office offered nothing worth snooping. The desk was bare except for an unplugged computer terminal. The desk drawers only contained forms waiting to be filled in. Karen sighed. Just her luck. If this was a movie, there would be something damning. She knew from what she'd read and heard that there would be plenty going on behind these walls to provoke her to outrage. The reports of the condi-tions endured by asylum seekers and illegal immigrants made her ashamed of the UK government. Calling them hostels made people think warmly of bunkhouses they'd stayed in on holidays before they could afford hotels. The reality was often overcrowded spaces unfit for human habi-tation. She shuddered to think of what COVID would wreak in those conditions. But none of it was visible on this side of the sally port.

At last the inner door opened again. Ryan led the way, followed by a tall man with thick dark hair, head bowed. He was dressed in dirty jeans and a thick brown polo-neck sweater. In one hand, he carried a plastic bag. Behind him came a burly woman in the uniform of a security guard – navy V-necked sweater, white shirt, black tie, black trousers and a utility belt that would have put the Batman to shame. 'Keep moving, pal,' she said loudly.

There was nowhere for Rafiq to move to. He flashed Karen a quick look, fear the most obvious element. 'I am a police officer. I need to take you in for questioning,' she said, brisk but not unpleasant. 'We have a statement from Miran that implicates you.'

He looked up again. This time she caught a glimmer of hope. 'Very well,' he mumbled. He held his hands out, wrists together.

Karen took his cue and produced a pair of plastic hand-cuffs and a spare mask from her backpack. 'Put on the mask, first.'

He did as she asked without a protest. She turned towards the outer door, glancing back at Ryan. 'You'll need to sign for him,' he said. He'd acquired a clipboard from some-where and had written Rafiq's name in block capitals. Her confidence almost slipped, but she reminded herself that nobody ever chased up illegals who vanished off the radar. She scribbled something that bore no relationship to her sig-nature and gestured to the door. 'Come on, Brian, I haven't got all day.'

And they were out and in the fresh air. 'What is going on?' Rafiq asked, his voice tight with tension.

'I'm a friend of Miran's. He sent me. We'll talk in the car, but just keep walking now.'

At the car, she put him in the back seat, carefully guiding his head inside. Karen took a quick look to either side of her. It being just past seven, the street was still mercifully quiet. She slipped her handcuff key out of her pocket, reached in and undid his restraints. Then she closed the door and went round to the driver's seat. 'Like I said, I am a police officer and I'm breaking a few laws and regulations right now—'

'Why are you here? What are you doing?' He was beginning to sound panicked. So he well might since there were people after him who probably had the capacity to bribe a police officer.

'Miran and Amina are friends of mine, and they're worried for you. I helped them set up their café. Aleppo. So they asked me to help you.'

'How can you do this? They know where I am. They will come for me.'

Karen shook her head. 'I have an idea about that. Would it help if you spoke to Miran?'

'I cannot go to him. They could be watching him, looking for me.'

Karen took out her phone and summoned Miran from her contacts. She pressed the call button and passed the phone through the small gap in the screen. 'Talk to him.' She started the car and drove off.

Rafiq looked astonished. Karen heard, faintly, the sound of the phone being answered. An explosion of gutturals and consonants followed from Rafiq, with occasional similar echoes from the phone. He kept throwing her unreadable glances. The exchange grew gradually less frantic. At last, he pushed the phone towards her. 'Miran will speak to you.'

Conveniently, they were passing a supermarket car park. Karen pulled off and took the phone back. 'Miran. It's me.'

'I told him he can trust you. But where are you taking him? You can't take chances with breaking the COVID rules, Karen.'

'I think I've done a wee bit more than that already, Miran. Which means I have to take even more care now.

125

Listen, I have a plan, at least in the short term. I know a safe place I can stash Rafiq for the time being. I'm taking him there right now. I'll call you later today, OK?'

A pause. Then a reluctant, 'OK. But don't scare him. He's had a terrible time.'

'I'll try.' Karen ended the call, then swung round in her seat. 'Wait here. I'm going to buy some food for you.'

It was like supermarket sweep. Milk, pitta bread, hummus, olives, apples, tinned tuna, a barbecued chicken, tinned soup and a box of tomatoes. It would do for now. On impulse, as she approached the till, she added a giant bar of chocolate. At least there was plenty of good coffee where Rafiq was going.

'Please, what is going on?' he asked as soon as she returned.

'I have a flat down by the sea,' she said. 'I'm not living there right now. I'm looking after a friend's place for him. I can't take you there because there's someone else there too. But you can stay in my flat without breaking the rules. You can leave for exercise outside for one hour a day. I know it will be hard for you. Boring. But at least it's safe. There's TV and a games console and there are plenty of books to read. There's a landline phone so you can call Miran. But tell him not to call you. That way, nobody can trick you.'

She started the car again and headed for the Western Harbour Breakwater. She drove into the underground car park and got out of the car, reaching in for the shopping bags. Rafiq was trying the door handle and looking panicked again.

Karen hurried round and pulled the door open. 'You can't open it from the inside. We transport prisoners in these cars as well as rescuing people.' She grinned and led the way to the lift. 'I can't come up with you. It's a breach of the COVID rules, and it would be just our luck to come face to face with a nosy neighbour.' She put down the shopping bags and produced a key card and a key. She ran through the procedure for getting into the building and told him her flat number. 'There are some men's clothes in the wardrobe. Just some joggers and T-shirts and stuff. They'll be too big for you but at least they're clean. They belong to my boyfriend. Help yourself. I'm going to call you every day at nine o'clock in the evening. Got that?'

He nodded. 'Nine in the evening.'

'I think we can meet outside occasionally if we keep two metres distance between us. Late at night is probably best. We can meet by the breakwater or somewhere round the harbour. Please make yourself at home. There's plenty of coffee beans in the cupboard and a grinder on the worktop. Now get yourself inside. I'll call you tomorrow morning. If you need me before then, my mobile number's on the back of the grocery receipt.'

For the first time, he looked her straight in the face. His cheeks were hollow, his eyes sunken. He looked like he could model for an El Greco painting. But his eyes were warm and dark, his lips full and mobile. Right now, they were smiling, in spite of the sparkle of tears in his eyes. 'I don't know why you are doing this.'

She turned away. 'I saw the photographs,' she said gruffly.

11

Karen arrived home to find Daisy in the thick of a Zoom call with Jason. 'You did say first thing, boss,' Jason said, looking wounded.

Daisy turned and flashed her a grin. 'Yeah, we were here on the dot of nine.'

Karen shrugged out of her coat and booted up her laptop. 'Sorry. I had to see to something and it took a wee bit longer than I expected.' She found the Zoom link and connected to the call. 'Morning, Jason. How are you doing?'

'Not bad, boss. It was good having something proper to do. I mean, it's OK having gaming time and time to spend with Eilidh, but it gets kinda boring, not being able to go out and about.'

'I know. I miss it too.'

'But you have been out and about this morning,' Daisy butted in from the borderline of chippiness.

'I've been out of the house on police business, Daisy. Not on a whim.' The temperature dropped a few degrees. 'How did your researches go, Jason?'

He studied his notebook with a frown. 'Jake Stein was one of the top-selling UK authors until the year before he died. He published fifteen bestselling crime novels. I think.

It's hard to be clear because some of them have different titles in America. According to the wee bit about him in his books, he'd sold more than ten million copies worldwide and his books were translated into seventeen languages. He took a bit of stick over the years for the way he wrote violence against women. Like he relished it. But he used to say he was highlighting the way society allowed those attitudes to persist in so many men. Not him, obviously, according to him anyway. Plus he said he was reflecting reality.'

Karen sighed. 'I don't think his particular brand of gruesome voyeurism had much to do with highlighting male attitudes. More about pandering to them. You said he stopped being such a bestseller the year before he died. What happened? Did he just write a couple of really bad books? Or what?'

'There was a massive scandal,' Daisy interrupted.

'I was getting to that,' Jason muttered, mutinous.

Karen nodded encouragement, then realised that on Zoom, neither of her junior officers could know who she was encouraging. 'On you go, Jason.'

'It started in the book world but it spilled out into the mainstream media. His latest book got pretty poor reviews. Readers turned on him on the socials about sadistic violence and sexual degradation. But what totally scuppered him was that this woman, Marga Durham, turned up at his publication party and walloped him in the middle of the celebrations. Boss, she totally went for it. A massive skelp then floods of tears. Turns out, Stein had an affair with her that went sour and he thought he'd get his own back by putting her in the book. People in the business would read between the lines and figure she was a masochistic slut, and he'd have got his own back.'

Daisy, clearly impatient at the pace of Jason's narrative, cut in: 'Except he didn't do a good enough job of disguising her. Everybody spotted who the character was based on, and Marga Durham was trolled mercilessly. Stein was publicly humiliated. His wife filed for divorce and he had to pay Durham a good-sized wedge to stop her suing the arse off him. And his wife's lawyers argued that the payment should come out of Stein's share, not out of the common pot. So he got stung both ways.'

Grimly, Jason grabbed the action back. 'And his publishers dumped him. He's with a wee Scottish imprint called Stooshie now.'

Daisy scoffed. 'Stooshie by name but not by nature. They haven't got the cash to stir up a publicity storm for their books. So Jake Stein suffered twice over with his next book.'

'OK. So much for the public scandal. What's the word behind people's hands?' Karen genuinely wondered how much Jason had been able to garner online.

'The wife of the guy who runs the book festival is a client of Eilidh's. They get on like a house on fire. Eilidh says she loves a good gossip, so she gave her a ring. She pretended another client was thinking about writing a biography of Stein, and Eilidh said she'd ask around to see whether anybody thought that was a good idea.'

'Nice idea,' Karen said. 'Might not work in normal life but in lockdown, everybody's desperate for a good blether.'

'No kidding, they were on the phone for nearly an hour, talking about all kinds of nonsense. But in the middle of it all, she said some interesting stuff about Stein. They always had to keep the good-looking young women away from him, apparently. It wasn't so much that he was handsy or that, it was just that he was very good at making them feel

130

special and whisking them off into the night. The flings never lasted long, and he could be brutal when it came to dropping the lassies once he'd got bored with them.'

'Not so different from plenty of other guys,' Karen mused.

'Except most of them haven't got the gloss of wealth and celebrity that Stein had. He had more effective armour against the knock-back,' Daisy pointed out.

'He was lucky that he'd never come up against one as gutsy as Marga before.'

'Maybe he'd just never been stupid enough to point the finger at them publicly,' Jason said. 'It must have been horrible, knowing that everybody was acting like they were grossed out, and they couldn't believe how stupid she'd been. Like, "Fancy thinking a cool dude like Jake Stein would be interested in the likes of you, Marga Durham?"' He slipped into a worryingly accurate impression of a young Edinburgh woman. It wasn't flattering to the breed.

'What else? Second homes? Hobbies? Pastimes?'

The flicker of notebook pages again. 'When he was still married, they had the big house in Ravelston Dykes. No holiday homes or weekend cottages. He said in one interview, "Why would I take on the bother of a second home? If I want to go somewhere for a weekend away, or to hide away and write, I'll rent someone else's place and let them have all the hassle." Hobbies were fast cars and eating out. He used to play rugby but he quit four years ago after he did his knee in. He was a chess champion when he was at school but there's nothing about him playing in recent years.'

Karen thought for a moment. 'Did he do any teaching? Any mentoring?'

Jason shook his head. 'Nothing recent. About five years ago, he taught a course up at Moniack Mhor in the

Highlands. He said – give me a minute . . . ' Jason frowned and peered into his screen. He'd clearly moved away from Zoom and forgotten they could still see him as he searched for his notes. Karen and Daisy exchanged a smile. Then his attention shifted back to them.

'Got it. "I had a perfectly pleasant time. There were a couple of promising writers there. But I came away firmly convinced that you can't teach people to write. You can help them become better if they're willing to listen, but that's about the size of it. And that's really the job of an editor, not a teacher. But it's a profitable racket for universities and colleges, so good luck to them. I don't see fleecing people of their life savings as being part of my role."'

'Mister Nice Guy,' Karen said. 'If he'd been murdered, there would have been no shortage of suspects. Is there anything at all that even hints at a connection between him and Lara Hardie?'

Jason hesitated. 'Maybe not a connection, as such?'

'Tell me.' Karen felt the frustration of not having direct eye contact with Jason. Two screens mediating their conversation did not allow her to fix him with her beady eye, she realised.

'I managed to access the photos the CSIs took of Lara Hardie's bedrooms. Her flat and her parents' home.'

'How did you manage that?' Karen butted in.

He flushed. 'I asked Tamsin.'

Tamsin Martineau was a feisty Australian who had somehow managed to worm her way into every department of the forensics unit at Police Scotland's Gartcosh campus. She knew everybody and they all seemed to owe her favours. Karen was torn between admiration for Jason's chutzpah, and annoyance that he'd dared to suborn *her* personal

132

contact. 'Since when have you been on terms with Tamsin?' she grouched.

'I always stop for a blether when you send me over there.'

'He takes her very chocolatey biscuits,' Daisy revealed.

Karen laughed. 'Fair enough.' Biscuits were the currency of the forensics unit; Tamsin was the equivalent of the Governor of the Bank of England. 'Good for you, Jason, I like a bit of initiative.'

He squirmed in his seat. 'It's what Phil would have done.'

But Phil had far more charm than you, Jason. What you did took courage too. 'So what did you spot in the pix?'

'She was a big reader, boss. Bookshelves all along one wall of her bedroom, and a bookcase in her room in the flat. One of those IKEA ones, by the looks of it. Anyway, I zoomed in as close as I could get. It was hard to make out all the titles, but she was really anal about how she sorted out her books. Eilidh organises hers by colour, which I think is mental because you can never find what you're looking for unless you already know what colour it is. But Lara was dead sensible. She arranged them alphabetically. Obviously, she liked some writers more than others. But in her shelves at home, there's a gap where Jake Stein would fit. There's not any other obvious gaps. And in her student flat, there's a whole block of Jake Stein. All his novels, in a row. She must have brought them to uni with her when she started there. Like she didn't want to be parted from them.' Jason looked triumphant. 'She was a real Stein nut.'

12

Karen sighed. 'I don't know. It's a bit thin. I've got a whole shelf of Chris Brookmyre's books but I don't expect him to pop round and murder me.'

'That's because he's never met you, boss,' Jason said, realising he'd gone too far as soon as he'd spoken. 'Sorry—'

'You will be,' Karen promised sourly. Never mind that Phil would likely have said the same. She didn't want Jason or Daisy to mistake a good working relationship for friendship, no matter how much they all liked each other. She had no intention of being a martinet like Markie, but the lines of command still had to be respected. Even if this was only an exercise. 'You need to go back and dig deeper, Jason. In the novel, Laurel Oliver says she'd been at a workshop with Cobain. But you said he hadn't done anything like that for five years. Maybe he started doing it again, trying to make a few bob? Can you get in touch with his agent—'

'His agent dumped him. As far as I can see, he did the deal with Stooshie without an agent.' Jason gave an apologetic grimace.

'OK. Well, talk to whoever does publicity at Stooshie and see whether they know anything about him teaching courses or workshops or whatever these guys do to part people from their hard-earned cash. And if you can get a list, so much the better. In fact, see if you can get a list of all the events he did in, say, the last six months before he died. If that goes nowhere, we'll go to his old agent and publisher.'

Jason nodded vigorously. 'Will do, boss. Sorry.'

'Don't grovel, it's unattractive. An apology will do.' Karen grinned. 'Just don't do it again.'

'I'll get on to it.'

'Boss?' Daisy leaned into her screen. 'The crime scene in the book – it's a cabin in the woods in East Lothian, Jason. Near Tyninghame Sands. It supposedly belongs to a writer called—' she looked at her notes.

'Mari Gibson,' Karen supplied. 'Good point, Daisy. Stein writes about Cobain supporting her writing her first novel. Maybe that's based on the truth. Let's see what we can dig up on that, Jason. Any newspaper stories about a writer giving Stein credit for helping them write a prize-winning debut novel. There can't be that many of them.' She straightened up in her chair. 'Right. I need a cup of coffee. Crack on with that lot, Jason. Me and Daisy are going to look at the notes Jake Stein left with the novel, see whether that takes us any closer.'

They all left the call and Karen headed for the coffee. Daisy ambled after her, leaning on the counter. 'Should we not talk to the ex?' she asked. 'If anybody knows about Stein's friends and contacts, surely it would be her?'

'She seems not to have known a lot of what he was up to.' She tipped her favourite ground mixture into the Aeropress and set the kettle on to boil. 'Maybe she's one of those women who chooses not to know. Anything for a quiet life. Either way, we have to be on more solid ground before we front her up. "Sorry to bother you, but we think

135

your ex-husband wasn't only a serial shagger. We think he murdered a lassie just to show he could do it and get away with it."' Karen raised an eyebrow.

Daisy conceded. 'Not going to go well.'

'Probably not.' Karen let the kettle go off the boil then filled the cylinder of the coffee apparatus. Daisy turned away and returned to the table where the photocopied notes sat in two neat piles. Karen finished making her brew and joined her. 'Right then, let's see if these notes give us a clue to what he was planning.'

The Vanishing of Laurel Oliver

The book features a pair of writers, good friends. JAMIE COBAIN and ROB THOMAS. JAMIE is attractive, smart, charismatic. Has had a stupendous international career. ROB is quiet, average but talented, at the start of a good-looking career. JAMIE takes pity on him, draws him into his circle and discovers they were both serious teenage chess players. Meet once a month or so, have dinner, play chess. Then JAMIE is disgraced – he loses his reputation over a written description of the rape and torture and murder of a young woman that everyone in the publishing business recognises as his former mistress. He loses his marriage, his publisher, his readers. He's determined to take his revenge on the world, and his ex-wife.

Then he finds out ROB is shagging his ex. Something inside him snaps.

The two men keep on meeting. Talk about the perfect murder. JAMIE says he knows how to do it. It takes two . . . ROB rubbishes the idea. Modern forensics make it impossible, etc. JAMIE is adamant it will work and what's more, it'll make a fantastic novel. JAMIE is writing the novel as a road map for the

136

police to uncover ROB's 'crime'. The disappearance is going to be unsolved until the novel is published and someone figures it out and JAMIE does the 'He talked about it but I never thought he'd do it' injured innocent line.

Karen looked up, baffled. 'I don't understand. This doesn't make sense. Why would Stein write about a perfect murder in terms that point the finger straight at himself? Even if he's doing it as a frame-up, he's putting himself in the driving seat.'

Daisy ran her hands through her hair. 'I know. The only thing I can think of is that he was planning to come back to it and change the character details so he'd be in the clear.'

'But if the point of all this is to take revenge by framing McEwen, how's he going to manage that?'

Karen shrugged. 'I don't know. Maybe his brain was already playing tricks on him? We don't know when this was written, after all.'

'What? You think he was hallucinating?'

Karen shook her head. 'Not really. When I googled the brain aneurysm, there was no suggestion of any precursors like that. I'm grasping at straws, Daisy.'

They stared glumly at each other. Then Daisy brightened. 'But boss, just because it doesn't make sense as a novel he was going to publish doesn't mean it's not a truthful account of Lara Hardie's murder. What if we treat it like a blueprint and follow it through? It might just lead us to the answer we're looking for.'

In Karen's head, that made no more sense than the manuscript. But they'd come this far along the road; it might be worth trying Daisy's suggestion. 'We've got nothing to lose, I suppose. Let's finish reading this, at least.'

JAMIE picks the girl at a book signing. Student in halls. Gives her the number of a burner phone he's already acquired in prep. The messages will be on her laptop but it doesn't matter! (Find a way to get the laptop into his hands.)

Borrowed chalet on the coast nearby. Drink, Roofies, smothers her. Or strangles her? Showers her, Tyvek suit. In the car boot. Back to ROB's.

Body disposal? JAMIE has it all worked out. Rob has an inspection pit in his garage. Wrap her in sheets, cover in rockery stone and the contents of his compost heap and replace the cover. They'll never notice it under the car.

Knocks on ROB's door and tells him what he's done. OMG it wasn't a joke after all . . .

ROB can't see a way out – his car has her DNA from when JAMIE drove her to the seaside. What's he going to do with the body?

ROB pretends to go along with it, knows he can never sell his house if he doesn't do something with the body. But he knows enough about forensic science to understand bodies always turn up. But moving it is phenomenally dangerous . . . Unless he finds a way to implicate JAMIE?

So he plans the double-cross . . . Not sure yet what that is but I'll know when I get there.

All going swimmingly. ROB thinks he's double-crossed JAMIE. Until the final killer twist.

HAHAHAHAHA

(Timelines. Where does the murder come in relation to the divorce, etc?)

Include in the text some of L's notes and poems because only the killer would have access to what's on her hard drive. Then it'll show up on the copy of the IRL hard drive which will totally incriminate Rob when the cops find it in his house. In his study, slotted in between his forensic science texts.

The notes have all sorts in. Notes on a workshop on how to adapt screenwriting structures to the novel. Musings on how we struggle to write people whose politics don't coincide with ours, we think don't really have emotional depth, don't feel things the same way. A couple of L's own jejeune poems. Never made public. But there are bits of them in the novel.

(NAMES are important, need to be encoded, don't get confused!)

Neither of them will dare sue for libel, because I have the constructed evidence that will prove ROB is the killer.

And then they will go down.

Perfection.

Karen put down the scant outline. 'It's completely bonkers. But I can see why Jason's Meera was concerned. Though we're all so bloody bored right now that we're seeing all sorts of shapes in the shadows. It's a pity Jake Stein didn't share his killer twists with us, though. It's clear these notes were earlier than the text too, because elements have changed, presumably because he thought they'd work better?'

'I guess that's how it works. Something occurs while you're writing that works better. Like he says in the notes, "Not sure yet what that is but I'll know when I get there."'

'First step is to confirm who Stein played chess with. If he played chess with anybody. We think it's Rob McEwen because of the other clues in the manuscript, but that could be a total red herring. Maybe it's time to go and see the ex-wife.'

Daisy frowned. 'Should we not find out who his chess opponent was beforehand?'

'I'd prefer that. But do you know any crime writers well enough to ask? I know I don't.'

Daisy shook her head. 'I did once get Doug Johnstone to sign a book for a birthday present for a . . . friend, but I don't think he'd remember me.'

'And there's no handy circumstances like book festivals or readings going on just now to take advantage of. So, the ex-wife it is.'

'How do we do that in lockdown?'

Karen shrugged. 'I think we can just rock up on her doorstep. We tell her we want to conduct a witness interview and that me and you are a bubble. We can do it indoors if she has a room big enough for us to be two metres away from her with the windows open, or we can do it outside if she's got a garden. I don't think it's too cold for that today.' Even as she spoke, she could see the bright light of excitement in Daisy's eyes. The prospect of getting out of the flat for more than an hour's tramp around the immediate environs was clearly appealing.

'I'll find out where she lives, will I?'

Karen nodded. 'You will, Daisy. You will.' Then she paused. 'I've just had a thought. Podcasts. Some days, it feels like everybody's got a bloody podcast. There must be some that focus on crime fiction. While you're tracking down Rosalind Stein, I'll check out the podcasts, see if there's any that look like they might give us a lead. I'll have to tread carefully, though. We don't want crime writers with time on their hands fancying their chances as Miss Marple.'

Daisy groaned. 'No kidding. What could possibly go wrong with that?'

13

Karen retreated to Hamish's study to delve into the alien world of podcasts. There was one that she did dip into from time to time; she'd stumbled on it by accident while looking for a school friend on Facebook. Hosted by a guy who had been in the year above her at school, it featured road trips around Scotland that ended up in weirdly interesting places. She'd never heard of most of them – The Man in the Bath in a loch near Oban; the Devil's Pulpit in Finnich Glen; the Garden of Cosmic Speculation – but she was familiar with others – the Chain Walk at Elie; the Electric Brae in Ayrshire; the Hermit's Castle in Sutherland. But listening to Johnny Spinks taking her for a tour was an entertaining way to spend an occasional half an hour on her night walks.

But she hadn't wanted to explore that universe any further. As far as she could see, there seemed to be a preponderance of true crime podcasts. The very description set her teeth on edge. Why did people think they could solve a crime better than trained detectives and forensic experts? Of course there were miscarriages of justice; Karen had worked her way through a few of those in her time. But these amateurs who thought they knew best simply muddied the waters more often than not. She reckoned the people who made the podcasts were every bit as blinkered and biased as the laziest of cops, and every bit as inclined to leave out what didn't suit their theory.

Then there were the political podcasts. Speculation and precooked opinions, she reckoned, acknowledging her own bias and prejudices. If she wanted to hang out in an echo chamber, she could just spend more time on Twitter.

She was aware that she was an anomaly. People her own age and years younger seemed to live their lives on screens, swapping the identifiable details of their lives on Twitter and WhatsApp and TikTok and Instagram. At least, she thought that's what it was right now. Next year, there would doubtless be another cool place in cyberspace to hang out.

But none of that stuff ever went away, not really. And Karen knew only too well from what she'd seen and heard at work that the toxicity of trolls spilled over into the real world all too often. Her problem was that she was a visible cop. Not good in a world where some of the people they were supposed to serve and protect didn't see those things the same way. As a woman, she'd always been the easiest to clock in any team she'd been part of. She had no intention of making herself more visible to the crazies. She'd given Daisy the lecture, but Daisy had given her the 'I know why we call you KP Nuts,' look and carried on as before. God knows who she was talking to on whatever 'swipe right, swipe left' dating app she was into. At least lockdown made her safer, Karen thought. She wasn't meeting up with anyone IRL, as they called it.

Sighing, she set off to explore further. There seemed to be podcasts about everything from the menopause to 1960s football, with everything in between. She actually found one for dogs to listen to. Even if you liked this stuff, how did you ever find anything? She tried searching for 'crime fiction' and was swamped with suggestions, none of which was really what she was looking for. But Karen never gave up and she kept on worming her way down the rabbit hole. Eventually she found what she thought she was looking for. *Black Thistles* promised in-depth interviews with Scottish crime writers, 'Complete with all the jaggy bits.'

Karen looked at a list of episodes reaching back more than two years. Sometimes there were two a month, sometimes only one. It was presented by two men, one from Glasgow, the other from Kirriemuir. They claimed to cover 'the gamut of the genre, from granny-pleasers to gruesome gothic'. She thought its faux jollity threatened to take all the joy out of murder mysteries. But looking down their list of past guests, she spotted a clutch of writers whose books she'd enjoyed enough to buy more than one. And then, to her delight, she found Jake Stein. Two years ago, before the sky had fallen in on him. Scrolling down the page, she found a Twitter handle and an email address.

Hastily, Karen knocked out an email.

Hi, guys. I'm DCI Karen Pirie with Police Scotland. I've got a quick query for you about a Scottish crime writer who's actually been on your podcast. Obviously, this isn't for public consumption, but I'd appreciate five minutes of your time. We can do a WhatsApp call, if that works for you.

She added her number, then clicked on the Stein interview.

It was illuminating, in the sense that she could detect

a depressing congruence between Jamie Cobain and his creator. Jake Stein had cultivated an air of hail-fellow-well-met camaraderie, but to a practised listener like Karen, the reality that lay beneath peeped out often enough for her to form a different impression. He had false modesty down to a fine art, but she reckoned it hid a pomposity that would be easily pricked and an insecurity that would readily turn to resentment. She'd have enjoyed facing him across an interview room table. It would have been a challenge to see how quickly she could puncture that highly polished ego.

She'd almost come to the end of the podcast with no mention of chess when her phone buzzed with a WhatsApp call. 'Karen,' a breezy voice greeted her. She recognised it immediately as the podcast co-host from Kirriemuir. 'This is Chesney here, from Black Thistles. I must say, we are honoured to be the podcast of choice for Scotland's top cold case cop.'

Karen chuckled. 'More like the podcast of last resort, Chesney. But I must admit, you do a very professional job. Nothing like the intensity of a real interrogation—'

'But then there's generally a wee bit more at stake when you've got somebody in the hot seat, Karen. All we're doing is feeding the reading machine. So, what's this burning question that's driven you into our arms?'

Bumptious as he was, it was hard to dislike his bounce. 'You'll understand that I can't give you any details about my reasons for asking what I'm about to put to you?'

He groaned. 'Aw, don't give me that "jeopardising an ongoing investigation" malarkey, Karen. We're in the middle of lockdown and you're a celebrity cold case cracker. How ongoing can it be?'

'I'm not a celebrity, sir. I'm a detective who deals with some of the most upsetting cases that Police Scotland investigates. And I don't work cold cases, I work historic cases. Because unsolved serious crimes are never cold in our eyes. So can you maybe dial down the flippancy a bit?'

'OK, OK. Sorry. I'm not used to dealing with people like yourself, who do this for real. Facetiousness is always my fallback. Can we start this again? You want to ask me a question but you can't tell me what it's about?'

'That's about the size of it. And the other thing is that I would very much appreciate it if this conversation went no further. If crime writers are anything like the polis, there's nothing you like more than a good gossip.'

He gave a roar of laughter. 'You nailed it there. The public think when we get together we talk about how to kill people and get rid of bodies. They couldn't be further from the truth. We're like a bunch of old grannies in the steamie. Nobody's rep is safe with us. We relish tales of disgrace and disaster. Authors being dumped by their publishers, publicists ratting out prima donna writers, true stories of whose books are really put together by their editors. And that's before we get on to the shagging.'

'I'm afraid you'll be very disappointed with my question. I'd put it at zero gossip value.' Karen tried to sound rueful to disguise how tedious she found cheery Chesney.

'Fire away, then.'

'Jake Stein had a regular chess opponent. Do you know who it was?'

A moment of stunned silence. 'That's *it*? You just want to know who he played chess with?'

'That's it. You could say I've got a bit of a chess problem he might be able to help me with.'

'If I'd tried to guess what you wanted to know, we'd still have been here at the next Bloody Scotland,' he scoffed. 'If there ever is another festival anywhere, thanks to this bloody COVID. Jake Stein used to play chess with Ross McEwen. You know who I mean?'

It fit. She wasn't sure how she felt about that. 'I know the name, yes.'

'Rising star,' Chesney said. 'It was weird – like their careers were mirror images of each other. Jake kind of took Ross under his wing when his first book took off. So it would look like he'd been his big supporter before the rest of the world caught up. Of course, it wasn't like that at all – Jake just heard the bandwagon approaching and leapt aboard early enough to look as if he'd been there all along. He's not the only one who does that, by the way – he was just a bit better at it than most. And then Jake got the legs cut from under him when he did that atrocious thing to lovely Marga Durham.'

'And is she? Lovely, I mean?'

'Honest to God, you couldn't meet a nicer lassie. Genuinely kind. Goes out of her way for folk. No way did she deserve that, even if she did bin him. But oh boy, did he pay the price. His career flushed down the toilet while Ross just kept getting bigger and bigger. He's another good guy too.' He ground to a halt.

'So Ross McEwen and Jake Stein played chess together?'

Another snort of laughter. 'I wouldn't say they played "together". More like "against each other". It was definitely a serious business. It's about the only thing Stein managed to hang on to from his old life. He basically got the frozen shoulder from everybody else.'

Karen was surprised. She hadn't thought this was a world

where a little light adultery would get a man thrown out of the club. She said as much.

Suddenly serious, he responded with a sober answer. '"He that toucheth pitch shall be defiled,"' he said. 'Guilt by association. Nobody in a relationship would want to explain to their other halves why it was still OK to hang out with a scumbag like Jake turned out to be. And if you were looking to find yourself a relationship, it'd be pretty hard to explain why he was one of your mates. None of the women wanted anything to do with him. Not even the groupies. I know they say everybody loves a bad boy, but you'd have to be terminally stupid to want to hook up with someone who might do to you what he did to Marga. And for all his faults, Jake wasn't interested in the terminally stupid.'

'So, Ross McEwen was his last remaining friend?'

'I suppose so. But I don't think it went much beyond the chess, to be honest. It's not like Ross was sharing platforms with him. He didn't even blurb his last book.'

Karen wondered how a man as invested in other people's business as Chesney could have let this one get past him unexamined. 'Did you ask him why?'

A brief pause. 'I didn't.' He sounded puzzled. Then a sigh. 'I think Ross is just one of those really reserved guys. He doesn't talk about himself. I honestly don't even know if he's with anybody. And I couldn't hazard a guess as to whether the somebody he's not with is male or female. So it would feel really intrusive to ask him about Jake.'

'Does Ross McEwen live in Edinburgh, do you know?'

'He does. He's got a lovely modern house out at Cramond. Architect designed. In its own grounds. It's not got the sea views, but the house is immaculate. It's got a

147

sort of turret on one corner, glass on all sides. I went out there one time to deliver him a set of my proofs. Do you want the address?'

'That'd be helpful,' she said, overcoming her natural resistance to finding herself obliged to anyone. Her phone pinged almost immediately with a contact card.

'You didn't get that from me, mind,' Chesney cautioned. 'Like I said, he's quite reserved.'

'Just one more thing,' Karen said.

That gust of laughter again. 'OK, Columbo. Fire away.'

'Can you think of any writers Jake gave a helping hand to when they were starting out?'

'There were a few. I don't think he did it out of the goodness of his heart, I think he was always looking for a bit of reflected glory. But he had a good eye, so it usually paid off. Ross McEwen was one. Deni Blackadder, she was another. And that lassie from Inverness, Josy Heriot. He'd get them on panels and blurb their books. So, is this like the genie of the lamp? I help you and I get three wishes?'

Karen couldn't help laughing. 'Not even one. I didn't come up the Forth on a biscuit, Chesney.'

'I've heard about you and your night walking,' he said. 'Can I steal it for one of my characters?'

Karen froze. What the fuck was this? Who would turn her insomniac wanderings into the currency of gossip? Anyone who knew about her nocturnal walking knew it had only started after Phil's murder. After she'd lost the gift of sleep. 'I don't know what you're talking about,' she said calmly.

'It's not a big secret, Karen. Scotland's a village, you know that. There's dozens of crime writers in Scotland now. We all have our tame contacts. And they tell us the quirky stuff as well as the dramatic scary stuff. Plenty people must have

148

heard about the woman who walks by night.' He dropped his voice to horror story hollowness.

'Is this the kind of bollocks that inspires your books? Look, fascinating though this is, I have to go. I've got work to do.'

'Take me on a walk with you one of these nights.'

Exasperated, she said, 'Look, Chesney. For one thing, we're in lockdown and it's against the rules to go for walks with somebody outside your bubble. For another thing, you've been misinformed. And since three's the charm, I don't go for walks with strange men even in the middle of the day. Thanks for your help, but goodbye, Chesney.'

She cut him off in the middle of, 'You can't blame me for—'

Karen dropped her head into her hands. Was this what keeping your own counsel got you? She was the talk of the steamie? 'The woman who walks by night'? Like she was some kind of freak? She knew she shouldn't care.

But she did.

14

Eilidh stretched provocatively on the sofa, pouting as if she was posing for a selfie. 'I don't get it,' she said. 'The whole country's on furlough but you're still knocking your pan in, working all the hours God sends. No, not God. KP Nuts.'

Jason looked up from his laptop screen, wounded. 'I'm a key worker, babe. I can work from home, mostly. But if I have to go out in the course of an investigation, I'm allowed.'

Eilidh sighed. 'I get that. But how come it's always got to be done this minute? You're looking at something that happened ages ago, it's not like anybody's going to do one in the next couple of days.'

'Phil always used to say that if it was your kid or your partner, every day without answers hurts as bad as the first one. If we give them some answers, they can start to heal.'

Eilidh snorted. 'Saint Phil. The way you talk about him, it's like the guy could walk on water.'

Jason was a placid man, inured to a lifetime of jibes from his older and smarter brother Ronan. But this was a barb that pierced his shell of politeness. 'Don't diss Phil,' he said. There was an unusual edge to his voice. 'If I'm any good at being a polis, it's because of what I learned from Phil.'

Eilidh pushed herself upright. 'Typical bloke. You don't give the boss much credit.'

He gave her a bleak look. 'That's because I'm still learning from her. But Phil's not here. So credit where it's due, Eilidh.' He turned his attention back to the screen of his laptop.

She sighed and turned on the TV. 'Well, I'm not waiting on you any longer. I'm going to start watching the third series of *Stranger Things*.'

Jason looked up in dismay. 'But we've been watching that together,' he protested.

'I know, but I'm fed up of waiting.'

He felt hard done by, but he knew from past experience that there was no point in arguing with Eilidh when she was in this kind of mood. His mum said she took advantage of his good nature. Mostly he didn't mind, but when it came to the world of the Upside Down, it was a different story. Jason scowled. 'Well, put the headphones on at least.'

She reached for the padded over-ear phones and Jason moved round the table so he couldn't see the TV screen. He sighed and reached for a fresh piece of gum. Stooshie Press named Ruaridh Brown-Grant as their publicity manager. It listed the switchboard number and the generic corporate email RuaridhBG@stooshie.scot. Jason had a feeling neither of those would be much use today. He found Ruaridh B-G on Twitter, followed him and asked him to follow back so Jason could send him a direct message. Then he leaned back in his chair, hands locked behind his head, and waited.

Staring at the unchanging screen, he wondered what cops had done to track people down before the internet. And slowly, it dawned on him that there was olden technology that still worked. He remembered fat phone books from his

151

childhood that listed people by name, address and number. He googled 'phone book' and entered Brown-Grant. He took a gamble on Edinburgh as his address, and was astonished when R. Brown-Grant appeared with an address in Gorgie, complete with phone number. Sheesh. Who knew?

Eagerly, Jason plugged his earphones into his mobile and called the number. A man's voice answered. 'Hello?'

He didn't sound nearly as posh as Jason had expected. Nowadays, being double-barrelled was no guarantee of class. 'Is that Ruaridh Brown-Grant?' he asked.

'Aye. Who am I speaking to?'

Jason introduced himself. 'You're the publicist at Stooshie, right?'

'For what it's worth right now, yeah. It's not the liveliest time for publishing new titles.'

'I need to ask you some questions about one of your authors. Well, he used to be one of your authors but now he's dead.'

A moment. Then Brown-Grant said, 'Five will get you ten you're talking about Jake Stein.'

Jason tried to parse the sentence but got nowhere. Except that he recognised the name. 'How did you know?'

'He's the only one of our authors who has died in the last three years. And to be honest, it doesn't surprise me that he'd have done something to bring him to the attention of you guys. So what's the hap? What's he done? And can I talk to the press about it?'

This was all going a bit too fast, Jason thought. 'No, you can't talk to anybody about it. This is an ongoing investigation and any unauthorised publicity could interfere with a potential arrest.'

A sharp laugh. 'You can't arrest a dead man.'

'I never said Jake Stein had perpetrated a crime,' Jason said sternly. 'Don't try to trick me, Mr Brown-Grant.'

'Call me Ruaridh, for Pete's sake,' he sighed. 'So what do you need to know? What's going on?'

'Were you in charge of Mr Stein's work diary? His appearances and interviews and things? Did they go through you?' Jason scrabbled for a pen and his notebook.

'Oh yes. Jake Stein might have fallen from grace, but he was still a prima donna in his head. Any requests for his presence, he punted them straight on to me. I had to sort out all the details and run them past him, to make sure he was happy. And then I had to do his bloody invoicing too.' The rising tide of bitterness broke on the final sentence. 'Why are you interested?'

'I can't tell you. Sorry. I'm not being difficult, it really is about not compromising an inquiry. Have you got a list?'

'Have you got a warrant?'

Jason closed his eyes and breathed deeply. 'No. But I can get one. Why are you bothered? Jake Stein's dead, he's not got any right to privacy now.'

Brown-Grant grunted acquiescence. 'Right enough. I do have a record, it's on my laptop which is in the next room. I suppose you'll be wanting me to send it to you?'

'I'd buy you a pint if I could.' Jason rattled off his email address. 'One other thing. I know he didn't believe you could teach someone to write, but I was wondering. Since he was pretty skint, was he doing any mentoring or workshops?'

A snort. 'You think anybody would send him a baby writer for mentoring after what he did? No, he never did one-to-one mentoring. But you're right, he was pretty skint. He'd put together a workshop – "The secrets of story

153

structure – how to tell a bestselling story." And he was touting it around anywhere that would have him. Colleges, second-division universities, that kind of thing.'

'Was he getting a lot of pickup?'

'A bit. Creative writing's all the rage now, and he had been a bona fide bestseller, even if he was also a bona fide scumbag. He was doing one or two a month. Maximum sixteen students.'

'Are they on the list?'

'They are. Complete with the contacts who booked them. Look, is this going to lead to a sudden burst of publicity for Stein's backlist? Because if so, a wee heads-up would help so we've got stock lined up.'

Jason grinned. 'Good try. But I can't tell you.' His email pinged and he checked. A message from Brown-Grant with two attachments. 'Thanks for your help.'

'You're welcome. I'll give you a bell next time I get a speeding ticket.'

Jason ended the call, feeling pleased with himself. Since Daisy had joined the team, he'd felt insecure. She had a degree, she knew way more than he did about all kinds of things and he worried that she'd push him out of the way in the boss's good books. Plus the Dog Biscuit had already tried to sideline him after he'd broken his leg. It still wasn't right, but at least working from home meant Markie couldn't see him limping at the end of the day. So every success he could chalk up made him feel a little less anxious.

He opened the attachments – one for readings and book events, the other for workshops – and printed them out. It would be a long tedious task to work his way through them, but Jason was good at tedium. Detail suited his temperament, which was how he'd got to know Meera at the National Library in the first place. He liked her attention to those small points that made a big picture.

Jason was about to make a start, working backwards from the most recent workshops, when his mobile rang. A glance at the screen and he groaned. His brother Ronan. What had he done now? Ronan was the stone in Jason's shoe. A bad lad, was the consensus of his fellow officers in Kirkcaldy, where Ronan still lived round the corner from their mother. He did things with cars, some of them legal, and had some dodgy pals. Jason wished he'd sort himself out, but knew there was nothing he could do to change his big brother. That was another reason he'd liked working with Phil and Karen. They knew Ronan wasn't Jason.

With a sigh, he answered the call. 'Jason?' Ronan's voice was edgy and strange. 'Jason, Mum's not well. She phoned me to come round because she wasn't feeling right. And you know she never complains about feeling like shite.'

'So did you go round?'

'I had a wee bit of business to sort but I went round as soon as I could. And she couldn't come to the door. I had to go round the back and let myself in with the key she keeps under the ash can.' They hadn't had a coal fire for years, but Jason knew what his brother was talking about.

'Get to the point, Ronan.' He was beginning to feel scared.

'She was lying on the settee in the living room. White as a sheet, Jase. And breathing like a wee puggy. She never even looked up when I went in.' Proof to Jason that something was definitely wrong with Sandra Murray.

'Did she speak to you?'

'I put my hand on her forehead and she was burning up, Jase. Like she was on fire. And then she started coughing.

Like she couldn't get a breath. I went and got her a drink of water, but it didn't help.'

Jason could feel a strange tightening in his chest. 'Did you phone the doctor?'

'I'm not fucking stupid,' Ronan shouted. He took an audible breath. 'I'm sorry. I'm just scared, Jase. The GP's on her way. Can you come?'

Jason felt a deep wrenching pain in his stomach. He knew the rules. He knew the price he might have to pay if he was caught out. Into the silence, Ronan spoke again, angry. 'Jeez, Jase. This is your mum we're talking about. When you broke your leg, she dropped everything and legged it to your bedside. Not a fucking thought for herself. Why are you still standing there?'

For once, Ronan was right. 'I'll get my coat,' Jason said and ended the call. He noticed his hands were shaking as he got to his feet and hurried across the room to the narrow hall. He was reaching for his puffa jacket when Eilidh grabbed his arm, headphones dangling round her neck.

'What's going on? Are you going out?' she demanded.

'It's my mum. Ronan rang. It looks like she's got the COVID. They're waiting on the doctor.'

'And? You're not thinking of going there, are you?' Her eyebrows rose in perfect curves of incredulity.

'I have to. She's my mum. When I needed her, she came like a shot. Now it's my turn.'

Eilidh shook her head. 'No. You can't go there. If she's got it and Ronan's with her, he's probably got it as well. You go, and you'll get it too, then you'll bring it home to me. And what use is that to your mum? Christ, Jason, people are dying of this thing. And you want to dive into the thick of it?' Exasperated, she grabbed his jacket and stuck it back on the peg.

'She'll be scared, Eilidh. She needs to know we're there for her.' He reached for his jacket again.

'Your mum loves you, Jason. She wouldn't want you to put yourself at risk for her sake. You know that.'

Jason shook his head, mulish stubbornness in his expression. 'I have to do this, Eilidh. How will I look myself in the eye if she dies and I ignored her?'

Eilidh made an impatient noise and neatly stepped around him, back to the front door. 'She's not going to die, Jason.'

'You just said—'

'Most people don't die. And she'd be mortified if she passed it on to us. Plus, if you get caught driving across to Fife, you'll be fucked. You'll get kicked out of the polis, no question. And then where will we be? No wages coming in, no furlough because I'm classed as self-employed. We'll lose the flat, we'll lose our savings. No way would Sandra want that for us. She'd never forgive herself. You know that, Jason.'

He felt on the verge of tears. Eilidh made a kind of sense. But Jason loved his mum. How could he decide? He took a step forward but could go no further without manhandling Eilidh out of the way. Jason had never lifted a hand to a woman and he didn't want to start now.

The sound of his phone cut through his indecision. Ronan. He took the call but before he could speak, Ronan was already gabbling in his ear. 'Fuck, Jason. They're taking her to the Vic. The doc took one look at her and called an ambulance. Dinnae bother coming, Jase, they'll not let you near her. They willnae even let me in the ambulance, the doctor says no way.'

'Is she worse?'

'She's burning up and when she's not coughing, she's

wheezing like grandad when he had the bronchitis.' He drew a breath in audibly and when he spoke, his voice shook. 'I'm scared, Jason. What if she dies?'

Eilidh, who had heard this exchange, grabbed the phone from a shocked Jason. She spoke calmly. 'It's Eilidh, Ro. She's not going to die. Sandra's a fighter, you know that. And the Vic's a great hospital. The best place for her. Just let the doctors and nurses do what they do.'

They heard Ronan choke back a sob. 'You're right, Eilidh. I'll phone back after the ambulance has been.' The line went dead.

Eilidh threw her arms round Jason and stroked his back. 'It'll be OK, darling,' she said softly.

He hoped she was right. He couldn't imagine how they would get past this moment of indecision if she wasn't.

15

When Karen returned to the dining room, Daisy was deep in the Lara Hardie case notes again. She looked up, distracted, and said, 'Any joy, boss?'

Karen nodded. 'I found out who he played chess with. Like you thought it might be. Ross McEwen.'

'I read his first novel,' Daisy said. 'He won a couple of awards for it. It was pretty good. A twist every fifty pages, you know the kind of thing. But he did it better than most. At least we've got an idea who "Rob Thomas" is meant to be, if this is properly based on a true story.'

'If it does map on to reality that closely, why haven't Stein's widow and McEwen gone public with their relationship? With Stein dead, there can't be any issue around it now. The podcast guy I've just spoken to, he said Ross McEwen keeps his private life under wraps. He didn't even know whether he likes guys or girls. It's all very odd. I want to speak to the widow before I front him up. Did you manage to track down her address?' Karen pulled out a chair and opened the case file. The answer was right in front of her. 'Oh, asked and answered. Nice job.' Karen recognised the address as one of the modern blocks built at Quartermile, on the edge of the wide green space of the Meadows. 'So she's up in the goldfish bowl, eh?'

'I imagine when she bought it she thought she'd have a relatively peaceful view,' Daisy said. 'Now I bet it's crammed from dawn till dusk with everybody taking their daily exercise with their kids and their dogs. By the way, she's reverted to her maiden name – Harris. She never stopped using it professionally, but now she's totally ditched the hyphenated "Stein".'

'Can't say I blame her. Let's see if we can set up a meeting for tomorrow.' She picked up the manuscript again and flicked through the pages. 'You know, another odd thing strikes me about this. Everything we've got – a few chapters, a bit of an outline, some notes? It's all computer printout. I can't believe he didn't make notes while he was still at the early stages. And if he did, there might be more connective tissue that positively links this to Lara Hardie's disappearance.'

Daisy frowned. 'That's a good point. I remember hearing a radio programme about Agatha Christie's notebooks. Apparently they found a box of them in the attic of her old house and a lot of what was in them was totally random. Like, she'd have a shopping list on one page, an idea for a plot on the next page. Then a list of spring bulbs, a recipe for a cake and finally some notes about what she was working on. And because she'd just scribble in whatever notebook she had handy, sometimes there would be references to the same novel in three or four notebooks.'

'Makes sense to me,' Karen said. 'The notes on my phone would be incoherent to anybody but me. So you think there might be notebooks in the archive?'

Daisy shrugged. 'Or Post-It notes. Or file cards.' She groaned. 'I know what comes next.'

Karen grinned. 'I'll get on to Bethan and make arrangements.'

'Me and my big mouth. Oh well, at least it'll get me out of the house.'

'I'll see whether she'll let both of us in. We are one household so it shouldn't breach the regs. With two of us working it, there's less chance of missing anything crucial.'

'That's if there's anything crucial to find,' Daisy grumbled. Clearly, she was a long way from being convinced that this was any more than a wild goose chase to keep them occupied. Karen couldn't blame her. But she'd followed slender leads to rewarding conclusions before. She still had hope for this one.

Jason didn't know what to do with himself. Eilidh wanted him to snuggle up on the sofa, but that felt wrong. How could he do that when his mother was lying in a hospital bed, struggling to breathe? He felt suffocated himself inside the four walls of the flat. 'I need to go for a walk.' As soon as he said it, he knew it was the right thing to do.

'I'll come with you,' Eilidh said immediately.

'No, I need to be by myself.'

She looked at him as if he'd turned into a stranger. 'How? Tell me you're not going to do anything stupid like sneak off and drive to Kirkcaldy?'

'No,' he snapped. 'I'll leave the car keys here, if you don't trust me. I just need air. It's not about you, it's about me.' He turned away and grabbed his coat. Pausing only to toss his car keys on the hall table, he marched out of the flat and took the stairs two at a time. He emerged into late afternoon sunshine that did nothing to take the chill off the air. The only others in sight were on the other side of the street; an elderly couple tottering towards Leith Walk, holding hands like teenagers.

161

Jason had no idea where he wanted to go. On automatic pilot, he turned up Leith Walk, his steps following his regular route to the police station at the top of the hill in Gayfield Square. He walked in a dwam, his thoughts and emotions churning chaotically. He'd never thought about the possibility of life without his mother. She was never ill. She kept the house like a palace, she worked three days a week in a care home, and on top of that she was always doing favours for her neighbours – minding their kids, shopping for pensioners, walking people's dogs when they had to take on extra overtime.

He came to himself as he arrived at the tiny park in front of the cop shop. He sat down on one of the benches, hands clasped between his knees, frowning. Scarcely a minute had passed when his phone burst into life: Ronan.

'What's happening?' Jason demanded.

'OK, so they've took her to the Vic, like we thought,' he said. 'The paramedics gave her oxygen in the ambulance and they said she seemed to pick up a wee bit. The doc was right, they totally wouldn't let me go in the ambulance with her. So I got in the motor and drove up there. Bastards wouldn't let me in. Bitch of a paramedic said they'd got more important things to do than argue with me.'

Jason could imagine. She had a point, though. 'Do you know anything?'

'She's on a COVID ward. I managed to speak to one of the nurses on the phone. They've got her on an oxygen mask. He told me she's holding her own. Like our mum would be doing anything else. He's going to phone me if anything changes.'

'We'll just have to wait, then,' Jason said, his voice hollow.

'Fuck all else I can do. But can you not get in? You're a polis, I've seen polis going in and out the hospital.'

'They've got regulations in place for a reason. It's to keep folk safe. Plus the cops going in and out'll be locals. They'll know I'm not one of them. And like the paramedic said to you, they've all got more important things to be dealing with than that.'

Ronan made a scornful noise. 'You've got no bottle, bruv. You've always been the same, ever since you were wee. "Don't tell on me, Ronan,"' he mimicked.

Jason swallowed hard. 'I'm not going to fall out with you, Ronan. Not at a time like this. We need to be strong for each other and for Mum.' The line went dead.

Fuck this. He wasn't going to rely on someone who only wanted to take their pain out on him. Jason found the number for the Victoria Hospital and dialled. When it was answered, he explained the situation. The woman on the phone was so gentle he almost wept. 'Give me a minute, son,' she said, putting him on hold. When she came back, she repeated what Ronan had said. 'Leave your number with me, son. If there's any change, we'll give you a call. I know it's hard, but try not to call us more often than once a day. We're all doing our best here.'

'I know,' he said, feeling bleak. 'Thank you.'

He leaned back and stared at the sky. This was unbearable. He needed something to fill his head. Something that wasn't Eilidh filling his ears with what she wanted him to believe. Jason jumped up and practically ran across the grass to the police station. All the information he'd managed to extract from Ruaridh Brown-Grant was accessible via his office computer. Rummaging in his pocket as he hurried, he came out with a mask Eilidh had made from an old blouse and fixed it in place over his nose and mouth.

Ignoring the unstaffed counter, he made straight for the

side corridor that led to the HCU office at the back of the station. He keyed in his access code and hustled down the hall, stripping off his jacket as he went. He saw nobody, which was a relief. Closing the door quietly behind him, he booted up his computer and printed out the lists that Brown-Grant had sent him. Considering all they were supposed to do was sit at a desk and write books, Jason was amazed at the amount of time a writer spent running about the place doing all kinds of weird things.

It was late in the day to be questioning librarians and arts administrators, but they wouldn't be in their offices anyway. They'd be stuck at home, probably bored out of their trees. Jason would be a welcome distraction, he reckoned. An escape from quarrelling kids and fractious partners. He went down the list, circling all the contacts who had provided mobile numbers rather than office landlines.

Then he started.

His colleagues a few streets away were having a better afternoon. Rosalind Harris had apparently been intrigued by Karen's call. She'd offered to set up a Zoom meeting for the morning, but Karen had said she'd rather talk in person, albeit at a safe distance. 'This is all very mysterious, Chief Inspector,' Rosalind had said.

'It's really very straightforward, Ms Harris. Your late ex-husband's name has come up in the course of an investigation, and I'm hoping you might be able to cast some light on the circumstances.'

'I doubt it. There were many areas of Jake's life that were a closed book to me. Even more than I realised when he was still alive. But frankly, anything that breaks the monotony of lockdown is a plus in my book. How do we do this within the rules? Shall we find a quiet bench in the Meadows?'

They settled on meeting at 10 a.m. on Middle Meadow Walk near the Swedish coffee shop. Karen noted the meeting in her diary, saying, 'That's the easy one dealt with. Now for Bethan Carmichael.'

Predictably, the librarian was not thrilled to hear from Karen again. 'I've already stretched the rules to accommodate your demands,' she objected.

If she believed that earlier request had been a demand, she was in for an education, Karen thought. 'I appreciate your desire to abide by the Scottish Government's rules and advice. But I must remind you that I'm also obliged to carry out my duties as a member of Police Scotland. Criminals are not too bothered about obeying the rules at the best of times, and we have to deal with that in the most practical ways we can. I'm no keener than you on being exposed to COVID.'

Bethan harrumphed. 'And yet you're asking me to ride roughshod over the systems we've set up to protect our staff.'

Karen closed her eyes and counted to five. Ten was out of the question most days. 'I've thought about this,' she said. 'If you can have the materials laid out in a single ventilated space, my colleague and I will work there alone. We're sharing a flat at present, so we actually count as one household. If you provide us with a diagram of how to get to the room, your security guard can let us in and we'll make our own way there. No need for anybody to come near us.'

A long moment while she digested Karen's suggestion. 'Normally, we'd insist you were accompanied by a member of the library staff.'

'These aren't normal times,' Karen said flatly. 'We will

handle everything with the utmost care. We're not silly wee lassies. We understand the importance of handling evidence and we'll bring that expertise to your archive.'

'And what happens if you find material you consider to be evidence?'

Karen was tempted to say, 'Then we'll stuff it down our pants and run. They don't call me KP Nuts for nothing.' Instead, she spoke calmly. 'We will photograph it in situ, replace it where we found it and rely on you and your staff not to interfere with it.'

There was a long frosty silence. 'I resent the suggestion that anyone employed by the National Library of Scotland would interfere with archive material.'

'I thought I was suggesting the very opposite, Bethan. My team, we love the National Library and its librarians. You're a phenomenal resource. Please trust us to respect that.' She rolled her eyes at Daisy, who was obviously suppressing a fit of the giggles.

Karen could hear Bethan exhale heavily. 'Let me talk to my people and see what can be done.'

'Thank you. I was thinking we might get started tomorrow afternoon.' There were few things Karen enjoyed more than pushing her luck with a sweet smile on her face.

'Not very likely. But I will see what might be possible. Perhaps next week.'

'I'm expecting to see you tomorrow. I know you won't want to be accused of obstructing a homicide investigation.'

'Wait!' Bethan exclaimed. 'Are you telling me this is definitely a murder inquiry now? I thought you were just on a fishing expedition.'

'It's looking increasingly likely.' It was still less than the truth, but closer than it had been when they'd last spoken.

'So can we maybe expedite our access to the rest of Jake Stein's papers?'

Sounding chastened, Bethan said, 'I will call you tomorrow morning.'

Daisy gave her boss a round of applause as she closed her phone down. 'Every time I see you in action, I feel like I used to when a tutor said something illuminating about an obscure bit of poetry. I'd lay money on us being in the archives before close of play tomorrow.'

Embarrassed at the praise, Karen shrugged. 'We've still got a long way to go. Which reminds me, Jason's not been in touch. The last time he went dark, he was lying at the bottom of a flight of steps with a broken leg.'

'Lightning doesn't strike twice, boss.'

Karen quirked a smile. 'You've not known Jason very long, have you? I'll give him a quick call. Let's make it three in a row for good results.'

16

It took Jason so long to answer his phone that Karen expected it to go to voicemail. She was already anticipating an uptick in anxiety when he finally answered with a gruff, 'Aye, boss?'

'Hi Jason. I thought you might have checked in before now? How did you get on with backtracking Jake Stein's events?'

He cleared his throat. 'Aye, I got a list from his publicist: book events and, you were right, he did do some workshops in the months before he died.'

'And? You got details?'

'Uh huh. I've managed to speak to some of the people who ran things.'

He sounded curiously flat, Karen thought. Normally, Jason resembled a puppy. Full of springiness or, when he fucked up, tail between his legs, crawling mournfully into a corner. Now, he was almost robotic in his responses. 'Are you OK, Jason?'

'I'm not getting very far with these inquiries, boss. The ones I talked to about events never noticed anybody like Lara Hardie talking to Stein longer than it took to sign a book. Nobody hanging about him that was remotely like

168

her. I've got lists of the people who attended his workshops and so far her name isn't on them. I've got a few to go. I'll keep at it.'

'It's maybe getting a bit late to be calling people, Jason. It's nearly nine o'clock. People might get a wee bit freaked out, getting a call from the polis at this time of night in the middle of a pandemic.'

He made a strange noise, almost like a choked sob. 'Aye, right,' she thought he said. And realised there were none of the usual Eilidh noises off.

'Jason – what's going on? You don't sound yourself.'

'It's my mum.' No mistaking it now, his voice was choked, the distress obvious.

'What's happened?' Karen had a feeling she already knew the answer.

'She's got . . . She's got the COVID.'

'Oh, Jason. That's hellish. How is she doing?' Her heart went out to him; in spite of his surface bounce, he was a man who felt things deeply, and she knew how devoted he was to his mother.

Now he was sobbing. Full-on sobbing like a small child. Where was Eilidh? Why was she not making soothing noises? Daisy was frowning a question at her. Karen held up a finger, demanding silence.

Jason managed to get himself under control surprisingly quickly. 'Sorry, sorry,' he mumbled.

'No need for sorry. I know how worried you must—'

'She's in the hospital. The Vic. She's got an oxygen mask on and she's running a temperature and we're not allowed anywhere near her and she'll be in a right state and . . .' He ran out of breath. He gulped for air. 'I'm scared, Karen. I'm really scared.'

169

That he used her name told her all she needed to know about the state of his emotions. 'Where are you, Jason?' Praying the answer wasn't, 'Kirkcaldy.'

'I'm in the office.'

'Our office? In Gayfield Square?'

'I had to get some fresh air. And then I realised I needed to occupy myself or I'd just totally crack up. And if I went back to the flat ... well, Eilidh would just keep going on about how it's all going to be OK and not to worry. And I was up the top of the Walk, so I thought, all my info is on the system, I can crack on with that. You know?'

Karen knew. She'd made her own negotiations with fear and grief. 'I understand. Have you told Eilidh where you are?'

A shuddering sigh. 'No. I couldn't face it.'

'OK. Here's what we're going to do. I'm going to call Eilidh and tell her not to worry about you. And you're going to finish up for tonight and put on your jacket. I'll meet you on one of the benches on the green outside the nick and we'll have a wee drink together and then I'll walk you back down to your flat. And if there's no news from the Vic, in the morning, you can come back up and we'll have a cup of coffee outside before you get back to the job. I think that's what Sandra would want – she's so proud of you, Jason. She'd be mortified to think she'd diverted you from your work. Is that OK?'

'Aye, boss. Give me ten minutes to finish up.'

Karen ended the call and let out a long breath. 'Jason's mum's in the hospital with COVID.'

'I figured it was something like that. And he's in the office, am I right?'

'He needed to get some air. And then he needed to

170

stay busy.' Karen was already on her feet, heading for the coat pegs.

'And he didn't need Eilidh wondering when she'd be able to cheer Sandra up with a new hairstyle.' Daisy's tone was acid.

'Poor lassie hasn't got much in the way of hidden depths.'

'He deserves better.'

'Aye, but he's got to work that out for himself.'

'This might be the perfect time. I gather you're going to meet him?'

Karen came back into the room and opened the drinks cabinet. 'With a wee bit of Scotch courage.' Gin was her spirit of choice, but not something she could drink neat. She took out one of Hamish's hip flasks and filled it with a Speyside single malt – what he would call a 'morning whisky'. Nothing too challenging for her or for Jason, but a good quality dram that would slip down easily. 'He needs to feel he's not facing this without support. Can you call Eilidh and let her know he's OK and on his way home?'

Daisy groaned. 'I get all the good jobs. Sure, I'll do that.'

As she descended the stairs to the street, Karen remembered she was supposed to make a phone call at nine. Would this day never end? As she walked, she speed-dialled her home number. For the second time, she feared she was about to reach voicemail, but then she heard Rafiq's voice. 'Hello?' Tentative, for obvious reasons.

'Hi, Rafiq. It's me, Karen. Is everything OK with you?'

'Better than OK. I thank you very much for this. Your flat is very comfortable and you are very generous.'

'You figured out how things work? The TV, the cooker?'

'It's good. I have used your shower and I feel really clean for the first time in a long time.' He chuckled. 'Your boyfriend is indeed much bigger than me, but it feels good to wear something fresh. And to eat proper food. You have saved my life. I do not understand why, but I am grateful.'

The warmth in his voice was embarrassing her. 'I'm happy to help. But we need to sort you out some clothes that fit better. I can meet you tomorrow evening at the breakwater and we can order some online.'

'I cannot pay for this,' he said. 'Perhaps Miran can lend me some?'

'Don't worry about that just now.' Karen did the time sums in her head. 'Meet me opposite the main entrance to the block, by the sea. Half past ten?'

'I will. Thank you. A million times.'

As she ended the call, she turned into the bottom of Gayfield Square. Jason was already hunched on one of the benches. As Karen approached, he shifted along to the far end. He greeted her with a small nod. She could see well enough under the street lights to notice his eyes were red and swollen.

'I'm truly sorry about your mum, Jason.'

He nodded again. 'She really likes you, boss.'

'Do you know how she got it?'

He shrugged. 'Must have been at her work. You know she's working in a care home now, three days a week?'

Karen took out the hip flask and a packet of disinfectant wipes. She cleaned the outside of the flask and the little cap that doubled as a cup. She poured some whisky into the cup then passed the flask to Jason. 'Help yourself, I've got plenty here,' she said.

He looked on the verge of tears again. 'You shouldn't have bothered.' Nevertheless, he accepted the flask and took a deep swig. He wiped his mouth with the back of his hand and said, 'Good stuff.'

'Hamish,' she said.

'Aye, well. You're a gin drinker, you'd know no different.' He managed a crooked smile.

'Any news?'

Jason shook his head. 'I don't want to talk about it.' He turned away.

'Oh my God, Jason.' She couldn't help herself. 'You've got cornrows up the back of your head.' She stifled a laugh.

He swiftly swivelled back to face her. 'I know. Does it look as stupid as it feels?'

'I don't know. Is it possible to feel that stupid?' They grinned at each other, a beautiful moment of escape from anxiety.

They finished the whisky in silence. 'Let's get away down the hill,' Karen said. As they stood, Karen put a hand on his arm. 'I've got your back, Jason. Any time you need to let off steam, I'm here.'

'Thanks, boss. That means a lot.'

'Just don't tell anybody, right?'

'Your secret's safe with me.'

They set off, Karen asking Jason for more details about the calls he'd been making. Work, the balm for all miseries. For a lot of people, its absence was going to be the hardest part of lockdown. For the briefest of moments, she felt lucky.

17

Karen was half an hour early for her meeting with Rosalind Harris. She liked to stake out the turf before she met people outside her usual stamping grounds. She knew the Meadows well enough, but the area had been in constant flux since the development of the former Victorian Royal Infirmary had been underway. Quartermile, so called because the site was quarter of a mile from the iconic castle and Royal Mile and also, by happy chance, measured quarter of a mile from corner to corner.

Some of the original buildings remained, transformed into luxury flats and offices; others had disappeared, replaced by geometric blocks of glass and steel containing glamorous flats with stunning views of the city and beyond. Karen had heard that dozens of the flats had been bought by foreign investors who had never set foot in the place. Certainly, on occasions when she'd walked through the Meadows late in the evening more windows had been unlit than illuminated. She wondered how many of the apartments were actually occupied in lockdown.

Karen walked along Simpsons Loan, figuring out which block held Rosalind Harris's flat. To get to their rendezvous point, Rosalind would have to leave the block and turn right towards Middle Meadow Walk. There was a short lane opposite the entrance to her block, with a walled-off bed containing young trees and plants. Karen perched on the low surround and took out her phone. Anybody looking would see a woman in a warm winter coat and a woolly hat checking her messages. Karen expected to see nothing except Rosalind Harris – available from several angles on Google Images – and that was fine. But it never hurt to cover all the bases.

Five minutes later, she was glad she'd done just that. The door opened and two people stepped out into the chill morning. Rosalind Harris emerged first, the door held open by a man. She turned towards him, obscuring Karen's view of his face. He bent down to kiss her then they turned in opposite directions. She caught a quick glimpse of the man as he turned away, for all the use it was; he was wearing a brown tweed butcher's boy cap that obscured the top part of his face and the bottom half was covered by a dark beard. He was dressed for the weather in a grey tweed overcoat that came to his knees.

Still, Karen mused as she hastened to follow Rosalind, it had been long enough since her divorce and the death of her ex-husband. Nobody could blame her for moving on. She'd eventually managed to do the same after Phil's death, and he'd never publicly humiliated her.

She'd almost caught up with Rosalind by the time she reached the wide path that led down to the Meadows. Her quarry stopped by the side of the path, scanning in both directions. Karen came to a halt the prescribed two metres distant, smiled and raised a hand. 'Ms Harris?' she ventured. Lawyers liked a bit of formality till they decided otherwise, in her experience. 'I'm DCI Pirie.'

Rosalind tipped her head in acknowledgement. 'Shall we walk?' She indicated the direction and they set off. 'There are some benches on Jawbone Walk,' she said. 'It's a bit early for the student population to be taking their exercise, so we should be lucky and get one to ourselves.'

Karen kept pace with her as they veered right on to the tree-lined path. Before long, they found an empty bench and sat at opposite ends, half-turned towards each other. It was her first chance to study Rosalind. She wasn't drop-dead gorgeous, Karen thought. But hers was a face you'd look at twice. And it matched the description in the manuscript. Glossy dark hair held back by a wide barrette framed a broad forehead with well-groomed eyebrows over hazel eyes. Her nose was short and pert, her mouth wide and full, bracketed with creases that promised smiles. She wasn't smiling now, though. She was gazing directly at Karen, who felt she was definitely losing by comparison. 'Now perhaps you can explain why you need to talk to me?' Rosalind asked, raising her eyebrows in a question that revealed faint lines across her forehead.

Karen gave a rueful smile. 'I'm not sure I can manage that in a way that doesn't sound almost random. But I'll try. You may remember the case of Lara Hardie? A student who went missing without a trace around a year ago?'

Rosalind frowned. 'It rings a vague bell. She went out one evening and never came back? Is that the one?'

'That's the one. Disappeared into thin air. My job is running the Historic Cases Unit, so whenever we get fresh evidence with something like this, it falls into my team's remit. Now something's turned up that we feel is worth looking into. But it's very circumstantial.'

'All very interesting, but what has it to do with me?'

'Can I ask you about your ex-husband's archive?'

'Jake's archive? What on earth has that to do with a missing student?'

Karen gave a one-shouldered shrug. 'Probably nothing. But there's some details that niggle. I don't know about you, but whenever I find something that feels ... I don't know how to put it. Out of kilter? Weird? I have to chase it down. I'm sure you have moments like that in your line of work?'

Rosalind nodded, but her face expressed doubt. 'It happens. Mostly it turns out to be nothing. A clerical error or a misunderstanding. But yes, I know what you mean.'

'The archivist at the National Library found something in Jake Stein's archive that set her wondering.'

Rosalind sighed. 'I'm sure there's plenty in there to set a librarian's mind wondering. My ex was not always a very nice man. What in particular are you referring to?'

'There was an unfinished manuscript in one of the boxes—'

'Let me stop you there, Chief Inspector. There were half a dozen partial manuscripts in the archive. Books he'd started that fizzled out when he realised the plot made no sense, or it was going nowhere, or he hated the characters too much to want to spend more time with them.'

All of which matched Karen's question marks about this particular manuscript. 'I'll have to take your word for that, I haven't been in the archive myself yet. The one I'm interested in is called *The Vanishing of Laurel Oliver*.' She let that hang in the air.

Rosalind shook her head. 'It doesn't ring any bells, I'm afraid. To be perfectly honest, it really doesn't sound like one of my ex's titles. He tended to go for more dramatic ones. *Steal the Dead*, that sort of thing.'

'It's about two writers who play chess together. One of them has a fall from grace. The other's career is on the up. The loser finds out his wife is having an affair with the other man. He decides to set his opponent up by framing him for murder.' Karen's expression asked the question her words hadn't.

Rosalind's face was blank. Neither bewildered nor taken aback. For Karen, that was as much a tell as a gasp of surprise.

'Do you remember coming across it?'

'No. But honestly, I didn't pay much attention to the fiction in the archive. What interest I had was in the letters and the diaries. And even then ... well, there's a limit to how much humiliation most of us can take.' Her voice was more clipped now. Karen couldn't decide whether she was hiding something or simply uncomfortable with the memory of what Jake Stein had been truly like.

'But your husband was a chess player, wasn't he?'

'My *ex*-husband did play chess, yes. Frankly, I imagine that's why he chose it as a proxy conflict for the two writers. Jake would have been writing from a place of knowledge. No research required.'

'Who did he play against? Did he have a regular opponent?'

She gave a merry little laugh. 'Chief Inspector, don't make the mistake of conflating the fiction with the reality. Even in a *roman-à-clef*. The character in the manuscript may have borne some superficial similarities to my ex, but there's no actual congruence. You can't map a character directly on to its creator. Nor the actual people in their lives. Trust me, I don't resemble any of the female characters in Jake's books.'

She had a point, Karen knew. Nevertheless, when a

witness used words like 'honestly' and 'actual' and 'frankly' as often as Rosalind was doing, Karen always heard the faint ringing of a bell that tolled the opposite message. 'You didn't answer my question. Did he have a regular opponent?'

She shook her head. 'I really couldn't say. Latterly, we led quite separate lives. He had his friends, I had mine. He was often on the road, promoting his books. I don't have much idea how he spent his time away from home, though I had always presumed it involved less cerebral pursuits than chess. Look, where are we going with this? What's the point of these questions?' She shifted, as if on the point of going.

'The point of these questions is that a young woman is missing. Based on my experience of these things, presumed dead. Based on my experience of these things, when a young woman with no history of mental health problems, with an active social life and perfectly adequate academic results – when a lassie like that ends up on the missing list, the chances are that somewhere along the way she crossed paths with someone, probably a man, who meant her serious harm.' Karen deliberately sharpened her voice and raised her chin. 'So when we find the slimmest evidential connection, we follow where it leads us.'

Rosalind's cheeks pinked up. 'Of course. Forgive me. I thought when they buried my ex, that I could finally close the door on him.'

Karen held her gaze. 'Does the name Ross McEwen mean anything to you?'

A couple of rapid blinks. 'He's another Scottish crime writer. I've met him a few times. Awards ceremonies, Edinburgh Book Festival parties.'

'Did you know he played chess with Jake?'

Her eyes widened. 'I don't remember either of them

179

mentioning it. To be honest, my brain tended to glaze over at those dos.'

She was lying, Karen thought. The question was why. 'Fair enough. By the way, I'm curious as to how you ended up in charge of your late ex-husband's archive.' She let the comment hang.

Rosalind gave a wry smile. 'Like many of us, Chief Inspector, Jake thought he would live forever. He never got round to sorting out his testatory affairs after the divorce. He probably thought there was no hurry. His will made me his literary executor, and he never got round to changing it. In fact, I inherited his copyrights and what little else he had too.'

'I wondered. Thanks for clearing that up. I've only got a couple more questions, then we're done. Did Jake have a place where he went to write? A cabin, or a wee bothy somewhere?'

She shook her head. 'No. He wrote at home. Or when he was on the road, he'd write in cafés. He liked people-watching and eavesdropping, he said it often gave him little tics and behaviours he could transplant on to his characters.'

'So he never borrowed anywhere from a colleague, to get away from it all and write? Maybe when he had a deadline?'

'No, never.'

'Not even one of the writers he'd helped in their early days?'

Rosalind raised her eyebrows in surprise. 'Really, no. He didn't much like the countryside, to be honest. He preferred the buzz of city life.' She gathered her coat around her. This time she really was about to leave.

'You don't seem to have a very high opinion of your ex. Tell me, do you think he would have been capable of murder?' It wasn't the sort of question Karen would normally pose. But she wanted Rosalind Harris rattled.

She stood up, her expression imperious. 'Jake was many things. Some of them frankly repulsive. But he was never violent towards me.'

'Push anyone hard enough, and they'll respond in ways we don't recognise,' Karen said mildly.

'Trust me, I pushed him hard on occasion and he never raised a hand to me. Why on earth would he murder a young woman?' Now she'd found the outrage button.

Karen stood up. 'Maybe to prove he could?'

Rosalind scoffed. 'Are you the best that Police Scotland can do? If so, God help us all.' She turned on her heel and marched off up the Jawbone Walk.

Karen sat down again and watched her go. She wondered exactly how many lies Rosalind Harris had told her. And more importantly, why.

18

Jason awoke to the sound of his phone. He scrabbled for it, almost falling on the floor, remembering as he grabbed it that he was on the sofa. Not because Eilidh had banished him, but because he couldn't sleep and didn't want her to suffer the same fate. He registered Ronan's name and stabbed the phone with his finger then jammed it to his ear. 'What's the news?' he demanded before his brother could speak.

'It's not good,' Ronan said. 'They let me talk to her for a wee minute on the phone but she could hardly say my name. She's still on the oxygen but they say she's not responding as well as they'd like.'

'So what does that even mean? She's responding a bit? She's not getting any better?' He squinched around and sat up, staring at the room without seeing anything. 'How can they not talk plain English? Like, on a scale of one to ten, how bad is it?

'They never tell you anything. That way you cannae kick off if it all goes to shit. All I know is she didn't sound like herself.'

'It's driving me mad, being stuck here and not able to see her.'

'I don't know, I think it's worse, being this close but still not able to sit with her and hold her hand.' He took a ragged breath. 'Jase, they're talking about maybe putting her on a ventilator if she doesn't start to improve.'

Jason felt a cold hand gripping his chest. He'd seen people on ventilators after road traffic accidents. They couldn't speak. Sometimes they weren't fully sedated and their eyes rolled like frightened horses'. The thought of his mother that scared made him want to cry. 'They know what they're doing,' he said, as much to convince himself as Ronan.

'But do they? Do they really? This is a new disease, it's not like having a heart attack or pneumonia, where they know what works and what disnae. They're just guessing, the same as the rest of us with our stupid masks and hand sanitisers. We don't know how to beat this thing.'

'They're doing their best, Ro.'

'Aye, but it's not *their* mum lying there all on her lonesome struggling to get a breath. You can bet your next fish supper that the First Minister wouldn't be so calm at the bloody podium every day if it was her mum in the hospital.'

'That's not the point. Nicola would be climbing the walls same as us if she was in our shoes.'

'They'd be working a bloody sight harder to find a cure,' Ronan said. Jason heard the sound of something being slammed. A hand on a wall or a table, experience told him.

'You're wrong, Ronan. We're all in this together. Even Boris bloody Johnson. Look, there's nothing we can do for her except not go off the rails. If I hear anything, I'll call you. You do the same, aye?'

'Sure.' He sighed. 'Stay safe, bruv, I cannae be doing with two of you in the hospital, eh?' The line went dead. Jason buried his head in his hands again. Maybe it was time to go back to Gayfield Square and pretend everything was normal.

Daisy had decided it was time to talk to Lara Hardie's flat-mates. Belle Kenzie and Paloma Duncan had both been interviewed at the time of their friend's disappearance but neither had been able to shed any light on it. According to the notes, neither had seen her over the weekend before she vanished; they'd gone down to Newcastle to a gig. 'Lara wasn't into the band,' Paloma had said. 'She was more into indie stuff. You know, whiny white boys with guitars.'

Beyond asking the obvious questions about boyfriends and anyone Lara might have had a problem with, in person or online, the investigating officers hadn't explored more deeply. Daisy couldn't blame them. There was nothing else to go on. Nothing suspicious about a clutch of books on a shelf by the same author.

But now there was a new thread to pull on.

Daisy had tracked down Paloma and Belle on Facebook. Like almost everybody else in lockdown, they were desper-ate for distraction. She'd arranged a Zoom call with Paloma while Karen was off questioning Rosalind Harris. The digital comms system did nobody any favours, but Daisy could tell Paloma was what she'd call pretty rather than beautiful, but that she was determined to make the most of herself. Even at ten in the morning, she was in full make-up, lips pouting at the screen. It wasn't a look that charmed Daisy, but then it wasn't aimed at her.

'Thanks for talking to me, Paloma.'

A flash of bleached teeth. 'It's good to see another face. This lockdown is doing my head in. But Lara was my pal, I'd do anything to help you find out what happened to her.' Pure Glasgow, with some of the rough edges smoothed off.

'And we're doing all we can to do just that. Do you mind if I record this conversation?' A shake of the head. 'I've seen the interview you did with my colleagues at the time of Lara's disappearance. I don't want to go over old ground, but is there anything, no matter how insignificant, that you've remembered since then?'

Paloma shook her head, disappointed. 'I've racked my brains, but nothing's occurred to me.'

'No worries. Now, you were doing the same English course as Lara, right?'

'Yeah, we were doing the Romantic poets that term.' She sniffed. 'Not that they were that romantic. Too much "half in love with easeful death" if you ask me. Lara thought Keats was cool, though.'

'Did Lara have any other favourite writers? I mean, ones that are still alive?'

'Oh yeah, loads. She loved crime fiction, she always said it was her dirty secret. I don't know why, because she never made any secret of it, and I wouldn't describe the crime novels I've read as dirty, but there you go.'

Hallelujah. Daisy hoped her excitement was well hidden as she asked, 'Were there any in particular she really liked?'

'She liked all that Tartan Noir stuff. Denise Mina, Ian Rankin, Chris Brookmyre, Jake Stein and that cute guy who writes about a bunch of women private eyes and undertakers. Weird shit.'

'Doug Johnstone,' Daisy said automatically.

'Yeah, she went to see him at Portobello Books when his last book came out. I don't get that – going to see writers doing their dog and pony show.'

Daisy didn't dare let herself hope that she'd uncovered a definite link between Lara and Jake Stein. But she was going to test it, nevertheless. 'Did she do that a lot? Go to book events?'

Paloma frowned in thought. 'Well, it's not quite that straightforward. We're students, we don't have, like, loads of money. So she'd check out events she could go to for free. Libraries are good for that. But if it was somebody she really rated, like Doug what's-his-name, she'd put her hand in her pocket. She really wanted to be a writer herself. It was like she thought if she went to enough events, she'd find the magic spell she could use to transform herself into a bestseller.' She scoffed. 'We all read too much Harry bloody Potter when we were kids. We really believed there were magic spells that would change the world.'

'I know what you mean,' Daisy said. 'It's not magic, though, is it? It's hard work.'

Paloma giggled. 'It's focus, not hocus pocus, that's what my dad always says.'

'He's not wrong, your dad. So, can you remember anybody else she went to see in the weeks before she died?'

Paloma gazed upwards at the ceiling. 'She went to see Denise Mina at the university. Lara thought she was the big kahuna. She used to retweet every single thing she said on Twitter. And she did a workshop with Ross McEwen.'

Daisy let the pause last. Then, 'Anybody else?'

Paloma's face lit up. 'Of course. She was going to see Jake Stein. I think it was around the time she disappeared. She'd seen him before, she was dead excited about seeing him again.' She sniffed disdainfully. 'I mean, why would you want to see somebody with his attitude to women? Did you see those stories about him and that woman he exposed in his book? But Lara said it had probably been exaggerated.' She shook her head, exasperated. 'I mean, it's weird. Lara had a real sense of self-respect, but if you wrote a book she loved, she'd forgive you anything, up to and including eating babies.'

Time to be cautious now. 'Had she ever met Jake Stein?'

Paloma scoffed. 'He'd signed a couple of books for her. Mind you, if he had chatted her up, she'd probably not have dared tell me and Belle. We'd have been all, "WTF?"'

'Did she have a friend that she went to see authors with?' Daisy was desperate not to let this peter out without more to work on.

Paloma shook her head. 'Not that she ever mentioned. And I think she would have, it's not like we'd have been jealous or anything. It was just, like, her weird little quirk. We've all got something lame in our lives, right?'

Daisy smiled. 'We do, Paloma. We do. You say Lara wanted to be a writer – did she ever go on one of those residential courses?'

Paloma shrugged. 'If she did, she never said. But maybe in the vacation? We all do our own thing then, mostly.'

'You said earlier that Lara had different tastes in music. Did she have mates that she went to gigs with?'

'She used to go with her cousin Liam. But he went off at the start of the academic year to do a Masters in Vancouver. So she just went on her own. It's not exactly an edgy scene.'

It felt as if they were running out of momentum. Daisy could always come back for more if she needed to. Besides, she was due to call Belle Kenzie in ten minutes. She wrapped up the call then punched the air. 'Cooking with gas, Daisy,' she muttered.

*

Twenty-six miles away on the other side of the Firth of Forth, Ronan Murray was in the grip of a ragbag of emotions. Fear at what might happen to his mother, rage at the failure of the medical profession to perform miracles, frustration at the refusal of his useless brother to exploit his position to get inside the COVID ward, and self-loathing for not being able to fix any of it.

The nearest he could get to his mother was to be in her house. He felt her presence here in a way he never did in his poky wee flat in Templehall, even though she was no stranger to it, regularly rocking up with a couple of frozen pizzas, a bag full of cleaning materials and clean sheets. She'd strip his bed, stuff the rancid sheets in a bin bag to take home then stand over him while he put on the fresh bedding. She'd go through the place like a tornado, then the pair of them would sit down to watch *EastEnders* with their pizzas. What if that never happened again? He knew he could take care of himself, he just stood back and let her do it because she loved to feel her boys needed her.

He made a brew. Two teaspoonfuls of Gold Blend, two teaspoonfuls of sugar, a slug of milk. It was only when he raised the mug to his lips that he realised the milk had turned. Reflexively, he threw it in the sink, but it splashed back, covering his white polo shirt in a scum of brown and cream. 'Oh, for fuck's sake,' Ronan yelled, hauling his top off and wiping his chest clean. He threw it in the washing machine and, still swearing, went through to his brother's old room. The wardrobe still held some of his clothes. There would be something there to fit him.

When he opened the wardrobe, he saw much more than he'd bargained for.

*

Belle Kenzie's long hair was the colour of marmalade, brushed to a shine. She had greenish eyes and a small mouth that made Daisy think of a self-satisfied ginger cat. But she was as eager to help as Paloma had been.

'Every now and then, we just sit with a bottle of wine and go through all we know about Lara. And we come up blank.' Her accent was posh North of England. Private school, Daisy reckoned.

She nodded. 'I know how frustrating that is, but I've just been talking to Paloma, and she told me Lara loved going to listen to authors talking about their books.'

Belle looked startled. 'What? You think that's got something to do with her disappearing? Have you ever been to a book event? They're about as dodgy as ... as ... as one of my granny's coffee mornings. And people hang around for ages afterwards, gossiping and wittering on. You'd never manage to abduct anyone there!'

'But maybe she met someone there who invited her for coffee, or a drink?'

Belle pondered. 'That's just not Lara,' she finally said. 'She wasn't into casual hook-ups. When we went out on the town together, we were like the three musketeers, we looked out for each other. We never went back with guys on a first encounter, we always made them meet up for coffee or dinner or something afterwards. Some people think we're freaks, but we're just careful.' She paused. 'We're not sanctimonious old fannies,' she added. 'We enjoy clubbing and tequila shots the same as anybody else. But we respect ourselves too much to take stupid risks. That's why it's so baffling, whatever happened to Lara.'

'What about those book readings? Did Lara go to them by herself?'

189

'Oh yeah. Sure, she did that. But that's not like going to a bar or a club or a gig on your own, is it? I mean, your mother never warned you against *readers*, did she?'

Maybe she should have . . . 'I take your point. But I've heard of authors having stalkers. Maybe somebody started stalking Lara at a book event?'

Belle looked doubtful. 'She never said anything about a stalker. And trust me, Sergeant, young women of my generation know all about stalker behaviour online and in the flesh.'

That 'my generation' stung. Daisy wasn't even thirty yet. Time for a different tack.

'Paloma told me Lara had ambitions to be a writer herself. Do you know whether she ever asked any of her heroes for advice?'

'I don't think she had the nerve. She did talk about maybe doing a workshop, but I talked her out of it.'

'Why would you do that?'

'It's just a scam for making money, isn't it? All that creative writing stuff. Everybody knows that you can't learn to be a writer.'

'I think the jury's out on that one,' Daisy said. 'A lot of very successful writers have done creative writing degrees or gone on courses to improve their work.'

'And a lot of them haven't,' Belle said mutinously.

'You might as well say art school or music college or theatre schools are all scams. You can always improve your craft.' Daisy kept her tone mild. She didn't want to alienate Belle even though she was talking a modicum of bollocks.

'Anyway, Lara took my advice.'

Oh no, she didn't . . .

'It's not that I didn't want to help her. I totally did. That's why she asked me to read what she was working on.'

Daisy's interest quickened. Lara's laptop had vanished along with her. Nobody knew what she'd been writing at the time of her death. 'What was it? Have you still got it?'

'She'd started writing a psychological suspense novel. You know, where somebody has a terrible secret in their past, only it turns out to be a completely different secret? She sent me the first hundred pages.'

'A hundred pages? That's quite a commitment. Have you still got it?'

'I think so. I might have cleared it out of my downloads, but I'll still have the email with the attachment. Why?'

'I'd like to take a look at it.'

'I get that, but why?'

'Because I'm interested in what she was working on.'

'You think there might be a clue?'

Daisy tried not to let her frustration show. 'Not really. But my boss is a stickler for crossing every t and dotting every i, and I've learned not to leave any stone unturned. Mostly it's a waste of time, but sometimes it isn't.'

'Oh. OK. I know what you mean. My dad's like that. God forbid you come home with half a tale.' Then suddenly, her face crumpled. 'I'll get that over to you soon as I can. Thanks for taking this so seriously, Sergeant. We loved Lara. Losing her has left a big hole in our lives. Not knowing what happened to her, that's the worst of it. At least if we had the answer to that, we could find a way to come to terms with it.'

Somehow, Daisy doubted that. Whatever the answer, one question would rub away at their hearts forever – how could we have saved our friend? Daisy wouldn't have swapped places with them for all the tequila shots in all the student bars in the country.

19

Karen was impressed with what Daisy had achieved on her own initiative. 'All that stuff about the author events – that fits with the version in Jake Stein's book.'

'And Belle was adamant that she'd talked her out of going to workshops because it was a money-making scam, which explains why Lara didn't share what she was up to. She'd have been too embarrassed to admit it.'

'And we've got the two lassies confirming independently that Lara was a Stein fan. It all moves us a bit further along the line. You said her pal has a copy of the novel she was working on?'

'That's right.'

Karen grinned. 'Oh joy. Another unpublished masterpiece to wade through.'

'There's only a hundred pages or so,' Daisy said. 'I'm smiling on the outside and crying on the inside. However, if Lara was serious about wanting to write, then it would make sense for her to look to one of her heroes for advice. Maybe even to try to get them to mentor her.'

'If we can put her and Stein in the same place, we might be getting somewhere. If we're lucky, Jason's researches might pinpoint that.'

Daisy sighed. 'Always supposing his mum doesn't take a turn for the worse. How's Hamish doing, by the way?'

Karen turned away and busied herself making a coffee. 'He's actually having to work the croft instead of leaving it all to his shepherds. One of them, Donny, buggered off to spend lockdown with his girlfriend, so that just leaves Teegan, who's not got a vast amount of experience.'

'I thought you just left sheep to their own devices on the hill?' Daisy opened the fridge and stared into it.

'That's what I thought too, until I met Hamish. But no. There's always something needs doing – making sure your walls and fences are in good nick, lambing, docking tails, castrating wee boy lambs, dipping them, marking them with dye and ear tags, shearing, crutching – and that's not what you think – and dealing with the multifarious diseases of sheep.'

'Who knew?'

'I suspect he's bloody hating it. Poor Teegan will be on a steep learning curve.'

'I thought you said he'd bought a distillery?' Daisy took out a pot of hummus and a box of sliced peppers left over from the night before.

Karen laughed. 'Distillery is a very posh word for Duggie Brewster's still. One step up from bathtub gin. It's a one-man band, so I bet he's got someone from the village doing all the donkey work. And his Edinburgh baristas have been repurposed as delivery boys for the online customers.'

'Really? I assumed he was making the hand sanitiser to donate to hospitals and charities. Like BrewDog are doing.'

Karen snorted. 'This is Hamish we're talking about. You can take the man out of America but you can't take America out of the man. There will be some people who will come out of this pandemic ahead of the game, Daisy, and I suspect Hamish will be one of them.'

'And how do you feel about that?' As soon as she spoke, Daisy knew she'd gone too far. She held out the box of peppers. 'Sorry, boss. Want a dip?'

Karen and Daisy found Bethan Carmichael outside the back entrance to the National Library, sheltering from a flurry of rain beneath a golf umbrella. The two police officers had opted for hats and raincoats; it was always a good idea to keep your hands free. You never knew what you might be walking into. Even on the deserted streets of lockdown. Karen introduced Daisy, reminding the librarian that they were a bubble. Carmichael gave a knowing smirk. 'That's handy,' she said.

Karen couldn't be bothered explaining their domestic circumstances. It was none of the woman's business. Let her imagine what she liked. 'I appreciate you organising this for us. I know it must have been complicated, in the present circumstances.'

Carmichael sniffed. 'We have a very efficient organisation here, even in lockdown. It was simply a case of moving the archive boxes from one location to another, more appropriate one.'

So why the fuss on the phone? Karen's smile was stiff. 'DS Mortimer and I can get straight to work, then.'

Carmichael dug into her satchel with her free hand and pulled out a laminated A4 sheet. 'I've drawn you a plan of the route from the back door here to the room you'll be working in.' Daisy took it. 'I've also marked the nearest toilet.' She stepped inside the door, where the security guard sat on a high stool, masked and gloved in bright blue latex.

194

She pointed to a hand sanitiser dispenser. 'Please use the sanitiser regularly. I'll let you make your own way.' She stepped back, leaving the regulation two metres between her and the security guard. 'And be very careful with the materials you'll be inspecting.'

'I think we can manage that,' Karen said. 'Thanks.' She took the map from Daisy and led the way down a long corridor leading into the bowels of the building. Down a flight of stairs, round a corner, two doors down. They opened the door on a gloomy room with a stack of archive boxes along one wall. A table and two chairs facing each other across it. The only natural light came from a pair of long windows at ceiling level, both currently cracked as wide as they would go. Daisy snapped the lights on, and the room brightened.

'Let's get started then. How are we going to divide this up?' Karen studied the wall of boxes. 'Meera told Jason she was doing a preliminary organisation of Jake Stein's stuff. So I'm guessing the numbers on the boxes indicate a timeline?'

'That'd make sense. I mean, they might decide ultimately to group the papers by other criteria – novels, short stories, letters, diaries. But the first step would be to sort them into date order.'

Karen nodded approvingly. 'I knew your misspent youth in the world of academia would come in useful one of these days.' She walked the length of the room. It was daunting. 'Twenty-two boxes. Let's start with the last ones first. And make a note of his friends and correspondents and anybody he's worked with. Radio producers, journalists.'

They took a box each and started working their way through. Karen's began with a small pile of flyers for events in the months before Stein's death. With a sigh, she took out her phone and photographed each one. 'I know Jason's been talking to his publicist about the events Stein was doing, but there are maybe some that came through a more direct route. We need to double-check, just in case.'

Daisy nodded. 'Will do, if I come across any. So far, all I've got is a bundle of Christmas cards and a pile of royalty statements.'

'Check the cards, there's always a chance Lara might have sent him one.' Karen moved on to a cardboard file of letters and emails between Stein and his erstwhile publisher. It was an ill-tempered exchange, covering the period after the showdown with Marga Durham. The publisher made it clear that once they'd published the second book in his current contract, there would be no more. They were done with him. Stein argued that they were killing the goose that laid the golden egg, that readers were even more interested in his books now he had the whiff of scandal about him. 'They love a bad lad,' he argued in one lengthy email. 'I've earned you a fucking fortune over the years, and this is how you thank me?' Wounded elephant syndrome, Karen thought. How was it that men who were outed for their appalling misogyny still managed to feel entitled?

Next she came to some manuscript pages. Written in tight block letters, each page consisted of a brief outline of a short story with a possible title and destination for the finished article. Karen skimmed them, but none seemed to have any connection to Lara Hardie's life or writings.

On they plodded, through newspaper cuttings, notes that meant nothing to either of them in the same cramped block capitals, printed-out emails from fans and other writers, a couple of short stories, bundles of receipts for travel and restaurant meals, VAT returns. An hour and a half in and Karen felt she was losing the will to live. She was certainly losing the power of concentration. She stood up and stretched her back. 'You'd have to wonder who's ever going to be interested in all this crap.'

'There'll be people queuing up to use it in their PhDs,' Daisy said. 'So many more MA and PhD students these days, all scrabbling around for something fresh to write about.'

'I get that but, his restaurant receipts?'

'I can see it now. "The role of Nando's in the composition of Jake Stein's fiction."' They both laughed.

Karen pressed her palms against the wall and did some calf stretches. 'How far down your box are you?'

'About halfway. You?'

'A bit more. This is going to take forever.' She returned to the table and continued the tedious task. The minutes dragged by but then, suddenly, sandwiched between a contract for a BBC radio comedy quiz and a brochure for a crime festival in Inverness, she came across a couple of pages that made her sit up and take notice. The first was a list of names. The hand was, by now, familiar.

LARA
LAURA
LAURIAN
LORI
LAUREL

HARDIE
LAUREL AND
STANLEY LAUREL
OLIVER HARDY
LAUREL OLIVER

It read like a free association on Lara Hardie's name, moving step by step till he arrived at Laurel Oliver. *The Vanishing of Laurel Oliver.* This was more than circumstantial. This felt like solid evidence.

20

For a long moment, Ronan stared incredulous at the contents of his brother's wardrobe. He imagined Jason would never wear most of the items again. Hell, Ronan wondered, why had he ever worn them in the first place? But right at the back, beyond the garish Hawaiian shirts Jason had loved in his late teens, beyond the terrible cords he'd once thought stylish, beyond his first proper suit, was the thing that had knocked him back on his heels.

It was the last thing he'd expected. Though, if he'd thought about it, it made perfect sense. Jason almost never needed it these days, so of course he'd dump it in their mum's house. But now, it felt like the answer to a prayer. Jason's police uniform, pristine in a bag from the dry cleaner, hanging there, calling his name. On the shelf above, the peaked cap with the familiar black and white checked band.

Ronan reached out tentatively, as if he expected the Police Scotland uniform to disappear in a puff of fluff. The plastic squeaked as he dragged it out of the wardrobe and threw it down on the bed. He ripped the covering away, and there it was.

They were roughly the same size, him and Jason. Ronan was maybe more muscled across the shoulders and an inch or so shorter in the leg. But who was going to notice that? He found a pair of elastic-sided black Chelsea boots. Ronan pulled on the trousers and squeezed his feet into boots that were a size too small. He didn't care. It wasn't for long and it was in the best possible cause.

Next came the black short-sleeved top, then the fleece jacket, zipping it up to the neck. Then he realised he didn't have the standard utility belt. Without it, he wouldn't look the part. The first genuine polis who saw him would know instantly he was an imposter.

He thought for a moment. Where the fuck was the high-vis jacket Jason had been issued during his brief stint on Traffic? Surely that was long enough to cover his hips and disguise the absence of the Batman belt? Where would his mother have it tidied away? He didn't like the obvious answer one bit.

Ronan didn't know whether he could face his mother's bedroom. If he didn't go in there, he could kid himself she was still around, maybe having a wee lie-down. Denial was a comfort that would be shattered as soon as he went into her bedroom. But he had to find the high-vis jacket.

Steeling himself, Ronan pushed open the door to Sandra's bedroom. The imprint of her head was still on the pillow, the covers thrown back where the paramedics had made her ready for the ambulance. What was almost as bad was that the room smelled uniquely of her. That combination of hairspray, perfume, the familiar mix of toiletries that said 'Mum' to him. Ronan clenched his fists and wrapped his arms around himself so tightly he couldn't give way to tears.

He fell to his knees beside her bed and reached underneath for the plastic storage boxes she kept there for clothes that weren't in the current cycle. He hit the jackpot in the third box. Folded neatly into a bundle was Jason's high-vis jacket. Ronan groaned with relief and pulled it out of the box. To put the cherry on the cake, the epaulettes were still in place, Jason's number in reflective silver.

He yanked the jacket on, zipping it up far enough to disguise what was missing and checked his look in his mother's cheval mirror. All he needed now was a radio to slot into the jacket. Ronan went through to his own teenage bedroom and rummaged around in the drawer where he dumped stuff he didn't use any more. Right at the back of the drawer, his fingers brushed against something he'd forgotten about. He'd had a brief spell as a bouncer at a local nightclub. The job had lasted until the management found out he was taking bribes from underage lassies who wanted to break the law. But he still had the lumpy walkie-talkie he'd been issued with and hadn't bothered handing back. It more or less fitted the slot on the jacket, and it looked the business, he reckoned.

Ronan took the cap from the shelf. With a mask on, none of the polis he'd ever had a run-in with would recognise him.

One last thing. He rang the hospital and put on his most polite voice. 'Hi. My auntie's been admitted with COVID. We wanted to send a get well message but we don't know what ward she's on. Can you help? Her name's Sandra Murray ... yes, I'll hold ...' Within a minute, he had the answer.

Jason might have bottled it. Ronan wasn't about to.

Blissfully unaware of what his brother was planning, Jason was ploughing on through Jake Stein's events diary. Late in the afternoon, he finally managed to contact the organiser of a writers' workshop in Dundee who apparently didn't believe in voicemail. Susie Donaldson was the senior administrator for the creative writing module at Invertay College. She made it sound as if it was only one step below being the national Makar. 'You're lucky to catch me. I don't believe I should be at anyone's beck and call outside office hours,' she told him imperiously.

'I assumed you'd be working from home,' Jason said, trying to keep the weariness from his voice.

'You know what they say, Constable? To assume makes an ass out of you and me. Now, what can I do for Police Scotland today?' She managed to imply that she was a constant source of help to the force.

'I work for the Historic Cases Unit and we're opening a new line of inquiry into a missing person. This is confidential, of course, but we're trying to establish where she may have crossed paths with someone involved in her disappearance. So we're backtracking through her movements. We have reason to believe she may have attended a writers' workshop at Invertay.'

'I see. I can't imagine someone with ulterior motives attending a writers' workshop, Constable. You'd soon be found out if you weren't committed to the work.'

Jason closed his eyes and tried not to sigh. 'Still, we have to pursue every possibility. I understand you ran a workshop led by Jake Stein a while ago?'

'That's right, yes. It was completely sold out. I suppose some people were made curious by his notoriety. I'll be honest, I had my doubts about hiring him, after his disgrace, you know. But on the plus side, his rates were much lower than anyone else with his track record.' She sounded very pleased with herself. Sure, why not put a sexual predator in a room with vulnerable egos?

'Do you have a list of the people who attended his workshop?'

'Of course I do. Good heavens, what kind of Mickey Mouse operation do you think we run at Invertay?'

'I'm sure you're very efficient. But it was a while ago.'

'What's the name of the woman you're interested in?' The acoustic had changed, as if Susie was looking away. Jason could hear fingers rattling on keys.

'I'm afraid I can't tell you that. What I'd like is for you to send me the list.'

A pause. 'I'm not sure I can do that. Data Protection Act, and all that.'

Jason wanted to crawl down the phone and scream in her face, but he took a breath instead and said, 'I'm not asking for any data. Simply a list of names. There's no issue of privacy. I've spent all day on the phone to events administrators who think that helping solve a young woman's disappearance is more important than just about anything else.'

'There's no need to be like that.' Her voice was frosty. He could imagine what she looked like and it wasn't an appealing thought. 'Very well. Send me a photo of your ID and give me your email address and I'll send you the list with all the contact details redacted.'

The call over, Jason folded his arms on the desk and laid his head on them. He was trying to block out all thoughts of his mother's predicament, but nothing was working. Not even a jobsworth like Susie Donaldson could silence his fears.

21

The ban on hospital visits meant that for once it was easy to find a parking space. Ronan tucked his car between a couple of SUVs and made sure there was nobody around to see him emerge from his souped-up Audi with its spoiler and its custom alloys. He walked briskly to the A&E entrance and went in. Nobody gave him a second look as he made his way through the department, following the signs to the ward he was looking for. He didn't want to risk the close quarters of the lift so he took the stairs, forcing himself to keep to a steady pace and not run up two at a time.

It wasn't hard to figure out where the COVID wards were. For a start, there were a lot more people encased in full PPE. He couldn't tell the difference between nurses, doctors, auxiliary staff and porters. They were all so focused on what they were doing, it was as if he were invisible.

He slowed a little, checking the signs for the ward his mother was on. But before he could go any further, a small Asian woman stepped in front of him, blocking his path. 'You can't come in here, officer,' she said, her voice authoritative and firm.

'I've to do an identity check on a patient,' he said.

'Somebody that was brought in earlier. There's some con- fusion as to whether the paramedics got the right name.'

'I'm sorry. That's just not possible. You'll have to go back. This is a quarantine area.'

'I've got a mask on,' he protested.

'Not good enough.'

'But if somebody's here under the wrong name, would that maybe not be dangerous for them? Underlying medical conditions, and that? The family are worried.' They were all familiar with the terminology these days.

The woman took a couple of steps forward, forcing him to move back. 'I tell you what I'll do. Tell me the name of the person you're interested in. Give me your phone' – she held out her hand – 'and I'll go and take a picture of them. And I'll make sure I wipe down your phone afterwards. You can take that back and make whatever checks you need back at the station or wherever.'

Ronan had been doing well up to that point. But now he reverted to form and panicked. He pushed the woman to one side and hurried down the hallway as she stumbled against the wall. Now people were paying attention to him. He made it as far as the door to his mother's ward before a burly man wrapped his arms around him from behind.

'What do you think you're playing at? This is hospital, not a rammy in the street.'

'I'm doing my job,' Ronan snarled. 'Let me go or I'll arrest you.'

And now the Asian woman was in his face again. 'Get out. Right now. Are you deliberately trying to catch COVID? You want me to call your colleagues and have them throw you out? Andy, show this idiot the way out.'

The man unwrapped him from the bear hug but held tight

to his arm. Half-leading, half-dragging Ronan he got him away from the wards and barred the way back. 'Just go,' he said gently. 'There's people seriously ill in there. We're trying to look after them. We don't need this.'

But Ronan was fired up with self-righteousness. He took a step forward and punched the man in the throat. He made a strangled gasp and fell to his knees.

And Ronan was off and running, pushing his way past anyone who tried to stop him. He was dimly aware of shouts of alarm, but he was past caring. At the door to the ward, he brushed the Asian woman aside as if she was a small child and burst into the room.

For a moment he was disorientated. At first glance, the occupants of the four beds looked the same. Old, grey-faced, features obscured by breathing equipment, like scuba divers on land. Then his vision cleared and he recognised his mother's faded brown hair on a pillow, stringier than he'd ever seen it before. He ran down to her bedside, ignoring the nurses trying to stop him. 'Mum,' he said. 'Mum, I'm here. We love you, Mum.' Sandra's eyelids fluttered but stayed closed. 'You've got to keep fighting, Mum.' He reached for her hand but before he could touch it, a strong arm gripped his other arm and twisted it viciously up his back.

'Enough, pal,' a thick Fife accent said in his ear as he forced Ronan to spin round and head for the door. 'You're gonnae walk the plank for this.'

'Let go of me,' Ronan hissed as they returned to the corridor.

'I'm reporting you,' the Asian woman said. 'I've got your number, I'll be speaking to your commanding officer. Now get off my ward.'

The brutal Fifer let go of Ronan and pushed him away, towards the far end of the corridor. As he staggered, Ronan caught sight of a real polis heading towards the commotion. He took flight. Down the hall, round a corner, down a flight of stairs, along another corridor, down more stairs and out an emergency exit. He emerged, panting, on a cement path alongside a shrubbery. He had no idea where he was in relation to the car park.

But going there would be a stupid move. That would be the first place they'd look for a man on the run. He put his hands on his knees while he caught his breath and considered his next move. Cautiously, he moved along the path in what seemed to be the direction of traffic noise. He emerged alongside a dramatic modern building, all concrete and strong lines. He recognised its unmistakable profile and knew he'd never be happier to see the Maggie's Fife cancer centre, the architectural star in the crown of the Vic. They wouldn't be looking for him round this side of the hospital. He could make his escape and walk back to his mum's house in less than half an hour. He'd get changed and come back for the car later, when all the fuss had died down.

As he walked, Ronan congratulated himself on at least managing to speak to his mum. She'd heard him, he knew it. Her eyes had nearly opened. OK, he'd maybe not managed to sit and talk to her like he'd planned. But at least he'd done better than his chicken-hearted brother.

Maybe not tell him that, though.

Karen took a photograph of the list of names then passed it over to Daisy. 'Bloody hell,' she exclaimed. 'That's solid.'

'That's what I thought at first sight,' Karen said. 'But if I was a defence counsel, I'd say, "My client was intrigued by the disappearance of Lara Hardie and merely used that as a jumping-off place for his imagination."'

Daisy considered this, her expression growing crestfallen. 'But surely, if we tie it to all the other pieces of circumstantial evidence?'

'It's an interesting point. Because here's the thing, Daisy. We're never actually going to be trying this in court. Jake Stein is dead. We might believe he killed Lara Hardie, but that's never going to be tested by the legal process. Now, you might argue that we could go down the balance of probabilities route and tell her parents we think we know what happened to her. But what if we're wrong?'

Daisy chewed her lip. 'We'd at least be giving them closure, no?'

'Which would be all very well, unless Lara's killer gained confidence from getting away with it, and did it again.' Karen sighed. 'We need to be certain. Copper bottom certain.'

Daisy groaned. 'And to think I thought the HCU might be more satisfying than live cases.'

'Trust me, it is. But because we have the opportunity to dig deeper, we have to make sure we dig wider too.' Karen looked at her watch. 'God, it's nearly six. Let's give it another half hour and call it a day.'

She turned back to her task and picked up the other loose sheet of paper, which was face down for some reason. It was a page printed out from a computer. At the top of the page was a fragment of narrative. Karen was no expert in the finer points of typography but she thought this was a different font from either of the ones she'd seen Stein using.

If you're a student of true crime, you've probably already read the official version of the events of the night of May 9th, 2014 in New Orleans, as outlined above. Trust me, the truth is far stranger than the fictions constructed by the powers that be. It had nothing to do with shrewd detection and everything to do with my pal Joey's natural-born instinct for mayhem.

But what I knew about that night was only one small piece of a jigsaw I only managed to piece together seven years and three deaths later. [Quote for LO?]

Beneath it, a few lines of poetry.

> *let them go – the*
> *truthful liars and*
> *the false fair friends*
> *and the boths and*
> *neithers – you must let them go they*
> *were born*
> *to go*

'Have you seen anything else in this font?' Karen passed it across. 'What do you make of it?'

'I've not noticed.' Then Daisy stopped abruptly, shock on her face.

'What is it?'

She visibly pulled herself together. 'I just … I recognise the poetry.'

'I didn't know you were a poetry buff. You've kept that quiet.' Karen's tone was teasing.

'I'm not. Someone sent this to me, years ago now. It's a stanza from a poem called "let it go" by e e cummings. He was an American poet. He didn't use capitals or much in the way of punctuation. It's about letting everything go that stands between you and your desire, your dreams.' Daisy spoke abruptly: 'It ends up saying the only way you can accept love is to let everything else go.'

'And did you?'

'I thought I did. But she didn't think I had.' Daisy's eyes widened as she realised she'd said more than she'd intended.

'Aye, well, more fool her.' Karen kept her tone light. Daisy had clearly guarded her sexuality with care. Not a whisper of gossip had crossed Karen's radar, probably because most male cops had a very particular idea of what a lesbian looked like, and it wasn't Daisy. So Karen was determined not to make her colleague fear her slip of the tongue.

They looked at each other across the table. Karen read dismay in Daisy's expression. 'So is he a good poet, this e e cummings? I've never heard of him.'

'He wrote a lot of love poetry. You've probably seen quotes from him on greetings cards, which I think would have driven him mad. "i carry your heart with me (i carry it in my heart)"? That's him. And "i like my body when it is with your body".'

Karen shrugged. 'Not the kind of greetings cards I get. I'm obviously doing something wrong.'

'He was a prisoner of war in the First World War. He wrote a novel about it. But his politics were a bit dodgy. He supported McCarthy in the 1950s in his communist witch hunt. It's one of those, "can you still admire the writing if the writer's got terrible politics?" things.'

'You seem to know a lot about this guy.'

Daisy flushed. 'I'm a detective, boss. When something crosses my path I don't know about, I find out what I can. I've seen you do the same thing.'

'Fair point. OK, so what's a bit of a poem by a politically

dodgy American poet doing in Jake Stein's files? I don't see any other sign he was interested in poetry.'

'Maybe somebody sent it to him?'

Karen thought about it. 'But he'd already lost everything. He'd had to let it go and what it brought him was the opposite of love.'

'Maybe they sent it before his downfall? Maybe it was actually Marga Durham who sent it to him?'

'That's possible, but it was in the box right next to the Laurel Oliver thing, which suggests it was later. What about the bit of text above it? It reads like the opening of one of those crime novels where the author goes all round the houses to avoid telling you what any normal person would say in the first sentence. "That night in New Orleans that Fred Smith got murdered, x, y, and z happened."' Karen was scornful; she'd thrown aside a few of those, infuriated by a twist that any decent detective would have picked up in the first fifty pages.

Daisy studied it, frowning. 'That bit in the end, in the square brackets – it looks like he was deliberately choosing it as an example of bad writing. Maybe the LO stands for Laurel Oliver? What if Stein planned to incorporate it in his novel as proof she was nothing special as a writer? In the notes, he says he's going to use quotes from her work, doesn't he?'

'That's a good idea. I can't tell you how much I wish we had more of the bloody thing.'

'Hopefully Belle will manage to find Lara's manuscript on her computer. Then we can check it against this and see whether Stein lifted it from Lara?'

Before Karen could respond, her phone rang. She rolled her eyes. 'Oh, God, it's Eilidh. I hope Jason's mum's no worse.' She answered the call. 'Hi Eilidh, it's DCI Pirie here.'

'Where's Jason?' she demanded, her voice as audible to Daisy as it was to Karen.

'He's not at home?'

'He went out first thing this morning and I've not seen him since. I tried phoning him, but it just goes to voicemail.'

'Gayfield Square.' Daisy, sotto voce.

'Has something happened? Has his mum taken a turn for the worse?'

'Something's happened all right, but it's not Sandra.' Eilidh sounded grim. 'I've just had the polis at the door. A pair of them, looking for Jason. They wouldn't tell me what they were after him for. I asked if Sandra was OK and they both looked as if they didn't know what I was on about. They asked to come in to check if he was there and I said no. Was that OK?'

'You were quite within your rights, Eilidh.' Karen thought it was a fifty/fifty. Let them in and they'd take that as permission to turn the place over; refuse and they'd assume you had something to hide.

'That's what I thought. They weren't very happy about it. One of them said something about "KP Nuts' awkward squad". Anyway, they said when he got in, he should report directly to Fettes. What's going on? This is scary.'

'I don't know, Eilidh. Nobody's been in touch with me about Jason.'

'How not? You're his boss.'

'I know, I'm as puzzled as you. Look, don't panic. Obviously nothing's happened to him. It'll be something or nothing. Just sit tight. Let me look into this and see what I can find out. I'll call you back as soon as I hear anything.'

'I'm scared, Chief Inspector. What if he's lying in the dark again, hurt, bleeding?'

'That's not very likely, Eilidh.'

'So where is he? It's lockdown, there's hardly any place he could go. I mean, he's not been walking round Sainsbury's for eight hours, has he?'

'I'll find out all I can, Eilidh. Soon as I can. And I'll call you back.' There was no arguing with Karen's tone. Instead, Eilidh simply cut the line. Karen gave a rueful smile. 'That'll be me off the Christmas card list.' She stood up and reached for her coat. 'Come on. Let's go and find the lost boy. And see if we can figure out why he's a wanted man.'

22

They were halfway over the hump of the Royal Mile when Karen stopped in her tracks. 'It's just dawned on me. Sorry, Daisy, but I think you need to go straight home. Jason isn't in our bubble, and I can only justify being in the same room as him because we're doing key work.'

Daisy smacked her forehead lightly. 'Duh. Of course, I wasn't thinking. I'll peel off at Picardy Place and go home. Maybe Lara's pal Belle will have tracked down the manuscript of her masterpiece.' Or maybe she could get online while she had the place to herself.

'Have an evening off,' Karen said. 'It's not like we're skiving. I'll sort out Jason, then I've got a bit of business to sort out down at the shore. I'll see you later.'

Daisy raised her eyebrows. What was this bit of business that was making her boss dodge around the lockdown rules? Yesterday morning she'd sloped off, now this. It wasn't anything to do with Lara Hardie, that was for sure. According to Jason, even when Karen went off on one of her hunches, she was quick to keep him in the loop. No, there was something else going on. Daisy decided to park it for now, but if it continued, she'd be doing a wee investigation of her own. Because it was always handy to have something on your boss tucked away in your back pocket.

'When are we going to talk to Ross McEwen?' Daisy asked as they passed beneath the railway tracks and headed under the Waterloo Place viaduct. The rain had given up the ghost; now the air simply felt damp against their faces.

'I haven't decided yet. It all feels kind of muddled in my head right now. I'm still struggling to make sense of this bloody manuscript. I need to sit down and work out what we actually know, what we think we know and what's fiction. I'm not there yet.'

There was no point, Daisy knew, in trying to push Karen in a direction she didn't want to go in. She headed off down Broughton Street, intent on picking up a fish supper to take home. It was one of the few pleasures available these days. Fresh fish in batter and a pile of chips, and she'd be ready for an evening of pleasure. She hoped whatever it was that Karen was up to, it would give her enough time for what she wanted to do.

Karen walked away from Daisy and turned down Leith Walk. She paused in the lee of a shop doorway and took out her phone. She dialled a former colleague from Fife who was now desk-bound in one of the intel analysis teams. 'Hey, Stevie. KP here.'

'All right, Karen? How's tricks?'

'Doing away. Yourself?'

'Ach, just bashing the keys and trying to flush out the scammers. Being stuck inside has given some of them a new lease of life. So, I'm assuming you're not just calling to say I love you? What can I do for you?' He sounded ridiculously cheerful.

'You still got your finger on the pulse down at Fettes?'

'Nobody better. It's a bit harder with the two metres distance. Folk do prefer to whisper the juicy stuff but what can I say? I've got a gift.'

Karen smiled. She knew all about Stevie Malcolm's gift. It had come to her rescue a couple of times in the past. 'My wingman?'

'The Mint?' A note of caution in his tone.

'The same. A couple of uniforms turned up on his doorstep looking for him this afternoon. He wasn't there because he was elsewhere doing his job. As instructed by me. The pair of polis at the door didn't actually kick the door in, but they were clearly not there to invite Jason on a night out. They told his fiancée that Jason should come in as soon as he got home. To see the Dog Biscuit.'

'Is Jason's mum in the Vic?'

Karen's heart sank. 'Aye. She's in the COVID ward.'

'I know what this is about.' He lowered his voice. 'Your man Jason broke all the rules and tried to get in to see his mother on the COVID ward. He assaulted a nurse and a doctor and legged it when the local lads turned up. The doctor clocked the epaulette number and it matched up with the Mint. A very pissed off local commander called the Dog Biscuit.'

Karen groaned. It was worse than she'd feared. It was infuriating that the local guv'nor hadn't had the wit to deal with it himself, though. Dumping it on Ann Markie was the sure and certain way of getting her to dump it more heavily on anyone she could blame. Somehow, Karen knew this would end up being her fault. 'Great. And now she wants him to turn himself in?'

'You'd know more about that than me,' Stevie said. 'But

I will tell you one thing – there's no point in him rocking up here tonight. She's away home in time for some Zoom meeting with the Justice Secretary. She'll not be back till tomorrow morning.'

'Thanks for the heads-up.'

'You want my advice? Get him here at seven in the morning. She usually gets in about twenty past.'

'Even on a Sunday?'

'Even on a Sunday. You know what she's like. In serious need of a life.'

'I'll get him here. Hangdog and grovelling. Thanks, Stevie. I owe you one.'

He sighed. 'If the pubs ever open again. Who knew I'd be nostalgic for happy hour?'

Karen chuckled. 'Anybody that knows you.'

After she ended the call, she leaned against the door jamb. What the actual was Jason thinking? She thought she'd talked sense into him the day before, but it seemed she was kidding herself. So where was he?

She presumed he wasn't so stupid that he'd have hung around at his mother's house in Kirkcaldy. But he wasn't at home either. She could only imagine he might have gone back to Gayfield Square because it was the only safe haven he could think of. What's the best place to hide from the police? Inside the nick, obviously.

Karen used her digital pass card to get into the station. Running a skeleton crew made it easier to come and go without raising eyebrows; tonight, she wasn't looking for a car, so there was no need to communicate her presence. She knew she was disregarding more COVID rules than she cared to count, but she consoled herself with the fact that she was keeping her distance and wearing a mask. Nor was she in crowded places; Gayfield Square felt like the aftermath of a neutron bomb – all the buildings left standing, all the people vaporised.

With every step closer to the HCU office, she grew more apprehensive. What if Jason wasn't here? Worse, what if he'd done something beyond the bounds of standard stupidity? She paused in front of the door and took a deep breath, squaring her shoulders. Then she opened the door.

For a moment, her breathing stopped. Jason was indeed in the office, but he was face down on the desk, head cradled in his arms. There was no sound and she couldn't see any movement. But she refused to believe the message her brain was receiving.

'Jason,' she barked.

He started up from the desk in a jumble of limbs, his chair shooting backwards on its castors, his head falling forward on to the edge of the desk with a wicked crack. 'What? What? Oh fuck,' he mumbled, grabbing his forehead. He looked across at the door, eyes bleary, expression appalled. 'What just happened?'

'I think I woke you up,' Karen said.

He cleared his throat noisily and rubbed his eyes. 'I fell asleep.'

'That's usually what you have to do to get woken up. Why are you sleeping here? You've got a perfectly good bed waiting for you down the bottom of the hill.'

'I didn't sleep much last night.' He shook his head like a dog emerging from the sea. 'Sorry, boss. I should have went home, but ... I don't know, I put my head down for five minutes.' He glanced up at the clock. 'Three hours ago.'

Karen dropped into her own chair and gave him a long

measured stare. 'Do you need to phone the Vic, to check on your mum?'

Panic gripped his features. He'd learned a lot in the last few years, but they obviously hadn't got to the 'hiding your emotions' module, Karen thought, making a mental note to address this another day. 'Has something happened?' he squeaked.

'Nothing, as far as I'm aware. I'm presuming Ronan would have called you if there was any change.'

'That's right.' Relief flooded his face, his eyes suspiciously damp. 'I'll wait to call till we're done, then.'

Karen tapped a pencil end to end on her notepad. Point, eraser, point, eraser. 'I'm going to ask you something and I need you to be absolutely honest with me. Whatever the answer is, we can sort it out. OK?'

He blinked fast then nodded. 'OK, but—'

'Did you go to Kirkcaldy today?'

'No.' He spoke without a second's thought. 'I never.' He frowned. 'Why would anybody think I did?'

Karen's heart went out to him. He was essentially so decent. And it got him into all kinds of trouble, particularly because of his brother. 'Somebody wearing your uniform tried to get into the COVID ward where your mum is. There was a scuffle and the imposter legged it. But they got the epaulette number. And it was your jacket. I don't know any more details than that. Except that the local boss decided it needed to be kicked upstairs and now the Dog Biscuit has you in her sights.'

'I don't understand. I've been here all day.'

'If it wasn't you, Jason, then who could it possibly have been? Who else has access to your uniform? Your high-vis jacket? Your epaulette number?'

219

She watched the light dawn then the mutinous darkness descend. His chin rose in defiance. 'I haven't got a clue, boss.'

'Where is your uniform?'

He looked away. 'I'm not sure.'

'Please, Jason. I can't help you out of the shit unless you start telling me the truth. Whole truth, nothing but.'

His sigh sounded as if it came from somewhere around his knees. 'It's at my mum's house.' His voice barely above a whisper. Then he met her eyes and spoke at his normal level. 'Ronan doesn't know that.'

'So, what? Some random broke into your mum's house, found your uniform and decided to visit your mum? Jason, I am not blaming you for the fact that your brother is a petty criminal and a fuckwit. But I am determined that you are not carrying the can for him. ACC Markie has summoned you. Now, I happen to know she's gone home for the day, so no need to show up till the morning. I'll meet you at seven sharp outside Fettes. And we'll sort it out then and there.'

He nodded, a picture of misery. 'Thanks, boss.'

'Now, I'll walk you home to make sure you get there. Eilidh's worried sick. She had two polis at your door this afternoon, looking for you. You're going to have to do some penance for that.' They walked out, Karen two metres ahead of Jason, and set off down Leith Walk on opposite sides of the pavement. 'I don't suppose you talked to anybody in Gayfield Square?' she asked.

Glum, Jason shook his head. Then he suddenly brightened. 'But I've been working. I've been phoning people up all day. I kept a log. Who I spoke to. When. The calls will be timestamped on my phone.'

Karen couldn't keep the smile from her face. 'And if it

comes to it, the phone mast will prove your phone was in Edinburgh. That's a relief.'

Jason's grin matched hers. 'No kidding.' He came to a halt. 'That reminds me, I just need to check one thing.' He took out his phone and started tapping, talking all the while. 'I was talking to a woman at Invertay College, they ran a workshop with Jake Stein, she was going to email me a list of . . . ' His voice trailed off and he thrust the phone at Karen. 'Bloody hell, boss.'

Karen stared at the screen. There it was, in black and white: Lara Hardie. They'd found the crossing point.

23

Daisy stretched out on her bed, her laptop open on the bedside table she'd shifted to provide a better angle. The woman on the screen was, like her, stripped to her bra and pants. They'd taken the best part of half an hour to get that far, savouring the pleasure of virtual seduction. Even if the hands providing the sensual touches were their own, the words that accompanied the actions were very definitely not. If lockdown had done one thing, it was to separate the sexually articulate from the herd.

'My hand's moving down your spine, fingertips caressing your soft, soft skin. And now I'm taking hold of your bra strap, squeezing the two sides together, easing the hooks out of the eyes, letting it fall away.' Daisy suited her own actions to Steph's words, letting her bra slip loose, revealing her breasts. 'Now I'm moving my hands round to your breasts, touching them, making them tingle. No, not your nipples yet, I need to tease you more.'

Daisy had met Steph two days before lockdown. A mutual friend's thirtieth birthday party had brought them together in a second-floor tenement flat in Marchmont. Daisy had always scoffed at the notion of love at first sight, ascribing to it a way of making lust respectable. But as soon as she started talking to Steph over the kitchen counter, they had connected. A lurch in the stomach, a spark in her head, a need to impress so this woman would not slip away. She'd never known that before. They'd talked and danced, talked and walked out into the freezing night, talked and crossed Bruntsfield Links to Steph's tiny basement flat where they'd fallen into each other's arms as if they were in some embarrassingly twee movie.

Steph wasn't even turned off when Daisy revealed she was a polis. 'If people like you don't do it, how's it ever going to get better?' Steph was a primary school teacher, responsible for thirty-three seven-year-olds. Daisy reckoned she'd be better equipped to keep public order than the entire HCU. Well, maybe not KP Nuts . . .

They'd spent the night together, reluctantly parting to start their respective work weeks. They'd arranged to meet up that evening. But the lockdown had been announced, and Daisy had agreed to move in with Karen for what she expected might be a couple of weeks. Now here they were, heading towards a month. The inevitable separations all over the country were hard enough to handle for long-standing commitments. Daisy thought she and Steph would stand no chance.

It was beginning to feel like she was wrong about that. They'd used lockdown to get to know each other better, faster than they might have done face to face. They'd spoken every evening, when Daisy could escape to her room or when Karen was out for her daily walk. And gradually, they'd started to find a way to explore their sexual relationship virtually. Daisy had worried it might feel tacky, but somehow they'd navigated the awkwardness.

Now, tonight, a treat – Karen was out of the house, sorting

out Jason then on her own private errand. A chance for them to explore, to enjoy, to experiment.

Daisy stroked her breasts, circling round her nipples, waiting for permission to touch them. Steph murmured soft words, teasing and tantalising. Daisy felt the heat rising in her, almost unbearable.

Then the front door slammed. Heavy footsteps in the hall. Definitely not Karen. 'Fuck,' Daisy exclaimed. 'There's someone in the flat. I'll have to call you back.' She cut the connection before Steph could respond. She grabbed her jeans and pulled them on, hauling a jumper over her head. Her dressing gown would have been quicker, but she didn't want to confront an intruder half-naked.

Daisy burst out of her room and covered the short passage to the living room in three rapid strides. It was empty, but somehow the air felt disturbed, the faintest trace of an alien scent. She looked down the other passageway towards Karen's room and realised the office door was open.

She approached cautiously, sidling along the wall. She could hear drawers opening and closing, the sound of rummaging among papers. She pressed her face to the door jamb and eased one eye round it.

Daisy had never met Hamish Mackenzie, but she'd seen photographs, and even from behind, she was pretty sure the man rifling through the desk was its owner. Wavy golden brown hair, broad shoulders in a tweed jacket, narrow jeans revealing well-shaped calves. As she watched, he found what he was looking for and turned towards the door, a thin leather folder of papers in one hand.

Daisy stepped clear of the doorway and said coolly, 'Mr Mackenzie, I presume?'

He stopped in his tracks. And gave her a wide grin. 'You

must be the redoubtable Daisy. Pleased to meet you.' He stretched out a hand and moved closer.

'Two metres,' she yelped, backing up.

'Sorry, I wasn't thinking.' He pulled a ridiculous tweed mask out of his jacket pocket. Daisy reversed up the hall and picked up one of their disposables, fiddling the elastic behind her ears.

'What are you doing here?' she demanded.

He chuckled. 'It's my flat.'

'That's not the point. You're in lockdown in the Highlands. At your croft. You can't be here. It's against all the rules.'

He shrugged. 'Look, I came to collect these papers. I'm in the middle of a deal and I needed access to them.'

'You could have got Karen to post them to you,' Daisy pointed out. 'You're not just breaking the rules, you're compromising her too.'

He smiled the rueful smile of a man accustomed to his boyish charm working wonders. 'I needed them in a hurry. And anyway, she doesn't appear to be here. I figured this was the time of day she might have gone for her permitted exercise – the twilight hour. And it seems I was right.'

'She's working. If you must know. Within the rules. And you're very definitely not within the rules. I could issue you with a fixed penalty notice, you know.'

He stopped smiling. 'But you won't. Just think how embarrassing that would be for Karen. And I doubt you'd still be in the HCU by the end of the week. Look, I've got what I came for. I'm going to get straight back in my van and make a necessary delivery to my team, and then I'm going to turn round and drive north. If Karen's out working, chances are she'll be tearing up any COVID regs that stand between her and resolving a case. Let's just keep this between us, Daisy. A small quid pro quo for all of this.' He swept his arm round, a gesture encompassing the living room and beyond. He stepped towards her, forcing her to retreat. His size was intimidating, whether he intended that or not. 'There's no need to make a big deal out of this.'

Daisy glowered at him. 'If you think this is me making a big deal, you've obviously led a very sheltered life. The only reason I'm letting you walk out of here without con-sequences is that I respect DCI Pirie far too much to tar her with your misdemeanours. Now, on your way. And for your sake, I hope you manage to avoid running into any more police officers on your way back up the A9.' She stood hands on hips, staring him down.

'Lucky Karen, having you around. What a barrel of laughs that must be.' He marched past her to the front hall, letting himself out and slamming the door behind him.

Daisy subsided on to the sofa, surprised to find her hands trembling. She wondered whether Karen had ever seen Hamish in that mode. Somehow, she doubted it. If there was one trait her boss despised more than any other, it was bullying. And Daisy felt bullied, no two ways about it. It wasn't only that he was physically big; he'd chosen his moment to remind her that she was here on his grace-and-favour terms. Such behaviour was, she thought, often the obverse face of charm.

With a sigh, she headed back to her room to tell Steph their plans would have to be aborted yet again. The last thing she felt like in this jangled state was sex, real or virtual.

Karen walked Jason to the front door of his tenement. 'Be honest with her, Jason. You're under a huge strain. We all deal with that in different ways. Me, I walk. And I'm not getting nearly enough of that right now, by the way. Explain to Eilidh that your way of coping is to opt out of people, even the ones you love.' She wanted to give him a reassuring pat on the arm, but she held back. 'You know how you've taken to asking yourself, "What would Phil do?" Well, his way of dealing with it was to go down to Tough Melville's boxing gym and beat the crap out of the heavy bag. I hated that. I thought it was so bloody boysie, but it worked for him and he came home in a much better state. Better you take yourself off the board than you stay put and lose the plot with Eilidh when it's no fault of hers.'

'I know, boss. I'm not very good at expressing myself when it comes to feelings.'

'You're not alone there. You'll be fine, Jason. I'll see you in the morning at seven.' She waited till he went inside and began climbing the stairs before she walked on.

There was no point in trying to deal with Susie Donaldson from Invertay at this time of the evening. She could wait till morning. A session with the Dog Biscuit would leave Karen in the perfect state of mind for dealing with an officious official. She checked her phone. No messages. It was almost time to call Rafiq. She carried on walking into the heart of Leith, the only other person in sight a woman walking a standard poodle on the opposite side of the road. When she reached the Commercial Street bridge, she leaned on it and called Rafiq. The lights shimmered on the water below in the constantly shifting pattern she always found soothing. 'Hi, it's Karen,' she said.

'Thank you for calling. Are you well?'

'I'm fine. How about you?'

A brief pause. 'I am ashamed to feel so well when so many of my friends are in bad places.'

227

'I understand that. Are you still up for meeting tonight? We can walk along the breakwater. We can easily keep two metres apart. But at least we can talk. And order you some new clothes.'

Another pause. 'I don't understand why you are taking such risks.'

'It's not a risk. It's not against the rules to have a conversation with somebody you meet on your daily exercise as long as you keep a safe distance. We all need human contact, and you can't get on social media like the rest of us because all my digital kit's elsewhere. Besides, it's good for me to talk to somebody fresh. Trust me, you're doing me a favour too.'

'Very well. I will do this.'

'I'll meet you outside the building, on the far side of the car parking spaces. Give me ten minutes to get there.'

She had to instruct him to stop thanking her as they began to walk along the breakwater. 'I don't want gratitude for behaving like a decent human being,' she protested. 'I'm uncomfortable with you constantly thanking me. Can we just take it that I understand you're grateful and leave it at that?'

He looked momentarily anxious then broke into a smile. 'I understand your position. I will hold my thankfulness in my heart. How bad is COVID in the city?'

'Nobody really knows. The last numbers I heard for the whole of Scotland were eight and a half thousand cases and more than nine hundred deaths. It's very frightening.'

'You're right. And it is one of the reasons I am so glad to be out of that hostel. Too many of us living at close quarters, no way of imposing quarantine or avoiding infection. All it takes is one person, and the infection will run through everyone. I never thought I would say this, but I am glad I am not practising in a hospital right now. I know this is selfish.' He sighed.

'After what you've been through, I think you're entitled to a wee bit of selfishness. Once this is all over, I hope we can find a way to let you practise again. We need skills like yours.'

He shook his head. 'That is a long way away. I will always be in hiding from my past now.'

'But Scotland has a proud record of helping refugees. Miran arrived here with nothing, and now he and Amina have a thriving business. Well, it was thriving before lockdown. And I'm sure it will be again. And they're not the only ones. Down in Rothesay, there's a community of exiled Syrians, and they've established a barber's shop and a bakery. I'm told the baklava is amazing.' She turned to smile at him.

He sighed. 'But these people do not have a price on their heads. I cannot think about the future, Karen. I can only live day to day.'

'I'm sorry.'

'One thing is good, though. There is nothing here that stirs memories of my wife and my boy.'

'I don't expect that makes the grief disappear, though.'

They walked on towards the lighthouse. Rafiq pulled Hamish's jacket more tightly around his thin body as the east wind gusted down the estuary. 'It is always there. I have heard patients talk about the ache of an amputated limb, as if it was still present. Grief is like that, I think.'

His words moved her. She knew that feeling only too well. 'That's a good way of putting it. My partner was murdered three years ago, and I still feel his absence. He felt

229

like the other half of me. He was a cop too, and whenever I'm actively working a case, like I am just now, I find myself talking to him.'

Her words seemed to energise Rafiq. 'Exactly. I talk to Ayesha in my head. When I found myself in a position to smuggle those photographs out of the prison, it was her spirit that gave me the strength to do it. I imagine what she would say, and it helps me. My boy, though – he is a stranger to me. I try to bring him to life in my head, but he is frozen the way he was. I have lost him twice.'

They rounded the lighthouse in silence and Karen led the way into the park. There was something soothing about Rafiq's presence. It felt unusual to be in the company of a man who didn't need to assert himself at every point. 'I imagine it feels very strange. The absence of your son, I mean.'

'It makes no sense. But then, the effects of death do not often obey the rules of logic.'

'I thought I'd reached the point where I could have a relationship with someone else,' Karen said. 'It's been fun. And interesting. He moves in very different worlds from me, personally and professionally. But lately, I've been feeling the distance between us is growing rather than getting smaller.'

'Then it is time to leave, while there is still some goodness between you.' His directness literally stopped Karen in her tracks. Rafiq knew nothing about her, and yet she felt instinctively there was sense in what he said. He'd carried on walking and now he turned to face her. He looked pained. 'I have offended you. I am sorry. It is my habit as a surgeon not to give patients false hope. My friends say I should stop treating the rest of the world like a patient.'

'I'm not offended. I'm afraid that you are right.'

230

'What are you afraid of?'

'Hurting someone who spends a lot of time and energy trying to please me.' She gave a soft chuckle. 'And often getting it very wrong.'

'You will hurt him in the short term, but you will hurt yourself more in the long run. You say your man felt like the other half of you. Does it not feel shaming to settle for something less?'

Karen started walking again, giving Rafiq a wide berth as she passed. She walked briskly to the end of the path, staring across at the silent bulk of the Royal Yacht *Britannia*. He was right. He'd barely had a conversation with her, and yet he understood something about her she hadn't been able to articulate.

Rafiq caught up with her. 'I am sorry. My command of English is fine for communicating with other medical professionals. I have not learned British ways.'

Karen shook her head. 'I appreciate your honesty.'

'Perhaps we should talk about something less sensitive. Miran tells me the Scottish people are very agitated about the question of independence from England. Why is this?'

Karen burst out laughing. 'You think that's less sensitive? Rafiq, you've got a lot to learn about Scotland.'

'Then you will have to teach me. If I am going to make a life here ...'

'I'd enjoy that.' As she spoke, Karen realised it wasn't an empty platitude. 'But first ...' she pulled out her phone and headed for Uniqlo. 'We need to sort you out with some clothes.'

231

24

Jason was wearing a path in the grass verge at the side of the pavement when Karen arrived outside the ugly brick and glass box that housed Police Scotland. There were rumours that property developers were circling the site and Karen reckoned there wasn't a serving police officer who would stand in their way. It wasn't only ugly, it was inconvenient, designed for an era when the digital age was barely a twinkle in anyone's eye.

She was pleased to see that not only was Jason wearing his best suit, but he'd persuaded Eilidh to remove the corn rows and give the back of his head a very close trim. 'Looking good,' she said.

Karen had also dressed to impress. She'd taken one suit to Hamish's on the off-chance she might have to do something that required more formality than black jeans and a Seasalt shirt, and she'd teamed it with a subdued navy layer. For all the good that would do either of them. 'Masks,' Karen said, putting on one of the blue disposables that she'd picked up from the pharmacy. She handed another to Jason, shaking her head at Eilidh's garish fabric version. This wasn't the time for individualism.

It took longer than usual to get across the threshold, but

once they were inside it was straightforward. Some poor soul had been given the task of taping lines up the middle of corridors, and the walls had sprouted notices about masks, hand sanitisers and keeping the correct distance. At least the Dog Biscuit couldn't sentence them to that.

There was no sign of life in the anteroom to ACC Markie's office. Karen and Jason sat down on the visitors' chairs, carefully placed well apart, and waited. 'How did she tell me to report here yesterday when she knew she wouldn't be back till morning?' Jason asked.

'At a guess, she wanted you to sit around getting more and more nervous till you were too scared to go home. And then you'd be sleepless and vulnerable.'

Before he could respond, ACC Ann Markie wheeled through the door with the precision of a parade ground manoeuvre. Her eyebrows rose as she took in Karen's presence. 'I wasn't aware of asking for you, DCI Pirie.'

'DC Murray is a valued member of my team, ma'am. I felt it was appropriate for me to be here.'

Markie strode past them and into her office. 'Come in. And don't bother sitting down, you're not going to be here long.'

They exchanged a look – Karen irritated, Jason apprehensive – and followed her. Her office was brighter than the anteroom and although Markie was as perfectly turned out as ever, Karen thought she didn't look exactly camera-ready. There were bags under her eyes, and her make-up, normally flawless, seemed to sit awkwardly on her skin.

'This pandemic is a national crisis. People are dying every day. And I have to waste my time on officers who think the rules don't apply to them.' Karen was accustomed to Markie's icy delivery, but this time she sounded genuinely angry. 'Do you know why you're here, DC Murray?'

Jason said nothing, suddenly beyond words.

'Shall I enlighten you? You're here because yesterday afternoon, you put on your Police Scotland uniform and forced your way into a COVID ward. In the process, you assaulted a doctor, a nurse and a member of the support staff. Does that stir any memories?'

He shook his head. 'No, because it wasn't me.'

Markie scoffed. 'That's it? "It wasn't me." That's the best you can do?'

'It's the truth. I can prove it.'

'Oh, do delight me with your alibi. No, let me guess. You were in your flat with your devoted fiancée.'

Karen was swiftly losing all patience. 'No, he wasn't. He was in the HCU office in Gayfield Square, working on a case we are investigating as a result of evidence that's recently emerged.'

Markie gave her a basilisk stare. 'Really? I know I instructed you to review old cases, but that doesn't mean abandoning lockdown. You're not supposed to be in the office.'

'DC Murray was working alone. He needed access to office files and computer equipment.'

'That's your alibi, DC Murray? You were alone in a police office?'

'I was making phone calls. I kept a log. You'll be able to confirm it with the phone provider. And the data from the masts will prove I was in Edinburgh, not Kirkcaldy, when I made the calls.' Jason had found his voice. Assertive, not aggressive. And not even slightly whiny. 'Believe me, I'd like nothing more than to sit by my mother's bedside. She's fighting the COVID with everything she's got and I'm not there to support her and I feel like I'm letting her down.

But I never broke the rules. I never went to Kirkcaldy.' Red-faced, hands balled into fists, frustration came off Jason in a wave.

'He's telling the truth,' Karen said.

Markie showed no sign of belief or its opposite. 'So if what DC Murray says is true, who walked into the Victoria Hospital and burst into his mother's COVID ward wearing his uniform with his number on the epaulettes?'

Jason took a deep breath. 'I couldn't say, ma'am.'

Markie tossed her head in a dramatic gesture. 'Well, that's certainly not the truth. I need a name, DC Murray. Who did you give your uniform to?'

'Nobody. I never gave anybody my kit.'

Markie made a noise of annoyance and stood up. 'I take COVID very seriously. *You* both need to do the same. I want a name.' Jason said nothing. 'Very well. DC Murray, you are suspended from duty until this matter is cleared up. Go home and stay there. Now get out of my sight.'

They both turned to go, but Markie said sharply, 'Not you, DCI Pirie. Not yet.'

Jason left the room, misery walking, and cast a glance back at Karen as she spoke. 'Ma'am?'

'Thank you for confirming what I'd already heard about your team. You're working a case, not simply reviewing files? You seriously think a cold case is important enough to break the COVID rules?'

'I'm doing everything I can to stay within the guidelines. But when it comes to giving families answers about the fate of their loved ones, I think delay is insulting. Ma'am.'

'It's more insulting in my book to risk spreading a potentially fatal virus.'

Karen breathed heavily through her nose. 'I can't point to

a single thing I've done in pursuit of this case that breaches the guidelines.'

'You've been working alongside DS Mortimer. In an enclosed space.'

Bloody Bethan Carmichael. 'That's quite true. But we're a bubble. We're sharing a flat. I thought it was better for both our mental health than being in lockdown alone. And there's plenty of room for two.'

Markie's mouth tightened. 'I assigned Mortimer to you because I thought she might be a counterweight to your maverick tendencies. You have to learn there's no I in team.'

'There is in Gaelic.' Karen couldn't help herself.

'What?'

'In Gaelic, ma'am. There is an I in team. Sgioba.'

'We're not in the bloody Gaeltacht.' Her exasperation was unmistakable. 'You know, if you could actually manage to stick to rules that are there for a reason, you'd be amazed to discover how much better a detective you'd be.' She sighed. 'So what's the case you're looking at?'

'The disappearance of Lara Hardie. You remember the case?'

'Of course I do. What's your new evidence?'

Karen looked up at the ceiling. 'It's a bit hard to explain, but I'll do my best.' As she outlined the position, Markie's expression shifted from sardonic incredulity to interest.

'And your theory is?'

'Jake Stein was eaten up with rage and pain at his fall from grace. Discovering his wife was having an affair with Ross McEwen, his friend – probably his only remaining close friend and his chess partner – that gave him an easy target to displace his anger. So he decided to take his revenge by framing his wife's lover for murder. But to make it stick, he'd actually have to commit the crime then lay the false trail for us to pick up.'

Markie almost twitched a smile. 'I think you and DS Mortimer have been spending too much time on the sofa watching box sets. You know this sounds deranged, right?'

Karen did smile. 'I do. But the further down the rabbit hole we get, the more it feels possible. And I never want to let any chance of solving a case go by me.'

Markie sighed. 'To my cost, I know that. Do you even know whether Rosalind Harris and Ross McEwen are an item? If they even know each other, come to that?'

'She admitted she's met him. We're working on it. I want to firm up Stein's encounter with Lara Hardie before I talk to McEwen. I'm trying to work this along the same lines I'd travel if Stein was still alive.' She spread her hands. 'I don't want to frighten the horses.'

Markie walked across her office and stared out the window at the uninspiring view of the Waitrose car park. 'I'll give you a week to get somewhere with this. But that's not carte blanche for you to ride roughshod over the COVID regs. Keep your nose clean, DI Pirie. Or it'll end up bloody.' She flicked her wrist in dismissal.

'That's a chance I'm prepared to take, ma'am.' *Not for the first time.*

But as Karen walked through the empty corridors, she realised the process of outlining events to Markie had shuffled the pack of cards in her head. A glimmer of a different outline had begun to take shape. She imagined Jake Stein out of his mind with rage and pain and deciding he needed to take revenge on the man – and the woman – he'd trusted. He'd frame Ross McEwen for murder. But to do that, he'd have to commit murder.

While he was still in a state of derangement, he'd carried out his heartless plan and killed Lara. He'd set everything up so all he had to do was make an anonymous call to the police and bingo, McEwen would be firmly in the frame.

It still begged the question – why the manuscript? Karen felt she was groping towards an answer. What if Stein had been hit by the runaway train of remorse? What if he felt the need to confess, if only on paper? Well, on screen, anyway? He could have found some penance in writing a sort of expiation that could only be published after his death. When, presumably, McEwen would have served his sentence and been a broken man. Maybe as a writer of fiction, he couldn't help transforming it into the form of a novel? To give himself some emotional distance?

She still had no proof of this; but finally it made a kind of emotional and psychological sense of what they'd read. She needed time and the rhythm of her footsteps by the water to test this mad theory. For now, she'd have to park it. There was other work to be done.

Karen prowled the hushed headquarters, looking for a private space to phone Susie Donaldson. She didn't want to go straight back to the flat. She wasn't ready to rerun the conversation with the Dog Biscuit yet. Even though she told herself Markie was nothing more than a jumped-up bureaucrat, her words still smarted. She didn't have the skills to last a week in the HCU, and yet she revelled in exercising her petty power.

Karen found a deserted office in a short dead-end corridor. It showed no sign of recent occupation, unless you counted a cardboard coffee cup that had things living in it that a biochemist looking for a new vaccine might profitably culture.

She sat as far from it as possible and opened her phone. Jason had pinged everything over to her the night before – 'In case they lock me up . . . ' – so finding Susie Donaldson was easy.

The woman answered her phone almost instantaneously, which Karen thought was impressive this early on a lockdown morning. So many people working from home had come to relish an extra hour in bed, not to mention showing up at their desks in office attire from the waist up and pyjama bottoms from the waist down. And who could blame them? She'd have been doing the same thing herself if sleeping in had been one of her talents. 'Hello?' Susie Donaldson sounded wary, which was hardly surprising. Unfamiliar number early in the morning probably isn't going to be revealing you've won the lottery.

'I'm sorry to bother you so early, Ms Donaldson. My name is Karen Pirie. Detective Chief Inspector Karen Pirie. I'm in charge of the Historic Cases Unit of Police Scotland.'

'I've already spoken to one of your lot. A chap called Murray.'

'DC Murray, that's right. And we're very grateful for the help you've already given us. However, since DC Murray spoke to you, the case has moved along. We now believe this to be a potential murder inquiry, and I'm sure you'll appreciate how much more urgency there is to our investigation.' Karen let that hang there.

'If you say so. Though Historic Cases doesn't sound very urgent.'

It was the opposite of a wholehearted response, and it pushed all Karen's buttons about the importance of what her team did. 'That means we do need to have access to the contact details as well as the names of all the attendees at Jake Stein's workshop.'

'I can't do that. I told your colleague already. There are data protection issues, as I'm sure you're well aware.' The response was brisk.

What Karen was well aware of was the practice of trotting that out as an excuse whether there were any genuine data protection issues or not. It sounded good, it sounded official, but more often than not it was, as Jimmy Hutton said, a fuckton of bollocks. 'No, there aren't. As I'm sure a sheriff will tell me when I waste their time asking for a warrant. This is a murder inquiry. That means withholding evidence is a criminal offence. But I'm in a good mood this morning. I'll give you an hour to run this past your line manager and absolve yourself of responsibility. If I've not heard back from you within the hour, I will be lodging papers with the sheriff court.'

'Don't speak to me like that. I'm not one of your low-life criminals. How do I even know you are who you say you are?'

Karen rolled her eyes. What was it with people just now? Was there a second pandemic of grumpiness brought on by lockdown? This woman had some brass neck. Karen sighed audibly. 'It's very simple. You have my phone number. You can call the police office at Gayfield Square in Edinburgh – or any other police office, probably. Ask them whether this number corresponds to the mobile number for DCI Karen Pirie. They'll be helpful, if you say you're concerned about being scammed. An hour, Ms Donaldson.' She ended the call annoyed with herself for letting a jobsworth wind her up. Still, if it got them further along the road, it would be worth it.

25

Karen was halfway up Leith Walk when her phone vibrated. It was Susie Donaldson, no cheerier. Likely as a result of a conversation with her line manager, whose job Karen did not envy. 'I can send you the list of attendees and their contact details if you let me have your email address,' she said, her voice tight.

'Thanks, that's very helpful,' Karen said sweetly. She recited her email address and got the administrator to repeat it so she couldn't use the excuse of having been given the wrong email. 'If anyone complains about hearing from us, just blame me.'

'Oh, I will,' Donaldson said as she ended the call.

My day for winding people up. By the time she got back to the flat, Karen was longing for a cup of coffee. It was after nine, and she'd skipped one on the way out, not wanting to wake Daisy at half past six. Her sergeant had been in an odd mood when Karen had returned late the previous evening. Whatever was bugging her, Karen hoped a good night's sleep had sorted it out.

She found Daisy already set up at the dining table, laptop open before her. She looked up when Karen came in, and offered a wan smile. 'Morning, boss. How did it go?'

'The Mint's suspended, my coat's on a shoogly peg. The Dog Biscuit wasn't keen on the alibi. As we speak, some poor polis will be trawling through phone mast records, trying to establish the whereabouts of Jason's phone when he was making those calls yesterday. Total waste of time and energy.' She carried on to the kitchen. 'I need coffee.'

Daisy stood up and followed her. 'How's Jason? Any more news about his mum?'

'No change, as far as they're telling him. Poor lad's climbing the walls.'

'Who wouldn't be, in his shoes? So was it his brother that "borrowed" his kit?' Daisy made quote marks in the air with her fingers, not trusting her tone of voice to do it for her.

'Jason's not admitting it, but it's obviously Ronan. He's been a bad boy since he was a teenager and he shows no signs of maturity yet. But Jason's too loyal for his own good – he's not going to grass him up to Markie.' She scooped coffee into the press. 'I might, though.'

'Really?'

'Aye, really. I don't mind Ronan fucking up his own life, but I do mind him fucking up Jason's. If this is still rumbling on by the time Sandra gets home then, yeah, I might just dob him in.'

Daisy looked doubtful. 'What if ... what if she doesn't get home?'

Karen gave her a hard stare. 'Then we'll all have more pressing issues to deal with.' She pressed the plunger with unnecessary vigour.

Back at their makeshift workspace, Karen started in on her coffee. 'So, I spoke to the woman at Invertay. I don't understand nice middle-class, law-abiding people whose instincts are to obstruct us. She's supposed to have sent me the list of people at the workshop,' she added, already distracted by the process of signing in to her laptop. 'Here we go.'

There was an email from Susie Donaldson with an attachment. Karen forwarded it to Daisy, then opened it herself. Sixteen names were listed, each with an email address, a mobile number and the amount they'd paid to attend. It looked as if there were discounts for seniors and for students. Seventh on the list was Lara Hardie. Daisy let out a low whistle. 'Good work, boss. What do we do now?' The arrival of the list had clearly perked Daisy up.

'Did that manuscript of Lara's arrive yet?'

Daisy nodded. 'Just before you got back. I'd barely started reading it.'

Karen paused for a moment. 'OK. You carry on with that, and I'll split the list with Jason. He needs something to stop him climbing the walls. And there's no point in him carrying on with checking out the other events Jake Stein did. We've placed Stein in the same room as Lara. If we're lucky, someone will have noticed an interaction between them.'

'I thought you said Jason was suspended?'

'I know, but he needs to keep occupied, for his own sake, never mind Eilidh's. And who's going to find out? These are just investigative calls. If we need probative statements, we can go back to the witnesses later and put it on the record.'

'Or I could share the calls with you?'

Karen shook her head. 'I need you on Lara's manuscript. You've read Stein's version of events and his notes. We need to check whether there's any crossover and you're best placed to spot that.'

Daisy shrugged. 'Wish me luck.'

'We all need buckets of luck on this one.'

*

This time, it was Jason who got lucky. He'd been anxious about the task; he didn't think he was sufficiently on the ball to do a great job. But Eilidh encouraged him. 'Just concentrate on what's in front of you, doll. You'll do fine.'

Lockdown meant that almost everybody was at home to take their calls; he reckoned it was taking about half the time it would usually consume to get through the preliminary interviews. After a couple of conversations, he'd learned that the workshop had begun with an ice-breaking session. Each attendee – three men and thirteen women – was paired with the person sitting next to them. They had ten minutes to find out some key information about their partner, then they had to introduce them to the group.

The workshop proper involved Jake Stein giving fifteen-minute lectures on aspects of writing, followed by him setting an exercise. They'd have fifteen minutes to complete it, then they'd all read out what they'd written; Stein and the others would give critical comments. 'They're supposed to be constructive criticisms,' Del Morrison had said. 'Mostly they were encouraging, but sometimes Jake cut through the crap and said things that felt a bit like a put-down. Nothing you could really pin down, but the kind of thing you don't want someone to say about your writing.'

'Like what?'

A sigh. 'I can't really remember but he did say to me after the dialogue session, "Such a shame *Take the High Road* isn't on any more."'

'Ouch!' Jason could barely remember the long-running Scottish soap, but he recalled enough to realise Stein's comment had not been complimentary. 'Do you remember anything specific he said to Lara?'

'Not off the top of my head. I don't honestly remember much about her. She was pretty quiet. You know the kind of lassie? Doesn't speak up much, nods a lot at what other people say. She seemed nice enough, just kind of beige.'

Del was the third person Jason had spoken to. Neither of the others had anything more informative to offer. But he struck oil with the fourth. Jenna Butt had been paired with Lara for the first exercise. 'She was very precise,' she said. 'She told me she'd been to a workshop before—'

'When was that?' Jason's ears pricked up.

'I don't remember exactly, but a while back. Anyway, she said she'd made such an idiot of herself the last time that she was determined to get it right this time if we were asked to introduce each other. So she'd prepped. Wish I'd done the same, I ended up babbling like a bubblyjock.'

Jason had no idea what a bubblyjock was, but he didn't think that mattered. 'What do you remember Lara saying?'

'She was a student in Edinburgh. She didn't say which uni or college, but she said she was doing English. She was doing a module in Twentieth-Century Scottish Fiction. Her favourite writer was Muriel Spark. I remember because I've never been able to get on with Muriel Spark. I don't get the way she writes. Do you like Spark?'

'I don't get much time for reading.' His English teacher had tried to get them to read *The Prime of Miss Jean Brodie* and he'd thought it was daft. 'What else did she have to say?'

'She wanted to write crime fiction, mostly because of Kate Atkinson. But she admitted that Jake Stein was her guilty pleasure. And she wished she could write with the kind of pace he had in his books.' Jenna chuckled. 'I thought she was just sooking up to Jake, but no, she really hung on his every word. She took loads of notes. Like he knew the

secrets of the universe and she was going to rip them out
of his hands.'

'Did she ask a lot of questions too?'

Jenna considered. 'Not that I remember. But she did kind
of hang around him at the tea breaks. On the fringes of
the group.'

'Did you talk to her outside the sessions? Like, at the
lunch break?'

'Not so much. There were a few of us hung out together.
We were talking about what we were working on, what
kind of writer we wanted to be.' She chuckled again. 'I said,
"a bestselling one". I don't remember what Lara said.' She
pulled a face. 'To be honest, I don't think I'd even remember
this much if she hadn't been all over the media when she
went missing. I didn't even notice it at first, it was one of the
other women at the workshop who DM'd me. We'd stayed
in touch because we're both writing sort of feminist coun-
terfactuals, and she called to say Lara was all over Twitter.'

'Do you mind telling me who that was?'

'She must be on your list, right? Alice Barker.'

'She's here, yes.' And he'd already spoken to her.

'She was talking to Lara outside in the car park at the end
of the event. That's why she remembered her.'

Jason put an asterisk next to the name on his printout.
Why would Alice Barker have pretended not to know
anything about Lara Hardie? 'Did she say what they
talked about?'

'Just that it had been a good workshop. Lara probably
didn't get a chance to say anything, Alice was so full of how
brilliant it had been and how much she'd learned about
story structure.'

'Fair enough. Is there anything else you can remember

about that day? Anybody else Lara talked to? Anything about what she was writing?'

'Sorry, officer. I've shot my bolt. Listen, good luck finding out what happened to Lara. She seemed like a nice lassie. It's hard to imagine her provoking anybody to violence, you know what I mean?'

'My boss always says it's never the victim's fault. Being violent is always an active choice, she says. So if something bad happened to Lara, it wasn't about what she did or how she was. It was about a choice somebody else made.'

A moment's silence. Then Jenna said, 'Wow. Your boss sounds amazing.'

'She is. Thanks for your help, Jenna, you've been a star.'

Jason sat staring at his phone. He needed to process what Jenna Butt had told him. He didn't want to send the voice recording of his interview to Karen until he'd cleared up the disconnect between what Jenna and Alice Barker had said. There had to be a reason for Alice not to be honest with him. Sometimes people lied about contact with victims for innocent reasons, like they were afraid of being caught up in something embarrassing. Or they didn't want their partners to find out.

But sometimes the reasons were less innocent. It was hard to work out how Alice Barker might fit into their theory of what had happened to Lara Hardie. Jason was well aware that he wasn't the sharpest knife in the block, and this was one of those times when he feared there might be a simple explanation he wasn't seeing. It wouldn't be the first time.

What would Phil do? It was his touchstone for so many of his decisions. The answer wasn't always immediately obvious. But this time it was. 'Talk to the boss,' he said aloud, picking up his phone again.

26

Frustration was buzzing in Karen's veins as she ended the penultimate call on her list. Yes, people remembered Lara, mostly because a few weeks after the workshop, her face had been everywhere. Online, in print, even on TV. Her parents making an appeal that almost everyone believed would be fruitless. But Lara's fellow aspirants on the writing seminar recalled almost nothing. Quiet. Not pushy. Attentive. 'Keen to write propulsive crime fiction,' was the most informative line she'd got. There wasn't even anyone trying to big-up their connection for a place in the limelight.

She was about to make her final call when her phone rang. Jason. Every time his name appeared on her screen now, she feared the worst. 'Jason. I hope you're having more luck than me.'

'A wee bit, I think. I've just pinged you a voice memo from my last call. When you've listened to it, can I talk to you? There's this lassie, Alice Barker. She denied that she'd even noticed Lara. But one of the others says different.' Hesitant, flat. He didn't sound at all like himself.

'Sure. Ronan been in touch? Any more news about your mum?'

'I spoke to the hospital earlier. She's still very poorly, they said, but she's not any worse.' A catch in his voice. 'She must be feeling like we've deserted her.'

Karen doubted whether he was right. If Sandra was consciously feeling anything, she suspected it would be abject terror. 'She knows you'd be there if you could,' she said, noting he hadn't mentioned his reprobate brother. 'I'll call you when I've listened to the interviews.'

Jason's interviews were less illuminating than she'd hoped, though it did seem clear that Lara was impressed by Stein. And like Jason, she also wondered what was going on with Alice Barker. She rang him back. 'Alice Barker,' she said.

'Yeah. When I spoke to Jenna, she said Alice had spoken to Lara outside. That it had been Alice who brought Lara's disappearance to her attention. But Alice told me she barely remembered Lara and didn't speak to her.'

'So either Jenna's being quite the bitch about Alice being self-obsessed or Alice lied to you.'

'Jenna's her pal,' he protested.

'I reserve some of my best bitchiness for my pals,' Karen said wryly. 'But you're right, it's way more likely that Alice is being economical with the truth. Call her back and confront her with it.'

A pause. 'You want *me* to do it?'

'Why not? You're more than capable. You want me to hand it over to Daisy?' Who immediately perked up, like a terrier whose leash has been taken off its hook.

'No, but I'm suspended. Alice Barker could turn out to be a probative interview. And then we'd be stuffed if it ever came to court.'

'The way this is going, it's never going to go to court because the man we believe to be the perpetrator is dead.'

'We might be wrong. Then we'd be stuffed.'

Karen was startled to be put on the back foot by Jason. But she couldn't deny he was right. 'Jings, Jason, you're more on the ball than me today. You're right. Leave it with me, then. I'll do it.'

'Is there anything else I can be doing?' His voice was plaintive.

She was momentarily at a loss. 'Tell you what, I'll drop off a copy of the original manuscript at the HCU office. You can pick it up from there and go through it. A fresh pair of eyes, and all that. Keep it on the down low, though. I doubt the crew at Gayfield Square will have heard you're on suspension, but let's not tempt fate.'

A sigh of relief. 'Thanks, boss. I'll do that.'

'And let me know if you hear any more from the hospital.' A pause. 'Or Ronan.'

Karen was itching to talk to Alice Barker, but she knew she had to get the manuscript over to the office. Jason would already be out the door and striding up Leith Walk. 'I'll be back soon,' she said.

'I could go,' Daisy said. 'You've already had to go out today.'

Karen sighed. 'I don't want you to lose the thread of what you're reading.'

Daisy pulled a face. 'Trust me, this is not going to win the Golden Thistle. I'd be glad of a wee break.' Karen simply handed her *The Vanishing of Laurel Oliver* and the accompanying outline notes. 'See you later,' Daisy said cheerily. 'I might have to make a wee detour on the way back to the Tesco on Picardy Place. We're out of crisps and chocolate. And I'd kill for a fruit scone.'

Not for the first time, Karen envied Daisy's ability to

250

consume massive amounts of fattening carbs without ever seeming to put on a kilo. The christening fairy had not given Karen the gift of a high-speed metabolism; all the things she most enjoyed eating took swift revenge. If it wasn't for her habit of long night walks, she'd be the size of a house. It wasn't fair. When she'd complained about this to Hamish, he'd laughed and said, 'But you got the brains instead.' Sometimes it didn't feel like an equivalence.

Like now. Karen wasn't easily discouraged, but this case wasn't playing to her strengths. When she conducted interviews, whether with witnesses or suspects, she liked to see them. The way they sat; the set of their shoulders; how the small muscles of their faces responded; the unconscious reactions of their mouths and eyes; when they were still and when they fidgeted: all of that helped her form a sense of when they were moving away from truth. Even the movement of their feet. She remembered once watching an episode of a cop series where the director had kept returning to shots of the suspect's feet. It had been strangely compelling, offering a previously unconsidered bit of body language to process.

Phil had once said she should write a book on how to read people. There were two problems with that. For one thing, everything she tried to write turned out like a police report, even Valentine cards. But more importantly, she didn't know how to formulate the way she arrived at her conclusions. The nearest she could get was that it was a mixture of experience and instinct, and those were two things that couldn't be taught.

She listened again to the recording of Jason's interview with Jenna Butt, making a couple of notes as it played. Then she put her earphones in, the better to hear variations in tone, and called Alice Barker's mobile. It rang out

251

half a dozen times then a voice said, 'Hello? Who is this?' Even in those four short words, Karen recognised educated Edinburgh, a voice accustomed to being attended to.

'Detective Chief Inspector Karen Pirie of the Historic Cases Unit of Police Scotland.' She scoffed. 'Sorry, it's a bit of a mouthful.'

'What's this about? I spoke to one of you already today. Don't you communicate with each other?'

It sounded to Karen as if she was moving as she spoke. The closing of a door confirmed that. 'We do. And that's why I'm making this follow-up call. I need to clarify some things you said to my junior officer.'

'Clarify what? He asked me about someone who was at a writing workshop with me more than a year ago. I barely noticed her.'

'I'm afraid that doesn't tally with what one of your fellow attendees remembers.'

'Well, they're wrong. What I told the other officer is all I have to say.'

'One of our other witnesses has told us that you talked to Lara Hardie for a few minutes after the workshop was over.'

A beat. 'They're mistaken.'

'All I want to know is what you talked about. What Lara Hardie said to you. It's probably nothing relevant to our inquiries, but I need to be sure I've covered every angle that might shine a light on her disappearance.'

'And I've told you the conversation never took place.' There was a nervous edge to her repeated denials.

'Alice, this is a potential murder inquiry. Lara's parents deserve to know what happened to their daughter. Withholding evidence isn't only a potential crime, it's also a cruelty.'

252

'This is harassment.' Her voice had thinned to a hiss. 'I could complain about this. My father's a minister in the Scottish Government. You didn't know that, did you?' Defiant now.

Karen hadn't known that, but it explained a lot. The last thing the daughter of a government minister would want was to be associated with a murder victim, no matter how tangentially. Being put on trial on the unregulated battle-field of social media wouldn't just be harsh for her; it could impact on her father. 'Then he'll understand the importance of telling the truth. Look, you needn't worry about this coming back to bite you. Nobody in my team is going to mention your name outside our office. And you're not going to end up testifying in court.' *Not unless Lara told you Jake Stein had threatened to kill her.*

'I'm going to report you for harassment.'

'Well, that's your prerogative.' Karen kept her tone light and warm. 'But that's when you *will* end up all over the socials. I can guarantee the silence of my team, but I can't say the same for the rest of my colleagues. It grieves me to say it, but some of them have a hotline to their pet journalists.'

A long pause. Karen was afraid Alice was about to hang up on her. Then she spoke, her words tumbling over each other in a rush. 'Yes, all right, I did speak to Lara. We both agreed it had been a fantastic day and that the takeaways had been useful for both of us. She said she'd been recommended to come by another writer she knew, because she needed to write with more pace.'

'Did she mention which other writer had recommended Stein?'

'I didn't ask. I said I'd been impressed with the clarity of

253

his session on story structure. And that was that. You see? No big deal. It's not like I was hiding some deep dark secret. It was just a little white lie.'

'Thank you. You were worried about how your dad would react if you got dragged into a murder inquiry, and I get that. But all that happened is that your little white lie made you stand out. Made you look suspicious.' Karen sighed. 'I don't think we'll need to talk to you again, Alice. But in future, if you're interviewed by the police, I'd recommend you not to try the little white lies.'

Alice cleared her throat. 'You don't know what it's like. Every time I do anything, even if it's just to make a comment in a seminar at uni, some dickhead tweets a sarky comment.'

'I'd hate that if it was me. But if it gets out of hand, you can report them. To the university, if it's fellow students. Or to us, if you feel threatened.'

Alice scoffed. 'Yeah, right. Have you ever *been* on Twitter? Anyway, I've told you all I know about Lara Hardie, so you can leave me alone from now on, right?'

'Thanks. I hope we don't have to talk again.'

'Me too.'

And the line went dead. Just like that line of inquiry. Alice Barker's reticence was nothing to do with Lara, and everything to do with a father who regularly garnered more than his fair share of negative headlines, a fate that rubbed off on his daughter. Karen felt a moment of relief that the only time her parents had ever troubled the media was when her dad had won the Men's Championship at the local bowling club.

She climbed the spiral staircase to the garden room on the roof and watched the clouds slowly moving up the estuary, driven by a strong east wind. It had been a rough day so far, and there was still more to come. At moments like these, when a case seemed to be hitting the buffers, Karen would normally seek the company of her friends. Not to discuss the case, but to loosen the tightened gears of her brain. A Thai curry with social work manager Giorsal; a Vietnamese meal with forensic anthropologist River Wilde; a gin evening with Jimmy Hutton; or a night in with a pizza and a movie with Hamish. All of those companions were available online but like millions of others, Karen had already come to the conclusion that digital meeting places were a pale simulacrum of reality. It was easy to have superficial conversations, albeit with limited gossip. But anything beyond that felt contrived and artificial.

COVID was taking far more of a toll than the lives of those who succumbed to it. It was already damaging the fabric of the relationships that bound people together, she thought as she gazed across the city. All the lonely people; wasn't that how the song went? COVID had turned everyone into Eleanor Rigby.

She was jolted out of her reverie by the phone. Jason. Had he spotted something in Jake Stein's manuscript that she and Daisy had missed? Karen took the call and heard ragged breathing. 'Jason? Are you OK?'

'It's my mum. Boss, they're definitely going to put her on a ventilator. They say it's to help her breathe, but I'm really scared.' His voice cracked and broke. He sniffed.

'They know what they're doing, the doctors. The ventilator, it's there to help her breathe. To make it easier on her.' She tried to sound as if she meant it, that it was no big deal.

'They're going to—' He choked back a sob. 'They're going to set up a FaceTime. On a tablet. Because . . . ' More throat

255

clearing. 'She'll not be able to speak after they put her on the ventilator. Karen, this might be the last time she gets to speak to me.'

'Don't be thinking like that, Jason. People go off ventilators all the time, they come out of ICU and go home—'

'Phil didn't. He went into ICU and never came home.'

Karen squeezed her eyes tight shut and gripped the phone so hard her fingers hurt. 'You have to be strong for Sandra. Help her to believe she'll make it through this. Have you heard from Ronan? Does he know what's happening?'

A hiccuping sob. 'I've not spoken to him. I don't know where he is. His phone's turned off. But he'll be phoning the hospital every day. Fuck, I hope he gets the message in time.'

'Are you still at home?'

'I was just about out the door on my way to the office when I got the call.'

'Stay put with Eilidh. Make your call. Tell her how much she means to you.' She forced a small chuckle. 'You'll be as embarrassed as hell when Sandra comes home and reminds you of all the things you said. But say them anyway. And when you feel ready, give me a call and let me know how you're doing.'

'Aye. I will.'

'And tell her I was asking for her. Not that she'll care, but I think a lot of Sandra.'

Jason ended the call with a strangled noise that might have been a farewell or simply the point where control had gone. Karen's eyes were damp; she cared about Jason and Sandra, and that made her think about her own parents. She'd grown apart from them in her teens. Not in a hostile way. Just a lack of common ground. They'd wanted her to go to university but she couldn't see the point. She wanted to become a polis, sooner rather than later. And in a way, she thought, they'd never quite forgiven her for not living up to their aspirations. But the thought of losing one – or both – of them to COVID made her feel nauseous.

How much worse it must be for Jason, whose bond with his open-hearted mother was so important to him. Karen wished there was something she could do. But she couldn't even give him a hug.

'Fucking COVID,' she murmured, sliding down the glass wall till she was sitting on the floor, arms around her knees. It had dawned on her that the person she really wanted to talk to was beyond her reach, and not because of the pandemic. The image of Phil Parhatka shimmered in her mind's eye. She gave up on blinking back the tears and let them fall.

27

The sound of the front door closing dragged Karen back into the moment. She rubbed her cheeks dry and wiped her eyes with the back of her hand. The last thing she wanted was for Daisy to see her vulnerable. She got on well with her sergeant, but not well enough to count her a friend yet. Karen blew her nose and descended the stairs to find Daisy emptying her backpack of all the things that didn't make it on to the supermarket shopping list that Karen had written. Three large assorted bars of chocolate, two family-sized bags of crisps, a macaroon bar, two packets of scones – one plain, one sultana – and, bizarrely, Flamin' Hot Wotsits Giants. Karen had always hated Wotsits of any description. She loathed the way the aerated corn snacks stuck to her teeth. No temptation there, then.

'I left the manuscript in the office. I didn't see Jason, so I stayed inside the rules,' Daisy said over her shoulder as she put her treasure trove in the cupboard.

'After you'd gone, I told him to stay put with Eilidh. He's not going to be in any fit state to scrutinise a manuscript. They're putting Sandra on a ventilator.'

Daisy's eyes widened. 'Oh no. That's really scary. How's he holding up?'

Karen shook her head. 'Not well. He's clearly terrified.' She looked away, staring through the window at the New Town roofs. 'All he can think about is that Phil – my partner, I expect you know the story – Phil was in intensive care on a ventilator after he was run over, and he didn't come out the other side. So Jason thinks this is a death sentence for his mum.'

Daisy stopped what she was doing and said, 'I didn't know the details about Phil. Poor Jason. And poor you, too. It must bring it all back.'

Karen turned to meet her stricken gaze. 'It never goes away, Daisy. It never goes away.' A wan smile. 'I hope you never have to find out.'

'Me too.' She cleared her throat. 'I'll just crack on with reading Lara's deathless prose, then.' She settled down at the table, a block of chocolate Turkish delight beside her, and frowned at the page. 'Stein must have chosen her because he thought she was so desperate to be a writer. It couldn't have been because of the writing.'

'I'd have thought that was obvious. If she'd had a genuine flair for it, somebody would have picked up on it earlier. Somebody who wasn't looking for someone to kill.' She returned to the kitchen and stared into the fridge. 'I need to do something with those chicken thighs,' she said, half to herself.

'Spanish chicken. We've got the end of a chorizo and there's peppers and onions. And I think there's a sweet potato too,' Daisy suggested.

'Good idea.' Karen grabbed the items and started prepping the vegetables. 'How are you getting on with Lara?'

'It's not what I'd call a fun read. It's all a bit immature, to be honest. Her protagonist is supposedly in a long-term

259

relationship with a guy who's suspected of murder, but honestly, it's about as passionate as sucking a gobstopper. Very teen romance.'

'There is a market for that, I'm told.'

Daisy pulled a face and groaned. 'Give me half an hour and I'll be done. Then I can read you some of the most toe-curling bits.'

Karen quartered onions, sliced peppers and was about to chop the sweet potato into chunks when a cry of, 'Oh, fuck!' rang out so loudly she nearly stabbed her hand.

'What is it?'

'You've got to come and look at this.' Daisy beckoned her to her laptop screen.

Karen looked over her shoulder and read:

PART THE SECOND

If you're a student of true crime, you've probably already read the official version of the events of the night of May 9th, 2014 in New Orleans, as outlined above. Trust me, the truth is far stranger than the fictions constructed by the powers that be. It had nothing to do with shrewd detection and everything to do with my pal Joey's natural-born instinct for mayhem.

But what I knew about that night was only one small piece of a jigsaw I only managed to piece together seven years and three deaths later.

'Is that not in Stein's notes? Or something like it?'

'Word for word,' Daisy confirmed. 'But look. Here's the next page.' She scrolled down and broken lines appeared on the page.

The only way I could make sense of what I'd seen with my own eyes was to throw out everything I thought I knew about Guy. I remembered an e e cummings poem that had stuck in my head for years.

> *let them go – the*
> *truthful liars and*
> *the false fair friends*
> *and the boths and*
> *neithers – you must let them go they*
> *were born*
> *to go*

If I cleared out everything I thought I knew, I could start afresh and come to the truth that way.

'How could Jake Stein have quoted these exact bits of text unless he'd read Lara's manuscript?' Daisy's tone was incredulous.

Karen took it as a rhetorical question. 'I suppose he could argue that he was quoting from her to make his story sound more authentic ...' She wasn't even convincing herself, never mind Daisy.

'Not quoting so much as stealing. He was thumbing his nose at Lara. It wasn't enough to kill her, he had to humiliate her, even if he was the only one who knew it.'

Karen stared at the screen, her expression grim. 'He'd found his victim.'

28

There was always a point in an investigation where Karen felt the tangle of evidence start to unravel. She had the sense that they were teetering on the edge of organising the disjointed bits and pieces they'd amassed. Get it wrong now, and it might never work out. But get it right, and they'd have the answer to what had happened to Lara Hardie.

Thrilled by her discovery, Daisy needed to let off steam and decided to go for her official exercise while Karen cooked dinner. 'I'm going to go up Calton Hill,' she announced. 'That'll blow the cobwebs away.'

'Enjoy yourself,' Karen said absently. She found shallots and peppers, a slightly soft beetroot and half a bulb of fennel and began peeling and chopping. But her hands were on automatic pilot. What was going on behind her eyes was a very different process. She was sifting and sorting, adjusting and adapting, searching for the right route to resolution. She turned on the oven, chopped up the chorizo, unwrapped the chicken and patted it dry. She paused in mid-action as something struck her afresh.

Chorizo into the hot roasting tin, followed by a generous slug of chilli and garlic oil. Then the chicken, followed by the vegetables. Karen gave them a good rummle around then

slammed them into the oven. Cooking was the best distraction, she reckoned. The only trouble was that sometimes she
was so rapt that a crucial ingredient went on the missing list.

That evening, though, everything went to plan. Daisy
returned just as Karen was giving the roasting tin a final
shake. 'Three minutes,' she said, reaching for a bottle of
full-on Australian Shiraz. Daisy's eyebrows rose. Wine was
usually reserved for the weekend, a mutual decision at the
end of the first week of lockdown after they realised there
were eight empty wine bottles in the recycling bin. 'We
deserve it,' Karen said. 'I'm worried about Jason and his
mum and his fuckwit brother.'

They said little as they ate, but once they'd cleared their
plates, Karen said, 'I'm starting to see the way forward here.
It's almost exactly a year since Lara went missing. I think
it's time we talked to the family.'

Daisy seemed surprised. 'Won't that be giving them false
hope? If we rock up after all this time, they'll be expecting
us to have something positive to tell them.'

'That's why the anniversary works in our favour. It's not
like we're showing up out of the blue for no reason, which
really would be a major indication of progress.' There was
no arguing with Karen when she adopted that tone of voice.
'I'm going to call them and ask for a meeting.'

'Face to face?'

'They live in Perth. The place is full of parks and outdoor
spaces. The weather forecast's good for tomorrow – I checked.
I'm going to call them now and see if I can set something
up.' She stood up and headed for the table laden with files.
A quick search turned up the Hardie family details. Janet
and Andrew, and their daughter Emma, still living at home.

Karen took a deep breath and keyed in the landline,

aware of Daisy's eyes on her. It rang half a dozen times, then a young woman's voice said, 'Hello?'

'Is that Emma?'

'Speaking. Who is this, please?'

'I'm Detective Chief Inspector Karen Pirie from Police—'

'Have you found Lara?' Excitement and trepidation in those few words.

'I'm sorry, I don't have any news to give you.'

'Oh.' Crestfallen.

'But I was hoping I could meet you and your parents. To reassure you we're still investigating her disappearance. I know it's coming up for a year since Lara vanished and it might be helpful for me to talk to you all.'

'Helpful how? We told you everything, again and again.'

Karen dug deep. 'Sometimes things surface after a while. Would you be willing to meet?'

A long pause. 'How can we meet? We're in lockdown, remember?' Frustration creeping in now.

'Police officers are allowed to travel further than the five-mile limit when we're working. I thought we could get together safely somewhere out of doors. The weather's quite mild, and I know Perth has a lot of green space in the city. I could drive up tomorrow and meet you in the morning, somewhere that suits you.'

'I don't know. I'll have to ask Mum and Dad if they want to.'

'I understand. I'll give you my number and maybe you could call me back?'

'OK. But I'm not sure they'll be up for it. My dad especially. But I'll ask.' She ended the call abruptly.

Daisy gave Karen the thumbs up. 'That sounded pretty positive.'

'I'm not holding my breath. The lassie was all over the place, and no wonder. Let's see what happens next. Come on, it's time for some crap telly.'

As instructed, at ten precisely the next morning, Karen walked up the path of the Hardies' house. It was a solid Victorian semi-detached villa set back from the Glasgow Road. In normal times, there would be a steady flow of traffic on the busy arterial road, but this morning scarcely a car passed. She rang the bell, took a couple of steps back and waited. The door opened a crack and a young woman's face appeared. The resemblance to Lara Hardie was striking. 'I'm DCI Pirie,' Karen said.

'Yeah, I googled you. Your photo in the papers doesn't flatter you, but I can see it's you. Come round the side of the house to the back garden, we can sit out there.'

Karen wanted to say that grief was the most effective diet she'd ever known, but thought better of it. Emma Hardie was allowed to be rude; she wasn't. There was a wooden gate in the wall leading to the garden, but it was unfastened. She emerged into a riotous flower bed surrounding a neat lawn. Crocuses, dwarf irises, varieties of narcissi and grape hyacinths. It was an unexpected riot of colour in April in Scotland. She had to drag her eyes away from the display to the two women standing by the entrance to a conservatory. Emma she knew; the other woman was an older edition of her two daughters. The same bone structure, the same dark blue eyes. The complexion was similar, except that a network of fine lines surrounded her eyes and her mouth.

'What a beautiful garden,' Karen exclaimed.

'It keeps me busy,' Janet Hardie said, her voice listless.

Emma waved towards a picnic table, the sort with an attached bench on either side, much beloved by pubs, not least because drunken rowdies couldn't throw the chairs. Karen didn't think that had been a consideration here.

'I thought we could sit here. Mum and me on one side, and you at the opposite end on the other side,' Emma said firmly.

The three women arranged themselves as Emma had suggested. 'What about Mr Hardie?' Karen asked.

Emma looked away, reaching for her mother's hand. 'Dad's not joining us. He doesn't have a very high opinion of the police anyway, and when we looked you up online and saw you were in charge of the Historic Cases Unit, he got really upset. You didn't tell me you were a cold case detective when we spoke last night.'

'None of us thinks Lara's disappearance is a "cold case", as you call it. It's not even a year since she was taken.' Janet Hardie fixed Karen with a disdainful look. 'And you're no nearer catching the person who took her.'

'It would probably be more accurate to call my team the Unresolved Cases Unit. But the powers that be think that draws too much attention to our occasional lack of success. So they call us the Historic Cases Unit. It's not because these cases don't matter. They do. We take them very seriously. We've had some remarkable results and we bring the same commitment to every case that crosses our desks.'

'Fine words. But what does that actually mean?' Now there was anger seeping through Janet's calm facade.

'It means we go back to the beginning and reread every statement and check that every loose end was pursued. But one of the most important things we do is go back to the families and the partners of the missing person and listen to them talking about the one who isn't there. Informal conversation sometimes brings new things to light.'

'You said that on the phone,' Emma said with a sigh. 'Do you not think if there was anything relevant we'd have told you by now?'

'I'm sure you would have. But we don't always recognise what's relevant. And that's why I wanted to hear you talking about Lara as you remember her.'

'She was a lovely girl,' Janet said. Karen noted the past tense. This was a family who had managed to admit their daughter wasn't coming home. It was unusual, in her experience, for families to be so pragmatic. 'People talk about hormonal teenagers arguing and getting into trouble, but Lara was never like that. She never slammed a door, never called us names, never gave us a reason to worry.'

'Not like me,' Emma said. 'I was the difficult one. "Why can't you be more like Lara," was what I always heard. Here and at school. But I didn't resent her. You couldn't resent Lara, she was too much fun. She could always make me laugh when I was getting on my high horse.'

'She was a clever girl.' Janet again.

'She worked really hard.' It was a gentle corrective. 'I always got better grades, Mum, and I was totally lazy. She wasn't stupid, don't get me wrong. But Lara had to graft for everything.'

'She was just more thorough than you. You've always been slapdash.'

Emma pursed her lips. It was clearly not the first time she'd felt diminished by the comparison with her sister.

'Why did she choose English at university?' Karen wanted to move away from the contention.

'She loved reading. From being a little girl, she always

had her nose in a book. She got that from her dad. Andrew's always been a big reader and he got both the girls started young, first on comics and then books. He'd have loved to go to university and do English, but he had to go into the family firm.'

'We make tourist tartan,' Emma said. 'Scarves, teddy bears, umbrellas. We supply the fabrics. It's a dying trade. The Chinese and the Bangladeshis undercut us all the time nowadays. Thankfully that means I won't be corralled into the family business like Dad was.'

'So Lara was following your dad's dreams?'

'It wasn't like that,' Janet said wearily. 'She was her own person. She loved words and she wanted to be a writer herself.'

Karen hugged herself inwardly. She hadn't had to drag the conversation round to what she wanted to talk about. 'Was that something she'd always wanted?'

'She was a great storyteller, right from being a wee lassie. Whenever we went anywhere in the car, Lara would see something interesting and make up a story about it. She kept us all entertained.'

Emma looked less entranced. 'She was always reading me poems she'd written when we were teenagers. They were pretty lame, but her ambition was real. And she worked hard at it. She used to tell me the trick of being a writer was in the rewrites, and she reworked everything she wrote. She'd sit with a thesaurus, trying to find a better way of expressing what she thought.'

'She was always writing short stories and sending them off to magazines. She even managed to get a couple published in *The People's Friend*.' Remembering this, Janet thawed.

Emma rolled her eyes. 'That was before she started uni.

She never mentioned *The People's Friend* to her cool student pals. And who could blame her? It's not exactly a ticket to a publishing contract.'

'Did she ever consider doing a creative writing course?' Karen steered the conversation away from Lara's juvenile successes.

'Edinburgh doesn't do creative writing modules at under-grad level. But Dad was so keen for Lara to go to Edinburgh, she went there to please him. She always wanted to please,' Emma said.

'That's not fair, Emma. Lara wanted to go to Edinburgh because it's one of the best universities in the world. And you don't need to do a degree in creative writing to become a successful writer.'

Emma shrugged. 'She was talking about doing a Masters in creative writing at Edinburgh. She thought it was the best way to hone her skills.'

'But a Masters? That was quite a way off, she still had more than a year of her degree to go. What was she doing in between? Apart from reading, obviously.'

Emma grinned. 'She was fangirling.'

Janet gave a sharp sigh. 'That's not a very nice way of put-ting it. Lara thought listening to other writers talk about their work would help her develop good habits. And quite right too.'

'She listened to a shedload of podcasts. And she went to readings, when she could afford it.'

'You make it sound like we kept her short of cash,' Janet complained. 'If she'd ever asked for a sub to go to a book event, I'd have happily given her the money.'

'She liked to think she was standing on her own two feet,' Emma said. 'I don't have the same issue, do I, Mum?' She gave her mother a gentle dig in the ribs.

Janet almost smiled. 'No, you certainly don't.'

'I'm going to be a fashion designer,' Emma said. 'I've got an internship at the V&A in Dundee.'

'Well done. Did Lara sign up for workshops as well as going to readings?'

Emma shrugged. 'She didn't have much cash for something expensive like that. But she did manage to scrape the money together a couple of times. She earned a few quid working in the kitchen at the Film House on Lothian Road and she spent the cash on doing a workshop a couple of months before . . . ' Her voice tailed off.

'Was that with Jake Stein? I saw something about that in the file.'

'No, that was the second one she went to. She signed up for his workshop on the recommendation of the guy who was running the first one. He told her she needed to work on pace and suspense and that Jake Stein was the master at that. It didn't hurt that she was already a big fan. She's got all his books.'

'Do you remember who gave Lara the recommendation?' Karen tried to keep her tone light.

Emma frowned. 'What was his name?' She looked up into the heavens for inspiration. 'Mum, do you remember?'

Janet shook her head. 'I know he won the Golden Thistle. All his books begin with Re-something . . . '

Karen felt the hairs on the back of her neck rising. *'Restitution. Revenge. Retribution.'*

'That's the one,' Janet said. 'Him. *Rendition*. That was his last one.'

Not De-something, like the fictitious Rob Thomas. But Re-something, like the chess-playing Ross McEwen.

29

Karen sat in her car, pondering what she'd learned from Lara's mother and sister. She didn't like the fact that Andrew Hardie had given their conversation a body swerve. She'd read the initial interviews with all the family members, and he'd been the least forthcoming. He kept repeating that he didn't know who Lara hung out with, he didn't know anything about any boyfriend. They mostly talked about books together. He didn't speak to her on the phone, that was her mother's thing. And he had an alibi for the evening of Lara's disappearance. He'd been at a trade fair in Stirling, at a reception in the castle. He'd provided the names of a couple of people he remembered talking to.

Looking at the interview now, Karen wondered about the timings. Andrew Hardie had got home after eleven and before midnight. Nobody could be more precise than that. It was possible that he'd arranged to meet his daughter somewhere en route, but the question remained how she'd got there. There was no sign of her on CCTV from Waverley or Haymarket stations. She didn't show up on any of the bus cameras either. And if her father had come to Edinburgh to pick her up, he'd have had to leave Stirling right at the start of the reception for the timings to work.

Perhaps more importantly, there wasn't the faintest shadow of a motive. Hardie was clearly proud of his daughter and they shared a love of reading, but there was no hint of anything beyond that. And now she'd met the family, Karen found it even harder to believe. In her experience, when there was sexual abuse within a family, something always seemed off-kilter. She'd have been hard-pressed to define it, but it was an undercurrent to be picked up on.

Right now, he felt like the least likely suspect, and since they weren't in an Agatha Christie novel, Karen felt confident in putting him to one side. So she turned instead to the nugget of information that had provoked a twitch of interest. Ross McEwen, Jake Stein's regular chess opponent, had led a workshop Lara had attended in the months before her disappearance. Mapping *The Vanishing of Laurel Oliver* on to reality revealed a parallel narrative. Rob Thomas had first met Laurel Oliver at a workshop.

It was time they talked to Ross McEwen. Not least because Karen's musings had shaken something loose in the back of her mind.

Daisy had managed to track down a mobile number for Ross McEwen. It had gone straight to voicemail. She left a message asking him to call back, simply identifying herself as Detective Sergeant Mortimer. She hoped he'd call back before Karen returned; Daisy always liked to have a bone to lay at the boss's feet.

McEwen rang back within twenty minutes. 'Sorry I missed your call, Sergeant. I was on a Zoom with my agent. I don't think we've met before, have we?' He sounded relaxed, his accent a bland Central Scotland.

'No, sir.'

'It's just that I know quite a few cops. In my line of work, it's always good to check things via the horse's mouth. Which unit are you with?'

She didn't want to say, but she couldn't lie either. 'Historic Cases Unit, Gayfield Square.'

'I see.' The second word drawn out. 'So how can I help you?'

'My boss would like to set up a meeting.'

'What's this about, Sergeant?'

'I'm sure DCI Pirie will be able to explain when she sees you. Would this afternoon be convenient?' It was an unfair question. Nobody had a good excuse to cover unavailability except actually having COVID.

'I'm in the middle of writing a book. Is this urgent?'

'It won't keep till you've finished your book, sir.' She let a hint of insolence creep into her voice. 'I'm sure your contacts would agree.'

He sighed, long and loud. 'Three o'clock, then. Do you know the causeway across to Cramond Island? Just by the mouth of the river?'

Daisy wasn't familiar with it, but she knew how to use satnav. 'Yes. Where exactly did you have in mind?'

'There's a car park, it leads past the toilets to an oval of grass. There's a mast in the middle of it. We can meet there and walk along the seafront. Plenty of fresh air between us.'

Karen walked in on the end of this exchange. 'Is that Ross McEwen you're talking to?'

Daisy nodded. 'I've set up a meeting for this afternoon.'

'Nice one. You know, I've been thinking about Rosalind Harris. She was so in command of herself, what you'd expect from a lawyer. But my gut tells me she wasn't telling me the truth, the whole truth and nothing but the truth. And it set me wondering about truth and fiction.'

'Wondering what, exactly?'

Karen prodded *The Vanishing of Laurel Oliver* with a finger. 'If you didn't know anything about the provenance of this text, you wouldn't necessarily think it paints Jamie Cobain in a very flattering light. He's a narcissist and he's a killer, he's misogynist and a bully. If that's Jake Stein writing about himself, he's got a monumental lack of self-awareness.'

'But isn't that a marker of a psychopathic personality?'

'In theory, yes. But he does somehow get under the skin of the rest of his characters; I don't think he's entirely lacking in empathy. I keep coming back to the timeline – when did he write this? Why isn't it finished?'

Daisy leaned back in her chair, frowning in thought. When she replied, she spoke slowly at first then speeded up as she got into her stride. 'Some writers have to feel their way into a story. One American thriller writer I heard on the radio writes a two-hundred-page outline before he starts in on the book itself. Maybe Jake Stein felt the need to write this down like it was a book so that he could make sure he'd considered all the pitfalls? Left no loose ends? Covered all his tracks? Like it was a blueprint for the act itself?'

Karen considered. 'Like a roadmap. And if he did, there would be no need to go back and finish it after the fact.'

'Exactly. So he planned it all out, then carried it out.'

'So why hang on to it?'

Daisy shrugged. 'No idea. But he had committed the perfect crime. He might have felt too proud of his achievement to destroy the rough draft of it.'

It made a sort of twisted sense, Karen thought. 'Except . . .' She let the word hang.

'Except what?'

'The name. He'd have had to go back and change the name so it fitted with Lara. I'm beginning to wonder if it's a kind of confession rather than a blueprint.'

'Not necessarily. He might already have had her earmarked after the workshop.'

Karen shuddered. 'That's cold.'

They drove down towards Cramond, Karen filling Daisy in on her interview with the Hardie women. In return, Daisy shared the fruits of her research into Ross McEwen. 'He's thirty-nine, he was born and raised on the Raploch estate in Stirling.'

'That's one helluva journey, from the Raptap to the bestseller list. You'd never know from his books that he'd ever set foot somewhere that deprived.' The Raploch was notorious among Police Scotland officers. 'The academy of crime,' Karen's first boss had called it. 'You name it, they've got graduates in it.' In fairness, though, the people of the Raptap had successfully campaigned for changes in recent years. Housing had been regenerated and residents had forced a level of respect on the anti-social. Now it was home to the Big Noise Raploch, a children's orchestra that had even played on a BBC Christmas Special. Still, Karen was surprised that McEwen had broken free of his past so comprehensively.

'His mum was a single parent and she was apparently ruthless about his education. He always credits her with his success. He trained as a teacher and he was working in Musselburgh when he published his first novel. His real name is Liam McEwen, by the way. Ross is his middle name. He used it because he thought some of the parents might not like the idea of their little darlings being taught by a man who wrote such dark thrillers.'

'Makes sense. These days, there's always some keyboard warrior ready to stir things up on Twatter. Did he take off right away?'

'More or less. His first one was a word-of-mouth success, and the second one shot up the charts and won the Golden Thistle.'

'Golden Thistle,' Karen scoffed. 'That's a crime in itself.'

'So McEwen jacked in the day job and started writing full time. And just like in the book, he was flying high while Jake Stein's career went into freefall. Only last year, he won the National Short Story Award, which is a big deal, because it's not just crime stories that are eligible.' They turned into a village of narrow streets lined with whitewashed cottages. 'I had no idea this was here,' Daisy said. 'I suppose the prices are sky high.'

'And the way things are going, you'd expect to be flooded on a regular basis.'

'What? Unlike your building?'

'I'm on the third floor. And besides, the clue's in the name. Western Harbour *Breakwater*.' Karen pulled into the car park with fifteen minutes to spare. Only a handful of vehicles were there; although people were permitted to drive up to five miles for exercise, most seemed to prefer to walk from their front doors. In this part of town, after all, they were spoiled for choice.

They walked to the base of the grassy oval and leaned against the wall and waited. The breeze coursing up the estuary cut through any warmth coming from the sun that was dodging the high clouds. Karen pulled her scarf more tightly around her neck. Five minutes before the hour, a man emerged from the car park and started walking towards them. Karen blinked, then drew in her breath sharply. She'd seen that brown tweed butcher's boy cap only the day before yesterday. And the grey tweed overcoat. That might possibly have been coincidence, but this man had the same bustling gait: small tight steps that propelled him along surprisingly quickly.

'What is it, boss?'

'I saw him – or his body double – the other day. Snogging Rosalind Harris.'

Daisy's eyes widened. He was less than fifty metres from them. 'Are you sure?'

'I'd go into the witness box with it.' As he approached, Karen fixed a welcoming expression on her face.

He stopped the regulation distance from them and spread his hands. 'Which measure do you prefer? Two Alsatian dogs or one Richard Osman?' His face crinkled in a smile. The beard hid a lot of it, but it made it to his eyes.

Karen acknowledged him with a nod. 'Mr McEwen? I'm DCI Karen Pirie from the HCU. Thanks for agreeing to meet us today.'

'I'm intrigued. Your sergeant' – he tipped his head towards Daisy – 'wasn't very forthcoming, but on the general principle that I owe so much to your helpful colleagues when it comes to researching my books, I thought the least I could do was agree. Shall we walk?'

Karen shook her head. 'I prefer eye contact, if it's all the same to you.'

He shrugged. 'I'm dressed for the weather. So what's all this about?'

'We've received some new information about the disappearance of Lara Hardie. Do you remember the case?'

'Vaguely,' he said. 'I'm not one of these writers who rips their stories from the headlines. I wouldn't want to run afoul of the laws of libel. So I just make things up.' He gave a rueful grin. 'I'm not a news junkie, especially when I'm nearing the end of a book.'

'Lara Hardie vanished without trace on the twenty-second of April last year. She told her flatmates she was going to the library but she never turned up. There was no sign of her on any of the CCTV cameras between her flat and the library either. She just disappeared from an Edinburgh street.'

'OK, I'll take your word for it. But what has it to do with me?'

'Lara had one ambition. She wanted to be a crime writer.'

He frowned. 'Wait a minute. That's ringing a bell. Lara . . . slim, blonde, twenty-ish? I think she came to a workshop I was running as part of Book Week Scotland. Would that be right?'

He'd got there quickly enough, Karen thought, given that he'd not responded to public appeals when she went missing. But then, he'd already covered his back on that one. 'What do you remember about Lara?'

He raised his eyebrows. 'Not a lot, if I'm honest. There were a couple of really promising writers in that workshop, but she wasn't one of them. I would have given her feedback, but I never had any further contact with her.'

'You didn't come forward when she disappeared.' Daisy stepped into the role of awkward cop.

His brow furrowed. 'Why would I? She came to a workshop months before, I had no further contact with her.'

Karen let that hang a moment. 'Did you make any suggestions about how she might improve her writing?'

He bit his top lip with his lower teeth in an obvious struggle to remember. Then his face cleared. 'She was having problems with pace. Pace and suspense. Neither of those are things that I teach – I've realised I achieve them by instinct, so I don't know how to teach them. I'm good on dialogue, story structure and sense of place. So I told her she'd get better value with somebody else.'

'That somebody else being . . . ?'

He pushed his cap back a little. 'Well, there are plenty to choose from. I suggested Jake Stein. Because I happened to know he had a workshop coming up.'

'You suggested Jake Stein as a mentor to a young woman? A man who had been so comprehensively disgraced for his sexual predation?' Daisy again.

McEwen shook his head. 'Not as a mentor, for fuck's sake. As someone running a workshop with more than a dozen other writers. Someone she could definitely have learned from.'

'Your chess-playing partner,' Karen said mildly. 'Is that how it goes in your world? Put business the way of your pals, regardless of their reputation?'

He sighed and started pacing. Five steps, turn, five steps, turn. 'I felt sorry for him. Jake did a really stupid, offensive thing. And it cost him everything. His reputation, his career, his marriage, his friendships. But he didn't stop being a good writer just because he was capable of something really shitty.'

'You didn't think people would wonder about you? Lie down with dogs, get up with fleas, that sort of thing?' Daisy again.

He stopped and turned to face them. 'No. My friends, my colleagues – they know who I am.'

'Fair enough,' Karen said. 'I was wondering—'

He cut straight across her. 'You haven't told me what's

come to light about this woman. And what it's got to do with me.'

'I don't know if you're aware that Jake Stein's archive has been bequeathed to the National Library of Scotland?'

He met her eyes in a level stare. 'I didn't know, but I'm not surprised. It's what happens with a lot of writers' papers. And Jake did have a high opinion of himself. He'd expect to be the subject of PhDs, and maybe even a biography. I know they'd approached him about his archive, but they do that to quite a lot of writers. Getting in first before the American universities come in waving wedges of cash. What's Jake's archive got to do with me?'

'There are a couple of unfinished manuscripts there. One of them looks like he might still have been working on it at the time of his death. It's called *The Vanishing of Laurel Oliver.*' McEwen shook his head as she continued. 'Bizarrely, it seems to map on to Stein's life in several respects. It's all about a plot to destroy the man the protagonist plays chess with.'

He gave a disbelieving little laugh. 'And you assumed he must be writing about me? Because we sometimes played each other? Why on earth would Jake want to destroy me? We were friends.'

Karen let the silence draw out. Then she said, 'You're sure there was no reason why Jake Stein would want to frame you for murder?'

'This is insane,' he protested. 'I've told you; we were friends. If he wanted to take revenge on anyone, you'd have plenty to choose from. Publishers, journalists, agents ... Take your pick.'

Karen smiled. 'But none of them was fucking his wife.'

30

The skin round Ross McEwen's eyes paled. 'That's an outrageous thing to say.' His jaw set hard.

'I think it's the truth. As you said yourself, why would he decide to write a plot to destroy you unless he had a very good reason.'

He shook his head, scowling. 'It's a helluva jump from a novel's plot to me screwing Jake's wife.'

Karen gave him a long, measured look. 'As you may have noticed, we were waiting here for you to arrive. It's a habit of mine when I'm meeting people on unfamiliar ground. Two mornings ago, I was waiting to interview Rosalind Harris. Opposite the entrance to the block where she lives. And—'

'Enough,' he said savagely. 'I know what you saw. Yes. Rosalind and I are together now. So what?'

'Jake Stein was trying to fit you up for murder. The perfect murder, he called it. Did he ever mention that to you?'

McEwen's eyes popped. 'Jesus,' he breathed. 'Yes. He talked about a novel celebrating the perfect murder. Where the killer framed someone flawlessly.'

'He was writing it and you were recognisably the man in the frame. Do you remember anything else about it?'

McEwen began his truncated pacing again. 'This is a

nightmare,' he said. He stopped abruptly. 'And you think this has something to do with Lara Hardie's disappearance?'

'We believe it may be connected.' Karen's voice was gentle now. 'What it is you've remembered, Ross?'

He swallowed hard and sank down into a crouch. 'He said ... He said he wanted to make sure it would work so he had to practise it.' His voice had dropped, as if he were talking to himself. 'I thought he was joking.' He clamped his hands over his face and groaned.

Daisy and Karen exchanged looks. Daisy had an air of suppressed excitement. Karen just felt the sadness welling up in her chest. They waited for McEwen to recover himself. Eventually, he stood up again. 'I can't believe it.'

'When did your relationship with Rosalind begin?'

'June 2018. It wasn't something we planned. It happened very quickly and it took us both by surprise. Look, can we go and sit down? I feel a bit shoogly.'

Karen led the way to a bench in an alcove in the wall. She told him to sit down and instructed Daisy to sit on the other bench. 'We'll give anybody else who tries to sit down the bum's rush.' She stood facing them both, hands in her pockets, looked as relaxed as if this was any other day at the shore. 'Tell me about it,' she said.

He stared at the ground between his feet. 'I'd met Ros a couple of times, just hello, goodbye, on our chess nights. I turned up one evening as usual to find that Jake's flight from Leeds had been cancelled. He'd jumped on a train and he wouldn't be back for another hour and a half. I was going to leave, but Ros said he'd been insistent that I stay. She said' – he looked up with a sweet smile – 'she was under orders to keep me there.'

It was a story not so different from the one in the book.

Rosalind had fed him a monkfish curry with coconut rice and he'd asked for the recipe. They found a common interest in eating well and cooking, an interest not shared by Jake. 'You know people who choose wine by the price tag, rather than the contents of the bottle? Jake was like that with food. He'd always choose the most expensive dish on the menu, and he'd just shovel it down without noticing. Ros was wasted on him in every possible way.'

Then they'd run into each other at a cookery writer's event in a bookshop. Jake was away on tour, and she'd invited Ross for dinner. They talked each other to a standstill and ended the evening dazed with infatuation. Jake's book tour lasted ten days; by the time he returned, they were lovers.

'We knew we had to keep our relationship a secret. Jake was incredibly possessive. As far as he was concerned, Ros belonged to him and that was that. If he'd found out, he would have destroyed both of us.'

They'd carried on snatching time when they could, tamping down their greed for each other to avoid taking undue risks. And then Marga Durham had brought Jake Stein's temple crashing down around his ears. And Rosalind walked.

'Why didn't you make it public then?' Karen had asked. She was pretty sure she knew the answer, but she wanted to hear McEwen's version of events.

'Jake was in a state of perpetual rage and pain, like a bull in the ring tormented by the *banderilleros*. He only ever seemed to calm down when we were playing chess. He would rant about Ros – how she was still his, how she could never be rid of him, how she still loved him deep down, how he would destroy any man she took up with.'

283

He spread his hands in a gesture of despair. 'A writer's reputation is a vulnerable thing. Ours is a gossipy world, and I've seen people cold-shouldered and brought down by nothing more than an ill-judged tweet. So I agreed with Ros. We'd keep our relationship under wraps until Jake took ownership of some other poor woman.' McEwen shook his head sadly.

'What I don't understand is why you're still under wraps,' Daisy said, a touch of belligerence to break the soft focus.

McEwen looked momentarily pissed off. Then he almost smiled and said, 'Like I said. Reputation. Jake's only been dead for a few months. I don't want it to look like I couldn't wait for him to drop dead before running off with the woman he professed to love.'

'So how long is respectable?' Daisy again.

He gave her a cool glance and said, 'We reckon about a year should be acceptable.'

Karen studied McEwen, frowning slightly. 'You've been very helpful, Mr McEwen. There's only one thing outstanding. In his manuscript, Jake Stein gave a very full account of the perfect murder he was planning. Right down to where he would dispose of the body to best implicate you.'

'You really think he went through with it? You think he actually abducted Lara Hardie and murdered her? Just to take revenge on me and Ros? That's sick.'

'I can't disagree with that judgement. But I'm afraid we're going to have to search your property. In particular, your garage. Now, we can do this the easy way, where you give us permission because you've got nothing to hide, and DS Mortimer and I come back with you and conduct the search ourselves. Or we can go to the sheriff for a warrant, which complicates everything. Not least, the media are bound to get wind of it. I'm sure you remember the BBC helicopters over Cliff Richard's house?'

'This is crazy,' he said.

'On the other hand, it might not be. And it's my job to find out which of us is right.'

31

Hamish Mackenzie loaded the last box of hand sanitiser into the back of his Land Rover. 'Nice work, Duncan,' he said to the man he'd granted the title of Head Distiller. It didn't matter that he was the only one; experience had taught Hamish that people liked a title. It made them feel their work was important and that made them work harder.

Duncan shut the Land Rover with a grunt. 'Aye. Teegan said she'd bring a sack of the sweetgall down this afternoon so I can get started on a new batch. It smells a wee bit medicinal, folk will think it's the business.'

'It's going gangbusters down in Edinburgh. Between the hand gel and Shona Macleod's tweed masks, we can hardly keep up with the demand.'

Duncan gave him a sideways look. 'Aye. There's always somebody gets the silver lining from the cloud.'

'Might as well be us, Dunc.' Hamish clapped him on the shoulder. 'I'll see you in the morning.'

'You driving back tonight? It's supposed to be blowing a hoolie.'

Hamish shrugged. 'Nothing to trouble the Landie.' He climbed into the driver's seat. 'Or I might just stay the night,' he muttered, his words lost in the engine clattering to life. In spite of torn-faced Daisy Mortimer.

They walked back to the car park, Ross McEwen leading the way. 'I wasn't expecting things to move quite so fast,' Daisy said.

'It wasn't what I'd planned, but it felt like the right decision. When things are moving, it's always worth sticking to the direction of travel. What do you make of him?'

'He seems pretty straightforward. Selfish, but then most men are.'

'To be fair – which always grieves me – he's the one with something to lose if the trolls turn on him. People are still going to go to Rosalind Harris for their wills and probate, regardless.'

McEwen paused by his car. Neither woman was surprised to see it was a silver Toyota Prius. It seemed that Jake Stein liked to be authentic when it came to detail when he could safely be so.

'You lead the way, sir. We'll follow. Give us a minute to get on board.'

They followed him back through the pretty houses of Cramond village and east to the more secluded houses that stood in their own grounds. McEwen led them between tall gateposts up a curving drive to a modern two-storey house with almost as much glass as wall. At one end was a tall white tower whose top storey had windows all round. 'Looks like somebody dumped a lighthouse in the wrong place,' Karen said. She drew up behind McEwen. If he decided to make a run for it, it would be slightly harder for him to swing his car round.

When she stepped on to the drive, Karen caught a glimpse

of the garage, set back beyond the house. She tipped her head towards it, and Daisy nodded. McEwen led the way round the side of the house to a door opposite the garage twenty feet away. 'I usually go in through the kitchen,' he said, hanging cap and overcoat on a hook as they entered. 'Saves me trailing mud or sand through the house.' They stepped into the kind of kitchen that features in interiors magazines. Instead of the usual granite and steel, this was all oiled woods and soft lines. Drawers had their uses carved into their faces in cursive script; cutlery, serving spoons, utensils, tea towels. The cupboards followed the trend – cups, plates, wine glasses, tumblers, pasta, sauces, baking, rice & noodles, oils, vinegars, herbs, spices. Handy for those days when you couldn't remember your own name. A shelf of high-end cookbooks confirmed McEwen's claims of sharing foodie tendencies with his lover, as well as both an Aga and a gas range cooker.

Daisy and Karen automatically masked up; McEwen didn't bother. Careful to keep her distance, Karen walked around the perimeter. There was no view of the garage; that wall was where the vast American fridge and the ovens were situated. 'You can't see the garage from the house, then?'

Ross looked up from the bench where he was unlacing his boots. 'It's not very scenic. There are good views in other directions, so it's not like it's a loss.'

'We'd like to start with the garage,' Karen said.

A flicker of irritation crossed his face. 'I'll just tie my shoes again,' he said crisply.

'Thank you.' They followed him back outside. Karen noted the bulk of what she took to be a large barbecue, equipped with wheels so it could be moved easily. The garage door was controlled by a numeric keypad; it slid up and over with hardly a sound.

It was a space large enough for two substantial cars. But there were no vehicles inside. 'You don't put your car in the garage?'

'I can't be arsed. It's not like it's a magnet for car thieves.'

At one end was a stack of banker's boxes. McEwen waved a hand at them. 'Copies of my books, manuscripts.' A wry smile. 'The start of my archive, I suppose you could call it.'

Workbenches occupied the near wall. They were fitted with vices and G-clamps that looked dusty. There were pegboards for tools, but the array was hardly impressive. A hammer, a couple of pairs of pliers, a wrench. An electric screwdriver and a hammer drill sat lonely on the bench top. He caught Karen's eye and shrugged. 'I'm not much use with my hands. GSI, that's me.'

'GSI?' Daisy asked.

'Get Someone In. At least these days I can afford it.'

Next to them was the gardening equipment. Ride-on mower, hedge trimmer, tree lopper, as well as the usual assortment of spades, forks and hand tools. Karen had a sneaking suspicion this was another area where Ross McEwen Got Someone In.

Karen pointed to the floor where a panel of chipboard sat flush with the concrete around it. 'Is that an inspection pit?'

He nodded. 'The previous owner's taste for modernity didn't go further than his house. He was passionate about vintage cars. He used to pick them up as little more than wrecks then restore them. When I looked at the house, there was a beautiful American car sitting here. A Duesenberg Model J sports coupe. Cherry red. It was a work of art. I'd have bought it on the spot, but it wasn't for sale. I have no interest in cars – you've seen what I drive, for heaven's sake. But this would have been like having a Picasso about the place.' He grinned, and at once Karen recognised the boyish charm that probably appealed to Rosalind.

'So, the inspection pit was there so he could work on his cars?' Daisy broke the moment.

'That's right. I got a local joiner to make a proper cover for it, to avoid any chance of an accident.'

Karen approached and studied the cover. There was the narrowest of gaps all the way round. 'What's in it?'

'Nothing. It's just a void. I mean, there are steps down at one end, but that's all.'

'You didn't think it would be safer to have it filled in?' Karen sounded absent, but her senses were on alert.

'Probably, but the plan is when Ros and I officially come out, we're both going to sell our places and find somewhere together. It might be a selling point, you never know.' He smiled. 'Would it be naïve of me to ask what's so interesting about my garage?'

'How do you open this?' Karen tapped her toe on the cover.

'There's a crowbar somewhere . . . ' He looked around and walked to the end of the workbench. 'Yeah, here it is.' He pointed at the corner and went to grab the tool.

'Don't touch it,' Karen shouted. Daisy hustled across the garage and stepped between McEwen and the crowbar. She snapped on a pair of blue nitrile gloves.

He looked affronted. 'Seriously? You think I murdered someone with a crowbar? Should I be talking to a lawyer?'

'At this point, Mr McEwen, you are not the person of interest to us. We need to be sure, however, that any potential evidence is not compromised.' She looked around and spotted what she thought was a trenching spade. Narrow flat blade that might fit the gap if she was lucky. And for once, Karen was feeling lucky.

'On you go, Daisy.' Younger, fitter, and possessed of less dignity to lose, Karen thought. She kept her eyes on Ross McEwen. He was leaning against the workbench, arms folded across his chest, expression mildly curious,

'Do you mind telling me what has drawn you to my garage so inexorably?'

'Let's just say, information received.'

'Received via a partial manuscript written by a man who hated me, and wanted revenge on his ex-wife for finding happiness elsewhere? I think you've been reading too many of our books, Chief Inspector.'

'I'll be the first to apologise if I've wasted your time, sir.'

Daisy approached, spade in hand, apparently a woman unaccustomed to horticulture. On the edge of the pit, she hesitated, looking to Karen for guidance. Her boss nodded as she gloved up.

'One of the short sides, if my memory of Higher Physics is correct,' McEwen said. 'Levers and fulcrums and all that.'

Daisy stuck the spade into the gap and leaned on the handle. Nothing happened. She shifted the spade a little and tried again. She grunted and heaved, and this time it moved. Karen stepped forward and crouched to get her fingers under the edge. Daisy dumped the spade and together they inched the board sideways. It was lighter than Karen expected; one person could manage it, she thought.

The cover slid aside. McEwen gasped. 'Fuck me!'

Instead of the void he'd claimed they'd find, they were staring down at an uneven concrete slab that occupied the bottom half of the pit.

McEwen's eyes were wide, his hands in his hair. 'I swear to God, I had no idea . . . ' He looked around wildly. 'You've got to believe me. Whatever's down there, it's nothing to do with me.'

291

32

Karen left Daisy wrapping a spool of crime scene tape round the garage and walked Ross McEwen back to his kitchen. He slumped into the captain's chair at the head of the kitchen table, head in hands. He looked up at Karen. 'You think ... you think Lara Hardie's down there? You think Jake put her there? Really?'

'I don't want to speculate. I would still like to search the house, if you agree?'

He gave her a searching stare. 'Do I need to be talking to a lawyer?'

'You're free to do so. But you're not under caution or arrest.'

'I wouldn't even know where to begin, this is all so bloody preposterous.' He got up and went to the fridge. He took out a bottle of vodka and Bloody Mary mix and poured himself what Karen thought of as a big drink.

'I need to organise a forensic team to excavate your inspection pit. And there will be an officer on duty overnight. I don't think any excavation will begin until tomorrow morning, but it will be disruptive, I'm afraid.' *And all of this without alerting the Dog Biscuit.*

He took a gulp of his drink and shuddered a little. 'Can I go and stay with Ros?'

'I'd rather you stayed here. I may have questions as things arise.'

A sardonic grin and a dark laugh. 'I see what you're about, Pirie. You don't want Ros and I to put our heads together to cover our backs.' He winced. 'Sorry, terrible mixed idiom. I'm not even sure that's anatomically possible.'

'I can't stop you talking to Ms Harris unless I arrest you and put you in a cell. Which I'm not about to do. But I would like you here until we've finished searching the house.'

As she spoke, Daisy returned. 'All done.'

Karen excused herself. She walked out of the kitchen and into an open-plan dining and living room. It appeared to have been furnished for comfort rather than to impress. She could imagine stretching out on those sofas or chatting comfortably over dinner on those generously padded dining chairs. The back wall was kitted out with bookshelves crammed with crime novels. Where most people would have had a giant TV screen, McEwen had a seascape. It looked like the Firth of Forth on a windy spring day, all blues and whites and greys.

She couldn't hear Daisy and McEwen. She reckoned she could make her calls without being overheard. She walked the length of the room and sat in an egg chair that looked out over the lawn to a golf course beyond. First port of call was the local station. She spoke to a duty sergeant and outlined what she needed. Lockdown made everything more complicated, of course. 'I only need one man to guard the perimeter. It's a formality, so I can stand up in front of the sheriff at some point and say nobody could have interfered with what's inside.'

The grumbling that followed felt like a dog marking its territory rather than a genuine attempt to evade the task.

293

'I'll have somebody there within the hour,' he finally conceded. 'They'll need to be relieved at shift change, obviously.'

'I get that, I wasn't expecting one poor PC to stay there till breakfast. Oh, and if the householder leaves at any point, I'd appreciate it if your officer could inform me.'

Next, the summoning of a forensic team. Who knew what challenges the inspection pit would provide? Karen explained carefully to the duty Crime Scene Manager what she thought might be waiting for them below the skin of concrete. 'Well, it makes a change from a dog walker finding a decaying corpse in the woods,' he said. 'We like a challenge. We'll be there first thing.'

That only left one job. Someone had to babysit Ross McEwen. There was always the outside chance that he was not the sweetly innocent soul he was presenting to them. Karen often recalled a poem they'd studied at school. 'The Smuggler' by Norman MacCaig. She could still quote the final couplet. *'Nobody with such luggage/has nothing to declare.'* It was one of the tenets she lived her professional life by. A smooth surface didn't necessarily denote innocence; it simply meant its owner had a better class of decorator.

She could only imagine the Dog Biscuit's reaction if it turned out there was good reason to charge Ross McEwen with something, only to discover he'd done a runner in the night. She didn't want to ask Daisy; they still had a search to carry out. And they needed to be fresh in the morning.

She wondered whether Jimmy Hutton could supply a body from the Murder Prevention Squad but immediately vetoed the idea. If this was all going to go seismic with the Dog Biscuit, she didn't want to spread the damage.

That left one option, and it wasn't one she relished, for more than one reason. She speed-dialled Jason and waited. 'Boss,' he greeted her. 'No change, that's what they're saying. The nurse I spoke to, she said that was a good thing.'

'I'm glad to hear it. Any word from Ronan?'

Jason sighed. 'A lassie that works in Asda knows him and couldn't work out why he was wearing a Police Scotland vest. She told her supervisor, her supervisor told security. The security guy challenged him and Ronan chinned him and legged it. It's a total clusterfuck. I still don't know where he is.'

'You don't know if he's got any mates that live near the Asda?'

A pause. 'I don't know who he pals about with these days.'

She thought he was lying but she saw no point in making an issue of it. 'He's his own worst enemy.'

'That's what my mum always says.'

'Listen, Jason. I'm after a big favour. I think we're making some solid progress on the Lara Hardie case. We're search-ing Ross McEwen's house and there's an inspection pit filled with concrete on site.'

'Holy shit, boss. That's a total tie-in with the book. I picked it up from Gayfield this morning and read it through.'

'Thanks for that. I've lined up one of the tackety boot boys from Drylaw to stand guard on the garage, but I need a body to keep an eye on Ross McEwen overnight. I don't think there's any reason to think he's going to do a runner, but—'

'You want to do belt and braces, I get it. You want me to sit outside the house and make sure he doesn't take off, or have any visitors?'

Relief surged through Karen. She hadn't had to make the ask; somehow, over the past few days, Jason had reached a point where he was willing to take the initiative. 'Exactly.'

'Are you forgetting I'm suspended?'

'No. And Ross McEwen isn't going to see your face. He's got a massive pile out by the golf course in Barnton. You'd just have to sit in the car with the end of the drive in sight. And if he comes out, follow him, but call me the minute you're on the move. How does that sound?'

'I could do that, boss. It's better than sitting about doing nothing but chewing my nails. I tell you, I almost wish I smoked so I had something to do with myself.'

More than anything else at that moment, Karen wished Phil could hear what Jason had become. 'You're a good man, Jason. Can you get here for eight? We're going to take a look at the study.'

'Like it says in the notes: the external hard drive.'

'Wish me luck. We'll see you down the road from McEwen's house at eight. And Jason – thanks for this. I won't forget it.'

He scoffed. 'I think you better forget it, boss. Before the Dog Biscuit comes sniffing around.'

She laughed. 'See you later.' She stared out into the gathering dusk and wondered how many more times she'd stick her neck out for this job. Sooner or later, Ann Markie was going to come along with a chopper to chop off her head.

Back in the kitchen, McEwen looked as if tiredness had come over him like a wave and left him stranded on the high tide line. 'What now?' he asked, his voice slowed by exhaustion or drink. Or both.

'We'd like to take a look at your study.'

'You mean my office? I'm not a bloody professor. I'm a jobbing writer. I work in an office.'

It was a strange thing to turn belligerent over, given the ground they'd already covered. 'Whatever you call it, the room you work in. If that's the room where you used to play chess with Jake Stein.'

'Now?'

'Please. The sooner we get to it, the sooner we'll be out of your way.'

He led them to the end of the passage and round a corner to a polished concrete stair that hugged the wall of the tower. There were doors in the inner wall; as they went up, McEwen said in a monotone, 'Utility room, wine cellar, filing cabinets, toilet and shower.' Narrow lancet windows gave glimpses of the world beyond. They emerged in the top room, windows angled round in an octagonal shape. It was spectacular. The sea, the woodland, the golf course; a view in every direction.

A functional desk sat off to one side, a scatter of paper on the surface and a printer table next to it. On the other side of the room were a pair of leather tub chairs, a table inlaid with a chessboard between them. All round the walls were waist-high bookshelves. 'This is where the magic happens. Well, that's how *The Times* supplement described it. I'd say it's more like sweat and tears. The blood stays on the page.'

It had the air of a line he'd uttered many times. Karen prowled the perimeter. 'How do you work on screen with the sunlight coming at you?'

He stepped across to the desk and took out a slim remote. He pressed a button and a semi-opaque blind descended on one window. 'They're independent of each other, so it makes no odds where the glare is coming from.' He sat down in the desk chair.

'It would be easier for us if you weren't in the room while we search.'

'I'll stay put. I think I've already made it pretty bloody easy for you.'

Karen and Daisy exchanged a look. 'You take the desk, I'll take the shelves,' Karen said. Daisy gestured for him to move away, and he pushed back, letting the chair do the work.

'Be my guest.' He made an ironic gesture towards his desk drawers. Meanwhile, Karen got down on her knees and began her scrutiny of the shelf contents. Mostly they were reference books: forensic science; OS maps of Scotland; a complete collection of the green-and-white Penguin Famous Trials series; critical writing about crime fiction; biographies of writers; and finally, poetry. It wasn't what she'd expected from a lad from the Raploch, and Karen chided herself for her knee-jerk prejudice. She was a working-class lassie herself, and she had no chip on her shoulder. Ross McEwen had simply reached his escape velocity by a different route.

She worked her way methodically along the shelves, pulling out anything that might have hidden an external hard drive. She ruled out all the standard format books, but considered slim books of poetry, folded maps, small guidebooks. It was time-consuming but she didn't care. This might be make-or-break time; the single item that drew a straight line between Jake Stein and Lara Hardie.

In the end, it wasn't even disguised. It was pushed in between the embossed leather spines of Walter Scott's *Ivanhoe* and *Heart of Midlothian*, barely visible. Karen, still in her protective gloves, pulled out the books on either

298

side to expose the hard drive. 'Mr McEwen, can you come here, please.'

He crossed to her side, frowning at the gap in the shelf. 'Is that . . . ? It looks like one of those hard drives people upload stuff to when it's just cluttering up their computer.'

Karen lifted it carefully off the shelf and showed it to him. 'Is this yours?'

He shook his head. 'That's a bit old school. All my stuff is stored on the cloud. Early drafts, old emails, research files – all tucked away. I can get to it easily enough, but it's not taking up space on a daily basis. Much more eco-friendly than back-up drives and paper copies.'

'Not really. I read that data storage uses more than one per cent of global electricity,' Daisy said. 'That's not nothing.'

He glared at her. 'Fine. Stick to your notebook.'

'Have you ever seen this drive before?' Karen dragged them back to the point.

'Not to my knowledge. It's certainly not mine.'

'I'm going to take this with me. I believe it may be relevant to our inquiry.' She took a brown paper bag out of the satchel she carried, slung low across her body. She slid the drive into the bag, then sealed it, signing her name across the join. She passed it to Daisy, who scribbled her signature as witness and tucked it away in one of her deep pockets. Karen took out her own notebook and wrote out a receipt, handing it over to McEwen.

He stuffed it in his pocket without looking at it. 'Are you done now? It's after half past seven, you've had more than half of my working day for a fishing trip. And tomorrow's going to be a bust, with your pals digging up my garage. I'm entitled to a bit of peace and quiet.'

'We're done for now. There will be an officer on duty

outside the garage. I'd advise you not to attempt to dispose of anything overnight. Right now, you're a witness, not a suspect. It wouldn't be a good time to start acting like you have something to hide.' She turned and made for the door. 'We'll see you in the morning, Mr McEwen. Give my regards to Ms Harris.'

And she was gone, taking the stairs at a good lick. 'Are we leaving it at that?' Daisy asked as they made for the kitchen door.

'If we push any harder, he's going to dig his heels in and tell us to fuck off. Bottom line, he's not the one we're looking at here. We got a double result today – the inspection pit and the drive. Let's take that for now.'

When they reached the car, Daisy leaned on the roof and said, 'He could do a runner with the lovely Rosalind. Just to avoid the nasty publicity.'

Karen's smile was wholehearted. 'I don't think so. I've got it covered. Get in, Daisy.'

They turned out of the gate and Karen spotted Jason's car, parked up a hundred yards down the road. Daisy saw it too. 'That's Jason!' Then she glared at Karen. 'He's suspended, you can't do that to him.'

'Nothing to say he can't sit in his car on a quiet road and contemplate the universe. He's under orders to call me if McEwen makes any moves.'

'Why can't we just level with the Dog Biscuit and get support from detectives in the division?'

'Because that would give our beloved ACC Crime the perfect excuse to argue that the HCU isn't really up to dealing with major complex cases. And that this case isn't really old enough to be cold, so it should go back to the team who first investigated it. And I suspect they made a hash of it.

"Just another stupid lassie leading the wrong guy on." I want justice for Lara Hardie, especially now, when we're being forced to confront the impact sudden death is having in people's lives.'

'Even so ... We're skating on thin ice, boss.'

Karen liked that 'we'. 'That we are, Daisy. But just think how good it will feel when we get back to solid ground.'

33

It still felt spooky to be driving along a main road with scarcely any traffic. Karen found it difficult to keep to the speed limit with no other vehicles to measure herself against. She was about to say as much to Daisy as they turned on to Telford Road when her phone rang. The dashboard display told her it was Hamish. She didn't want to talk to him in the car with Daisy, so she rejected the call. 'I'll catch him later,' she said.

They said nothing for the rest of the journey, both lost in their thoughts. It was almost time for Karen to call Rafiq; they'd be back in good time for that. She parked in the same space she'd left earlier, checking her phone as she got out. There was a voicemail from Hamish. He sounded peremptory and upset in equal measure. 'Call me back as soon as you get this. It's important.' Karen sighed and waved a hand towards the front door.

'I'll catch you up, I think I've got some ruffled feathers to smooth. Maybe he's had his distillery raided by the local boys.' She connected to Hamish's number and before Daisy had closed the street door, he was on the line. 'What the actual fuck is going on with you?' His voice was cold and furious. She'd heard him like this once, when a supplier let him down badly, but this was a new experience for Karen.

'What? I've been working a case—'

'Really? Is that what you call it?'

'Call what, Hamish. You're not making much sense.'

His voice was tight, every word a block of ice. 'I drove down to make a delivery today. I thought I'd swing by your flat, see if I could maybe catch you there. You told me you'd been checking it out on your "official exercise".' The last two words were laced with vicious sarcasm.

Her stomach clenched and she felt sick. 'You went to my flat.'

'And imagine my surprise when I unlocked the door and discovered the chain was on. So I banged on the door in case you were in the bath or something and hadn't heard me. And guess what?' He'd lowered his voice, but somehow it held more anger.

'There's a very good reason—'

'What? For you installing a fancy man in your flat while you're pretending to be whiter than white in your bubble with Daisy? You must think I'm as stupid as the Mint.'

'Don't badmouth Jason. He's had none of your advantages.'

He scoffed. 'And don't you try to deflect me with the working-class hero card. There's a man in your flat. When he saw me through the crack in the door, I swear he looked like he was going to shit himself. I guess you told him about me, right? Which gave him one hell of an advantage since you hadn't bothered telling *me* you'd found somebody to keep you company in lockdown.'

'You could not be more wrong. If you've scared him—'

'Oh, come on, Karen. You can do better than that. What?

Is he one of your Syrian chums from Aleppo? One of the ones who made it over here and left their wives and kids behind? Very convenient.'

'Will you shut the fuck up for a minute and let me speak?' She shouted without thinking, then realised most of her neighbours could probably hear.

'I should have listened to Teegan.'

'What has the expert in the diseases of sheep got to do with this?' Her turn for sarcasm.

'Teegan said there was something dodgy about you not being in my flat the other night. Bloody Daisy covering for you.' She heard the disgust in his voice.

'You were in the flat? Your flat?'

'I needed to pick up some urgent paperwork. And you weren't there. So where were you? Snuggled up with your bit on the side?'

'This is absurd. I'm not having this conversation. There's a perfectly good explanation for what you saw this evening. Which, by the way, there can't possibly be for you being in either your flat or mine. I'm hanging up now. When you're up to having an adult conversation at an adult volume, I might consider speaking to you.' Karen ended the call, really missing the days when you could slam the phone down on someone.

She leaned against the car, her legs wobbly, her hands shaking. What just happened there? She tried to breathe deep but it was momentarily beyond her. 'He frightened you,' she said under her breath. 'Is this what it feels like to be one of the women the MPU takes under its wing?'

She closed her eyes and considered her options. She could call Rafiq, but he'd probably be too rattled to answer. She could drive down to her flat and try to talk to him there.

But Hamish might still be lurking and she definitely didn't want to confront him. Besides, she had no excuse to be driving. If a police car stopped her, she'd struggle to avoid trouble. Walking was a better option; it was easier to cut through back streets and vennels, easier to avoid being intercepted by police or other walkers. She was making mincemeat of the COVID regulations in one sense but at least she was keeping her distance and wearing a mask when she was with others.

She set off, calling Daisy to say she had to deal with something and she'd see her later. The question of what Daisy knew about Hamish in the flat could wait. At nine o'clock on the dot, she was cutting down Henderson Street. She stepped into a shop doorway and called her flat. It rang out. Once, twice ... six times. Twice more and the answering machine would kick in. Seven—'Hello?' An apprehensive question.

'It's me. I am so sorry about what happened earlier. The man who came to the door – it was nothing to do with you. He has no idea who you are. He had no right to be there and I'm really angry about it.'

'I was scared. He was surprised to see me but he was also very angry.' His words were tumbling over each other. 'I tried to close the door but he kept pushing against the chain. Shouting your name. I didn't know what to do. I said you were not here. He shouted, "Liar." He stepped back like he was going to attack the chain, so I slammed the door shut. He banged into the door but then he went away. Was he there to frighten you?'

Karen gave a dry laugh. 'No, not to frighten me. Just to see me. Listen, I'm going to walk down to the breakwater and check out the garage and the walkway. If he's not around, I'll call you back in about twenty minutes and you can come down and we'll have a conversation. OK?'

'If you are certain it is safe?'

'I won't call unless I'm positive.'

She set off at a brisk pace and covered the distance in record time. The supermarket was closed and Hamish's Land Rover was not in any of the public parking areas. So far, so good. She couldn't see it in the visitor slots near the apartment blocks, nor in the underground car park. Finally, she took a turn along the breakwater. No Hamish. Karen walked up towards the lighthouse. There was no cover and no sign of another human being. She called Rafiq again. He picked up and said nothing. 'It's all clear. Walk up towards the lighthouse, I'll be sitting on the first seat past the bushes. You can't see it till you're almost there.'

Karen walked back and sat on the wooden plank bench, turning up her jacket collar against the night air coming off the water. As if she didn't have enough to deal with, now she was going to have to sort out bloody Hamish. Rafiq was straightforward by comparison.

Following someone on foot always looked easy on screen. It was, Daisy knew, a lot harder than it seemed. Following someone on foot in lockdown was fiendish; being on the streets was instantly obvious. But when Karen had called her, Daisy figured she was off on her mysterious business again. This was her chance to find out what the boss was up to that was so secret. It had to be more than just checking her flat – she'd always been open about that until the past few days. She checked the window that gave on to the street to make sure Karen hadn't taken the car. Daisy caught sight of her heading towards Broughton Street, grabbed her coat and sprinted out of the flat and down the stairs.

She hit the street just in time to see a figure emerge from one of the basement stairs further down the street. He was wearing black jeans, a black hoodie and black Nike trainers. Proper lockdown ninja, she thought with a smile. Karen disappeared round the corner and he went the same way. Still she thought nothing of it, keeping her distance automatically.

Karen was striding out down the pavement, past the pubs and across the street past the Mansfield Traquair Centre with its stunning murals that were currently off-limits, and on down towards Canonmills. It dawned on Daisy that it was an odd coincidence that the black-clad man was heading in the same direction. She wasn't worried yet, just taking note.

But as Karen cut down Warriston Road past the Water of Leith and across St Mark's Park to join the waterside path, the man stuck on her tail, except that he crossed the road and stayed close to the walls. As someone would who didn't want to be spotted, Daisy thought with a thrill of apprehension. Was the lockdown ninja friend or foe, or just a weirdo? The one good thing was that he was so intent on Karen that he wasn't looking over his shoulder to clock Daisy, also sticking close to the wall.

Karen hurried on, oblivious. She was, Daisy recalled, learning Gaelic on her walks. Maybe she was too absorbed in her latest lesson to be as alert as usual about her surroundings? Daisy felt any qualms she might have had about tracking her boss disappear in the glow of having Karen's back.

As they approached Leith, Karen peeled off and wove

through side streets. Now there was no doubt about it. Daisy was not the only one on her tail. Karen suddenly ducked into a doorway; the man stopped in his tracks and dived behind a skip. Daisy nipped into a handy loading bay and peeked round the corner. She still couldn't see the man's face; his hood was pulled forward to protect his profile. One thing she was certain of – he wasn't Hamish Mackenzie. Though maybe he was one of Hamish's minions? Skinny and lithe, he had the look of someone who could have been a barista.

Karen set off again, picking up the pace. Ninja followed, and so did Daisy. If this wasn't on the edge of scary, she thought, it would almost be funny. Nobody on the streets but the three of them, moving through the night like shadows. She was pretty sure this wasn't what Nicola Sturgeon had meant when she advised them that an hour's exercise daily was what they were allowed.

By the time they grew close to the Western Harbour Breakwater, Daisy was almost convinced she was wasting her time. The boss was just heading for her flat to check it over. Unless she was planning on confronting Hamish in a lockdown showdown? Daisy liked the sound of that. She'd have to work 'lockdown showdown' into her conversation somehow. Steph might be amused.

All at once, everything changed. From brisk walking, Karen had shifted to prowling the supermarket car park and the parking areas around the flats. The man had taken cover among some bushes. Daisy crouched behind a car, waiting to see what would happen next.

What happened next was a weird sort of ballet. Karen moved along the breakwater, checking every place a car might be hidden. It was definitely a vehicle, not a person, for she wasn't bothering with doorways or loading bays. The man trailed behind her, stealthy and cautious. And behind him, Daisy dodged and hid. All the way along the breakwater, past the blocks of flats, the routine only broken when Karen briefly disappeared into an underground car park. Both of her followers bottled out of that pursuit; there would be no secure place to hide. And besides, Daisy thought the man likely had Karen in his line of sight. If he stayed put, so would she.

Karen re-emerged and carried on up the breakwater; the routine resumed. At last they left the apartment blocks and car parks behind them. Karen followed the path. The man walked on the verge close to the bushes, careful not to make a sound. Daisy, who had been there before with Karen, reckoned she could circle round the other side of the bushes and emerge with a clear view of the path.

She was right. At the far end of the scrubby shrubs, she saw Karen stop and scan the headland that led to the decommissioned lighthouse. As far as Daisy could see, her boss was the only person in sight. Wherever the lockdown ninja was, Karen hadn't spotted him.

Karen took out her phone and spoke to someone. Then she turned back and sat on the first wooden bench in the open. She turned up her jacket collar and waited. Whatever was going on, Daisy reckoned it was fuck all to do with checking Karen's flat. Or having that lockdown showdown with Hamish.

The minutes dragged past. Karen wished she had a pair of gloves. She thrust her hands in her pockets and huddled into her coat. She'd taken her earphones out, so she heard the running footsteps coming down the path towards her.

She stood up and half-turned in time to see Rafiq approaching. He stopped abruptly a couple of metres from her.

'I'm so sorry,' Karen said. 'The man who came to the flat – we're sort of together. But he's supposed to be a couple of hundred miles from here. He had no right to come to my flat.'

'I think he was very unhappy to see me there.'

A voice loomed out of the gloom. 'Damned right I was unhappy,' Hamish boomed as he appeared out of the darkness. 'Karen, are you going to be straight with me? What's going on here? Who is this guy?' Now he was upon them, poking Rafiq's shoulder with a finger.

'It's complicated. But not in the way you think.' Karen spoke calmly, trying to take the heat out of the moment.

Hamish stepped closer to Rafiq, forcing him off the path and on to the top of the breakwater slope. 'Who are you, pal?'

Rafiq struggled to keep his footing as Karen grabbed Hamish's arm to pull him away. In that moment, a black-clad figure ran into their midst and lunged at Rafiq. But Rafiq was already turning and the blow barely caught him.

'What the fuck?' Hamish roared.

Karen caught a flash and shouted, 'He's got a knife!'

Rafiq backed away, the only option towards the sea that lapped the bottom of the breakwater slope. The hooded man moved to follow him but before he could reach him, Daisy barrelled down the grassy incline and threw herself at him. In a chaos of limbs, Rafiq, his assailant and Daisy tumbled down the slope and into the freezing waters of the Firth of Forth.

34

For a moment, Karen was stunned. Then she shouted at Hamish, 'Get help.' She headed gingerly towards the bottom of the breakwater, but nearly hit the ground herself when Hamish pushed right past her, shedding coat and shoes.

'Fuck that,' he yelled, hauling off his heavy fisherman's sweater. 'You get help.'

In the dark, it was impossible to make out who was who. They were all struggling with the cold, the current and the shock. Already they were a few metres from the shore, clearly out of their depth. Hamish waded in and struck out with his powerful California-honed crawl towards the bobbing heads and waving arms.

'Oh Christ,' Karen said, reaching for her phone and calling the police control room. 'DCI Karen Pirie here. I'm at the far end of the Western Harbour Breakwater, near the lighthouse. Three bodies in the water ... Yes, alive ... Yes, it's a bloody emergency – get me some support here now.'

Hamish had someone by the neck and was swimming back to shore. He hoisted a body on to the breakwater and headed straight back. Karen crouched down to help and realised it was Rafiq, on his hands and knees, coughing up water and retching. She dragged him to his feet. 'Get back to the flat right now, and stay there. I'll call you when I can. But get the fuck out of here before the police arrive.'

He staggered, stumbled to the path and set off in a slow trot towards the flats. Karen saw the blue wash of emergency service lights and prayed he'd have the sense to cut round the back of the apartment blocks.

She turned back to the scumbled black and grey of the sea. Hamish and Daisy were making for the shore in a strange embrace. He was on his back, kicking strongly; she was clasped to his chest, her arms free to perform the most pathetic doggy paddle Karen had ever seen. As they drew close, Karen waded in and took Daisy from Hamish. Her teeth were chattering and she was shaking with cold and fear. Karen held her close. 'You're safe. You're OK. I've got you.'

Hamish stood up unsteadily and gazed at the sea. 'I can't see him. Fuck, I can't see him. Can you see him?'

Karen didn't want to see the man who had come at Rafiq with a knife, but she had too much respect for human life to turn away. The choppy water made it impossible to discern a human head but Hamish wasn't giving up.

'Over there,' he pointed. 'Is that him?' The waves parted and what might have been a human head disintegrated into a lip of water edged with foam. Hamish's shoulders dropped. 'Fuck,' he muttered. 'He's gone.' He wrapped his arms round his body and shuddered. Then he turned to Karen and demanded, 'What the fuck was that?' He looked around, seeing the blue lights growing closer. 'And where's your wee pal?'

Karen was in the grip of adrenaline and she was determined they'd all come out of this in one piece. 'Later. Listen.

Here's the line: Daisy and I walked down here to pass on some paperwork to you. We walked along the breakwater and a stranger came jogging towards us. He slipped. Lost his footing and went in. He appeared not to be able to swim. You two went in after him. Nobody mentions Rafiq. Is that clear?'

'Why should we lie for you, Karen?' Hamish, still nursing his anger.

'For fuck's sake, it's not for me. I promise, I will explain it all to both of you. But a man's life depends on us. Please believe me.'

Before any of them could say more, a pair of police officers in high-vis jackets came running into sight. 'What's happening?' one demanded. 'Control said, three in the water.'

'These two went in to rescue a guy who slipped and went into the water. But they couldn't find him in the dark. Is there a police boat coming?'

'It's been dispatched. Who's the man in the water?'

'We've no idea,' Daisy said through chattering teeth. 'He was jogging along the path towards us and he sidestepped—'

'Presumably to keep his distance,' Karen said.

'And he skidded. He just went straight in and he was over his head in seconds.' Daisy burst into tears. Karen had no doubt they were genuine. Though what in the name of actual fuck was Daisy doing there?

One of the police officers turned away and had an indecipherable conversation with her radio.

'What were you three doing here? You do know we're in lockdown?'

'Before we get into that, have you not got any space blankets in the car? These two are perishing here.' She spoke with the authority of rank. 'I'm DCI Pirie, by the way.

313

Historic Cases Unit. And this is DS Mortimer, also of the HCU. And the big guy is Hamish Mackenzie. DS Mortimer and I are in a bubble, living in Hamish's flat. Hamish is an entrepreneur—'

'I own the Perk coffee shop chain and I've got a croft in the Highlands where we're currently making hand gel. I urgently needed some paperwork for a deal I'm putting together, and I asked Karen to bring it down on her daily exercise.' As he spoke, he pulled on his jumper and his shoes. 'Until I had to dive into the Forth, we'd all been religiously keeping our legal distance, officer.'

Karen gave silent thanks. The fiction was holding so far. She looked out at the sea and spotted a boat heading their way, its searchlight carving a cone of light across the water, its edges as wobbly as a child's drawing. 'Officer, we need to get warm and dry. Space blankets for these two, and then I suggest we give you our details before I drive them back to Hamish's flat where we can all get warmed up. Statements in the morning?'

The policeman was taken aback, but not unhappy to have the responsibility for decisions taken from him. His colleague joined him. 'This where he went in?' she asked.

'Right here,' Karen said. 'It all happened so fast.' She shook her head and turned back to the officer she'd been talking to. 'Let us know if you find him, yeah.'

'Aye, Chief Inspector. I'll get the space blankets.'

The woman officer's eyebrows climbed but she said nothing.

The heat-retaining blankets were produced, contact details provided and Karen led the other two away from the scene. 'Where's the Landie?' she asked Hamish as soon as they were out of hearing.

'Round the back of the serviced apartment block,' he said, having the grace to look sheepish. 'I've been lurking down the side of your block for bloody ages. You walked right past me, you were only looking at cars.'

They piled into the Land Rover. As they drove out past the supermarket, Hamish demanded once more to know what was going on. 'I'll tell you when we're back at your flat and everybody's warmed up and in dry clothes,' Karen said forcefully.

'And we've got a big drink in our hands,' Daisy added. 'I've no idea what you've been up to, boss, but I know you well enough to know there's a good reason why a guy with a knife ended up drowned in the Forth tonight.'

'There's never a good reason why anybody drowns in the dark yards from the shore in the Firth of Forth,' Karen said bitterly. That silenced everyone.

While Hamish and Daisy were both showering, Karen tried to call Rafiq. There was no reply. She left a message saying simply, 'You've no reason for concern. Call me when you can.' She forced herself to sound unruffled. She could only imagine the state he was in. He'd just begun to feel a modicum of security and it had been ripped from him.

They reconvened in dry clothes, Hamish in a brilliant white shirt, black trousers and waistcoat. Daisy looked the same as every other evening – sweatshirt and jeans, grumbling about the wreckage of her favourite Converses. Karen had changed into trackie bottoms and slippers, pouring the drinks each requested. Once they were settled, Karen began. 'I promised I'd tell you why tonight happened. In exchange, I want you to agree to listen and not keep interrupting. OK, Hamish?'

315

He rolled his eyes and took a mouthful of Bowmore. 'You drive a hard bargain, Karen.'

'OK, Daisy?'

'Sure. Not knowing is driving me crazy.'

Karen laid out the events that had led to Rafiq lodging in her flat. 'I couldn't see what else to do. This isn't the best time to be a refugee whose life is under threat. And if anybody doubted that, tonight should have settled the matter.'

'So that guy tonight? The lockdown ninja? He was an assassin?' Daisy's voice rose in incredulity.

Karen sighed. 'It looks that way. I'm told the Syrian government has form for tracking down its enemies.'

'So where is what's-his-name now?'

'I sent Rafiq back to my flat and told him to lie low.'

'Will they not be looking for him? At the hostel? When he doesn't go back?' Daisy asked.

'I told them he might not be coming back. I made out that he was being moved to a secure location because he was a witness. Besides, nobody cares when illegals disappear. It's just one less body to worry about.' There was a moment of silence as they all thought about the implications of that.

Then Hamish shook his head. 'You can't blame me for jumping to the wrong conclusion,' he grumbled. 'A strange man in your flat? And you nowhere to be seen when I came round here before.'

'Yes, let's hear what that was all about. You came round before? Is that what you were shouting about earlier? Badmouthing Daisy? Did you show up here when I was out?'

He shrugged. 'It's my flat, Karen. Yes, I popped round. I hoped you'd be here, but you weren't. And Daisy gave me the bum's rush.' He tipped his glass towards Daisy. 'Sorry I doubted you, doll.'

'Don't call me "doll",' Daisy muttered. 'My name's Daisy and my rank is detective sergeant. Either will do.'

Hamish looked offended. 'There's no need to be like that.'

'Why not? You turned up, breaking all the rules, and you acted like I owed you for being allowed to stay here when it was nothing to do with you really. It was her who suggested I move in, not you.' She waved her glass extravagantly at Karen, almost showering her with red wine.

'She has a point, Hamish.' Karen couldn't help herself. 'And I will be having words with you, Daisy, about dividing your loyalties.' She felt like the headmistress in a bad Ealing Comedy, which pissed her off even more. 'Your place is at the croft just now, Hamish. You can legitimately come down to Edinburgh to make hand gel deliveries. You can even arrange to encounter me – at a distance – on my daily exercise. But what you can't do is come swanning round here, or my flat, whenever it suits you.'

'I'm here now—' he paused and knocked back his drink, defiantly pouring another. 'And I can't drive now, can I?' He grinned wolfishly.

'I'm out of here,' Daisy said, topping up her glass and heading for the door. 'You two need to have a conversation without me.'

They stared at each other across the room, Hamish visibly pleased with himself, Karen hoping her face was impossible to read. All she felt was the emptiness of knowing she'd failed and that failure had cost a life, and the man she'd been sharing her bed with was more interested in angling his way between the sheets with her than abiding by the rules designed to keep them all safe. It wasn't just them; if Karen had picked up COVID in one of her several encounters over the past few days then passed it on to Hamish, he

could infect a swathe of people in his small crofting community, a community that had remained untouched by the
virus thus far. 'You're irresponsible,' she said wearily. 'We're
all in this together, until somebody decides the rules don't
apply to them.'

'Oh, come on, Karen. You know the village is free of
infection.'

'But Edinburgh's not. I don't have a choice about going out
into the world. It's my job. You do have a choice, Hamish.'

He gave a boyish grin. 'I just couldn't stay away, Karen.
You know how I feel about you.'

'You forced me into lying on your behalf. I told those two
polis a string of lies about your involvement. If this comes
to light, my career is over.'

'If I hadn't been there, the outcome could have been a
bloody sight worse.'

'That doesn't alter the fact that you've acted outside
the rules.'

He scoffed. 'And you've never crossed that line in a noble
cause? Busting an illegal immigrant out of a detention
hostel, for example?'

'Your cause wasn't noble. You didn't pop down on the
off-chance somebody would be drowning in the Forth. And
you didn't just want to hang out because you missed me. I
know you, Hamish. You wanted a shag and you thought you
could talk me into it if you were here in the room.' There
was nothing flirtatious in her tone, only a weary acceptance
that she couldn't excuse his presence.

He spread his hands, his eyes imploring. 'I love you,
Karen. Is that a crime?'

She gave him a level stare. 'No. But it's a mistake.' She got
to her feet, but before she could leave the room, her phone

rang. She didn't recognise the number but she picked up anyway. It was the policeman who'd answered their call for help earlier.

'I hope you're all recovered from your ordeal?' he said.

She forced herself to sound as natural as she could manage. 'Yes, thanks. Nothing a hot shower and a large whisky couldn't fix. Any news of the man who went into the water?'

'That's why I was calling. The rescue boat found him a hundred yards from shore. I'm afraid he was dead at the scene. It looks like he drowned.'

'I'm sorry to hear that. We did our best.'

'Nobody's questioning that, ma'am.'

'Did he have any ID on him?'

'Nothing. His phone's probably at the bottom of the Forth. He looks Middle Eastern or Arabic. It's hard to tell.'

'Maybe an appeal to the public, if nobody comes forward?'

'Aye, that's probably the way we'll have to go. But it's early days yet. I was wondering, could you come in and make a formal statement tomorrow at some point?'

'All three of us?' Karen frowned. She wanted Hamish gone, not hanging around waiting to talk to a polis.

'I don't think that will be necessary. From everything you've said, it looks straightforward enough. I just need to get something on paper.'

She established when he was on shift and agreed to meet him at Gayfield Square to give her statement. Karen ended the call. 'You'll have gathered he didn't make it.'

Hamish shrugged. 'Probably just as well. It makes life a lot simpler for all of us.'

She stared at him in blank incomprehension. How could she have thought she might love this man? How could she

319

not have seen the self-serving attitude that lay beneath his apparent kindness and generosity? She remembered a friend once arguing over dinner that there was no such thing as altruism; there was always something in it for the giver, even if it was just the warm glow of having done good for some poor soul who couldn't manage what life had thrown at them. She'd thought it cynical but now Hamish was forcing her to reconsider. Right from the start there had been a niggle at the back of her mind but she'd swept it into a corner because she was so bereft after Phil's death. She'd wanted someone to make her feel valued again, and Hamish was good at that. Because it suited him.

'A man's dead, Hamish. It might be convenient for you because you don't have to confront your serial lockdown busting. And yes, he was probably there to kill a decent man. But who are we to judge his unknown life? The pressures that drove him here?' This time she made it to the door. 'You know where the spare duvet and pillows are kept. The sofa's very comfortable, so Daisy tells me. I want you gone when I get up.'

He stood up then and took a step towards her, arms spread in invitation. 'Karen?'

'Don't. Not now.' *Maybe never again.* 'As soon as lockdown is lifted, Daisy and I will be out of here and you can have your flat back to do what you want with.'

His face crumpled. His eyes sparkled with tears. She nearly cracked. Then she remembered Rafiq's frightened face, and her resolve returned. She shook her head. 'We'll talk later, Hamish. But neither of us can pretend this night hasn't happened.'

35

The last thing Karen did before she got into bed was to try to reach Rafiq. No reply, again. She wasn't surprised. He must be consumed with fear. Where there was one assassin, there could easily be two. His opponents had a long reach – someone in the hostel must have had sufficient access to discover who had sprung him. Presumably they'd googled her and found images online of good enough quality to identify her. They'd had the patience to wait for her to appear at Gayfield Square then follow her home. More waiting till she finally led them to Rafiq.

The guilt was tremendous. She'd tried to help, and maybe she had saved his life, but the price was high. And it could get higher still if someone had happened to see the drama playing out on the breakwater. Or even simply passed a dripping Rafiq on his way back to her flat.

And, on a much more trivial level, what was she to do about Hamish? The pressures of COVID had revealed aspects she'd never seen before. She'd always known he was a businessman, but she hadn't really considered how that might lead to ruthlessness. She'd never had cause to interfere with his businesses in the past; she thought now she had probably engaged in wishful thinking. She'd taken him at face value as a decent man with a reasonable attitude to his staff. Sure, she'd been uncomfortable from time to time when he'd organised some extravagant treat for the pair of them that she'd explicitly not wanted, but she'd thought that was because he wanted to give her pleasure. Now, she had to look at that in a different light. There was, she thought, an element of control in that sort of kindness.

This was the kind of tumult that usually drove her to walk the night streets. But she was almost growing accustomed to the enforced lockdown limitations on that. Her body and her brain were slowly learning that the nightly battle with sleep wasn't necessary. At first, she'd had a panicky couple of nights but once she'd understood she wasn't exactly imprisoned, she'd learned to let go. Like the poem in Lara's novel. Only, it wasn't love that had come in its wake; it was even more letting go.

When she emerged, freshly showered, just after seven, there was not a trace of Hamish in the flat. He was there on her phone; three missed calls and half a dozen texts she was scrupulously avoiding. He'd clearly not slept on the sofa, defiantly driving back north in spite of being over the limit. Not clever, just exasperating, Karen thought. She called through to Daisy. 'Coffee's on, we need to be out of here by half past.'

Daisy appeared in jeans and a dark green roll-neck jumper, dark smudges under her eyes. She yawned a 'Good morning' at Karen. 'Did you get much sleep?'

'Oddly enough, yes. I closed my eyes and I felt like I'd been unplugged. You?'

Daisy pulled a face. 'I kept dreaming I was drowning and waking up gasping for breath.' She reached for a mug of coffee. 'I guess I'm more sensitive than I thought.'

'Yeah, well, it was quite a night. By the way, you never did explain to me what you were doing in the thick of it.'

Daisy pinked up. 'I followed you and the lock-down ninja—'

'Don't call him that, it diminishes what he was doing.'

Daisy looked stung. 'Sorry. I followed you both.'

'Why?'

She wrapped her hands round her mug and took a sip. 'I thought you were up to something. And I wanted to know what.' A quick look up from under her brows. 'Because I'm a detective,' she said in a rush. 'I'm trained to think secrets are dangerous things.'

Karen couldn't suppress a smile. 'Bollocks, Daisy. It was nothing to do with training and everything to do with being a nosy wee shite. Just admit it.'

'Mostly. But there was a bit of me wanted to cover your back in case you fell into bother.'

'"Fell into bother"? That's a new one on me.'

'There's a lot of it about,' Daisy said with an acidic edge. 'Between you and the Mint.'

Karen shook her head, drained her coffee and put the mug in the dishwasher. 'Good to know that's where I sit in your top cop charts. Now get your coat on, we've got work to do. First, though, we'll have to swing by Leith. I need to check up on Rafiq.'

'I'm going to pretend I didn't hear that, if it's all the same to you, boss.' Daisy turned away to grab her coat and bag.

Karen did likewise and said, 'Heard what, Sarge?' They shared a wry conspiratorial smile and headed out the door.

Karen took a deep breath and unlocked her flat. The chain wasn't on and her heart sank. She shut the door behind her. She knew before she spoke that he was gone; there was no mistaking the feel of an empty space. Nevertheless, she called out, 'Rafiq? It's Karen.'

Silence. She walked through to the living room. Everything was in its place. On the table, a sheet of A4 lined paper, folded in half, weighted down with her front door key. Karen opened up the note and read,

> Dear Karen
> I can never thank you for what you have done for me. You and your friends saved my life. But I cannot be responsible for putting you in danger. I must take my leave of you now so you can be safe. Do not worry about me. I will send word when it is possible. Mamnounak.
>
> Rafiq

The words upset her more than she could explain. She felt she'd failed him, and was sad at the thought she would never see him again. She picked up the paper and took it through to her bedroom, where she folded it in half and tucked it in her bedside drawer. Her wardrobe was open, and she saw one of her backpacks was missing. Another note lay on the bed:

> I have taken the clothes you bought me, and I have taken a bag so I don't look so much like a street person. I am sorry for this, I hope you understand.

She walked back through and noticed the door of the washer drier was ajar. Curious, she looked inside. In a crumpled tangle were the terrible clothes Rafiq had arrived in.

They weren't even fit for the charity shop. Karen bundled them up and stuffed them in a plastic bag. She'd bin them on the way out.

She called Miran's number. When he answered, his voice sounded strained. 'Karen. Thank you, a thousand times. I think it is better that we don't talk right now. I want you to know that we have this. Come and have brunch when the lockdown is over and we can share our stories.'

Karen read between the lines and hoped she was right. She wasn't quite sure why she cared so much about Rafiq's fate, but she did, and there it was.

And they had to get on. The last thing she wanted was to keep the scene examiners or the search team waiting. Nobody wanted to be hanging around in the wee small rain that soaked to the skin in no time at all. She preferred her technicians not to hate her.

They made it to Barnton with a few minutes to spare. Karen stopped in front of Jason's car and got out to speak to him. 'All quiet, boss,' he said, stifling a yawn. 'Nobody in or out except the changeover boys.'

'Thanks, Jason. Any news from the Vic?'

He shook his head. 'No, nothing. The nurse says she's a fighter.'

'Well, we knew that. Away with you and get home now. Any change, let me know.'

Karen had noticed a terrace at the back of the house, sheltered by a glass canopy. She gathered her teams there, making sure they maintained their masked distances. 'What we're looking for is anything that connects Ross McEwen to the disappearance of Lara Hardie a year ago. Any mention of her name, any pieces of writing with her byline. Photographs, cards. I want you to work a room each, searching in a grid pattern. I know it's a big ask, but it's important. The owner is in residence; I'm going to ask him to stay in the kitchen.'

Then she turned to the scene examiners. 'I hope you got the message about the drills?' They nodded, glum.

One of them said, 'Just what we've been longing for.'

'At least you're working under cover in the garage. There's a possibility that the body under the concrete is inside a snowboard bag, but we don't know that for sure. I'm sorry, it's going to be a bitch of a job.'

'We'll manage,' the senior examiner said. 'Come on, people, we've got a job to do.'

Karen waited till they'd all moved off, then headed for the kitchen herself. Ross McEwen was sitting at the kitchen table, a pile of printouts in front of him, pencil in his hand. He looked surprisingly well-rested, smart in a ghillie shirt and black trousers. He pursed his lips and threw his pencil down when he saw Karen. 'How long is this going to take?'

'I don't honestly know. We'll probably be out of the house by close of play, but the garage could be a very different story, depending on what we find buried under the concrete.'

His mouth twisted in a sardonic line. 'You're going to have a right riddy if there's nothing there. If it's all just a mega wind-up on Jake's part.'

'I'll take my chances. I'd like you to stay in the kitchen while we search. DS Mortimer will be staying here with you. And I'll be with the search team in the garage. Thank you for your cooperation.'

He looked mutinous, but nodded agreement. 'I'll stay here. I can plan out my next murder.'

He wasn't nearly as entertaining as he thought he was. Karen left Daisy to it and went back outside. The garage was open and the SEs were standing around the inspection pit, masked, gloved and suited up. Karen knew their boss, Shane Brown, from a course she'd attended on body recovery. 'What's it looking like, Shane?' she asked as she approached.

He turned and sucked his breath in over his teeth, like a plumber about to reveal precisely how much of a cowboy the last plumber had been. 'Hard to say,' he said. Karen was accustomed to his general level of despondency so she tried not to let it knock the wind from her sails.

'Tell me the worst.'

'Well, we don't know how thick it is. And we don't know how dense it is. What we're going to do is drill some investigation holes in the corners. Because if there is a body in there, chances are it's not going to be rammed into the corners.'

'Makes sense. And then?'

He shook his head, a pitying smile on his face. 'I shouldn't have to tell you, DCI Pirie. That depends on what we find. Did you bring a book with you? We're going to be a wee while yet.'

Karen walked back to the patio where she'd given her briefing. There were a couple of rigid plastic chairs there that looked far too stylish to have come from the local garden centre. She picked one up, surprised at its weight, and carried it back to the garage. She set it down in a spot where she could watch the crime scene specialists and also keep the driveway in her peripheral vision.

The drills started with all the insistence of a visit to the dentist. What made it worse was that they all kept stopping and starting but not in synch. It seemed to go on forever, and they had no spare ear protectors. Karen could feel a headache starting at the base of her skull. But she needed to be there, to testify to what was revealed. Not for the benefit of the court, who would likely never hear a word about this case. But for the record. For Lara Hardie's family.

When the drills stopped, Karen's ears took a few moments to decide it was over. A faint smell of sour decay reached her. She got up in time to see Shane inserting a flexible cable into one of the holes. It had a light and a tiny camera lens on one end; the other was plugged into a USB slot on a laptop. He looked up as she approached. 'We're in luck. It looks like a relatively thin skin of concrete.'

'What's down there?' Karen drew closer, answering her own question by studying the screen.

'Well, there's definitely something down there. You know how you said there might be a snowboard bag? I think you might be right but it's hard to be sure because, look' – he pointed at the screen with a pen. 'See all this yellowy stuff? I think it's expanding polystyrene foam. But whoever put it there wasn't as thorough as they should have been. They've not achieved an all-round seal. You can see bits of red fabric where it hasn't completely covered the bag. So we know now that we can cut the concrete very carefully and remove it. Then we'll have a better idea what we're dealing with.'

He stood back and nodded to the colleague he'd left holding the flexible snake. 'Take it out and let's look down the other holes to be sure before we start cutting.' He grinned at Karen. 'Makes a change. Life in lockdown's been a wee bittie dull.'

'I wish I could say the same,' she sighed. 'It smells like there's something more than a snowboard bag down there.'

'Aye, well . . . concrete's porous, so there's going to be aerobic decay. You're not going to get a nice neat mummified corpse. We're likely going to need Dr Wilde before we get answers on this one. You might as well away and get yourself a cup of coffee. I bet his nibs in there has got all sorts of magic machines. There'll be nothing to see here for at least half an hour. Probably longer.'

'I'll stick around, if it's all the same to you, Shane. You know me, I hate to miss the chance to watch experts at work.' She turned back to her chair but before she could sit down, a car turned in at the gate and headed down the drive. The PC who had been standing guard at the crime scene tape looked at Karen and said, 'You want me to see who that is?'

'You bet.'

He broke into a trot as the car reached the turning circle at the head of the drive, Karen on his heels. The Lexus slowed to a halt and the driver emerged. 'Oh, fuck,' Karen groaned.

36

Rosalind Harris was in full lawyer battledress. Black suit with a swirling full skirt, white shirt with a jabot of lace at the neck, and an olive drab mac with the sort of dramatic cut that German designers favoured. Karen knew it had been chosen to put her on the back foot, and she wasn't having any of it.

The PC had placed himself between Rosalind and the front door. 'I'm sorry, ma'am,' he said, polite but firm.

'Thanks, officer,' Karen said, drawing alongside. 'Morning, Ms Harris. I presume you're here to see Mr McEwen.'

'Is there a problem with that?' The chill in her voice could have given the Dog Biscuit a run for her money.

'I'm afraid so. You'll see from the tape around the garage that this is potentially a crime scene, and you'll appreciate that it's in everyone's interests to keep that as pristine as we can.' Karen sounded as affable as a server at a coffee morning.

'There's no tape round the house,' Rosalind pointed out, sidestepping the PC.

'I don't think we've got a roll long enough. We are in fact conducting a room by room search of the house as we speak.

We have already found what we believe to be a significant piece of evidence.'

'Evidence of what?' She tried to move closer to the house. Karen neatly cut off her approach. Her steady expression made it clear that Rosalind would have to resort to physical contact to get past her.

'That's not entirely clear at present.'

'I insist on seeing Mr McEwen,' she said. Karen could see her dander was up, but that her lawyer's instincts were keeping it under control.

'You're not a criminal lawyer. I can't let you into the house. And I need Mr McEwen to be present while the search is under way. And besides, you'd be in breach of COVID regulations. You and Mr McEwen are not living together, am I right?' An almost imperceptible nod. 'So you're not in a bubble. So the only way you can legitimately communicate is if you're out in the open air two metres apart.' Karen smiled sweetly. 'And I've got a feeling the pair of you don't want to have a conversation at that volume.'

Rosalind blinked several times in quick succession. She knew when she was outmanoeuvred, Karen thought. 'There's no reason why you can't speak to each other on the phone, FaceTime or even Zoom. But I can't let you into the house.'

'You're not making any friends here, DCI Pirie.'

'I didn't join the polis to make friends, Ms Harris. I did. join up to solve crime and give people answers about the fate of those they love. To that end, I'd like to interview you again.'

'I don't think so.' She moved towards her car.

'You're not getting it, Ms Harris.'

Rosalind swung back to face her, two spots of colour on her cheeks. 'What am I "not getting"?'

'When we met before, you misspoke. More than once. I don't have to tell you how much of a mistake that is. I'd like to give you the opportunity to correct your statements before you dig a deeper hole for yourself.'

Rosalind put her hand on the door of her car, a clear preparation for departure. She pulled her lips tight, showing a thin line of white teeth between the dark red.

'I could arrest you and interview you under caution, but I don't want to do that. You know what the Edinburgh legal world is like. I don't want to embarrass you. So why don't we meet up later today and we can iron out those errors?' Karen let the steel in. 'And I may even have some results to share with you.'

'Carrot *and* stick. Very well done. I know your old boss. Simon Lees. He's quite glad not to be your boss any longer.'

'That makes two of us. Shall we say four o'clock? Middle Meadow Walk, like before?'

Rosalind got into her car and started the engine. 'Make it four thirty. I have meetings.'

Karen watched her go, wondering again just where she fitted in this jigsaw. Right now, she was very definitely sky.

'So, we cut away the polyurethane foam with craft knives, as close to the snowboard bag as we could manage,' Shane explained. 'Then we moistened it all over with a dissolvent, left it for ten minutes or so then wiped it off with industrial cleaning wipes. Et voilà. One zipped-up snowboard bag.' He made an extravagant gesture with his arm, indicating the bag, still in situ.

'Amazing. Will you be able to open it up where it is?'
Karen peered down into the pit.

'We'll have to, I think. Given what's likely in there.'
Karen looked a question at Shane. He pulled a face. 'Think a
bundle of bones submerged in the kind of sloppy soup that'll
put you off minestrone for life. As for opening it up, I'm not
keen to apply more solvent to the zips. The foam's invaded
the wee spaces between the teeth and there could be forensic evidence there. I'd suggest we make a very careful cut
along the bag next to the zip. That way, we'll see what's in
there, but we'll still preserve any possible evidence. The
photographer's taken plenty of shots as we've gone along,
and she'll do video of the opening up. Do you want us to
get started?'

'Can you guys take a break first? I need to bring the
householder out to see this. I want to see his face.'

'Sure. I'm dying for a vape. Better now than after we open
it up.' He turned to his team. 'Time out, everybody. The
DCI needs the room.' They did as they were asked. Karen
watched them climb back aboard their van then returned
to the house.

Ross McEwen was still sitting at the kitchen table, the
remains of a cheese and tomato sandwich next to his iPad.
He looked up as she entered. 'Tell your sergeant she's not
compromising herself if she accepts a sandwich,' he said.

'She's on a diet,' Karen said. 'We're making some progress
out in the garage. I wonder if you'd mind coming out and
having a wee look.'

He seemed alarmed. 'You're not going to tell me
there's a body there?' He stood up and took a couple of
steps backward.

'Is that what you're expecting?'

He looked anguished. 'I'm not expecting anything! Christ, I thought it was just an empty space till you rocked up yesterday.'

'I'd like you to come and take a look at this stage. There's no human remains. Not yet, anyway.' Karen fixed him with a hard stare. She knew it would be hard for him to refuse. 'Think of it as research for your next novel.' She gestured towards the kitchen door and followed close on his heels as he reluctantly made for it. Daisy brought up the rear, conscious of her role as the corroborating officer for whatever might come next.

Looking at the garage through his eyes, she thought it must be a shock. There were a couple of heaps of broken concrete to one side, and a scatter of strangely shaped chunks of polyurethane foam. The smell of solvent hung in the air, and it wasn't hard to imagine the taint of something else. Ross hesitated in the doorway. He licked his lips and turned to Karen, a beseeching look on his face.

'On you go,' she said. It wasn't a tone of voice designed for argument.

He took a few shuffling steps forward, craning his neck to see what lay below. Then all at once, he relaxed his shoulders. 'What is that?' He pointed at the scarlet bag. Curiosity appeared to trump fear in the moment. 'Is it a golf bag?'

'It's a snowboard travelling bag. Does it belong to you, Ross?' Now her voice was gentle.

'No way. I've never been snowboarding. I hate the cold. When I go on holiday, I head for the sun. The Mediterranean in the summer, Morocco or Sharm El-Sheikh in the winter. I've never even seen a snowboard up close and personal. Swear to God.' He kept staring into the pit, the very picture of bemusement.

Then suddenly it dawned on him. 'Is there a body in there?' He faced Karen, his mouth open, his eyes panicked. 'Are you telling me Lara Hardie's down there?'

'I don't know yet,' Karen said. 'What do you think?'

He backed away, careful where he was putting his feet. 'I don't think anything. This is mad. If there's anybody down there, it's fuck all to do with me.'

Karen raised her eyebrows. 'It's your garage.'

He squeezed his eyes tight shut, twisting his mouth into a grimace of fear. 'Whatever happened here, it wasn't me. Far as I was concerned, it was just an empty hole.'

'Shall we open it up and see what's inside?' Karen moved forward. There was a short flight of concrete steps at one end of the pit.

'No,' he howled. 'You can't do this to me, you've got no right.'

She shrugged. 'I thought you'd be interested to see what's buried in your garage, Ross. I would, if it was me, wondering whether there was the body of a young woman down there.'

He convulsed, hand over his mouth. He ran for the door, pushing Daisy to the side. He barely made it to the door before he vomited copiously on his lovely gravel drive. He stood panting, hands on his knees. Finally, he looked round at Karen with an expression of absolute hatred. He straightened up and staggered back to the kitchen door.

'You don't think that was a bit harsh, boss?' Daisy asked.

'He's almost certainly got a dead lassie in his garage. How else do you expect me to be?'

When Shane and his team returned, Karen was ready. In their absence, she'd rung Dr River Wilde, forensic anthropologist and probably the nearest Karen had to a best friend.

She'd sort out the budget for bringing her up from the Lake District afterwards; if they got the result she expected, the Dog Biscuit couldn't kick off too much. Karen had outlined what they had so far and what she was expecting. 'We're about to open the bag but I thought I'd give you time to get packed.'

'At least we know I'm not going to get caught up in traffic. Let me know as soon as you've got more info.'

Shane looked at the pit, and called over one of his colleagues. Even though the foam had been cut away, the space around the bag was still tight. 'Isha, you're about half my size. Are you OK with getting in there and making the cut?'

It was hard to read her reaction behind the mask and the goggles she was wearing. But she nodded and took a breath. 'Nae bother, Shane.' All eyes were on her as she made her way down the steps and edged round the bag.

'Take the cut about a centimetre in from the zip,' Shane said.

Isha took the plastic protector off the scalpel blade. She placed it where she planned to start cutting then looked up for approval. Shane nodded and she started the long cut. The bag parted and the full stench assaulted them in a wave of rot. Karen felt her gorge rise and had to swallow hard. 'Bloody hell,' she heard one of the scene examiners say. Another ran from the garage; she heard him retching. Karen stared down at the disgusting mess that had once been a human being. A few bits of bone emerged from the grisly slurry, including the unmistakable curve of a skull, but there was nothing to give a name to the remains.

'That's enough for now,' Karen said. 'Thanks, Isha. River will be here soon as, and she'll figure out how to preserve the remains. All you can do now is process the garage itself, see whether there's anything of use to us. Not that I'm hold-ing out much hope. But if that's who we think it is, at least one family will have the start of an answer to the question of what happened to their lassie.' Karen turned away, and walked back to the house, knowing full well that the start of an answer meant little without the end.

37

Ross McEwen had been stricken when the search team had departed with his laptop, his desktop, his iPad, his mini iPad and his phone, protesting that he couldn't work without the tools of his trade. 'We're not taking your pens or your paper,' Daisy had pointed out.

'I can hardly read my own writing,' he'd complained.

She'd shrugged. 'Sorry. You could probably pick up a reconditioned laptop relatively cheaply. If you're desperate.'

'But how can I do that if I can't get online to buy it?'

'Good point. Maybe Ms Harris could buy it for you and have it sent here?'

Karen walked in at that point. 'Lacking a laptop is probably the least of your worries right now. In fact, it might be a benefit, since it'll make it harder for the press to contact you.'

'You're talking to the press?'

'It's going to be impossible to avoid it. As we feared, there are human remains in your garage.'

McEwen seemed to shrink visibly. He crossed his arms over his chest and curled in on himself. 'Jesus,' he whispered. 'I can't believe he really did it.'

'At this point, we have no idea of the identity of the person whose remains we've found.'

McEwen stared at Karen. 'You want *me* to look at the body? No way. It's nothing to do with me. I spent one day in a room full of people with her, I can't identify her.' He tugged nervously at his beard. 'I had nothing to do with this.'

'Nobody could identify her right now, except for a forensic anthropologist.'

He looked nauseated. Any crime writer would have understood Karen's words. 'This is a nightmare,' he groaned.

'I find myself in a very difficult position, Mr McEwen. On the face of it, you're prime suspect in a suspicious death. A young woman known to you who disappeared without a trace a year ago may well have turned up dead in your garage. In normal circumstances, you'd be under arrest right now and on your way to a police cell. But on the other hand, we have what appears to be a confession from someone else. However, we can't confront him with what we think we know because he's dead.' Karen sat down opposite McEwen. 'You see my problem?'

He scoffed. 'Your problem is not my problem. It's not that I don't want to help – it's just that I can't. I don't know how it got there.'

'Are you still driving the same car you had a year ago? The Prius?'

'Yes, but—'

'I'm going to have the crime scene techs go over it too. We have to look for any traces of Lara Hardie.'

A sudden look of horror spread across his face. 'My car . . . I never thought about it before. I lent my car to Jake for a couple of days round about then. I can't be sure about the date, but I can check with my diary. I was out of town, doing an event in the Borders, in Melrose. I went on the train.'

339

The broken light of hope appeared on his face. 'I never made the connection.'

Daisy and Karen exchanged looks. It felt like a convenient recollection. 'You're now telling us that Jake Stein had borrowed your car on the night of the disappearance?' Karen asked, her voice flat. 'Really?'

He swallowed hard. 'Yes, his car was in the garage, having something done to it. And he asked if he could borrow mine. I wasn't using it, I told him he could have it for as long as he needed it. Ask Ros, she'll remember. Because we had to use her car to go out to dinner at Jamie Scott's in Newport later in the week. You've got to believe me!'

'Sergeant, come with me,' Karen said. 'Wait here for now, Mr McEwen.'

The two women stepped outside. 'What do we do next?' Daisy asked, her face eager.

'In an ideal world, I'd kick it upstairs. But the Dog Biscuit is so fucked off with me right now, she'd just take it off us and let an MIT wrap it up.'

'Would that be such a bad thing? I mean, we're not in it for the glory, and everybody would know it was an HCU operation.'

'This isn't a vanity project, Daisy. I don't care who puts it to bed as long as they've nailed it down on all four corners. But I'm not convinced the MIT will take it seriously enough. If I'm honest, I probably wouldn't have if I hadn't been desperate for something to get my teeth into. In the normal run of things, I probably wouldn't have chased it like we have. Now, I have no reason to doubt this was part of a nasty plot by Jake Stein to take revenge on his wife and her new love, to get his own back for his chess partner betraying him. But we have to be even-handed about it. Stein's not here to defend himself so we have to take on that role. Pick holes in our own case wherever we can.' Karen threw her hands in the air in frustration. 'We're the prosecution and the defence. I've never had to do this before.'

'So what do we do, practically?'

Karen began pacing, thinking aloud. 'The media are going to be all over this. Somebody will leak it.' Pause. 'And then Ross will be fair game. If he was under arrest, they couldn't get to him.' Pause. 'But I don't want *him* under arrest because of something Jake Stein did. And I don't want to open us up to accusations of wrongful arrest either.' Pause. A sardonic smile. 'That really would be a budget buster. But we are going to have to leave at least one officer on site. He could keep an eye on things.'

'Why don't we try to do a deal?'

Karen paused and gave Daisy a speculative look. 'What kind of a deal?'

'Well, technically, he can't go someplace else anyway, because of the lockdown restrictions. He'd probably want to hole up with the lovely Rosalind, but that's not an available option, is it? Why don't you tell him he has to stay put, where we can get our hands on him at any time? And tell him that if he does try to leave, the officer on duty has orders to arrest him on suspicion of murder? The deal is we won't arrest him yet . . . '

'Respect,' Karen said with an air of surprise. 'That's smart. You've spent more time with him. D'you think he'd go for it?'

'Short of chaining the Mint to his ankle, I don't see what other option we have.'

'Let's give it a try. And then I need to shoot off. I've got to get to Gayfield Square to spin a yarn to the bobbies who turned up at the breakwater. And then I have to go and interview Rosalind Harris.'

Daisy headed for the kitchen. She paused, fingers resting on the door handle. 'Is he OK? Your pal Rafiq?'

'He's in the wind. I don't know where he is and that's probably as well. I hope he finds a safe place. I liked him.' She turned away and headed for the car. Over her shoulder, she said, 'Stick around a bit longer, but make sure he understands that he's effectively under house arrest. Maybe see if he fancies a game of Scrabble. Or chess, if you're up to it . . .'

Karen arrived at Gayfield Square to find a uniformed sergeant waiting in the reception area for her, masked and properly distanced. 'Are you comfortable talking in my office? There's a good three metres between two of the desks.'

'That'll be fine.'

She put his stiff response down to awkwardness at being in someone else's station. She led the way and entered first, pointing him to Jason's desk. 'It's still weird, trying to do things by the rules,' she said.

He sat deliberately, and produced his notebook. 'I don't think you were entirely managing that last night, were you, Chief Inspector.' His voice was gruff, his eyebrows rising with the question.

So it was going to be like that. 'On the contrary. Until the man went in the water, we were being scrupulous. Sergeant Mortimer and I are in a bubble. We're staying in a flat that belongs to Mr Mackenzie. He has a business that produces hand sanitiser, so he comes to Edinburgh regularly to make deliveries. He contacted me and asked me to collect some urgent paperwork from his desk. We arranged we'd meet

342

down at the Western Harbour Breakwater for the handover. We kept our distance. I put the papers down on a bench and stepped back so Hamish could pick them up.'

From what she could see of his face, he didn't seem convinced. 'What was so important about these papers?'

'All I know is that Hamish said he needed proof of ownership of his new business. It involves a still, so I'm guessing it might be something to do with his licence.'

'Why the Western Harbour Breakwater? The address I've got for you is Forth Street. That's quite a step. More than an hour's exercise there and back, I'd have thought.'

'I have a flat there. It's permissible to check on unoccupied property. I thought I'd kill two birds with one stone.'

He grunted. 'Take me through what happened.'

Karen had run through it so many times in her head she'd almost come to believe her version of events. 'The three of us walked out towards the lighthouse. We were strung out across the path, keeping our distance. When we came out of the shelter of the bushes, I saw a jogger running towards us, from the direction of the lighthouse. He moved on to the breakwater to avoid getting too close to us. I'm not sure whether he tripped or slipped but suddenly he was tumbling down into the water. Hamish stripped off his coat and jumper and his shoes and dived in. Daisy followed. They swam out to where they'd last seen him, but they couldn't find him. The current's strong there ... I called the control room and asked for assistance. The rest you know.'

He sat back in his seat with an air of dissatisfaction. 'And you say you didn't know this jogger?'

'Never seen him before, as far as I'm aware.'

He produced a folded sheet of paper and opened it out for her to see. 'As far as you're aware?'

Karen studied the photograph. The mortuary technician had done a good job. He didn't so much look dead as CGI'd. His skin was pale brown, his brows heavy. A trimmed beard covered the lower part of his face. There was nothing particularly distinctive about him except that the bottom part of his right ear lobe was missing, as if it had been neatly sliced off. She genuinely had never seen him before. She shook her head. 'It was dark, he had his hood up. A lot of people run along the breakwater these days, I don't pay much attention to them.'

He took the picture back. 'We're releasing that to the media tomorrow and putting it up on the socials.' Then almost as an afterthought, he said, 'Are you not the woman that helped the Syrian refugees set up that café down Duke Street?'

'That's right. And no, he's not one of the café crowd, I'm sure of that.'

'I'll maybe take a turn down there and see if they can help me.'

'Good idea. Would you like me to type up my statement and email it to you? Rather than sit here laboriously writing it out? I can have it with you first thing.' She pushed her chair back, indicating she was done here.

'That'd be helpful. Thanks, DCI Pirie. I can see myself out.'

She watched him leave. Please God, let there not have been one of her boat-spotting neighbours at their window. There had been a couple of moments there when she'd felt the thin ice cracking beneath her feet.

Karen stirred herself and checked her watch. She reckoned she had time enough to swing by the flat and brew herself a coffee to go. It was turning into a long and stressful day and she felt seriously undercaffeinated. Sometimes she

wondered if the effect was as much psychological as physical. Literally, wake up and smell the coffee. Whichever it
was, she had to confess she was an addict. Growing up, she'd
known no better than instant. But her present requirement
for really good coffee was more a marker of her shift into the
middle class than anything else she could think of. Maybe
if Hamish had been a distiller from the word go instead of a
coffee entrepreneur, she'd never have fallen for his charms
in the first place. Seduced by a Brazilian single estate ...

It was a depressing thought for all sorts of reasons.

Karen shoved Hamish to the back of her mind and set off
across town to the Meadows, sipping from her keep cup as
she went. She managed not to think about Hamish except
when she was passing Perk, his hole-in-the-wall coffee
shop on George IV Bridge. Closed now, of course. In spite
of that blip of memory, she felt her energy levels rising and
by the time Rosalind came in sight, she was ready for the
next round.

Rosalind launched straight in. 'So you found the body.
Right where Jake's manuscript said you would. So why are
you holding Ross in a kind of house arrest? Either arrest
him or let him go.'

'Go where? We're in lockdown, as you seem to keep
forgetting.'

'Oh, so it's good practice to leave him in the middle of a
crime scene?'

Karen sighed. 'I don't like this any more than either of
you does. But the scene examiners have finished with the
house. They're not underfoot any more.'

'There's still a body in his garage.'

'Let's walk,' Karen said, tired already of the other woman's combative approach. She led the way down Jawbone

345

Walk, where they found an empty bench. Karen plonked herself down at one end, gesturing that Rosalind should do likewise at the other end. 'You're a lawyer. You know the dangers involved in lying to a polis. I'm giving you one more chance to come clean. Otherwise the next interview will be under caution in a police station.'

'You're quick with the threats, DCI Pirie.'

Karen sighed. 'It's not a threat. It's an explanation of the next stage on the route map. When I asked you if your husband had a regular opponent at chess, you lied. You told me you really couldn't say. But you knew very well that he played every couple of weeks against Ross McEwen.'

Rosalind shrugged. 'As I said at the time, I really didn't pay attention.'

'Not even when you started sleeping with Mr McEwen? You didn't tell me about that either.'

Rosalind's eyes narrowed in anger. 'You never asked me about Ross.'

'I asked you if you knew him. You said you'd met him a couple of times. Another lie. And an interesting one. Apart from anything else, it provides motivation for why your ex-husband wanted to destroy you. And your lover. So why deny it?'

'Because I thought it was none of your business,' she snapped.

Karen chuckled. 'It's easy to see you've never practised criminal law. In my world, Ros, everything's relevant until it's not. When did you and Mr McEwen become lovers?'

She stared at the ground. 'You've read the book.'

'I thought you hadn't?'

'You told me enough.'

'It's not what you'd call precise.'

346

Rosalind squeezed her eyes shut momentarily, then raised her head. 'It was well before the divorce. I was still living in the Ravelston Dykes house, trying to figure out how I could get to be a free agent. Because Jake would never have conceded that. It took the very public Marga Durham incident to make that possible.'

'Do you think your husband might have known you were lovers?'

She looked everywhere but at Karen. 'I thought not. I believed he would have gone off like a thermonuclear explosion had he known. But obviously, I was wrong. Once I was out of his reach, his warped mind had to come up with something else.'

There was a long silence. There was something about this version of events that wasn't sitting right with Karen. 'Do you have any idea how Lara Hardie's body might have ended up in your lover's garage? If it is her remains.'

'Dear God. No, I don't. I didn't know Jake was writing a bizarre story about a perfect murder, though I'm not entirely surprised you think he had it in him to kill someone. But if you're looking at Ross for Lara Hardie, you're looking in the wrong place.' She stood up, wrapping her coat around her. 'Try the Dean Cemetery. That's Jake's address these days.'

38

Karen watched Rosalind Harris stalk off down Jawbone Walk, her coat swinging around her like a flag. This was clearly her week for pissing people off. But something the lawyer had said had provoked a niggling thought. *I believed he would have gone off like a thermonuclear explosion had he known. But obviously, I was wrong. Once I was out of his reach, his warped mind had to come up with something else.*

Because warped was the perfect word to describe the revenge plot Jake Stein had come up with. She'd been swept away by the idea of Stein trying to destroy the happiness of his ex-wife and her lover, but the only truly ruptured reputation in the fraction of the book that had been left behind was that of its supposed author. Although all they had was a partial manuscript; who knew what twists and turns Jake Stein had planned? In the world of crime writers, maybe coming up with the perfect plot would be sufficient to restore his damaged name, even if it meant delivering a posthumous confession to a murder.

Before she could explore that idea further, her phone rang. A quick glance at the screen told her she needed to answer it. Tamsin Martineau extended her favours to the HCU in exchange for nothing more than a supply of premium chocolate biscuits because she was as committed to bringing the dead home as was Karen. So when the HCU's woman inside the forensic unit at Gartcosh called, Karen was always quick to respond. 'Tamsin,' she said, unable to keep the weariness from her voice.

'Bloody hell, Karen, you sound like you lost a dollar and found a cent.' Mostly, Tamsin had acquired the idiom of her adopted country but every now and again the Aussie in her slipped out.

'Tough week,' she said. 'Complicated case, Jason's in trouble, I think me and Hamish have hit the buffers.'

'That's harsh. And I'm afraid I don't have much to lighten the load.'

'Damn, I thought bad things only came in threes.'

'No, but listen, this isn't all bad, it's only "not good". We've got a new bloke in digital, just joined us from the private sector. Devon. Not only is he greased lightning, he seems to have a soft spot for me.'

Karen wondered what kind of space cadet would have a soft spot for a tattooed and pierced post-punk whose hair changed colour and style as often as a computer geek's T-shirt. Then scolded herself for being so superficial. Tamsin wasn't just a hotshot in the lab, she was smart and kind too. Devon might end up being a very lucky boy. 'No accounting for tastes,' she said, making sure the tease in her voice shone through. 'So has he made some headway with the external drive?'

'He has. It's quite interesting. On the face of it, what you've got appears to be a mirror drive of Lara Hardie's laptop. Data files, apps, etc. You could run a brand-new machine off this.'

'But? I can hear a but.'

'Everything is clean. There's no history. You try to roll out

349

the version history of a file or a folder, and there's nothing there. There's no trace of anything having been erased. No "recently deleted" emails. Nothing in the trash.'

'The manuscript said something like that,' Karen recalled. 'A bit over my head, Tamsin.'

'One of these days you're going to have to go on a digital forensics 101 course, Karen. What it means is that, at first glance, this looks like a back-up hard drive. But in reality, it's a carefully curated version of a hard drive that's been scrubbed of anything the person who made it didn't want you to see. It's been painstakingly moved across chunk by chunk. None of the fragments that inevitably get left behind when you erase something are there.'

'You mean, it's a fake copy?'

'That's exactly it. Hard to say why anyone would go to all that trouble; you know and I know that there's no *good* reason for creating an artefact like this. It's all about the appearance of candour without being candid.'

'I think it makes sense. It gives us access to what the killer wants us to know but he's obviously not copied anything that calls that version of events into question. It's clever.'

'It would fool most people at first or even second glance. But put it in front of a wizard like our Devon and it falls apart in his hands.'

'Sounds like the soft spot is mutual.'

Tamsin snorted. 'It's his expertise I've fallen for, and that's all. So, does this take you any further forward?'

'I don't honestly know. But if your Devon's at a loose end, there's a fine digital harvest en route to Gartcosh. All the devices we could lay hands on belonging to one Ross McEwen. That should keep him busy for a while. Not least distinguishing truth from fiction.'

'We like a challenge out here in the Crime Campus. To be honest, we're not overwhelmed right now, we're actually managing to clear some of the backlog. And the guys who came home from Italy with COVID before we even knew what COVID was, they're all back at work.'

'No lasting effects, then?'

'Hard to say. One of them is complaining about reduced lung capacity and a couple seem to be permanently knackered, but none of them was exactly Mr Sparky before. I will say, though, that it's made me a bit more religious about masking up and hand sanitising.'

Karen grunted assent. 'Jason's mum's on the brink of going on a ventilator. He's terrified.'

'Who wouldn't be? Give him my best, would you? He's a good egg. But what's with you and Hamish?'

'Long story. For another day. I'll be fine.'

'Course you will, girlfriend. If you need me, you know where I am. Now bugger off and figure out what Devon's discovery means.'

Jason was lying on top of the bed, still fully dressed. He'd been drifting in and out of sleep for a few hours, his exhausted body at odds with his troubled heart and fearful thoughts. What would he do without his mum? OK, he'd still have his dad, but since their parents had split up, the two boys had been clear in their allegiance. Ronan was his father's son; slippery, over-confident, economical with the truth, great fun on a night out. Jason wanted to be like his mother; loyal, reliable, hard-working, kind and honest. Losing Sandra on top of Phil, his mentor, would leave him adrift. Karen was great, but she was always his boss ahead of being his friend.

351

Eilidh was lovely, no getting away from that. But she didn't know what to do in a crisis. OK, when he'd had the accident that had left him in a dark cellar with a broken leg, she'd turned up at his bedside in Stockport with his mum. And then she couldn't get away home quick enough. The women whose hair she had to cut took precedence over Jason in his hospital bed. Not that he blamed her – she had her job to consider and there was nothing she could do for him. But Sandra had stayed. They'd watched stupid TV programmes together, had a good laugh about people they knew, even watched football on his laptop. She'd been a comfort.

He turned over again and tried to settle, punching the pillow into submission. He recited Scottish football goal scorers of the previous decade in his head, and he'd begun to drift off to Shaun Maloney, Steven Fletcher, Steven Naismith, Chris Berra, when his phone cut through the reverie. He jerked upright and freaked out when he saw the hospital's number on the screen. His heart raced and he felt sweat breaking out on his forehead. 'Uh huh, this is Jason,' he gabbled.

'Hello, Jason. This is Abu from the COVID ward. We spoke before about your mum?'

'How's she doing? Is she—'

'I'm sorry to say she's having increasing issues with her breathing. We want to help her, and the best way to do that is to put her on a ventilator, as we discussed before. We hoped we could avoid it, but now it's the best thing for her. She'll be more comfortable.'

'Is she going to die?' He'd blurted it out without meaning to.

'Not if we can help it. The thing is, Jason, she'll not be

able to speak once we get the ventilator up and running. So what we're going to do is a FaceTime call for the two of you. Have you got a tablet? A phone will do fine if not, you just get a better picture on a tablet.'

He leapt up from the bed and ran into the living room. He snatched up his iPad and ran back, leaving Eilidh trailing a battery of questions in his wake. It was a matter of a few minutes to set up the call, and suddenly Jason was face to face with a woman he barely recognised as his mother. Gaunt and pale, sweating and panting, she was a strange distortion of the woman he loved. 'Hi Mum,' he said through dry lips. 'It's me, Jason. I'm sorry I'm not there beside you but they willnae let me in.'

Sandra croaked something that might have been, 'I love you, son.'

'I love you too, Mum. The doctors say you're a fighter, like I needed telling. I know you're gonnae beat this thing, Mum. Everybody's rooting for you. Eilidh, Ronan. Even the boss, she can't believe you've not sent the COVID packing.'

Her eyelids fluttered and her mouth worked, as if she wanted to say something but it was lost in translation. A gloved hand moved into shot, a moistened sponge dabbing at her lips. 'Jason,' she said, clearly this time. 'I'm so proud of you. Best son a woman could—' she broke off to cough, a harsh bark that felt like it would never stop. At last, she lay gasping. 'Best . . . boy.'

Then a Black man he took to be Abu appeared in the corner of the screen. 'I'm sorry, Jason, Sandra. But it's time.' He gave a wee self-conscious wave.

'I love you, Mum,' Jason said desperately.

She moved her head in an almost-nod. 'I know.'

Then the screen blanked for a moment, then Abu

reappeared. 'Thanks, Jason, it meant a lot to you both, I could see that. Now the doctors and nurses have to do their work. We'll speak to you this evening.'

And it was over. 'The kindness of strangers.' He remembered there had been a film called that last year. Now he knew what they meant. It eased his heart a little to know that his mother was surrounded by kindness. But he wouldn't know peace till she was back home, surrounded by love.

Karen sat on the bench on Jawbone Walk. She was trying to make sense of the disparate pieces they'd uncovered over the past few days. If she arranged the pieces in their logical order, everything seemed to fit. It wasn't as if something was rammed into place in a spot where it really wasn't supposed to go. Her father had been guilty of that when they'd done jigsaws together in her teens. If he thought a piece belonged somewhere, then he'd do everything short of hitting it with a hammer to make it so. This case didn't appear to suffer from that problem.

And yet when she ran through the story in her head, something niggled. Maybe it was nothing more than that the run-through was simply too neat. She was still troubled by Jake Stein writing himself into the role of the bad guy if he was simply trying to fuck up McEwen and his wife. Was it enough to pin her conviction on the unwritten section of Stein's book?

In the end, she got to her feet, intending to return to the flat and pick up her car. Now Rafiq had disappeared, her flat was empty and she'd offered it to River. She'd wait for her in the underground car park and they could walk round the breakwater while Karen filled her in.

As she walked down George IV Bridge, Karen called her friend. 'What's your ETA?'

'According to the satnav, twenty-three minutes. Do you want me to come round to Hamish's flat to collect your key?'

'No, I'll meet you in the underground car park at my place.'

'Very Deep Throat,' River chuckled. 'I'll see you there.'

River made it to the breakwater flats four minutes ahead of Karen, who pointed her towards her designated space. She parked two cars away from River; she knew that neighbour had gone into lockdown with his fiancée in Glasgow. They kept the two cars' distance between them as they greeted each other. It was strangely poignant to meet up without opening their arms to an embrace.

'I want to give you a massive hug,' River said.

'Me too. It's been a shit few days. And Jason's mum's gone on a ventilator – I just got a text from his fiancée with the news.'

River groaned. 'That's not good. What's her health like generally?'

'I'd have said she was tough as old boots, but COVID's knocked the feet from under her. All we can do now is wait. And poor Jason's under suspension thanks to his fuckwit brother.'

'Tell me,' River commanded as they walked up the ramp out into the dark skies of evening. So Karen did.

As if on cue, her phone rang. The screen read DCI TODD. Daisy's old boss before Karen had stolen her. He ran the MIT team in Fife, which could only mean one thing right now. She rolled her eyes at River. 'Charlie,' she said, accepting the call. 'Tell me my mum's not gone on a shoplifting spree in Aldi.'

'I wish,' he said, a chuckle in his voice. 'No. It's a courtesy call to let you know we've lifted Ronan Murray.'

A sharp intake of breath, then Karen said, 'Where did you pick him up?'

'He checked in with the hospital and they said Mrs Murray was going on a ventilator but he could speak to her on FaceTime if he was quick. So he rang back five minutes later to talk to his mum.'

Karen groaned. 'I can guess what's coming.'

'The background. He was in the Beveridge Park. By the kids' play area.'

'All those unmistakable turrets … I take it you sent a patrol car down?'

'We did. They picked him up swaggering out the park with his two best mates. He's cooling his heels in a cell. I know it's tough on your boy Jason, but we're going to have to charge him. Impersonating a police officer, and three counts of assault against hospital staff, it's too much to ignore. We'll probably not bother with the fixed penalty notice for breaching COVID restrictions in the circumstances.'

'Poor Jason.'

'Aye. Do you want to pass on the glad tidings?'

In the hierarchy of stupid questions, that one was up there with, 'Apart from that, Mrs Lincoln, how did you enjoy the play?' Karen sighed. 'No, but I will. In exchange, if Ronan lets Jason off the hook, will you tell ACC Markie that he had nothing whatsoever to do with his brother's string of stupid offences?'

'Aye, I'll make sure I get that loud and clear from the eejit. And I'll pass it up the line.'

'Thanks. And thanks for letting me know, Charlie.' She ended the call, and explained the situation to River. 'I'm going to have to go round and tell Jason. Can we pick this up later? I'll call you when I'm clear and we can huddle on one of the benches?'

'Sure. Give me the key and I'll get settled in to the flat. Good luck.'

Karen walked back to her car. Luck was in short supply that week, she thought. It was about time the wheel turned in her favour. Trouble was, she couldn't imagine what luck looked like right now.

39

It was almost reassuring to find herself trailing the 36 bus, Karen thought. It was a moment of normality on the otherwise quiet streets of Leith. The bus pulled up at a stop to pick up a passenger, and Karen overtook it, finding herself back on a ghostly street. She double-parked outside Jason's building. Nobody would be going anywhere, and she wasn't planning on being there long. She called the landline and Eilidh answered. 'Hi Eilidh, I need to speak to Jason. Could you ask him to come downstairs?'

'Is it about his mum? Because he knows, he spoke to her on FaceTime before they put her on the ventilator.'

'No, it's not his mum.'

'Because if it's his work, he's not coming down. You should have stood up for him in front of Ann Markie, not let her put him on suspension for doing nothing. And then you've got the cheek to sit him outside somebody's house in Barnton all night.' A muffled sound, a small struggle, then Jason spoke.

'Sorry, boss. Eilidh's just ... you know?'

'It's OK, Jason. But I do need to speak to you. Can you come down, please?'

'Sure. Be right there.'

As he hung up she heard him say, 'You can't talk to—'

She could fill in the blanks herself. But Karen wasn't about to dodge the knowledge that Eilidh had a point.

Jason appeared at the door, clearly having run down the stairs. Hair askew, face grey with worry where it wasn't scribbled with ginger stubble. He looked as if he'd lost weight since that morning. 'Boss,' he said. 'Sorry about Eilidh.'

'I'd probably have said the same in her shoes. Strange days, Jason. We're all strangers to ourselves. I've got some news that I wanted to tell you face to face. It's not your mum,' she added hastily, seeing his face crumple.

He frowned. 'What, then?'

She repeated Charlie Todd's information. 'I'm sorry, Jason. Charlie's going to pass it up the line to the Dog Biscuit as soon as Ronan lets you off the hook.' She worried that might seem insensitive, with Sandra on a ventilator and Eilidh on the warpath, but she saw a spark of relief in his eyes.

'Thanks, boss. It's better for my head if I've got something else to think about. Like when Phil was in the hospital and we went to Oxford. Because that's what he would have wanted us to do. Right?'

Karen remembered the white-hot burn of fear that had sat inside her; the only thing that had dampened it down was knowing Phil would have been cheering on from the sidelines. 'I remember,' she said.

He nodded. 'I can't believe Ronan. He's pulled some stunts in his time, but this? He's going to go to the jail. No getting away from that. And so he should. Fighting with nurses, for fuck's sake. My mum's going to give him a right tongue-lashing when she gets out of the hospital.'

It was a brave line. She hoped it would come true.

*

Ross McEwen got to his feet. 'Are you moving in?' he asked Daisy, more brusquely than he'd spoken before.

'No. Now the scene examiners have gone, and we've not found your secret stash of Class A drugs, I think I'll call it a day. I'll just remind you that we'd prefer you not to leave the premises, but you're not under arrest so you're free to leave the house for your one hour's permitted exercise. But you should be aware that there are a couple of journalists with long lenses sitting at the end of your drive. Two metres apart, obviously.'

'Who told them there was something to see here?'

Daisy shrugged. 'Wasn't the HCU team. Probably a nosy neighbour seeing the comings and goings, put it together with the small announcement from Police Scotland that human remains had been discovered in a property in Barnton.'

'Well, thanks a bundle, Police Scotland.' No attempt to hide the sarcasm.

'It's the routine response to something like this. If you want to talk to the press, I'm not going to stop you. You probably won't like the end result, though. The insinuations they'll come up with . . . let's just say you'll wish you'd kept your head down.'

He sighed and walked to the door. 'I might as well try and get some work done.'

'There will be a police officer on duty overnight, protecting the integrity of what's in your garage. Tomorrow, you'll have more forensic officers on site. The poor sods who have to figure out how to deal with what's down there.'

'This is a like a bad dream,' he said. 'I make up this kind of thing for a living. Being at the heart of it for real makes me ashamed of how glib I've been about the whole business of murder.'

Daisy almost felt sorry for him. 'We don't know that these remains are those of a murder victim. We'll need to see what the forensic anthropologist and the pathologist have to say.'

He snorted. 'Aye, right. Why else would you go to all the trouble of such an elaborate disposal if you hadn't murdered someone?'

'It might be an accidental death.' Another snort. 'In compromising circumstances. It could have been a suicide, again in compromising circumstances. We don't really know anything for sure until the forensics team have done their jobs. And we've finished our investigations.'

'Bloody Jake Stein,' McEwen spat. 'He hated us so much. He could just have bitched and moaned about us all over town, but no. It wasn't enough to make Ros's life a misery, with his snide little messages. He had to keep his mouth shut until he'd worked out the best way to properly destroy us.'

Daisy looked away so he wouldn't see the eye-roll. She'd had a day of listening to McEwen whingeing and she really had had enough. She picked up her coat and her bag. 'I'll probably see you in the morning.'

'Be still, my beating heart. I can hardly fucking wait.' He hurried from the room, slamming the door behind him.

That was when Daisy realised she had no means of escape from Ross McEwen's property. Karen had taken the car, the forensics teams were gone. The only vehicle around was the liveried car the officer on guard had arrived in. And she couldn't take that, for all sorts of reasons.

There was nothing for it but to run the gauntlet of the journalists at the gate and walk down to the nearest bus stop. She could catch a 41 on Whitehouse Road. If they were still running.

She stepped outside the kitchen door. At least it had stopped raining.

For now.

Finally, Karen and River settled at opposite ends of a bench on the breakwater. Karen tried to put from her mind that she had last sat here waiting for Rafiq. She had no idea where he was; she hoped he was safe.

River snapped her fingers. 'Hey, you're miles away.'

Karen managed a smile. 'Sorry, I've got a lot going on in my head at the moment. This case, the one I've asked for your help with, it's like a cat chasing its tail. It started with a librarian phoning Jason.'

'OK, you've got me. Not a sentence I ever expected to hear.'

So Karen ran through the complicated accumulation of information that had occupied them since she'd first heard of *The Vanishing of Laurel Oliver*. 'It's like a bloody kaleidoscope. At first, it all looks straightforward. Jake Stein wanted to take revenge on his ex-wife and her lover, who happened to be his chess partner and probably his only remaining friend. So he decided to implicate them – or at least, his successor in his ex-wife's bed – in the murder of a young woman, taking care to ensure there would be no direct evidence against Stein himself. So far, so straightforward.'

River nodded. 'That makes perfect sense. What's the problem?'

'Stein set all of this down in a first draft of a novel, describing the planning and process of the murder. But the person in the cross hairs isn't the Ross McEwen character – it's Stein himself. And that makes no sense.'

River ran her hand through her thick auburn hair and frowned. 'It's a novel, though, right? So Stein could argue that it was a fiction, not a confession and the only reason he knew all the details was that his wife's lover had confessed to him.'

'But why would he try to disguise McEwen's role in it?'

River sighed. 'What if he's still in love with his ex? He knows that if he makes a direct accusation, she'll just accuse him of vindictiveness. He has to find a way to make it real for her. So he writes something that will provoke you guys to search McEwen's garage, et voilà.'

'That's beyond twisted.'

'So are his plots. Byzantine doesn't even begin to cover it. We're as bad as him, coming up with these convoluted scenarios. Maybe he never intended to publish it? Maybe he was just getting it out of his system. People always talk about writing as therapy, don't they?'

Karen pulled a face. 'But why keep it once it had served its purpose for him? It's a hell of a risk. Why would he leave it lying around among his papers? What are the chances that anybody coming across it would get that it's just a fantasy?' Karen stood up and started pacing, careful to keep her distance. 'And what's McEwen's motive supposed to be here? Why on earth has he murdered a young woman who wants to be a crime writer? Did he nick a plot from her, or what?'

River shrugged. 'I'm only a simple bone counter. You're the ones who are supposed to know what makes criminals tick.'

'Traditionally, it's sex or money. But crime fiction has become such a big deal, on the telly and in books. So the motives have grown more complicated. And they make it look like murder is the reasonable answer.'

River laughed. 'What? You think Agatha Christie didn't go in for baroque murder motives? Everybody on a train murders the victim? Somebody murders three people with matching initials as a cover for murdering, what's-his-name, Donald Duck? Somebody murders a teenage girl because they're in love with her and can't bear to see her wasting her love on an unsuitable bloke?'

'OK, you have a point. But those old-fashioned detective stories, everybody knew they were nonsense. That people didn't really behave like that. But crime writers now, they're obsessed with realism. Get the police procedure right. Get the forensics right. Get the street names right. It's all made to look real and even ... yes, reasonable.' Karen sat down heavily on the bench, tilting her head back to look at the sky.

'So why do you think Jake Stein murdered Lara Hardie?'

'If I was making this up, I'd say he killed her purely to frame Ross McEwen for a murder. To punish him and his ex-wife. And I don't know how I prove any of it.'

'Let's walk. I'm getting cold, sitting here.' River stood up and they headed for the lighthouse, a quick circuit of the point before they headed back. 'I really miss sitting across a table from you, thrashing stuff out. It's just not the same without a big bowl of pho and a cold beer.'

'I know. I still can't get my head round how quickly the world has changed. If you'd run this lockdown stuff past me six months ago, I'd never have believed how obedient people would be. I'd have thought we'd all be going, "Fuck it, I'm getting my pals round and we're going to get tore in to the G&Ts." Every day, I'm gobsmacked. I'm glad, don't get me wrong. But I'm gobsmacked.'

River shrugged. 'It's not rocket science, Karen. People are afraid of dying.'

'I get that. And I don't want to die. That's why I'm doing my level best to stick to the rules. But I'm a polis, River.' She stopped; River turned to face her. 'I have to be out on the streets doing what I do. Because I want the world still to be a decent place when we come out the other side of this. And that's why I'm trying to make sense of what's going on here. Because tomorrow, or the day after, I'm hoping you can tell me the bones swilling around in that board bag belonged to Lara Hardie. Then we can see about bringing her home, and punishing whoever's done this to her. If they're still within reach.'

40

Karen woke the next morning with a sense of having dreamed something important. But as always, she couldn't piece together anything that had happened in dreamland. She stood under the full blast of the power shower in the en suite bathroom; that was when her subconscious woke up. Two thoughts followed in swift succession. 'You're not seeing the wood for the trees.' Then 'Look through the other end of the telescope.'

Neither seemed at first to open any kind of crack in the case, but by the time she'd dressed and made her first cup of coffee, more thoughts were rumbling through her head. What if she had indeed got everything back to front?

When Daisy emerged from her room, towelling her hair dry, Karen was clear what she needed to do. 'How did you get on with McEwen after I left?'

'He's channelling Mr Grumpy. He's mostly pretty pissed off about losing his liberty. I pointed out that lawfully he could only go outside on his own for an hour. And that there were a couple of journos parked at the end of his drive, so good luck with that. He said he was going to do some writing, but I think he was actually loading up Assassin's Creed.' Her expression was scornful.

366

'I'm going to send you back out there today. River's going to examine the scene and sort out how we move the remains. It's seriously disgusting, but it's got to be done.'

'You want me to witness it?' Daisy sounded horrified.

'Somebody has to. Chain of custody, and all that. I've got other things to do, including a word with your old boss.'

'DCI Todd?'

'The same. They got hands on Ronan Murray last night. I'm hoping he'll have made a statement that gets Jason off the hook. And then I'll have to talk to the Dog Biscuit to get Jason back on the books.'

'Then he can take over at Barnton?' She looked hopeful.

'One step at a time.' She picked up her phone. It was still too early for the other call she had to make but she might as well get Charlie Todd out of the way. 'Morning, Charlie,' she began.

'Good to hear from you, Karen. You're on my list. You'll be pleased to hear Murray copped to the lot last night, and he was very clear that your Jason had nothing to do with it. He knows he's going down, he's just trying to get some Brownie points.'

Karen gave Daisy the thumbs up. 'That's great news, Charlie.'

Karen and Daisy high-fived like teenagers. 'At least something's working out,' Daisy said, heading for the fridge and breakfast.

Karen settled for a second cup of coffee as a bracer, then called ACC Markie. 'Good morning, ma'am,' she said, as bright and cheerful as she could manage. 'DCI Pirie here, bringing tidings of comfort and joy.'

'You're either a bit late or ridiculously early with the Christmas spirit, Pirie.'

Not in the face of that much frost. 'I'm just off the phone with DCI Todd in Fife. He tells me they've arrested Ronan Murray, and the good news is that not only has he admitted all the charges, he's said categorically that DC Murray knew nothing of his plans and made no contribution to his crime.'

A pause. Then, 'So how did he get his hands on DC Murray's uniform?'

She wasn't giving up easily, Karen thought. 'It was in storage at his mother's house. With her being in hospital, it was a simple matter for Ronan to help himself. Jason has no complicity here, ma'am.' Unspoken, *so un-suspend him.*

'I will confirm this with DCI Todd. And if it is the case, I will restore DC Murray to duty.' Every word sounded like it cost Markie dear.

'Thank you, ma'am.' Karen's response was equally grudging. An ACC who wouldn't take the word of one of her DCIs spoke volumes about her lack of respect for Karen. She couldn't help wondering how she dealt with the many senior officers whose success rate fell well below Karen's. She had a suspicion they saw a very different Ann Markie.

Daisy was frying bacon and potato scones, an egg balanced on the worktop next to the stove. 'That sounded good. Want anything while I've got the pan on?'

'No thanks, I'll have a banana.' She took the fruit through to Hamish's office and sat at the desk, staring out at the back side of the houses further up the hill. The patchwork of aged sandstone, the different tones taken on by years of coal smoke and weathering. The visible stain of the days when Edinburgh was called Auld Reekie. The regulation windows, four panes to each, shedding light on the very different lives beyond them. Karen was coming to love her adopted city in all its variety. How many wounds would this pandemic inflict on its people, on the very fabric of the city itself?

She was starting to have a glimmer of an idea about this case, an idea that contradicted what she thought she knew. There was only one place where she could check her hunch against the evidence. If that evidence existed.

Karen picked up her phone and made the call.

As before, Bethan Carmichael was waiting by the rear entrance, sheltering from the rain under her umbrella. 'We must stop meeting like this,' she said. 'People will talk.'

Taken aback by the evident warmth in the greeting, Karen grinned and said, 'Let them.'

Bethan led the way inside. 'My book club has taken to meeting online,' she said. *And?* 'We were discussing Belinda Bauer's *Snap*, and we got talking about how the police are represented in fiction. And one of our group is Ruth Wardlaw.' She threw a look over her shoulder.

Karen smiled. 'Fiscal Depute. I've worked with Ruth a few times.'

'Yes, she said. She gave you a glowing reference.'

And you realised I might be somebody worth paying attention to. 'That was kind of her. I appreciate you opening up the archive to me again.'

'It wasn't a problem, everything's where you left it. I'm trying to avoid making work for the staff.' They reached the room where Karen and Daisy had been before, and Bethan threw open the door. 'There you go, Chief Inspector. Any problems, drop me a text.' She pulled the door closed behind Karen.

Every now and then in an investigation, Karen felt she was standing on the very edge of something and almost wished she believed in someone she could say a prayer to. But wishing and hoping were for the country and western singers; they were no substitute for hard graft. She pulled on a pair of nitrile gloves and turned her phone off. She wanted no distractions this morning.

She had two initial targets. She knew where one was, but not the other. She knew it wasn't in the boxes they'd already worked their way through, so she started going backwards from there. Halfway down the second box she tried, she hit pay dirt. Held together by a large elastic band was a bundle of printed paper. Scribbled on the top right-hand corner in Jake Stein's characteristic block letters was CULLED TO ORDER.

Karen took out the bundle and sat down to work her way through it. On the second page, she found the first example of what she'd hoped to discover; 'broken' was scored through. In the right-hand margin, a mark Karen thought was called a carrot sat next to SHATTERED. Three pages further on, the word 'looked' was underlined three times and there was an X in the margin. Another four pages and a double line ran down the length of a paragraph. CLUMSY, REJIG appeared alongside. She turned back to the beginning and began photographing the marginalia.

By the time she reached the end of the three hundred and fifty-nine pages, she'd taken sixty-two photographs. Approximately an eighth of the pages in this first draft had flagged-up alterations ranging from single words to, CHECK WITH DAVE BRYANT RE CORRECT PROCEDURE.

Karen replaced the MS in the right place and carried on working backwards. By noon she'd worked her way through three of Jake Stein's first drafts. The notes in the margins appeared in comparable quantities in each. And looking at the remaining boxes, it seemed likely she'd find more examples.

She leaned back in her chair and allowed herself a moment of congratulation. It had been Daisy who had mentioned in passing the lack of corrections on the pages they'd seen but Karen hadn't paid attention at the time. But the sight of Ross McEwen working on his manuscript at his kitchen table had lodged in the back of her mind and she'd recalled what Daisy had noticed.

There were no corrections on the manuscript that was supposedly by Jake Stein.

OK, maybe it was the very first draft and he hadn't gone back over it. Or else it was a revised draft that already incorporated corrections. If it was the latter, it didn't make sense that all they had was a partial. It didn't prove her hypothesis one way or another, but it was suggestive.

She packed up the boxes she'd opened that morning and replaced them. Then she went back to the original manuscript of *The Vanishing of Laurel Oliver*. It sat in its original position within the box, the material that had been on top of it to one side. It had occurred to Karen that because they'd had a photocopy, they'd never studied the original. Perhaps there were notes too faint to have been picked up?

As she read, what struck her was how tonally wrong it seemed. She'd learned a lot about Jake Stein since she'd first read the novel, and nothing she had learned made her think it likely that he'd paint himself in such an unfavourable light. Even if he was supposedly ventriloquising Ross McEwen, Karen struggled to imagine Stein wanting the world to see him like this. And did he even have the insight into his own narcissistic personality to access this image? OK, he was a writer of fiction. It was his business to create characters who provoked reactions in readers – from love to hate, and every shade in between. But could he have projected those characteristics on to someone who was supposed to correspond to himself? She wasn't convinced.

But literary criticism wasn't evidence.

She turned the page that read:

THE VANISHING OF LAUREL OLIVER

PART 2

7

And there it was. In faint pencil, too faint to have left an impression on the front of the page. The same block capitals Jake Stein used throughout the archive. The same block capitals that would be so much easier to forge than cursive handwriting.

> SO, ANONYMOUS PHONE CALL TO POLICE: 'HERE'S WHERE YOU'LL FIND THE BODY'
> WHEN THEY SEARCH 'ROB'S' HOUSE, THEY'LL FIND THE HARD DRIVE. DIFFICULT TO SEE HOW HE WON'T GO DOWN.
> BASTARD WILL GET LIFE. THEN TVLO WILL BE PUBLISHED WHEN I'M DEAD AND GONE, HE'LL BE EXONERATED BUT HIS LIFE WILL BE UTTERLY FUCKED. AND HERS TOO.

On the surface, it looked like confirmation of the theory she'd developed. But it felt too obvious. Stein wouldn't have needed belt and braces; events would simply have unfolded as he'd set them up. If this was supposedly the posthumous manuscript that would tell the truth, why not let it speak for itself? He was an author, after all. He wrote novels that reached a conclusion that made sense, that didn't need auxiliary explanations. Taking it at face value meant tying herself in knots again.

But there was another way of looking at this.

The crazy idea she'd been keeping at arm's length all morning unfolded in front of her in one pencil note. It was as treacherous as walking out on thin ice. But it made more sense than anything else.

It was the mirror image of what they'd all fallen for.

41

Karen took the long way home. Down the gloom of the Cowgate to the eye-catching modernism of the Scottish Parliament; round the front of Holyrood Palace (they could probably house every street sleeper in Edinburgh in there since the Queen wasn't going to be around for a while); through the New Calton burial ground; a tip of the metaphorical hat to the Burns Monument; across the back of Calton Hill to Royal Terrace, then across the top of Leith Walk and home. The rain had stopped and she was pleasantly surprised to see how many people were on the streets, determinedly pursuing their daily exercise. Were people getting the hang of this now?

She let herself into the flat and brewed a coffee she didn't need but craved before she sat down and turned her phone back on. Voicemail from Jason. 'Boss, I got a call from the Dog Biscuit's PA. I'm back on the team. No news about Mum. What needs doing?' *Nothing you can do, son.*

And from Daisy. 'All quiet on the Western Front. McEwen was murdering Irish Druids when I looked in on him and River has been taking samples of that horrible muck and figuring out how to preserve the bones.'

And from Hamish. She debated whether to listen but in

the end she realised it wasn't fair to keep ignoring him. 'Karen.' A pause. 'My heart's hurting. We were all over-wrought the other night. We need to sort this out. Call me, please.' Overwrought? That wasn't the word she'd have come up with. She'd get round to calling him soon. Probably. She thought of all the things she liked about him. Then remembered the things that made her uncomfortable.

Later.

Right now, she had to think. She went back to the files. Ross McEwen had told Daisy he had no alibi for the night Lara Hardie disappeared. Ironically, that was less suspicious than having some elaborate timetable supported by car park payments, theatre tickets, restaurant reservations, a bar full of mates. Which of us, a year after the event, would remember what we were doing on a particular Monday evening unless there was something in our diary? What had he said? Karen zipped through the interview notes. 'If it was a Monday, I'd have watched *Only Connect* and *University Challenge*. That's all I can tell you.' Great. Even if he could remember the questions and what frock Victoria Coren had been wearing, in these days of streaming, it was no proof that he'd watched it live.

Back to the notes. The last time Lara Hardie had been seen by anyone other than her flatmates was at a Jake Stein book event in Dunbar, the night before she disappeared. Jason had spoken to the organiser, who had said she hadn't paid much attention to the signing queue because her daughter was over from East Kilbride for the weekend.

Karen reached for the phone and dialled. 'Jason,' she said.

'All right, boss. Thanks for getting me back on the team.'

'Thank Charlie Todd for persuading your fuckwit brother to get you off the hook. Don't you ever try to protect Ronan again, Jason. You've seen now where it gets you.'

'Aye, sorry about that. So, what's the score? Is there any-thing I can be doing?'

'I take it there's no more news about Sandra?'

'I spoke to them this morning, they said she'd had a better night, so maybe she's turned the corner?'

'I hope so. Listen, there's one wee detail you can maybe clear up for me. You spoke to the woman who organised the Jake Stein event in Dunbar? The night before Lara Hardie disappeared.'

Pause for thought. 'Yeah, I did. She was the bookseller on the night. I don't think she noticed anything funny.'

'That's what your note said. Did you get on OK with her? Is she somebody you could go back to?'

There was almost a laugh in his voice. 'You know me, boss. I'm good with women of a certain age. They all want to mother me.' A sudden intake of breath, then he recovered himself. 'I got on fine with her. How?'

'I want you to speak to her again. I want you to ask her whether she noticed any other writers there that night?'

'You mean Ross McEwen? Is he in the frame now?'

'No leading questions, Jason. No names. Just, did she notice any other writers there. Try to keep it casual.' A big ask for any of them, especially for Jason. 'Tell her it was on your list of questions and somehow you missed it off and now your evil boss is on your case.'

'Good cop, bad cop,' he said. 'Will do, boss. Soon as I get off this call.'

'There's something else I need you to ask her. The one thing we haven't chased down is the actual crime scene. You remember the cabin in the woods where the Laurel Oliver murder took place in the book?'

'The converted shipping container, right?'

'Exactly. The manuscript sites it in the Tyninghame woods, but there's nothing in that area that even resembles that description. Not even any cabins or bothies. The local lads couldn't come up with anywhere, so we had to give up on it. There's just too many miles of empty coast along East Lothian to scour for something so nebulous. And it might not even be in East Lothian, he might have made that up. And we don't know who owns it, which ruled out a search at the Land Registry. Do you think you could drag the conversation round to whether any writer she knows has a wee bolthole on her patch?'

'I could try,' he said, dubious.

'Come on, Jason, you said yourself that women of a certain age take to you. You are so the man for the job. Me and Daisy, we'd never get anywhere. This is our best shot, short of checking out every blip on the Ordnance Survey map between Musselburgh and Torness.'

'I'll do my best. By the way, boss. I had this thought. I'm probably totally off the page here, and you've likely junked this idea already. But we've been fixated on the idea that Lara Hardie was picked out at random. What if she was the real target after all, not just some lassie who happened to fit the killer's requirements? And then the book got written to cover up the real motivation?'

It hardly seemed credible, but Jason had come up with an apparently feasible theory that turned the case on its head. They'd all fallen for the neat version of events laid out in *The Vanishing of Laurel Oliver* without even considering that it might be a staggering double bluff. Karen had come close, but even she hadn't made that final crucial leap.

Karen combed the file again, trying to find the loose

thread that might provide something that was actual proof. If Lara had been a genuine target, there must have been a motive. There was nothing to suggest she'd had any kind of relationship with either McEwen or Stein. Nothing to indicate any sexual or emotional connection, and nobody had even hinted that she was the sort of woman who would revel in the secrecy of such a thing. Reading her work had squashed any idea that either man might have wanted to steal it for himself. She was biddable, it was true. But Karen couldn't think of a single reason why that would have made her a victim of such a cold-blooded killing. Jason's suggestion was tempting, but she feared she was being lured down a dark cul-de-sac.

Nothing to do but think. Karen hated inactivity so she got into the car and drove down to Barnton to check on River's progress. There were even more white-suited bodies in the garage than before. River was in the inspection pit. At least, Karen thought it was River. Mask, goggles, hood, elbow-length protective gloves. A pair of video cameras on tripods were recording what was happening. River put her hands into the stinking mess and emerged with a curved bone. She passed it up to one of the other techs, who bagged it and passed it on. 'Another rib,' River said.

She looked up as Karen approached. 'Pity we couldn't have lifted it out intact. But it would probably have leaked everywhere.'

'In fairness—' Shane started.

'Oh, I know, Shane, I'm not blaming you. With all that bloody polyurethane foam, it wasn't an option.'

'How is it going?' Karen asked.

'It's definitely human remains,' River said. 'At this point, one human. I'm taking out the bones by hand.' She frowned at the bag's contents, slopping gently against the margins. 'I think we're at the point now where we can start taking some of the sludge out. Isha – I'm getting out now, and you can take over. Sorry, you're the only one small enough.'

Isha said nothing. She merely went off to the van and returned with another pair of elbow-length gauntlets. River edged out of the pit and said, 'Here's how we're going to do this. Isha's going to scoop up the liquid a cup at a time and pass it up to one of you. You, the guy with the earring.' A quiet ripple of laughter as a broad-shouldered man pointed to his chest. 'Yes, you. You sieve it into a jug, check that there are no small bones in it, then transfer it into that big plastic bucket. I need this to be done carefully. I don't want to lose anything. Once we get the level down a bit, I'll swap with you, Isha. Is everybody clear on that?'

A murmur of assent, and Isha continued the grisly task. River walked across to Karen, stripping off her rubber gauntlets to reveal another pair of protective gloves beneath. 'I don't envy you this job,' Karen said.

River shrugged. 'I'd rather have this than maggot masses. We're making good progress. Once we clear the bones and the liquid around them, we'll get them off to the lab and Shane's team can extract the bag and take it over to Gartcosh.'

'You're not taking the remains to Gartcosh?'

'No. All my kit is in Dundee. There's nothing they can do there that we can't, and the one bonus I get from working for Police Scotland is that events like this make good teaching opportunities.'

'Aye, well, you wouldn't be doing it for the money,' Karen sighed. 'How long till you can give me some answers?'

'Basics? When I get her on the table. Gendering of the

bones, approximate age, any obvious bone injuries. DNA?' River pulled a face. 'We'll certainly get it from the teeth. Maybe tomorrow.'

'Speaking of teeth, can you get a chart across to me asap? If it is Lara Hardie, we've already got her dental records on file. What about CoD?'

'Unless it's something macro like a skull fracture, not much chance. I suppose it's possible there might be some drug residue in the soup, but I wouldn't put money on it having much evidential value.' Seeing Karen's disappointed face, she added, 'She didn't put herself in that inspection pit, Karen. You're a good bit down the road already.'

'I know. But we've come so far, I really need a result. A "case closed" I can put to the Dog Biscuit. When she sees how much of her precious budget I've blown on this body recovery, she'll stroke out if she doesn't get some good head-lines out of it.'

'You've never held back before because you might upset the bosses. Simon Lees used to be in a perpetual state of red-faced rage when he was in charge.'

'I know. But the Macaroon had a grudging respect for us. Ann Markie acts like we're the cross she has to bear, the price she has to pay for something she can't even remember breaking.'

River patted her shoulder. 'Look on the bright side. When this bloody pandemic is over—'

'You think it will be over? It doesn't show any signs of dying down.'

'It's early days yet. It's not the big one, Karen. There will be a big one, the perfect balance between infectivity and lethality, but this isn't it. To be brutal, it's not lethal enough. And when it's over, people are going to be making choices about their priorities. There are going to be all sorts of job vacancies all over the place. If we're lucky, Ann Markie will end up running some poor benighted English force.'

'I can dream.' Whatever she was going to say next was lost when her phone rang. 'Jason, my man. What have you got for me?'

'You're going to like this, boss. You're going to like this a lot.'

42

With an apologetic shrug, Karen stepped away from River and the forensics team. 'Fire away, Jason.'

'The bookseller, she's called Louise Fairbairn, she was a bit surprised to hear from me again, but she wasn't bothered about it. I said we were trying to fill in some gaps about Lara's disappearance and I wondered whether she could remember anybody else who was there who might be able to help. Turns out half the audience were her customers and she's going to email me their contact details.'

Karen chuckled. 'Good approach.'

'I said did they ever get other writers turning up to events. Just in a chatty kind of way, you know?'

'And, she goes, "Funny you should ask, Ross McEwen stopped in that night. He wasn't there from the start, which is why I sort of forgot about him." She said . . . ' The sound of pages being turned. 'She said he showed up at the beginning of the Q&A, hung about for a bit then went outside while Jake was packing up and saying his goodbyes.'

'Did he make any contact with Lara Hardie?'

'She didn't see anything. But she was busy dealing with book sales.'

'And did you record this, Jason?' *Please.*

'I did. I'll forward it to you.'

'Nice work. That takes us another wee bit further forward.'

'But that's not all.' He sounded lively for the first time in days. 'I went on about how lucky she was to live down the coast and how lovely it was and how me and Eilidh like driving down for a walk and a fish supper or a nougat wafer. And I said it must be a magnet for writers wanting to escape from the city. And she was off.'

'You've been playing a blinder today, Jason. Who did she finger?'

'Duncan Drysdale and Jess Hawkins live in North Berwick. Linda Marshall, J. P. Logan and his wife, Rona Balfour, they live in Dunbar. There were a couple of others in Haddington and somebody in Skateraw. I asked about boltholes and she said Deni Blackadder has a place at Cockburnspath and some Olga lassie from Belarus has a caravan at St Abb's Head. I've got it all on the voice recording.'

'That's terrific work. Are you OK with doing all this?'

'Uh huh. It takes my mind off my mum. Do you want me to see what I can find out about the Blackadder lassie and Olga what's-her-name?'

'That's a good idea. Start with Deni Blackadder – she's a crime writer, I think.'

'According to Louise the bookseller, Olga's a poet and a translator.'

'Less likely to have been pals with either Stein or McEwen, then. They all seem to stick to their silos.'

'I'm on it.'

She hung up, feeling a little burn of excitement in her chest. She turned back to the garage, where River was readying herself for a second round of delving into the horrors of the human slurry. There was nothing Karen could do there, so she made for the house. She found Daisy in the kitchen, reading a Sri Lankan cookbook. 'He's in his study, playing on the X-box,' she said. 'He made a big performance of leaving his phone on the counter, going on about he didn't want me thinking he was sneaking phone calls behind my back. Like I don't know you can message people in-game.' She rolled her eyes. 'Somehow, I don't see Ros Harris playing console games in office hours.'

'He's too savvy to be having incriminating conversations with anybody,' Karen said. 'Jason's got a statement putting him at that event the night before Lara went missing.'

Daisy sat up sharply, letting the book fall from her. 'You're kidding!'

'It's only circumstantial. He wasn't seen with Lara. But Jason's chasing something up that might help us further along the way.'

Daisy looked momentarily put out. 'Nothing I can help with?'

'No need, he's got it covered. It's something to focus on that isn't his mum in the COVID ward or his brother in custody.' Karen settled in one of the armchairs by the window and took out her phone.

She googled Deni Blackadder. Thirty-two, single, born and raised in Stirling. A distant cousin of the exceptional Scottish artist Elizabeth Blackadder, and author of three crime novels. She clicked through to her webpage, where the first thing she saw among several endorsements was one from Ross McEwen. 'Just when you thought there was nothing new under the crime fiction sun, along comes Deni Blackadder.' So there was a link.

It didn't prove anything. But it was suggestive. She went back to the Google results and spotted a recent podcast Deni had featured on. She popped her earphones in and pressed play. She was 'in conversation' with the Mystery Maven, who talked to crime writers about their life and work. There was nothing that caught Karen's interest till they got to the bit about how Deni was first published. 'I did a masterclass with Ross McEwen, and he was incredibly supportive. He said he loved what I'd written but that there were a couple of issues. One was structural, and hearing that made me want to go outside and howl at the moon because *nobody* loves a structural rewrite!' Laughter. 'But when he broke it down for me I could see it was more about moving bits of text around to change the order of when we get to know what we get to know.

'The other issue was that the protagonist was too clichéd. That was hard to hear but surprisingly easy to fix. So I did the rewrites with Ross's encouragement and sent it to Katya Green, who is now my agent. And she did the rest. I'd never have made it without their input.' This, Karen thought, was investigative gold.

She listened to the rest of the podcast but heard nothing of interest, except that Deni was doing lockdown in her cabin. 'I couldn't face seeing the city so denuded of people, of personality. So I took off to my tiny wee but and ben down the coast, looking out over the North Sea. I feel very privileged.'

Karen looked across at Daisy. 'How do you fancy a wee run down the coast tomorrow? Cockburnspath?'

'Will it involve fish and chips?'

It was time, Karen thought as she climbed the stairs to Hamish's flat. She couldn't ignore him forever. She fixed herself an Arbikie's AK gin with ginger ale and went through to the study. Long swig, short text.

Is this a good time to talk?

Almost as soon as she'd sent it, the FaceTime alert sounded. Karen connected and Hamish grinned out at her. 'I knew you wouldn't be able to ignore me forever,' he said.

'This isn't capitulation. It's a truce.'

He shrugged. He was looking particularly well, she thought. Beard trimmed, hair artfully tousled. It was almost as if he'd been expecting her. 'Call it what you will, we're talking. And that's how we fix things.'

'We fix things by making changes, Hamish. And I don't know whether the two of us are capable of making the kind of changes we need.'

'We won't know until we try.' He frowned. 'And I'm willing to try. You know how I feel about you. I love it when we're out and about, enjoying ourselves. Or staying in, enjoying ourselves. My friends think you're the best thing that ever happened to me. I'm sure when you meet my parents they'll think the same.'

'Whoa! Who said anything about meeting your parents? You're rushing at things we've never talked about, making out like they're the logical next step when they're a massive jump.'

He threw his hands in the air. 'That's because it feels like the next step. It's what people do when they're serious about each other. I've met your parents, haven't I?'

Karen's heart sank. 'Only by accident.' Her parents had come over from Kirkcaldy for lunch one Saturday. Hamish had arrived unexpectedly – although she'd told him they were coming – just as she was serving the rhubarb crumble and custard. He'd been effusive and charming and her parents couldn't get out the door fast enough. Later, her mother said, 'He's a smooth operator, right enough.' Her father had just grunted. The next time they'd been alone, he'd said, 'Are you sure about yon lad? You seem different when you're with him. Not like when you were with Phil. Then, you were yourself. Just more.'

For her father it was a major speech. It had given her pause, but maybe not enough. 'They've not met many folk like you.'

'What? Because I grew up in the US? Because I'm a businessman? Because I've made money? Come on, Karen, they're not as small-minded as all that.'

'We're different, Hamish. And you don't always get it. I grew up in a working-class home in a working-class town here in Scotland. I look at the world through a different prism to the one you use. You think throwing money at a problem is a solution. I've grown up without that option so I have to work at things to sort them out.'

'Karen, I work hard for what I have. I'm not going to apologise for enjoying the fruits of my success.'

She sighed. 'And there's nothing wrong with that. But you make assumptions all the time about what *I'll* enjoy. Half the time I feel like you've got a completely different woman in your sights. You don't *see* me. You don't *hear* me.'

There was a long pause. 'But I love you,' he said simply, all the bombast stripped away.

'But do you? I think the person you love is not me.'

'When we make love, none of that matters. We fuse. We're a perfect match.'

'When we make love, it papers over the cracks because it's so good.' Karen was beginning to feel cornered, and not for the first time. 'Your reaction when you found Rafiq in my flat frightened me. Not because you were scary – which you clearly were – but because it was a side of yourself you'd kept hidden from me.'

'No, that's not—'

'Let me speak, Hamish,' she said, raising her voice to bat him away. 'I've seen men who bully women too many times to take that behaviour lightly.'

'I don't bully you.'

'Not now, you don't. And I'd like to think I'd be strong enough to stand up to you. But jealousy is an ugly thing and you had absolutely no reason to distrust me. Absolutely no reason to be jealous of Rafiq. A guy on the run from people who had murdered his wife and son, a man living in constant fear. And you freaked him out. What happens the next time you think you have grounds for jealousy? What happens if the other man is not somebody you can bully? Will it be me you turn on?'

A long silence. 'All I've done is to love you.' His voice was quiet.

'I know that's how you see it. And I thought I could maybe love you. But I don't think I can. So I think it would be better all round if we stuck to what I said the other night. When lockdown is over, I'll move back to my place and we'll shake hands and call it a day.'

'You're making a terrible mistake here, Karen.'

And that was the moment when a woman's voice called out from off-screen, 'Dinner'll be on the table in five minutes, Hamish.'

'Who's that? Is it Teegan?'

His eyes flicked in the direction of the kitchen. 'That's right. She's cooking the dinner.'

'Why is she cooking your dinner? I thought she was shacked up in the yurt?'

'She is, yeah, but we've been taking turns with cooking the dinner for each other a couple of times a week.'

Karen could hardly believe her ears. 'Hamish, that's a total breach of the regulations. Teegan and you, you're not a bubble.' A horrible pause. 'Or are you?' She'd never doubted him before, not for a moment.

There was nothing artificial about his laugh. It was Hamish, loud and hearty as always. 'God, no. How could you even think that?'

'So there's no excuse for you completely ignoring the COVID rules? Hamish, they're in place for a reason. They apply to everybody—'

'Not you, when you're out and about chasing a case.' He was still grinning.

'Yes, me. There are certain exemptions for policing, but that doesn't extend to getting one of the neighbours in to cook my tea. What gives you the right to trash the rules?'

'Karen, Teegan and I work the sheep together every day. Anything I've got, she's got. It's just bureaucracy.'

'Your attitude is the reason people like Jason's mum are in hospital right now. Everything you've said has made me realise I was absolutely right to say this thing is over,' she said coolly and broke the connection.

43

They were about to leave for Cockburnspath when Karen's phone pinged. The message from River said,

I've emailed you the dentals for the remains. More later . . .

She called Daisy back to where they'd been working and asked her to pull up Lara Hardie's dental records, routinely acquired by the initial investigation. Just in case. Meanwhile, she opened the email attachment River had sent. Both used the same format for recording the mouth; they were a perfect match. The upper left canine was, usefully, an implant. 'It's Lara,' Karen said heavily.

'Are we going to see the parents?'

Karen sighed. 'I think I want to wait for DNA.'

Daisy was shocked. 'But you always say, every day a family waits—'

'Is a day too long,' Karen chorused with her. 'I know. But I'd like to get this interview out of the way before the world and his dog know whose body we've found. I'll call the Dog Biscuit when we get back and then we'll go and see the parents.'

'You don't think it'll leak?'

'Right now, it's just us and River who know. And I'd trust her with my life.' *Or my career.* 'Come on, let's make tracks.'

The cold case detective's visit had left Emma Hardie wondering whether she'd been painting too much gilding round the memory of her sister. She'd been determined to protect Lara from the easy assumption of her being the kind of stupid wee lassie who'd let the wrong guy give her a lift or slip her a spiked drink.

A few months after Lara's disappearance, a uniformed PC from the local station had delivered a cardboard carton to the Hardie home. He'd explained it contained material the detectives had examined and had decided had no bearing on whatever had happened to her. Her mother had gone through the contents: lecture notes and essays; a clutch of poems her father had dismissed as 'sub-Liz Lochhead'; a Moleskine notebook that said 'Writing diary 2019—'; and a couple of heavily annotated drafts of short stories.

In spite of her desire to find an answer among the papers, her mother had been forced to concede there was no smoking gun. But their encounter with Karen Pirie had fired Emma with the desire to find the missing key that would unlock Lara's absence. And the box of papers was all she had.

Painstakingly, she'd studied every piece of paper. She read her sister's essays, even the ones about modernism that made no sense to her. She struggled to read Lara's scribbled lecture notes which often consisted of a single word, waded through endless pages of draft essays headed clearly and legibly but which soon degenerated into illegibility, and poems she could make neither head nor tail of, often using seagulls as metaphor whether they made sense or not.

She left till last the writing diary. On the first page, Lara had printed, *I commit to writing every day. Only practice will make me better.* Emma's chest contracted at the thought of her sister's determination. It reminded her yet again of what had been taken from her. The entries varied in length; some a couple of sentences, describing work on a piece of prose; others, the opening paragraphs of a story; yet others, the outline of something bigger. There were notes of author events she'd attended, almost exclusively novelists. Then, to Emma's astonishment, *Tomorrow I go north to the Cairngorm Centre for Creative Writing. I'm using my birthday money for a residential course.*

Lara had said nothing of this. She had such little faith in her writing abilities, Emma thought. She cast her mind back to September 2018. Lara had said she was going to spend her birthday money youth hostelling in the Highlands with one of her university friends. Instead, she'd paid for the writing course, taught by Louise Welsh and Zoe Strachan, a couple of writers based at Glasgow University. Emma read the diary entries, all infused with excitement at workshops and tutorials, all making copious notes about what she'd learned. And there, in the middle of the week, a guest reader who had spent the evening reading his work and listening to the students reading short excerpts from their work. Ross McEwen had been so taken with the opening of a short story of Lara's that he'd invited her to send it to him when she'd finished it.

Lara had copied out what she'd read – the opening paragraph of a short story called 'Memorial Garden': *It wasn't the first time Katya had seen the stranger in the Garden of Remembrance. Their paths had crossed occasionally, him leaving as she was arriving, or arriving as she was leaving. It had never occurred to her that the man she exchanged polite nods with was the man who had killed her son.*

Emma had to admit it was arresting. She read on, hurrying now to find out what had happened with the story. She had to wade through a lot of inconsequential notes before she found out it had taken Lara the best part of a month – and a lot of despair and cursing – to reach a draft she was happy with. When she'd got that far, she'd gone to an event McEwen was doing at a bookshop in Edinburgh. She'd handed over the story. A couple of days later, he'd suggested she come to a workshop he was running in the city in a couple of weeks' time.

The entry after that workshop read, *RM thinks MG is really promising but it lacks pace and suspense. He doesn't teach those. Suggests I go to Jake Stein workshop. I can't afford it!!! RM said he'd square it with Jake. Amazing!*

It might be completely innocent, Emma realised. Buried away in the diary, it was easy to dismiss. Lara had gone to the workshop, then there was no further reference to either of the writers. Her focus was all on a new story she was writing for a competition. A few weeks later, she'd disappeared.

Emma burned with anger that, as far as she knew, nobody had followed this up. Pirie had asked a couple of half-hearted questions but nothing pointed. Emma felt tears pricking her eyes and she determined to confront the police officer with her failings. Lockdown or no, she was going to show Karen Pirie what she'd missed.

Karen let Daisy drive so she could plan her line of approach. That took until they reached the far side of the ring road. It was a sunny morning, the hills of East Lothian and the distant outline of Fife crisp in the spring light. But Karen had no eyes for the landscape that day. All she had space for in her head was Lara Hardie and how to establish who had killed her. Her thoughts kept running like a hamster in a wheel, so absorbing that it came as a surprise when they reached the end of the dual carriageway and arrived at the hamlet of Cockburnspath. All Karen knew about it was that it was important geologically, a random fact dredged up from schooldays. Daisy made a right-hand turn off the main trunk road, a manoeuvre that would usually take several minutes for a gap to appear in the oncoming traffic. Lockdown had reduced that stream; today, she crossed the carriageway without pause. There was not a soul in sight.

'What do we do now?' she asked.

'When in doubt, chap a door.' Karen got out and followed her own suggestion. She scanned the skyline till she saw the tell-tale curl of smoke emerging from a chimney. Karen crossed the road, fixed her mask in place and rang the door-bell. A pause, then a man's voice said, 'Who is it?'

'Sorry to trouble you, sir. I'm Detective Chief Inspector Karen Pirie of Police Scotland. Don't worry, it's nothing to do with you. I'm just looking for directions for somebody who lives here.'

'Nobody's supposed to be outside their houses just now.'

'It's police business. We're allowed. Could you maybe open the door?'

'No way. Look, see the living room window on the left there? Show me your ID through the glass.'

She couldn't blame him. Karen stepped over a rose bush, catching her coat on a thorn. 'Fuck's sake,' she muttered under her breath as she disentangled herself. She made it to the window and held up her photo ID. The man who appeared on the other side of the glass looked to be in his

394

mid-thirties, a faded Scottish rugby shirt stretched over the beginnings of a substantial beer gut. He peered at her ID then gave her the thumbs up. He waved at her to step back and when she was a good three metres away, he opened his window. 'Who are you looking for?' he demanded.

'Deni Blackadder. She has a wee place here, overlooking the sea.'

'I know fine who you mean. She writes books, eh? Dresses like a jumble sale?'

'I know about the books,' Karen said. 'Where will I find her?'

'Back to the roundabout, last exit. Turn left and just before you get to the harbour, you'll see a wee track off to the left. Go down there about quarter of a mile and you'll see her place tucked in against the cliff. It's two of they shipping containers welded together and turned into a kind of house. You wouldnae catch me living there.' He closed the window without further explanation.

Five minutes later, they'd reached the end of the track. On the outside, the containers were unmistakable, right down to the fading logos of shipping companies. A Harley Davidson trike was parked under a wooden lean-to. 'That must be a bloody cold way to travel in winter,' Karen said.

'Not to mention spring, summer and autumn. She's obviously doing well, those things aren't cheap.'

As they spoke, the cabin door opened and a woman emerged. She was tall and rangy, dressed in leather trousers, biker boots and a heavy sweater that appeared to have been knitted from a bag of remnants of many colours. Her hair was a chaos of black curls, her face lean and angular. 'What's going on here? Who the fuck are you? This is a lockdown and this is private property.'

Karen produced her ID again. 'We're the polis. We're from the HCU.'

A frown flashed across her face then she grinned. 'Historic Cases Unit. The lassies that wake the dead. So what's this in aid of? It's fiction I write, you know. I don't dabble in true crime.' She sat down on her doorstep. 'Sorry I can't invite you in. Lockdown, and all that. Plus I haven't made my bed since a week past Tuesday.'

In spite of the spikiness, Karen warmed to Blackadder. 'We'd like to ask you some questions about a case we've reopened. Well, technically it wasn't actually closed but it wasn't what you'd call active. And we need to check some details with you.'

'Me? I know fuck all about fuck all. Who's dead?'

Karen shook her head. 'I can't tell you. It's complicated and I don't want anything leaking until we've spoken to the relatives.'

Blackadder pulled a battered silver cigarette case from her trouser pocket, followed by an equally battered old Dunhill lighter. She opened the case to reveal a row of roll-ups. 'Smoke?'

Daisy and Karen both shook their heads. Karen really hoped the smell of dope wasn't going to hit her. 'So, do you mind answering some questions?'

'If I can, I will. Least I can do, living as I do on the proceeds of crime.'

She'd used that line before, Karen could tell by the smirk. 'You live here alone?'

'I do. Before we all became prisoners of our own company, I brought women back occasionally, but mostly I tried not to. I like the emptiness. I write better here than anywhere else.'

'So you don't invite friends, colleagues to join you?'

'Nope. If they want to write by the sea, they can find their own bolthole.'

'Not even if they're mentors, like Ross McEwen?'

Her face sharpened and she took a deep drag of her blameless cigarette. 'What's Ross got to do with it?'

'I did my homework. I know he helped you with your first novel.'

'I didn't even have this place then. After I had this craned in, everybody wanted to come and have a look, but I wasn't about to have a housewarming party. That cheeky bastard Jake Stein turned up out of the blue one day, but he didn't even get a cup of tea. I let him take a piss but that was all. I had a cup of coffee with Ann Cleeves at the picnic table—' she gestured beyond the containers to where a basic picnic table sat near the edge of the cliff. 'She was researching locations for one of her Vera books. Lovely woman, but she didn't get inside.'

This was going nowhere, fast. 'Does anyone else have a key? Someone local, in case there's a problem?'

She shook her head. 'I'm pals with the folk up at the campsite. If there's a problem, they've got my phone number.'

'No spare key under a plant pot?'

She grinned and waved her arm. 'No plant pots, Karen.'

'Ever had an intruder? Burglary? Local kids?'

'Nope. People round here think I'm mad but they're not hostile. And besides, I've got three locks on the door. Reinforced glass on the windows, because when it blows here, it really fucking blows.'

'Were you here last April? Around a year ago?'

Deni pulled an iPhone out of her hip pocket. 'Give me a minute ...' She frowned at the screen. 'Yeah, I was suffering from rewrites. I was here from the third to the thirtieth. My editor came up for a few days, but apart from that, I was locked into my bloody fucking binfire of a book.' A crooked smile.

Karen looked at Daisy, who gave her best blank look. Definitely nowhere to go. She smiled. 'It's been a pleasure to meet you. Thanks for your cooperation.'

'Your books are great,' Daisy said. 'I love the characters, especially Sophy. I totally get her.'

Blackadder looked startled. 'Wow. Thanks. I never thought I'd have a police officer fan.' She jumped to her feet. 'Wait a minute.' She disappeared inside.

'I never had you pegged as a fan girl,' Karen teased.

Blackadder appeared with a book in one hand and a Sharpie in the other. 'The courier just brought these yesterday. It's my new book.' She flipped it open. 'What's your name?'

'Daisy.'

Karen couldn't quite credit this breathless version of her sergeant. Blackadder scribbled something, signed with a flourish then shut the book. 'It's been fun, girls. Now I know where to come for professional advice on cold cases.'

'Any time,' Daisy said. Karen nudged her back towards the car. Deni Blackadder leaned in her doorway, arms folded, a knowing smile on her lips.

'What was that?' Karen asked.

Daisy managed a three-point turn without ending up at the bottom of the cliff. 'I think she's a really interesting writer. Challenging. You should give her a try.'

As they reached the end of the track, Daisy said, 'Do you mind if we drive down to the harbour? I feel like stretching my legs.'

'Sure. I'll wait in the car, I'm not in the mood for a face full of North Sea spray.'

When she'd parked, Daisy took a quick look at what Blackadder had written. Karen spotted the familiar pinking of her cheeks. 'What did she write?'

Daisy passed it over. '*To Daisy. Who really does get it. In sisterhood, Blackadder,*' Karen read. 'Looks like you've got a fan too,' she said, handing it back with a grin. 'Away you go and walk off the excitement.'

She watched Daisy head into the wind. Jake Stein had been inside Blackadder's shipping container home, albeit briefly. But long enough to realise it made good copy as a crime scene. It wasn't an exact match with the book, but it wasn't far off. And he'd have known about the connection between Blackadder and McEwen. He might well have told McEwen all about the bolthole, for that very reason. Nevertheless, it proved nothing.

Then, in a bid to divert herself from her frustration at their failure to make progress, she googled 'Olga poet Belarus Scotland'. Up came Olga Kotova, a poet in her forties who had been resident in the UK for a dozen years. She taught at the Open University, and seemed to appear regularly at book festivals. No blurbs from Ross McEwen, obviously. She didn't seem a likely fit for a friend of his.

Karen scrolled on. Olga doing events; Olga publishing a new translation of some poet Karen had never heard of; Olga chairing a panel at the Edinburgh Book Festival; Olga winning a prize for a translation of a book of short stories; Olga—Karen stopped and went back. The short story prize was sponsored by an Edinburgh legal firm. Binns McIndoe Harris.

Hardly daring to breathe, she opened another window

and googled the law firm. BMH were a blue-chip outfit with offices on George Street. Their selling point was 'Cradle to the Grave – all your legal needs. From Family Trusts to Wills & Probate, and everything in between.' She clicked through to 'Who we are' and halfway down the page, she found herself looking at a very stylish headshot of Rosalind Harris. 'Rosalind heads our Wills & Probate team. She is an expert in ensuring your testatory desires are met in every respect.' A part-time job that didn't bring in the kind of money Jake Stein could earn? It didn't sound like it to Karen.

She went back to the page about Olga's prize. This time, she googled the prize itself. On the 'history' page, she found not only the details of the winners but also the photographs of the presentation events. Four years ago, there was Olga, accepting a crystal trophy and a cheque from Rosalind Harris. The following year, in one of the 'candid' shots from the reception, Olga and Rosalind faced each other, laughing and toasting each other with champagne flutes. Nothing the year after, but last year, Rosalind and Olga were seated next to each other at the celebratory dinner.

Had they been looking at the wrong bolthole?

44

At least they had a proper address for Olga Kotova. She'd been living in her caravan for long enough to be on the council tax register. Karen had set Jason the task of finding where it was; he had developed a certain expertise at negotiating his way round lists, usually by charming some woman into doing the searching for him. In spite of almost everyone working from home, he'd tracked down someone with the right database access, and he'd found the details by the time they'd arrived at St Abb's.

'"Twinned with New Asgard"?' Daisy exclaimed as they entered the village. 'What the actual?'

'It's a sort of joke. They filmed the *Avengers: Endgame* movie here and renamed it. I think we've gone past the caravan site.'

Daisy groaned and turned round. 'Sorry, got carried away.'

A hand-lettered sign said the site was closed due to COVID-19. A long chain extended across the gate, a central padlock presumably there to give existing residents access. The office seemed deserted. They left the car on the grass verge by the entrance and walked in.

There were only a handful of vans parked up. The place had an air of empty desolation. Apparently, few people

were prepared to weather lockdown in the teeth of expo-
sure to the vicious winds that beat against this coast. Karen
had dug deeper into the images of Olga online and found a
Scottish magazine feature about the poet that showed her
sitting in a folding chair outside her van with the sea in the
distance. At the far end of the site, she spotted a couple of
smart-looking static caravans that matched the one in the
photograph.

They approached on gravel paths that were beginning to
sprout weeds. The nearer of the two showed no sign of life,
but there was a light on in the farther one. 'Sometimes,'
Karen sighed, 'I wish I was a private eye, not a polis.'

'How?'

'Well, I could roll up to Olga's front door and pretend to
be a journalist researching a big feature on Rosalind Harris.
Desperate to know the woman behind the wills. We could
sit and have a proper blether about how Ros loves to come
down to the seaside for a fish supper. So much so that Olga's
given her a key to come and go as she pleases.'

'I can see the attraction,' Daisy admitted.

As they grew closer, they could hear the insistent beat of
a drum and bass track. 'Really?' Karen said.

'Don't be so judgemental,' Daisy scolded.

'Judgemental is what I live for, Sergeant.' She grinned.
'Come on, let's chap the door.'

The music stopped. The woman who opened the caravan door couldn't have been more different from Deni
Blackadder. For starters, her hair was arranged in a French
plait and her round face above the dramatic black and silver
mask was devoid of make-up, emphasising her large grey
eyes. She was elegant in black slacks, ballet slippers and a
sweater in a fine marled grey wool. 'I'm sorry, I think you

have the wrong van,' she said, her accent faint but very definitely present.

'Are you Olga Kotova?'

She seemed to withdraw. 'I am. Who is asking?' Karen and Daisy went through the usual rigmarole while Olga grew more obviously wary. 'I don't understand. Why are you here?'

Karen recited the same spiel she'd given Deni Blackadder. It seemed not to alleviate Olga Kotova's unease. Karen wondered what in her past had left her with so little trust of a police officer on a sunny afternoon. 'You're not suspected of any crime,' she tried. 'I'm sorry we can't be more explicit about the case we are investigating, but there are good reasons for that. We want to ask you a few questions, that's all.'

'Do I need a lawyer?'

'I don't believe so. But if that would make you more comfortable, that would be fine, provided we can organise it within the lockdown rules.'

Olga gave her a long hard stare. She seemed to be memorising Karen's face and matching it against some database in her head. 'Wait there,' she said, disappearing back indoors. Karen and Daisy exchanged looks, shrugged. Waited.

At length, Olga reappeared, struggling with three folding chairs. 'Please, make way.' She leaned the chairs one by one against the outside of the van. She took one and marched round the end, out of the wind. 'Help yourselves,' she called as she vanished.

They grabbed a chair each and followed her, setting themselves down more than two metres from her. She seemed to think Daisy was too close and waved her back a few centimetres. Then she took out her phone and laid it on the arm of the chair. 'I will record this,' she said.

'That is your prerogative,' Karen said. 'How long have you lived here, Ms Kotova?'

'It has been my home for six years. I know some people think it's strange, not to want to live in a house. But I like liminal spaces.'

Whatever that meant. 'Do you live here alone?'

She nodded. 'Always.'

'What happens when friends come to visit?'

'Why do you care? If they are staying, I have an arrangement with the owners here. They give my visitors the use of a caravan at a very competitive rate. But not many people come to stay. They prefer to meet in Edinburgh.'

'So you go up to Edinburgh often?'

She crossed one elegant leg over the other. 'In normal times, yes. More or less every other week. I take the bus. It's better than taking my car into the city.'

'I can't say I blame you. Edinburgh traffic's terrible. I walk everywhere I can.'

Olga nodded her approval. 'It's a good city for walking. When the festival isn't on, at least.'

'Who looks after the place when you're away?'

She frowned. 'No one. I lock the door and away I go. I take my laptop and my notebook with me when I leave. I live very simply here. Who is going to break into a caravan with nothing to steal except books?' She snorted with laughter. 'I don't think there's anyone in St Abb's who would have any interest in stealing my books.'

'Does anyone else have a key?'

'Why are you asking this? Why do you care who has my key? Do you think something bad has happened here?'

'It would help if you would answer the question.' Karen spoke mildly but her expression was severe.

'Would it help me? I think not.'

'You're not suspected of any crime, Ms Kotova.' Daisy spoke gently. 'But we are investigating a very serious crime and we want to bring the perpetrator to justice. We think whoever has your key may have been exploited or coerced into handing it over.'

Karen didn't always like these unscripted 'good cop, bad cop' routines, but Daisy was good at offering people a sort of sanctuary. Olga's eyebrows rose, her eyes widening. She planted both feet firmly on the grass, and said, 'And if that were to have been the case?'

'Then there would be no blame attached to them.' Daisy's words hung in the air.

Aye, right. Karen picked up the ball and ran with it. 'And it might be that you were protecting them from further coercion or control.'

Olga shifted in her seat. 'And what if they were already safe? What if the person who had been putting pressure on them is no longer in a position to do so?'

'It would ease their conscience,' Daisy said. 'And that's no small thing.'

Olga stared out over the fields towards the sea. 'I have a friend who loves the extremity of this coast. For some time, it was an escape for her from a difficult marriage. We share a taste in books, and I always think it nourishes her. About two years ago, I was awarded a residency in Banff in Canada. It meant I would be away for a couple of months or more, if I extended it elsewhere. It was advantageous to both of us for me to give her a key so she could come here and decompress. And I knew there would be someone keeping a watchful eye on my home.'

'Would you tell me the name of your friend?'

Olga's fingers wound themselves around each other. 'I do not want her to think I have betrayed her.'

'We won't tell her,' Karen said. 'She need never know.'

'Of course she would know, only we know this,' she snapped.

'Not necessarily. Your friendship isn't a secret, surely? People know you're close. She's probably spoken to friends, to colleagues about her love of this area. She'll have mentioned you, before she ever had your key. This is not a betrayal, it's a way to help her to get rid of her guilt,' Karen said, picking up Daisy's theme.

Olga sighed and wrapped her arms around her chest. The two polis kept silent, scarcely daring to breathe. This could be the moment that made sense of their case. At last, she spoke. 'My friend is called Rosalind Harris. She is a lawyer in Edinburgh. She used to be married to a man called Jake Stein who made her life very difficult. She divorced him but still he tormented her. And then he died. So she need fear no more the heat of his temper. But she still comes to visit because she loves it here.' She paused. 'Do you think he . . . did some evil here?'

'I'm truly sorry, but I can't say anything more now. I wonder, can you tell me whether you were away last April?'

'Something happened last April, then? Something . . . here?'

Karen couldn't see a way of avoiding the question. But if she was right, all that would do would be to postpone the poisoning of this sanctuary for Olga. 'It's possible,' she said. 'Were you at home for all of April last year?'

In reply, she picked up her phone and tapped the screen. 'I was here until April sixth. Then I went to Burgundy, in France. I was there for a four-week residency. Many of these chateaux, they like to visibly support the arts.' There was a wry note in her voice. 'It's rather splendid bed and board for a small amount of work.'

'You bring them prestige,' Karen said. 'So, for most of April, you were not here?'

'I was not.'

'But your friend had access to the caravan?'

Olga nodded, eyes downcast. 'And why not? She had always respected it.'

'Did you notice anything different when you came back? Anything missing, anything out of place?'

Olga pondered briefly then shook her head. 'I don't remember anything amiss.' She sounded sad; bereft, almost.

'I know how difficult this has been for you,' Karen said. 'When it's possible to explain, I hope you'll appreciate we came here with the best of intentions.'

Olga stood up, straight as a rake. 'Ah yes. Those things that pave the road to hell.'

They walked back to the car, Karen feeling a spring in her step. They were getting closer. 'Did you notice the security cameras on the admin building?' she asked.

'They're quite well disguised but yes, I did. What are the chances, do you think?'

'A year ago? Not good. Depends on the system, depends how organised the curation is.'

They'd arrived at the office by the gate. Still no sign of life. There was a number to ring but before Karen's phone connected a man walked round the side of the building. He had the lean, wiry build of a fell runner, an impression emphasised by his outfit of lycra running pants and a wind shirt. 'What can I do for you, ladies?'

They produced their ID. 'DCI Karen Pirie. We're making

inquiries about an incident that may have taken place here last April.'

He turned down the corners of his mouth. 'No incidents here last April, officer. We run an orderly site.'

'But none of us knows for sure what happens behind closed doors, do we? Humour me, Mr . . . ?'

'Garside. Doddie Garside. I'm the owner here. And manager. If anything kicked off here, I'd know.' He took a pack of chewing gum from his pocket and offered it to them. They declined and watched him strip off the wrapper and slip the stick into his mouth.

'I see you've got security cameras,' Daisy said.

'State of the art, pal. Motion-activated, digital cloud storage. You can't be too careful in this game.' He chewed vigorously, slack-jawed and ugly. 'Every car, every van that rolls up to that entrance, it's locked and loaded on the system. Even youse two. It's got a wide angle of capture.'

'How far back do you store images?'

'Got them all, pal. Since I installed it in November 2018. What's your interest?'

'We'd like to look at last April,' Karen said. No point in beating about the bush. 'Would you be amenable to that?'

'Do you not need a warrant for that?'

Silently cursing armchair criminalists, she smiled and said, 'Not if you give permission. All we want to do is check whether a particular person was here on a particular date. If you've got it on cloud storage, presumably working through it wouldn't be difficult?'

45

Twenty minutes later, they were back on the road. Jason was primed with the login details for the security camera footage, and was already trawling through the data. It would have been an appropriate task for him at any time; today, it was the perfect distraction from worrying about his mother.

Karen knew that she should speak to Ann Markie, if not face to face, then at least via FaceTime or Zoom. But she wasn't in the mood for confrontation. It was enough that she was going to have to do the death knock with the Hardies without getting into a ruck with the Dog Biscuit about budget-busting and making arrests on thin evidence. So as they sped back down the A1 to Edinburgh, she propped her laptop open and composed an email.

Good afternoon, ma'am. We've just had confirmation from Dr Wilde that dental comparisons leave no doubt as to the identity of the human remains found in the garage of Ross McEwen's home in Barnton. It is Lara Hardie, who you will remember disappeared apparently without trace a year ago. I'm on my way now to speak to the family, and I will then be pursuing the lines

VAL McDERMID

of inquiry my HCU team and I have opened up and developed over the past few days. The forensics team have taken possession of the remains and will be carrying out all necessary tests, including confirmatory DNA. I will keep you informed of our progress.

DCI Karen Pirie

She read it back to Daisy, who grinned. 'She's not going to like it.'

'She's going to have to lump it. She should be pleased to have some positive news in lockdown. Solving crime's what we're supposed to be for, after all.'

'So we're on our way to see the Hardies?'

Karen nodded, clearly unhappy at the prospect. She hated nothing more than seeing the light of hope extinguished in people's eyes. And although Janet Hardie had schooled herself to speak of her daughter in the past tense, she would be less than human if she didn't have a flicker of hope left in her. At least lockdown rules meant the Hardies would be at home; no need for an awkward phone call first. 'I'll set the satnav. We're going to Perth.'

Karen slumped into the passenger seat, all the stuffing knocked out of her. 'That was hellish,' she said. Emma had crumpled into a sobbing heap; all the colour had drained out of Peter Hardie's face and he'd started to tremble. He'd tried to speak but couldn't get past a teeth-chattering stutter. Janet had been the strong one, holding it together for her husband and daughter. She'd dragged Karen through the details of the discovery; Karen, fearing she'd come to regret having those images in her head, had tried to keep it

410

as clinical as possible. But there was no way of sugaring the pill of this particular death.

They'd wanted to see her, of course. Karen tried to deflect them; there was nothing to see of the Lara they'd known, after all. But Janet would not be diverted.

They wanted to know how she'd died. Karen couldn't answer that yet, not until she'd heard from River and the pathologist. Peter Hardie had recovered himself and shouted angrily about their failure to save his daughter.

And Emma had rocked and sobbed, great gulps of misery.

It had been one of the worst death knocks she'd ever had to deliver. 'Let's go home,' she said.

'Are we not going to arrest them? Ross and Ros?' Daisy had the upbeat energy of someone who has not had to give a family confirmation of their worst fears.

'Not tonight.' Karen looked at her phone. Three missed calls from Ann Markie. She was already in the doghouse. She might as well leave the return call till she'd assembled her ducks in something approximating a row. But before Daisy could pull away, Emma Hardie came running out of the house, shouting at them to stop. 'Cut the engine,' Karen said, opening the car door and facing Emma, who skidded to a halt, face scarlet, eyes swollen.

'You missed this.' Emma waved a leather-bound note-book, accusing.

'What is it?'

'It's her writing diary. You lot had it in your hands and you didn't get it. You just dumped it in a box and brought it back to us.'

Karen shook her head. 'I've never seen this, Emma. What is it that's upset you?'

Wildly, Emma flicked through the pages. 'Look, here. She

411

was getting help from Ross McEwen and Jake Stein. You asked about them, but you already had the answers. Right here.' She brandished the notebook in Karen's face. Daisy got out of the car and approached warily. Just in case.

'Like I said, I've never seen this. Who gave it to you?'

'You lot. You brought back all her uni stuff because there was nothing in it that had anything to do with her disappearance.' Emma was shouting now, tears leaking from the corners of her eyes. She stabbed a page with her finger. 'But it was all in here. Her hopes and dreams and the people who were inspiring them.' She waved the book in front of Daisy's face. 'Look. She was even sending them her stuff.'

Daisy gently took the notebook from her and read the passage Emma was pointing to. It was the opening paragraph of a short story called 'Memorial Garden': *It wasn't the first time Katya had seen the stranger in the Garden of Remembrance. Their paths had crossed occasionally, him leaving as she was arriving, or him arriving as she was leaving. It had never occurred to her that the man she exchanged polite nods with was the man who had killed her son.* With a jolt of surprise, she realised she recognised the title. And its significance.

'You even asked about them when you sat in the garden here and talked to us,' Emma shouted. 'You just ignored what my sister had written.'

'Nobody knew this mattered in the initial investigation,' Daisy said, passing it to Karen, who read it with a puzzled expression. 'Emma, can we take this with us?'

She gave them a piteous look. 'You promise you'll look after it? Take it seriously?'

'We'll take it seriously,' Karen said, still uncertain what had put Daisy on full alert.

Janet Hardie appeared in the doorway, clinging to the

jamb as if it was a spar in a stormy sea. 'Emma,' she called. 'Emma, come away in.'

Emma turned to look at her. 'I need to go. Just do your job this time.' Then she spun round and stumbled back up the drive to her mother.

'What are you seeing that I'm missing?' Karen demanded as the front door closed behind the two women.

Daisy pointed to the page. 'This, here. The short story opening that Lara read to Ross McEwen's workshop. The title?'

'"Memorial Garden"? What about it?'

'That's the title of the story that won the National Short Story Award for Ross McEwen. And Lara sent her story with the same name to him months before she died.'

'Are you saying what I think you're saying?'

'We'll need to look at Ross McEwen's story. If the first paragraph is the same . . .' Daisy took a deep breath. 'He maybe stole her story. Then when it got to the shortlist, when it was going to be broadcast on the radio . . . Plagiarism's still a massive sin in the world of books.'

'But a motive for murder?'

Daisy nodded. 'There have been some massive scandals in recent years. It would destroy him.'

'Then that's a motive right there. Now we've got a two birds, one stone motive.'

'If we're right, it's the very definition of ironic. She actually learned enough from those bloody workshops to write a short story good enough to win an award.'

They sat facing each other across the table, each with a notebook and a pencil. Karen stared at the thin bundle of pages Daisy had printed out from the award website. The first paragraph was identical to the one in Lara's notebook. Now it was time to focus on what they knew and what they suspected. Karen looked up and said, 'Well spotted, Daisy.'

Daisy shrugged, but she pinked with pleasure. 'It was pure chance, I read about it when I was researching McEwen and the title just stuck.'

'It's a shame we don't have the full text of Lara's story.'

'We would have had if he hadn't killed her. She was so self-effacing about her writing, I don't think she'd have had the courage to show it to anyone else.'

'Low self-esteem. I think maybe her father's "encouragement"' – Karen made rabbit ear air quotes – 'actually made her more afraid of disappointing him. She didn't value her work, which made her easy prey for Ross McEwen to pillage.' She frowned. 'We need to work on the timeline. When did he know he was going to be shortlisted for the award, in relation to when Lara disappeared?'

'Do you want me to check it out tomorrow?'

'I think we need to. Here's what I think happened. I think Ross McEwen and Rosalind Harris were fed up with Jake Stein. He was bitter about the divorce, bitter about his career going down the tubes, bitter about the desertion of so many of his friends. More than that – he regarded Rosalind as his property, even after the divorce.

'He took every opportunity to make Rosalind's life a misery, and he was savvy enough to do it under the radar of the stalking legislation. The kind of social media insinuations that can be laughed off, that no court's going to grant an injunction against. Rosalind's experience made them both deeply anxious about what he would do and say once he knew about their relationship. He'd do everything in his power to destroy them.'

'But did he really have that sort of power?' Daisy cut in. 'He was a busted flush, surely? Why would anyone care what he thought?'

'Come on, Daisy, you know what a poisonous bear pit social media can be. He'd have painted them as a pair of Machiavellian plotters trying to get him out of their way. Before you know it, there would be a whole conspiracy theory about McEwen bribing Marga Durham to attack him in public, bringing him down so he'd be the bad guy when the evil lovers went public.'

'I suppose.'

Karen was glad of Daisy's grudging response. Ahead of them would be stronger arguments than this to counter. 'So, how to get rid of Stein? I think Ross McEwen was maybe not prepared to take extreme measures but he was certainly fantasising about it. And I suspect it was the kind of pillow talk he and Rosalind shared. "If only he was dead." "But darling, don't you know fifty ways to kill your rival?" And somewhere along the line he came up with the idea of framing him for murder.'

'And from there, McEwen decided to kill an innocent young woman as collateral damage?' Daisy's tone of scepticism was matched by her expression.

'If he was already thinking murder, it must have seemed like the perfect way to escape Lara accusing him of plagiarism.' Karen ran a hand through her hair. 'You've spent time with him. He's got a streak of cold arrogance. Partly, I wonder whether he did it to see what it would feel like. To do what his characters do. To prove he could commit the perfect murder.'

'That's quite a jump.'

'Is it, though? Lara had the power to destroy his

415

reputation. What kind of writer steals a student's work to lift his own status? He's never expressed any sympathy for Lara, has he? Did he ever say anything to you about how terrible it must have been for her? How frightened she must have been? Anything that showed a shred of empathy?'

'No,' Daisy said slowly, letting Karen's words sink in. 'Now you point it out . . . It's all been about him. The impact this is going to have on his reputation. The disruption of his work. It's like the inconvenience to him is what matters way more than Lara's death. It feels like you could be right.'

'But my feelings don't count for anything. It's evidence that matters. I think it played out something like this. He'd been playing with the idea of murder for a while, trying to figure out every detail and every possible pitfall. Almost as an exercise in imagination. He'd need the right victim – young, ambitious, vulnerable and malleable. When Lara turned up at his workshop, he maybe started to think he'd found her. She was desperate to be a writer, so she'd do anything he asked of her – keep their connection under wraps to protect him from being bothered by other, less talented baby writers. Follow his advice about other events to attend. She probably showed him more of her work and he'll have told her it was promising. Then he realised quite how promising. It's classic grooming. Classic psychopathy.'

'So how did Rosalind not see through him?'

'Habit. All those years with Jake Stein had moulded her expectations. McEwen's more subtle about it than Stein, I suspect. But coercive control only ever works because the victim's primed for it. And Rosalind Harris has been well primed.'

Daisy scribbled a note on her pad. 'She thought McEwen was her saviour but he's just another captor. Why else would she play along with keeping their relationship under wraps even after Stein was dead? He wanted to prove to himself she was under his thumb.'

'I think so. Going back to Lara: once he'd picked her out, McEwen primed her to make a very public connection with Stein – another workshop. Meanwhile he says he'll look at her wannabe novel. I assume he used an anonymous emailer to set up a fake ID online. And at some point, she shows him the story and he submits it for the prize—'

'Not really expecting it to win.' There was excitement in Daisy's voice now. 'Then he hears it's been shortlisted and disaster looms. This will totally destroy his reputation.'

'Suddenly the fantasy looks like a good option. And his affair with Ros shows us a man who gets off on taking risks. He's worked it all out, he's ironed out the pitfalls. He's ready to roll. So McEwen tells Lara to go to Jake's event and shows up himself right at the end. He asks her to send him the new version of her novel and slips into the night.'

'And then he arranges to meet her to work on it together, just like in the manuscript? And tells her to keep it all to herself, not just to save him from other writers but so she can take all the credit when it's a runaway success.' Daisy was up and running with it now.

'He has access to Olga Kotova's caravan because Rosalind has the key. Either with or without her knowledge, he does what it says in the manuscript and uses Olga's caravan to kill Lara. Then he buries her in his own inspection pit, makes a sort of copy of Lara's hard drive and "hides" it in his house. I think the plan was to wait for Lara to drop out of the headlines to cover his back in case anyone had spotted the two of them together. If it was clear they were home and dry, then they would send the manuscript anonymously to the police. Or phone in a tip-off about the body dump. And Jake Stein would almost certainly be convicted of murder.'

'Only, he died before they could complete their plan. Are we absolutely sure that was natural causes, by the way?'

Karen nodded. 'There was a post-mortem because it was a sudden unexplained death. Both pathologists agreed it was natural causes. Bolt from the blue kind of thing.'

'So they didn't need to fit him up. Why didn't they just destroy the manuscript?'

'Because they had Lara Hardie's body in McEwen's garage. If the body was eventually discovered, by then the archive would have been catalogued. If the archivist didn't make the connection, Rosalind could say, "Didn't my late ex-husband write something very similar to that?"'

Daisy mulled it over. 'It makes a horrible sort of sense. But how do we prove it?'

Karen went through to her bedroom and returned with a substantial box of chocolates. 'This, Sergeant, is a three-layer problem.'

46

'How many lies does it take to turn circumstantial evidence into truth?' Karen asked, contemplating a salted milk chocolate praline.

Daisy chewed her chocolate treacle toffee, swallowed it and said, 'How many have we got?'

Karen bit into the praline and made an appreciative noise. 'Rosalind Harris said she vaguely remembered meeting McEwen at a few crime writing functions, when he'd been coming round her house for two years playing chess with her husband. She denied knowing whether Stein had a regular chess partner. Me, I think I'd notice if the same guy kept turning up at my house once a fortnight, even if we didn't have much to do with each other.'

'Plus she omitted to mention that she was in a relationship with this guy that she only vaguely remembered. I've never managed to pull that off,' Daisy said. 'Though heaven knows I've tried.' She grinned. 'The reason for keeping things secret was a bit shoogly too. I've only ever kept somebody I was sleeping with a secret when there was what you might call an overlap. And there's been nothing like that since Rosalind divorced Stein, and certainly not since he died.'

'Let's not forget I saw Ross McEwen coming out of her

apartment block at Quartermile with her. Snogging on the doorstep.'

'Total breach of COVID rules,' Daisy said solemnly. 'Social media would lose its tiny collective mind over that. Plus McEwen never came forward at the time Lara disappeared to say he knew her and he'd definitely seen her the night before she went missing. That's a big sin of omission.' She reached for a dark chocolate strawberry cream.

'OK, so that's the relationship lies. I want to talk about this,' Karen said, pulling the photocopied MS in front of her. 'I've seen the original now. And I've seen some of Stein's other first drafts. You mentioned this right at the start, and I'm sorry I didn't pay attention at the time. Not in my wheel-house, as the cliché goes. You said *The Vanishing of Laurel Oliver* was amazingly clean. But his other first drafts – they don't look like this. There are small corrections – words swapped for similar ones, that sort of thing. And there are much bigger changes. Whole paragraphs deleted, sentences turned about. One where a minor character's name was changed. Wee notes to himself to check things. So this manuscript doesn't match the others. I'm not a literary critic, but that seems significant. What do you think? Am I talking shite?' Apparently without thinking or consulting the guide, Karen went straight for a nut cluster.

'No, you're on the money, I'd say. If there's no earlier ver-sion of this MS, it'd be really surprising if he got it so right straight off the bat. Where did you get these, by the way? They're lush.'

'They were in a gift bag at the back of the wardrobe. If they weren't for me, they should have been.' A tart note in her voice that made Daisy's eyebrows rise.

'Finders keepers, boss ... Something struck me as well,

going through it again the other day. I didn't have Jake Stein marked down as a man with much self-awareness. Now, maybe this was a double bluff but I don't think he would have been able to picture himself as the loser in the way he's portrayed here. I think we should think about getting a textual analysis of the manuscript, compared to Stein's published works and to McEwen's.'

'That's not going to be cheap.'

'There's bound to be some geek at the university who knows how to do it. Plus there's software for it now,' Daisy said. 'With the availability of text on the internet, student work is routinely checked for plagiarism. I'm sure you can run comparisons in the same way.'

'What? To see if they copy each other?'

'It's more to do with the way they compose sentences. Grammatical formations. Favourite words. The algorithms work it out. Do you not remember a few years ago there was that big stooshie about that political thriller that came out under a pseudonym? And people were making all kinds of wild guesses about who it might be? Everybody from George Osborne to Janey Godley. And it turned out to be some Glaswegian down-table hack on the *Telegraph* that nobody had heard of? And they got him on language. We could do the same, get him that way?'

Karen wrote *EVIDENCE* on her pad and underlined it. She added *textual analysis* underneath.

'And there's that pencil note you found on the back of the Part 2 page. There might be something there. Handwriting comparison maybe?'

Karen bit into a liquid centre and screwed up her face in revulsion. 'I thought that was rum baba, but it's horrible.' She studied the list. 'Pisco sour,' she revealed in disgust. 'Who would do a thing like that?' She pulled a face and grabbed a chocolate mint cracknel to take the taste away. 'Handwriting analysis isn't a science, it's an art. All depends on the level of experience. But it's worth bearing in mind. The bottom line is, if we can prove McEwen wrote *The Vanishing of Laurel Oliver*, it all becomes much more straightforward.'

'And if Jason finds security camera footage of Ross McEwen's car going in and out of Olga's caravan site, at the very least he's got questions to answer.'

'If the gods are smiling.'

'So what's our next step?' Daisy's hand crept towards the chocolate ginger, but Karen got there first.

'Two things. In the morning, you see what you can find out about the timeline on the short story. And we wait for Jason. If he finds what we need, and your timeline works, we bring them both in. Interview under caution. If they won't come, we arrest them. She's the weak point. He won't budge, I'd put money on it. But she might be persuaded that she can have a life after this if she can lay it all on him.'

'If she knows about it?'

'If she knows about it. I'm inclined to think she knows enough.'

'First thing in the morning?'

Karen shook her head. 'I'd rather do it in the evening. Provided you and Jason get the goods. That way, we keep them hanging about into the small hours, let them stew. If their lawyers kick off, we'll bed them down in the cells.'

'You have a very dark streak.' Daisy put the lid on the chocolates with a look of regret.

'Someone should probably have told Hamish I come with a government health warning.'

'He's a big boy, he can take his chances along with the rest of us.'

'Aye, and if you find him floating face down in the Water of Leith, don't come looking for me. I'll be the one with the alibi with a cast of thousands.'

47

Jason had come up trumps, Karen told Daisy over the first coffee of the day. 'So no pressure there, then, Sergeant Mortimer.'

'I've already made a start,' Daisy protested. 'I've googled the prize and got a contact email for the administrator. I sent her a message before I came through, asking her for an urgent call.'

'I'm impressed,' Karen said. 'Between you and Jason, I'm going to be redundant soon.'

'When are you going to tell the Dog Biscuit where we're up to?'

Karen pulled a face. 'As late as possible. Ideally not till I've got them both in custody. And we've had a forensic team taking his car to bits. There'll be something there. No matter how many times he's had it valeted since.'

Before Daisy could challenge this, her phone rang. She snatched it. 'Unknown Caller' made her grin. 'Either it's my African prince seeking access to my bank account or it's Gina Donizetti from the National Short Story Award.' She accepted the call, putting the phone on speaker.

'Hello? Is that Detective Sergeant Mortimer?' Southern English, beautiful enunciation.

'Speaking.'

'I'm Gina Donizetti. You emailed me?'

'I did, thanks for responding so promptly. Do you mind if I record this call?' Daisy asked. Karen pulled out her own phone and set the voice recorder running.

'I don't see why I should mind. I have nothing to hide. But now I'm even more intrigued. Why on earth might a detective sergeant from the Historic Cases Unit in Edinburgh want to talk about short stories?'

'It's part of an ongoing inquiry. I'm afraid I can't go into details, but I have some questions about the timetable of your judging process.'

'How very intriguing.'

'The prize is awarded in May, is that right?'

'Correct. The fourth Monday in May, to be precise.'

'And when is the shortlist announced?'

'On the fourth Monday in April.'

'And the stories are broadcast on the radio in the same week?'

'That's right, Sergeant. Is there some suggestion of corruption at the heart of our award? Because I can assure you—'

'Nothing like that,' Daisy hastily interrupted. 'There's no question of any wrongdoing on your part. Am I right in thinking that the stories are read by the authors themselves?'

Karen leaned in to better hear the reply. Gina Donizetti gave a little laugh. 'That's the idea,' she said. 'Wherever possible, they read the stories themselves. That can be quite demanding.'

'I imagine some people are better at it than others.'

'Yes. But we work very hard with them to make it happen.'

'So I guess the writers know they're going to be on the shortlist well before the public does? To make time for the recordings?'

Gina sighed. 'Inevitably. The writers are told in the last week of March.' A dry chuckle. 'We managed to squeeze it in this year just before lockdown.'

Daisy let out the breath she didn't know she'd been holding. 'So last year, 2019, your shortlisted authors would have known by the end of March?'

'Just a moment.' The whisper of fingers on keys. 'March twenty-fifth, the messages went out to the authors and their agents, where applicable.'

Daisy raised an interrogative eyebrow at Karen, who nodded. 'Thank you so much, Gina.'

'It was one of yours who won last year.' Now there was an alert edge to her voice.

'One of ours?'

'A rather dashing Scotsman. Has he done something wrong?'

'I really can't comment on an ongoing case.' Daisy's tone was repressive. 'I've taken up enough of your time. Thank you for your help.'

'You're welcome, but—'

'Have a good day.' Daisy managed to make it sound like she meant it, and ended the call. She nodded at Karen's phone and her boss turned off the recording function. 'He knew he was fucked if Lara was still alive when that story was broadcast. He might be able to persuade her he'd done it to show how good she was, that he still intended to give her the credit, but even someone as biddable as Lara would have her limits.'

'And he had an oven-ready plan,' Karen said wearily. She pushed her chair back and stood up. 'Poor Lara. It's a bloody good story too. She should have had the chance to be proud of herself.'

*

Karen paced the length of Simpson's Loan and back again, waiting for the call from Daisy to say she was about to move on Ross McEwen. Like Karen, she had a uniformed officer from Gayfield Square with her. Karen wasn't expecting confrontation but it was always best to be prepared. Karen, Jason and Daisy had spent much of the day on Zoom, working their way through the evidence and putting together an interview strategy.

Her phone buzzed with a text. A glance showed it was from Miran, and she opened it with a mixture of dread and hope.

I wanted to let you know everything is well. Thank you for all you did to help. Your friend, Miran.

She was taken aback at how relieved she felt. Before she could interrogate the response, the screen lit up with Daisy's number. 'I'm on the doorstep,' Daisy said.

'Don't let him make a phone call now. Tell him he'll have to wait till he gets to the station. See you back there.'

She squared her shoulders and pressed the buzzer for Rosalind Harris's flat. It felt like a long time before she answered, but it was probably less than a minute, Karen thought. 'Ms Harris, it's DCI Pirie. Can you come down, please?'

'Why? I've had my exercise for today.'

'I need you to accompany me to the police station.'

Absolute silence.

'Ms Harris? Did you hear me?'

'I heard you. But I can't imagine what is so important that it trumps the lockdown rules.'

'Crime, Ms Harris. I'm investigating a serious crime and I need to interview you under caution.'

'Under caution?'

'I can caution you via the intercom if you like? It's equally valid. I have a witness here.' She winked at the uniformed PC, who gave her the thumbs up. 'I am detaining you under Section 14 of the Criminal Procedure Scotland Act 1995, because I suspect you of having committed offences punishable by imprisonment, namely abduction, murder and the illegal disposal of a body—'

'I know what the bloody caution is. Are you insane?'

'The reasons for my suspicions will be explained to you in full at a police station. You will be detained to enable further investigations to be carried out—'

'Shut up. This is madness.'

'If you don't come down of your own free will, we will be obliged to enter the building and arrest you. I'm sure that someone in your position wouldn't consider that a good look.'

The intercom went dead. 'What do we do now?' the PC asked.

'We give her ten minutes to get herself together and phone a hotshot criminal lawyer.' She leaned against the glass wall next to the door and studied her watch. Eight minutes passed and the intercom crackled into life. 'Which police station are you taking me to?' Rosalind Harris demanded.

'Gayfield Square,' Karen said. 'Your brief will know it.'

Another three minutes and Rosalind emerged from the lift. She was wearing the same swagger of winter coat, only this time over indigo jeans, a cowl-necked sweater and a pair of scarlet New Balance trainers. Her hair was tucked into a cable knit turban against the chill. She gave Karen a look that would have sent the dogs of the city howling for the suburbs and strode to open the door.

'You are going to regret this, Pirie. I won't call you DCI,

because I suspect by the end of this you're going to be the same rank as your minder.' She cast a disdainful glance at the squad car parked in the street. 'I'm not travelling in that, either.'

'Fine. Where's your car?'

'I'll walk.'

'Then I'll walk with you.'

Rosalind stalked off at a fast pace. 'What do you want me to do?' the PC asked.

'Your best.' Karen hurried off in Rosalind's wake. She was a brisk traverser of the city streets, but Rosalind was heading towards George IV Bridge like a race walker. She didn't bother waiting for the little green man to cross the Royal Mile, which was perfectly reasonable as the only vehicle in sight was the police car on their tail. She cut through to the New Steps, taking them two at a time. No one to give them a second look. Ten o'clock at night in the heart of the city and scarcely a body was stirring.

Down past Waverley Station, up to St Andrew Square with its massive column paying homage to a man who delayed the end of the slave trade, past The Stand comedy club, its stages silent. No laughs to be had in the city tonight. Finally, Gayfield Square.

Karen caught up with Rosalind as she was buzzed into the station. Confronted with two masked women, the sergeant behind the bar looked shaken. Karen broke the ice. 'Hi Sarge. I've brought Ms Harris in for questioning under caution. Interview room one?'

'No can do, Chief Inspector. Sergeant Mortimer just brought someone in. You'll have to settle for room two ...'

Karen shrugged. 'Confessions sound the same, whatever room they're made in.'

'I'm going nowhere till my lawyer gets here,' Rosalind said, the heat of her anger doing nothing to melt the frost in her voice.

'Would that be Ms Considine?' the sergeant asked sweetly.

'Yes.'

He nodded. 'Aye, she's already in Interview Two.'

'Better get going. Ms Considine's clock's running,' Karen said cheerily, leading the way down the hall.

48

Karen shut the door on Rosalind Harris and her lawyer. They were entitled to private conference and Karen was doing this by the book. She crossed the corridor to the other interview room, tapped on the door and stuck her head round. Ross McEwen sat on one side of the table, what she could see of his face stony. Daisy sat opposite, arms folded, file in front of her. Eyes unreadable. In the corner stood a uniformed PC.

Daisy looked around. 'Mr McEwen's lawyer hasn't arrived yet.'

'There's no hurry. Can I borrow you, Sergeant?'

'How long is this going to take?' McEwen demanded. 'I don't even know why I'm here. A body in my garage with no connection to me, and you're accusing me of murder?'

'Let's have this conversation when your lawyer's in the room,' Karen said, as Daisy stood up and followed her out of the room, closing the door firmly behind her. 'How's he handling it?'

'He's bloody furious but he's keeping the lid on it. I think he thinks we've got nothing on him.'

Karen's expression was grim. 'We'll see about that.' Her phone beeped with a message. River.

Hyoid broken.

She knew what that meant. The small wishbone-shaped bone, protected by the structures of the throat. A bone that could only reasonably be broken if the throat was crushed. It was the de facto marker of strangulation. Karen showed the message to Daisy.

'So it's murder, then.'

Karen nodded. 'Come with me, let's see where we can get with Rosalind.'

Rosalind leaned forward, forearms resting on the tabletop. She was clearly wound tight. Her lawyer, Mary Considine, had recently started wearing glasses, and the oversized black frames had turned her from a jolly round-faced Irishwoman into a darkly scary creature, especially with the black mask she'd opted for. Karen hadn't dealt directly with her previously; her clients tended to be at the high end of the social scale. Legal Aid didn't come near her hourly rate.

Daisy sorted out the recording equipment and Karen reminded Rosalind that this was an interview under caution. 'When I first interviewed you in connection with the disappearance of Lara Hardie, you lied to me about your relationship with Ross McEwen. Why did you do that?'

Rosalind looked to Considine, who nodded encouragement. 'No comment.'

'When did you and Ross McEwen become lovers?'

'No comment.'

It was going to be a long night. Made all the more difficult by the wearing of masks, guarding at least half the facial expressions. 'When did your husband discover your affair?'

A flicker in the eyes. 'No comment.'

'When did you and Ross McEwen decide to murder Lara Hardie?' Considine opened her mouth to protest but Karen talked through her. 'I'll rephrase that. When did you and your lover decide to frame your ex-husband for murder?'

This time, the 'No comment' was definitely shoogly.

Karen sighed. 'Rosalind, you're not helping yourself here. As things stand, you look like an equal partner in a criminal conspiracy to abduct and murder Lara Hardie and dump her body in your lover's garage. This is your only chance to escape those charges. If you had nothing to do with it, you need to tell me what you knew and when you knew it.'

Considine leaned in and whispered something in Rosalind's ear. She shook her head.

Karen continued. 'You need to protect yourself. Ross is going to jail for a very long time and unless your version of events gets you off the hook, so are you. Goodbye liberty, goodbye legal career, goodbye lovely Quartermile apartment and goodbye friends.'

'That's enough,' Considine said. 'Let's have some questions rather than threats.'

'That wasn't a threat. It was an offer. And it's an offer that won't be repeated. Ros, we think that Jake was wearing you down. He still treated you like a possession and he wasn't a man who would back off. But Ross thinks like a chess player. The only way to defeat your opponent is to take them off the board. Murdering Jake was a non-starter because the pair of you would have a solid gold motive. But Ross has a devious mind. You only have to read his books to know that. He thought it would be much smarter, much more effective, to send Jake to jail for life.' Karen scoffed. 'From what I've seen of him, it's an idea that would have made him positively gleeful.'

'No, you've got it all wrong,' Rosalind blurted out, then covered her mouth with her hand. 'I mean, no comment.'

Karen let the pause spool out. 'He thought he could commit the perfect murder. Perfect because it would make your husband the fall guy. You'd be rid of him for good. Only Lara Hardie would pay the price and really, she didn't count, did she? She was just a nobody, a wannabe, the perfect victim. Poor Lara Hardie, whose only crime was to write the short story Ross McEwen stole.' A flash of shock in Rosalind's eyes. 'Did you not know about that? It wasn't Ross who wrote that clever, tender "Memorial Garden". It was Lara Hardie. He passed it off as his own.' A pause. 'I'm going to ask you again. When did he draw you in to this conspiracy?'

'No comment.' Rosalind couldn't meet her eyes now. Her hands were tight fists clenched on the tabletop.

'It wasn't enough that he dragged you into this. He had to draw your friend Olga Kotova into his mess too. How do you think she'll feel when the forensics team rip her caravan to the bare bones looking for traces of Lara Hardie's murder?'

Her head came up and her face was a mask of horror. 'Olga? What do you mean, Olga?'

'We believe that's where he lured Lara. Using the key she'd entrusted to you. It loosely resembles the account in the manuscript.'

'You've got this all wrong,' she said. Considine put a hand on her arm and she shook it off. 'Ross didn't kill Lara Hardie. Jake did.'

'When did you realise that, Ros?'

'Ros, I must advise you—' Considine didn't stand a chance. Not now the floodgates were opened.

'Ross told me. Jake had gloated that he'd murdered Lara

434

Hardie and framed Ross for it. He told him all the details except for where he'd hidden the body. He said if Ross didn't give me up, he'd tell the police where the body was. And there would be enough there to incriminate him.'

The room fell quiet for a long moment. Mary Considine leaned in to her client and spoke too softly for them to hear. Rosalind shook her head and whispered something in return.

'I need a moment with my client.'

Karen didn't want to relinquish the momentum but she knew she had no choice. She stood up. Daisy turned off the recording and together they walked out.

'We've got her,' Daisy said. 'She's admitted knowing about the murder.'

'And I hope that's what Mary Considine is impressing upon her right now.'

Daisy squatted down, leaning against the wall. Karen was too fired up with adrenaline to stand still, and she paced back and forth, running the options for the next phase of the attack. Five minutes. Ten minutes. Then Mary Considine emerged. 'What can you do for my client?'

'That depends on what she can do for me.'

'If I was to posit that she had no knowledge of who killed Lara Hardie or when, but that she believed what her lover told her and acted out of fear, how would that play for you?'

Karen shook her head. 'Why would that play anything but a bum note for me? We've already got her admitting to knowing about a murder she didn't report to the police. We've got her lying to us about their relationship. We're convinced we can prove that Ross McEwen wrote the manuscript account of the murder. It's a stretch to believe he could have got so many details right if he hadn't committed the crime. Trying to hide behind Jake Stein as the killer just won't play.'

Considine held her stare. 'If you're still open to discussion, let me talk further to my client.'

'Take your time. We're off to have a conversation with Mr McEwen. Maybe he'll be more forthcoming.'

Considine scowled. 'That I doubt, unless you've suddenly discovered some interrogatory skills.' She turned on her heel and returned to the interview room.

'Harsh,' Daisy said.

'Lawyers' games. Come on, let's see what Ross McEwen has to say for himself.'

McEwen's lawyer had arrived, a pudgy, pink-faced man. His hair sat in a fluffy blond halo round his head and his round tortoiseshell glasses perched on the end of his nose. He'd have to be bloody good to overcome those handicaps, Karen thought. The evidence of that lay in a beautifully tailored suit and massive gold cufflinks engraved with some fancy crest. 'I'm Richard Balfour,' he announced in a tone that implied they should recognise his name and tremble. 'I'm here to represent Mr McEwen and I must protest at the way my client has been dragged here from his home and kept waiting for a significant amount of time for an interview that could equally well have been conducted under his own roof.'

Karen wanted to ask whether he was paid by the word, but told herself it was too soon for that. 'Duly noted,' she said. Daisy set up the recording and they all recited their names. Karen reminded them that this was an interview under caution.

'My client has no idea why you are interviewing him under caution.'

'He might not have told *you*, but I'm sure he does. Mr McEwen, can you explain how the remains of Lara Hardie came to be in your garage?'

He leaned back in his chair and shrugged. 'I can't be sure, but I think they were placed there by the late Jake Stein in an attempt to incriminate me in her murder.' Balfour was scribbling away on his legal pad with a Mont Blanc pen, frowning all the while.

'Interesting that you use that word. I don't recall anyone involved in this investigation talking about murder.'

'What can I say? I'm a crime writer. Human remains in unexpected places shout murder to me.'

'Why would Jake Stein want to incriminate you?'

'Because he was a nasty, mean-tempered bully who resented the fact that his ex-wife had found happiness with me.'

Balfour squirmed in his chair.

Karen made a note. 'That's not quite the timeline though, is it? Ms Harris had "found happiness" with you some time before her marriage ended. You were having an affair behind his back.'

'We didn't realise he knew. Until he told me he was going to make me pay for it, I thought we'd managed to keep our secret to ourselves.'

'What was your reaction to his threat?'

McEwen shrugged again. 'I laughed and told him not to be pathetic. That Ros was a grown woman who could make her own choices.'

'But that wasn't the end of it, was it?'

He drummed a tattoo on the table with his fingers. 'Obviously not or you wouldn't be wasting our time here in the middle of the night.'

'You decided, like any serious chess player, that the only strategy was to take Jake Stein off the board.'

He laughed. 'Really, Pirie, you should consider a new career in stand-up. It's true that I write about murder. I probably know more undetectable ways to kill than you do. But I don't do it for real.'

'Not even to see what it would feel like?'

Balfour leaned forward. 'That's a very offensive question, Chief Inspector. Are you planning on presenting any evidence at any point?'

'I was working up to it, but we'll cut to the chase.' She opened her folder and took out the printouts of the jpegs Jason had sent her an hour earlier. She laid them out in front of McEwen, who had suddenly stilled. 'You see the date stamp in the corner?'

He nodded.

'Mr McEwen, would you speak, for the recording?'

'Yes, I see it.'

'That is the date that Lara Hardie disappeared. Is that your car? You can see the number plate quite clearly.'

He glared at her. 'It's a car like mine with the same number plate as my car.'

'What? Someone cloned your car?'

'I think this is when Jake Stein borrowed my car.'

'It doesn't look like Jake Stein in the driver's seat.'

He scoffed and waved the photograph at his lawyer. 'It doesn't look like anybody. It could be Prince bloody Charles.'

Balfour nodded. 'You'd struggle to get a Fiscal Depute to agree with you there, never mind a jury, Chief Inspector.'

Karen shrugged. 'Fair enough. I didn't really expect you to cop to that. But you'd agree that there is someone in the passenger seat? Someone with light-coloured hair?'

'I suppose,' McEwen said, sulky now.

Karen took the second picture from the file. The second camera was assisted by the spotlights on the facade of the office that lit up the entrance at night. 'Same date stamp, three hours and twenty-seven minutes later.'

She laid it down, face up. 'Just you, this time.'

McEwen stared at the picture. His car, his car's number plate and his face clearly illumined. 'You've faked this,' he said.

'No, we haven't. Unless you're going to claim this is Jake Stein in a Ross McEwen mask?'

'I was at the caravan site perfectly legitimately, checking on our friend Olga's caravan.'

'And your passenger? What happened to her?'

He shook his head. 'I had no passenger. It's obviously a trick of the light.'

'We think your passenger was Lara Hardie. That you took her to that caravan for the sole purpose of murdering her.'

His laugh was confident. 'Really, this is beyond bizarre. Why on earth would I murder Lara Hardie? She was a virtual stranger to me. I barely remember encountering her.'

Karen closed her eyes momentarily and breathed heavily through her nose. 'Lara Hardie came to you for help because she idolised you. She wasn't just any other wannabe, though. She had real talent.'

His lip curled in scorn. 'You wouldn't say that if you'd read her novel.'

'I've read her short story.' Karen enjoyed the tightening of his shoulders. 'The one that won the National Short Story Award last year.' Karen let the pause grow. 'You must remember that one, Ross? "Memorial Garden" – the one you stole from her.'

'Is this the sort of bullshit your usual customers fall for? You're living on fantasy island. I wrote "Memorial Garden".'

'I don't think you did.' Karen produced Lara's writing diary and opened it at the page she'd bookmarked. She pushed it towards him. 'Would you like to read that?'

He looked away. 'I'm not playing your stupid game. Lara copied that from my story, not the other way round.'

'She'd have had to fake the whole diary to get the dates right.' Karen riffled the edges of the pages.

'People with obsessions have done more than that. She copied me.'

He was good, she had to admit that to herself. But was he good enough?

49

Dawn, and Karen was sitting on a bench on the grassy patch outside the Gayfield Square police station. Not for the first time, she marvelled at the rich variety of birdsong in the city centre. There were enough trees and green spaces to provide habitats for all sorts of birds. She'd even seen the iridescent flash of a kingfisher on the Water of Leith.

She'd sent Daisy back to the flat for sleep and food. But she had to wait for Ruth Wardlaw, the Fiscal Depute, to read through the docket of evidence Karen had prepared. Then she would decide what, if any charges should be laid against Ross McEwen and Rosalind Harris. Usually by the time they reached this point in a case, Karen had little doubt what would be presented to the court. But this time, she wasn't certain she'd put together a strong enough case.

They'd have had next to nothing without the security camera footage. It was hard to imagine why McEwen had been so careless about that. He'd been so meticulous about every other detail. Maybe he'd thought the police weren't smart enough to join up the dots to Olga's caravan. Maybe he'd not been quite as well prepared as he thought; the success of Lara's story had caught him on the back foot.

Maybe he'd underestimated the quality of the image on the cameras after dark. Whatever the reason, it had been disastrous for him. All the clever plotting that worked on the page wouldn't be enough to get him out of this. She hoped.

McEwen had to be going down. Jason's digital trawl had made that happen. He'd gone back through the CCTV footage and found a previous visit to Olga's caravan two days earlier, presumably to do the set dressing.

It would be a complicated trial, but Karen thought a good advocate could make sense of it for the jury. But if Rosalind Harris stuck to her story, they'd be hard-pressed to charge her with anything more than obstructing justice. A jury might buy her version of events – the psychologically abused woman who hadn't been able to stand up for herself twice over. A sympathetic jury might let her walk free.

She tilted her head back and savoured the city air, clearer than she'd ever known it. Having virtually no traffic had transformed the quality of life. Would everyone simply return to their old habits once the pandemic was over, or would they have learned what Karen already knew – that walking the city was its own reward? Time for thought, time to spy on the lives of others, time to discover new routes and expand the mental map.

One thing would definitely not be the same for her. She was done with Hamish. Even before the moment Teegan had demonstrated how he thought he was above the letter of the law, she'd been stifling doubts and tamping down resentments. She was tired of capitulating, tired of feeling there was something wrong with her.

He wasn't a bad man. Just not the right man for her. She could see now that she'd allowed herself to let him into her life precisely because he was so different from

Phil. There would never be any real comparison. And Hamish had helped her to heal. She would never take that away from him.

He was, she hoped, an interregnum. Someone else would touch her heart; she believed that now in a way she hadn't when she took up with Hamish. He'd filled a space and they'd had a lot of fun. And that was no small thing.

Her thoughts were interrupted by her phone. She saw Jason's number and felt the cold hand of fear crush her heart. 'Jason,' she said.

'She's away,' he said, his voice cracking. 'Twenty past four.' He sniffed.

'I'm heart-sorry, Jason.'

'I know, boss. She thought a lot of you.'

'It was mutual. She's going to leave a big hole in your life.'

'I've got to live up to what she wanted me to be.' A sob caught in his throat.

'It's going to be tough. But you can do it. If there's anything I can do to help, with the arrangements, or anything else, let me know. I mean it.'

Now he was crying, his sentences coming in broken phrases. 'We cannae even have a proper funeral. No chance to celebrate her. To swap stories.'

'Soon as we can, we'll do that, Jason. I promise. We'll give Sandra the send-off she deserves.'

'I better go. I've to let people know what's happened. I'll not be at my work for a few days, sorry.'

'Take as long as you need. Oh, and Jason? Those images you tracked down? They did the trick. Sandra would have been proud.' A pause. 'And so would Phil. Be kind to yourself. We'll talk soon.'

Karen felt the weight of loss. Her eyes shone with unshed

tears. She knew from bitter experience that she'd get past this. She had friends. She had a job that mattered to her. She had come to love her adopted city, with all its subterranean problems. But right now, she just wanted to close her own front door and sleep. Sandra Murray had been a good woman, a woman with a big heart and a genuine warmth. How many more Sandra Murrays was this fucking virus going to take? Would there be enough left to pick up the burdens?

The prospect of rest receded even further as Ruth Wardlaw emerged from the police station, unhooking her mask. Karen stood up to greet her. 'How's it looking?' she asked.

Ruth grinned. 'I think you're over the line. I'm going to recommend the full slate of charges. Your team's done a good job.'

'Not bad, considering they tried to tell us it wasn't historic yet.'

'Well, I reckon it'll be a historic victory in due course. You're going to get an absolute shedload of publicity on this one.' She pulled a face. 'And somebody's bound to publish poor Lara Hardie's novel now.'

'The National Short Story Award people have already presented her parents with the trophy that should have been hers. It's not much of a consolation, but I think it's been a wee bit of a help, especially to her sister.'

'Don't underestimate the power of consolation.'

Karen shook her head, 'Ross McEwen, with his sense of entitlement. What a trail of pain he's left in his wake. And what about Rosalind Harris? What are you going to do with her?'

Ruth sighed. 'I want to go with art and part. The law's

clear enough. "Any person who aids, abets, counsels, pro-
cures or incites any other person to commit an offence
against the provisions of any enactment shall be guilty of
an offence and shall be liable to the same punishment." I
think I can make it stick. Whether a jury will feel the same,
who knows? All we can do is the best we can do, Karen.'

Karen nodded. 'Aye. All we can ever do is the best
we can do.'

Epilogue

September 2021

Karen stood on the Royal Mile outside the High Court, letting the sun spill down on her face. In front of her, set in the cobbles, the mosaic Heart of Midlothian marked the Old Tolbooth, where countless judgements and executions had taken place over the centuries. Today's judgement would have a different ending, but not one that was necessarily easier. Ross McEwen would be an old man before he'd be eligible to be released on licence. Rosalind Harris would serve only a few years, but that would be enough to take her life from her.

For the Hardie family, hunched together on the public seats, a different kind of life sentence lay ahead. Every milestone Emma clocked up – graduation, first job, love, maybe children – would be matched by the grief of never seeing Lara on the same road. At every family occasion, there would be an absence that shouted louder than any celebratory words. Karen didn't think the punishment meted out to the pair in the dock would feel like justice to the Hardies, but then, nothing could.

There had been times when she had wondered whether

they would ever reach this point. Lockdowns, restrictions on public places, her own unpleasant experience of COVID, delays in the criminal justice system that brought home painfully the adage that justice delayed was justice denied – they'd all conspired to make this an even tougher wait than usual.

She felt a touch on her arm, and there was Jason. 'Let's go,' she said, leading the way down the Royal Mile towards the bridges. It had been a strange time for Jason too. The whole shape of his life had changed; his mother's death had brought many aspects of it into sharp relief. He loved his brother but without his mother's love to intervene between them, he'd finally realised he couldn't trust him. He'd thought he loved Eilidh, but lockdown and crisis had combined to force a realisation that when the going got tough, she didn't know how to handle it. She'd tried to brush off Sandra's death as something they 'just had to accept', but Jason had realised what he just had to accept was that she was never going to be there for him. As he'd said to Daisy, 'When you realise you've got more support from your boss than your fiancée, you know something's not right.'

But recently, he seemed to have turned a corner. The grief was less insistent. He'd decided to try for sergeant, because Sandra would have wanted him to. And he'd been out on a couple of dates with Meera Reddy from the National Library. Just a movie, and dinner at that nice Italian in Leith. But it had been good fun. And she liked football too. Although he wasn't sure he could work up the same enthusiasm for the women's game, he was open to conversion.

The truly good news for all of them was that Ann Markie had departed. She'd taken up the reins as chief constable at a small force in the South of England. 'It's the obvious next step on the road to world domination,' Daisy had said in the pub on the night they'd gone out to celebrate the news. The new ACC (Crime) hadn't been appointed yet; Jimmy Hutton had heard on the grapevine that it was going to be a proper copper who'd had boots on the ground in the recent past. At least, thought Karen, they wouldn't have any personal beef with her.

Daisy had surprised them all by installing herself not in her own flat in Glenrothes but in the Bruntsfield flat of a teacher Karen had yet to meet. She was still reticent about her private life but lockdown romance, love on the Zoom, seemed to have worked for Daisy.

Life without Hamish was going just fine for Karen. At the end of the first lockdown, Daisy and Karen moved out of his flat. It had felt like a good decision at the start of lockdown, but she'd felt a genuine sense of relief to close the door on his home for the last time. Only when she returned to her own flat did she realise the weight of being under someone else's roof, even so luxurious a roof as Hamish's. She still stopped in at his coffee shops if she was passing and needed a caffeine fix, but so far, their paths hadn't crossed.

Six months after the terrible night at the breakwater, a letter had arrived at Karen's flat. It was postmarked Montreal and the handwriting seemed familiar. She turned it over and saw the return address: *Yasin, Prince Arthur Est, Plateau Mont Royal, Montreal.*

After the end of the lockdown, when Aleppo reopened, Karen had sat down with Miran. He explained that one of their group knew a crew member on a container ship about to unload in Grangemouth. He'd managed to persuade the captain they needed a doctor on board – 'a nod and a wink, I think you say, Karen' – and Rafiq had found a berth. Miran assured her he'd be safe and she almost believed him.

And then out of the blue, a letter. She'd ripped it open and read it with an eagerness that took her by surprise. He'd travelled from Grangemouth to Antwerp. From there, he'd found a place on a container ship bound for the Port of Montreal. Within a month he'd been on Canadian soil. As soon as he'd arrived in Montreal, he'd claimed asylum. Because his life was in danger if he'd returned to Syria, his claim had been accepted. *They welcome refugees here*, his letter said. *They treat us like human beings, not animals or prisoners. I feel safe here.*

More than that, he'd been placed on a programme that would ultimately restore his professional life to him. Within the year, he hoped he'd be back in the operating theatre, doing what he did best. And he was writing to thank her and to hope that they would meet again. His email address had been at the bottom of the letter.

It had taken her three days to reply, mostly because she didn't know why it had so unsettled her to hear from a man she'd spent such a small amount of time with. A man she thought was gone from her life. But she had replied, and somehow they'd found a way to cross the distances between their experiences.

It would be a while yet before Rafiq would be able to get a passport. But she had amassed plenty of holiday leave over the past couple of years. And she'd promised that, as soon as the McEwen trial was over, she'd book a slab of leave and visit Montreal. After all, she'd grown up to the sound of her father playing Leonard Cohen albums; she always thought he was more sexy than miserable, and she'd always fancied visiting his home town. There must be somewhere she could sit down with Rafiq and enjoy tea and oranges while they watched the sun pour down on Our Lady of the Harbour.

Acknowledgements

Past Lying is set in the lockdown world of April 2020, but I needed some clear blue water between then and now so I could write about those frightening and constantly changing days.

I wrote this novel in 2023 in New Zealand, where I spent four months thanks to the Centre for Irish and Scottish Studies at the University of Otago in Dunedin. Huge thanks to my boss, Professor Liam McIlvanney, whose conversation and friendship helped the book on its way.

Thanks too to our landlady Jill for providing a home from home at the top of the hill!

Tania Mackenzie-Cooke organised an amazing book tour round both islands in the excellent company of Michael 'Screamer' Robotham and Josh Pomare; thanks, Tans, to you and the family for lending us your home. We loved our first Christmas at the poolside!

Amina Shah, National Librarian and Chief Executive of the ever-helpful National Library of Scotland, was generous with her knowledge and experience and will forgive me, I hope, for playing fast and loose with their facilities.

As always, I'm indebted to my forensic friends. My dear pal Sue Black, who now has so many honorifics I don't quite know how to address her formally, provided invaluable help – blame her for the human soup – and Professor Lucina Hackman of Dundee University also offered her assistance.

My team at Little, Brown saw *Past Lying* through the editorial process and beyond – thanks in particular to Lucy Malagoni and Cal Kenny. Lizzy Kremer and Stephanie Glencross at DHA added their valuable voices to the mix, as did Amy Hundley at Grove Atlantic. Anne O'Brien and Laura Sherlock both hoisted me over the finishing line – I couldn't have seen the wood for the trees without you two!

To my writing friends, I tip my hat. You bring me endless pleasure and marvellous fun. None of the fictional characters in *Past Lying* is based in any respect on real writers, living or dead. Cross my heart and hope to die!

And finally, to Jo. Thanks to you, I'm living my best life. You always have my back, and you mix the best cocktails. Here's tae a' oor lucky puckies; I'd raither be here than gaitherin' buckies.